THE FAR WEST

PATRICIA C. WREDE

THE FAR WEST

SCHOLASTIC PRESS · NEW YORK

All rights reserved. Published by Scholastic Press, an imprint of Scholastic Inc.,
Publishers since 1920, SCHOLASTIC, SCHOLASTIC PRESS, and associated logos
are trademarks and/or registered trademarks of Scholastic Inc.

Library of Congress Cataloging-in-Publication Data Available

ISBN 978-0-545-03344-2

10 9 8 7 6 5 4 3 2 1   12 13 14 15 16

Printed in the U.S.A.   23
First edition, August 2012

The text type was set in Griffo.
Book design by Christopher Stengel

For Sayoko, with thanks

CHAPTER 1

It is a true thing that the Far West is a strange and danger-ous place. Everybody knows that, which is a little odd. In my experience, the things everybody knows are just exactly the ones that are most likely to be mistaken in some important way or other, if they're not flat-out wrong right from the start.

But folks are mostly right about the Far West. If anything, it's an even stranger and more dangerous place than everybody says. That's why whenever someone makes it a little farther west and comes back alive, they have tales of new wildlife no one's ever seen or heard tell of. Sometimes they're harmless, like prairie dogs and chameleon tortoises; sometimes they're useful or beautiful, like jewel minks. Most of them, though, are like swarming weasels and saber cats and dire wolves and steam dragons — deadly dangerous and not anything you'd be advised to stand around admiring, beautiful or not.

The critters have never stopped people from heading West, though. By the time I turned twenty, the settlements and tinytowns stretched a hundred miles west from the Mammoth River, and dangerous new wildlife was showing up every couple of years instead of every decade or so. The mirror bugs that ate every plant over an eighty-mile-wide strip from the middle of the Red River Valley almost all the way to the Middle Plains Territory caused the most problems, but the medusa lizards we'd only just found out about were the ones that scared the bejeezus out of everyone.

The medusa lizards turned animals and people to stone — and not just one at a time, but in bunches. Worse yet, they absorbed magic, so normal spells were no use against them. We were lucky there'd been only two of them, and even so we'd lost two horses while we were trying to shoot them. We almost hadn't managed.

My twin brother, Lan, and I had been part of the group that killed the medusa lizard pair, and just having been there was enough to get every newspaper and broadsheet in Mill City after us. One reporter cornered me halfway home from my job at the college menagerie and kept me standing in the hot August sun for ten minutes while he asked the same questions we'd been answering for days — "Why were you up at Big Bear Lake?" and "Did your brother sense the medusa lizards before anyone else?" Then he had a bunch of personal questions about what it was like to be the twin of a double-seventh son.

"What's it like not to be a twin?" I said, trying to hide how cross I was. "I don't have anything to compare it to."

"Er," he said, looking startled. He drew a line on his notepad, then looked up at me. "It's just something our readers would be interested in."

I was about ready to say something when he added, "Because you'd never know from looking at the two of you that you're twins, and —"

"If I could grow a pair of muttonchop sideburns and

about five inches in height, we'd look exactly alike," I snapped. That wasn't strictly true — Lan and I both have brown hair and eyes, but I have Mama's straight little nose and Papa's narrow chin, while Lan's nose is flatter and narrower, like Papa's — but we have as much resemblance as any other brother and sister, and maybe more than most.

"But Miss Rothmer —"

"Good day, sir." I turned and walked briskly off before I lost my temper even worse and hit him with the hotfoot spell Lan used on the school bullies back when we were thirteen. By the time I'd gone twenty feet, I was regretting it, but it was too late. I just hoped no one at home heard about it.

Of course, I wasn't that lucky. Everything I said got written up in the papers. My mother and my sister Allie both scolded me for being rude and unladylike, and my older brother Robbie spent three weeks teasing me about growing sideburns. I was just glad that the reporters hadn't counted up all Papa's children and figured out that I was an unlucky thirteenth child. It didn't seem to matter as much to folks in the West as it did back East, but I still didn't like the idea of people finding out.

Lan hated the notice even more than I did. He was still getting over the accident back in the spring that killed one of his college professors out East. It was partly Lan's fault — he'd been messing around with advanced Hijero-Cathayan magic, and it had gone out of control and burned him and a lot of students, as well as killing Professor Warren — and he didn't think he deserved to be remarked on for helping out with the medusa lizards after doing something like that.

3

So I wasn't too surprised when he told me he was going back out West for the rest of the season as a sort of assistant circuit magician.

I was surprised by Mama's reaction, though I shouldn't have been. She never liked it when anyone in the family went west of the Mammoth River, and she was still fussed about Lan having been hurt.

"No," she said firmly when Lan told her over dinner. "You're not well enough."

"Mama, I was well enough to go out with Professor Torgeson two months ago," Lan said, surprised.

"And look how that turned out!" Mama said.

Lan frowned. "It turned out fine."

"Fine? Chasing off after creatures that turn people to stone? That's not fine!"

"It would have been worse to wait for them to come to us."

"It would have been better not to go at all!"

"Better for who?" Lan said. "We didn't come to any harm."

"You could have," my sister Allie put in.

"I could have fallen down the stairs and broken a leg, too," Lan told her. "Or been hit by a runaway horse cart while I was crossing the street, but I don't see you worrying about that."

Allie scowled at him. "You shouldn't be making Mama fret."

Lan got a curdled look on his face, like he really wanted to say a whole lot of things that he knew he shouldn't, and was having trouble keeping them in. I decided I'd best step in before he exploded. "The Settlement Office wants everyone who faced up to the medusa lizards at Big Bear Lake to go out and warn other settlements about them. Lan's one of the people who was there, so of course they want him."

Mama's eyes narrowed and she gave a skeptical sniff. "They send out warnings all the time. They don't need eyewitnesses to do it."

"I believe they want to prove that it is possible to kill the creatures and survive," Papa said mildly. Then he added soberly, "Without turning to stone, in whole or in part."

I breathed a quiet sigh of relief. I'd figured that Papa knew what the North Plains Territory Homestead Claim and Settlement Office intended, because he was one of the magicians the Settlement Office called on regularly to help out with things like improving the settlement protection spells. He'd been West himself, too, when there were emergencies out in settlement territory that the settlement magicians and regular circuit riders couldn't handle alone. But I hadn't known until right then that he didn't object to Lan going West that summer.

"They don't need Lan to prove anything," Mama said. "There was a whole group of people who went after those lizard things. Some of the others can go; they don't need to send a boy who hasn't even finished his schooling yet."

Lan's face darkened, and I knew he was about half a second from losing his temper, so I said quickly, "Lan and I are twenty, Mama; that's older than a lot of the folks who file for settlement allotments. And there were only six of us who went out hunting the medusa lizards, and Professor Torgeson has to stay here and study the one we brought back, Mr. Grimsrud has his allotment at Big Bear Lake to tend to, and Greasy Pierre went back out in the wildlands right after we got back to the settlement. I don't think anyone could find him even if they wanted to. That leaves Lan and Wash and me."

"Wash can't cover all the settlements by himself in two months," Lan said, and I could see he was trying hard to sound reasonable. "It's . . . it's my responsibility to help, Mama. And it's not as if they can ask Eff to go."

Mama pressed her lips together for a second. Then she opened her mouth and took a deep breath. Before she could say whatever she was going to, I said cheerfully, "But they did ask me."

Everyone sat there looking stunned, even Papa. "Mr. Parsons came around to the menagerie late this afternoon," I went on.

"Eff, you can't possibly be thinking of going!" Allie said in a horrified tone.

I shrugged. "Mr. Parsons said they've sent Wash out to take care of the far edge of settlement territory, but they want someone to go to settlements closer in, too. It didn't sound like it would be too bad." All of which was quite true; I just didn't say that I'd already told Mr. Parsons that I'd be staying in Mill City to help Professor Torgeson and Professor Jeffries. I figured that by the time everyone finished up yelling at me and making me stay home, Lan wouldn't have as much trouble getting Mama to let him do what he wanted.

Just as I'd hoped, Mama and Allie were even more fussed about me going out West again than they were about Lan, but it was a lot easier for me to keep my temper because I didn't really want to go this time. Riding around to different settlements wasn't as interesting as studying the dead medusa lizard we'd brought back, and I'd only ever have just one chance to help study the very first medusa lizard anyone had ever seen.

Lan left for the settlements a week after that dinner conversation, and for a while it looked as if everything was going to work out just exactly the way I'd wanted. Mama still wasn't best pleased about Lan leaving, nor about me going back to work at the menagerie (she thought Professor Torgeson and Professor Jeffries were a bad influence on me), but she couldn't do much about either thing.

The first sign that things were going wrong came in early September, when Professor Jeffries walked into Professor Torgeson's office waving a letter. "The Frontier Management Department wants one of us to take Lizzie to Washington," he said. Lizzie was what we'd started calling the dead medusa lizard. It was a lot shorter than saying "medusa lizard" all the time, and it made it feel less dangerous than it'd been when it was alive.

"What?" said Professor Torgeson, frowning. "That will take a good two months! It's going to be hard enough to develop the lizard-repelling spells the Settlement Office needs before spring without wasting that much time."

"I believe they expect us to take the train," Professor Jeffries said mildly.

"Bureaucrats!" Professor Torgeson said, like it was a really horrible swear word, and her Vinland accent got thicker, the way it always did when she got angry. "Don't any of them remember more than two paragraphs of the magic theory they learned in day school? Let me see that letter."

Professor Jeffries handed her the letter and winked at me. I smiled back, but I could understand why Professor Torgeson was upset. The preservation spells on something as big as the medusa lizard were easy to disrupt, and one of the most sure-fire ways of disrupting them was to move the thing they were cast on. Moving it as fast as a train went would pretty much guarantee that the spells would fail. On top of that, the medusa lizard was resistant to magic; it had been hard getting the spells to work in the first place, even with Lan helping.

"I don't know what they can be thinking," Professor Torgeson muttered. "Train tickets! And of course it didn't occur to them that we are teachers and classes have started."

"Theirs doesn't seem like the wisest course of action, does it?" Professor Jeffries said. "Would you like to tell them so, or shall I?"

Professor Torgeson got a gleam in her eye. "I'll be happy to let them know, if you're quite sure you don't want the pleasure yourself."

"I'm sure you'll be far more convincing than I would be," Professor Jeffries told her with a perfectly straight face, and Professor Torgeson laughed.

Professor Torgeson was convincing, all right, but what finally made the Frontier Management Department reconsider was the fact that the medusa lizard we'd brought back was a female, all ready to lay a whole lot of eggs, and the preservation spell Lan and Professor Torgeson had put on it had worked so well that Professor Jeffries thought some of the eggs could be hatched.

The Frontier Management Department didn't want live medusa lizards anywhere near Washington, not even baby ones. They weren't all that happy about the possibility of having them east of the Great Barrier Spell. As soon as they got Professor Torgeson's letter about the eggs, they sent a very nervous little man out from the headquarters in Washington to talk to the professors and Mr. Parsons at the North Plains Territory Homestead Claim and Settlement Office about the best way to proceed.

They talked for the rest of September, while the medusa lizard sat in storage and Professor Torgeson got madder and madder and even Professor Jeffries started walking around with a frown. By then they'd agreed on letting the lizard — and the lizard's eggs — stay at the Northern Plains Riverbank College, provided we took it back west of the Barrier Spell just as soon as we could. And that was where things bogged down.

Once he understood about the preservation spells and the eggs, the man from the Frontier Management Department didn't want anyone to so much as *look* at the medusa lizard until it was back on the other side of the Great Barrier, and until the new study center was finished, there really wasn't anywhere on the west bank to take it. He also wanted to pick a bunch of experts from out East to do the studying, though I surely didn't see how anyone could be an expert in a critter no one had ever seen before. The professors wanted a proper scientific study done, but they wanted to be the first ones doing it, and they were itching to get started. Mr. Parsons didn't care who looked at the medusa lizard or where they did it as long as somebody figured out how to stop the critters real soon, before more of them showed up out of the Far West and started turning settlers into statues.

It took until early October for them to come to an agreement, and what they agreed on was that the Northern Plains Riverbank College professors could observe the medusa lizard at the college as much as they wanted as long as they didn't remove or disrupt the protection spells even for a second. That meant no dissection and no testing, especially not magical tests, but at least we didn't have to move Lizzie to a warehouse on the far side of the river and ignore her. The Frontier Management Department promised to get its list of experts together and start sending them out in a month. The nervous little man shook hands on the arrangement and went back to Washington to tell them about it, and the rest of us went back to work on other things.

I couldn't help feeling cheated, though. If I'd known that the Frontier Management Department was going to make us wait until November to work on the medusa lizard, I could have spent the last couple of months out in the settlements with Lan and Wash. I was very grumpy for the rest of October.

CHAPTER
· 2 ·

THREE WEEKS AFTER THE MAN FROM THE FRONTIER MANAGEMENT Department left, right before Halloween, we had an early snowstorm. It was only about half an inch, and it melted off before the next morning, but it put Mama and Allie in a considerable taking, because Lan still hadn't come back from the settlements. Nothing anyone said made any difference; they were both convinced that Lan would be stuck out West for the whole winter. Papa and Robbie and I couldn't make a dent in their notions.

"Even Mr. Parsons doesn't know for sure where Lan is," Allie announced. "I saw him after church yesterday, and I asked."

"Allie, I thought you knew better than that," Papa said. "Mr. Parsons isn't likely to have the whereabouts of a settlement rider at his fingertips, especially this late in the season."

"Well, he should!" Mama said in a cross tone that meant she knew Papa was right but she didn't like it one bit. "Anything could happen out there." Robbie made a face behind her back that nobody saw but me.

Before Papa could reply, there was a knock at the door. Papa frowned; no one in Mill City came calling during the dinner hour. "I'd better see who it is," he said. A minute later, we heard muffled voices in the front hall, but Papa didn't come back. Just when Mama was about to send me or Allie to find out what was going on, the door of the dining room opened.

"I'm home!" Lan announced.

Allie burst into tears of relief. Mama gasped, then stood up to give him a hug. "My stars, Lan, you gave me a turn! Why didn't you let us know when you were going to be back? We were expecting you a week ago!"

"Allie had just about convinced herself that you'd been eaten by saber cats," Robbie put in.

Lan winked at me over Mama's shoulder, then let go of her and turned to Robbie. "Things happened, and by the time I knew for sure when I'd get here, there wasn't a mailbag heading east that would have beat me home."

I was looking from Lan to the doorway. Papa hadn't come back yet, and Lan had an expression on his face that he only ever got when he was planning to surprise someone. "Lan?" I said. "What sort of things happened?"

"Oh, this and that. No saber cats, though," Lan said, and grinned. Now I was positive he was up to something. He stepped to one side and said in a too-casual tone, "I brought you a surprise, Mama."

"Is *that* why you're so late?" Allie sniffed. "I can't imagine what would make up for all the worrying we've done."

Lan shot me a look; then he turned to Allie and his grin broadened. "You tell me if it was worth the wait," he said, and called back down the hall, "Come on in!"

There was a rattle of footsteps, and six people crowded into the room, two adults and three childings, with Papa bringing up the rear.

"Rennie?" Mama said, her eyes going wide. "Rennie!"

"Auntie Eff!" my almost-eight-year-old nephew, Albert, said importantly. "Uncle Lan brought us. We came in a giant wagon! It took *weeks*, and there was a whole herd of mammoths. I was hoping they'd follow us, but they didn't."

My niece, Seren Louise, aged six, was right behind him. "Auntie Eff, we saw a lady with a feather on her hat!"

"Annie Eff, Annie Eff!" yelled Lewis. He was the littlest of the childings, barely three, and he seemed more interested in having an excuse to shout than in understanding what was happening.

All three of the childings had grown enormously in the year since I'd last seen them, and they were all happy to be admired and wondered at. When Mama finished exclaiming over Rennie and passed her along to Allie, I told Albert and Seren and Lewis to come and meet their grandmother. Mama and Allie and Robbie had never met Rennie's childings before, because they'd never made the trip out to the Oak River settlement, and neither Rennie nor Brant had been back to Mill City since they'd run off together eight and a half years before. I'd been to visit them at Oak River twice in the last two years.

While Mama was busy hugging the little ones, I sat back. Brant was standing quietly beside the door, just watching. His brown eyes were tired, and there were lines in his face that hadn't been there a year ago. My stomach clenched. He looked much too sad and worried for this to be an ordinary family visit.

I glanced at Lan. He looked just as tired, which didn't surprise me if he'd just spent a week helping ride herd on Rennie's brood, but there was something else. His shoulders were tense, and a second after his eyes met mine, he looked away. I felt more uneasy than ever, in spite of the way the childings were bounding around.

After a bit, Lan pulled some extra chairs up to the table for the grown-ups and offered to take the childings to the kitchen for some dinner. As soon as they were out of the room, Allie fairly exploded into questions. "Oh, Rennie, it's so good to see you, but why didn't you tell us you were coming? Or did the letter get lost? Settlement mail isn't always reliable, I know. Why haven't you come before?" She gave Brant an unfriendly look, like she thought he was to blame — as if Rennie wouldn't have just upped and come home if she'd really wanted to. "How long are you staying? And where?"

Rennie looked down at her plate and picked at the carrots she'd just served herself. "We — it was kind of a last-minute decision. We haven't settled much yet."

Mama's eyes narrowed, and I could see that she'd gotten over her surprise and was starting to add things up . . . and I didn't think she liked the total she was getting any more than I did. "Rennie," she said, "I hope you and Brant know that you and your children are welcome here, no matter what has happened."

"I — thank you, Mama," Rennie whispered without looking up.

"Now, why don't you tell us what is going on?"

Allie opened her mouth to say something, and Mama shot her a glance that made her close up again real quick.

"The long and short of it is, we've parted company with the Oak River settlement," Brant said heavily. "They're buying out our share, but . . . well, it wasn't exactly a friendly parting."

There was silence while everyone waited for him to go on. Before it got awkward, Papa said, "I see. Have you had time to consider what you're going to do next?"

"Not really, except looking for work as soon as I'm able." Brant hesitated. "I was hoping that Rennie and the childings could put up here for a few days, until I can get a place lined up for us to stay."

"With Jack and Nan and Hugh gone, there's plenty of room for all of you. I won't hear of you staying anywhere else," Mama said firmly. "I expect you'll have enough to do without househunting on top of it, so don't argue."

"I wouldn't dare, ma'am," Brant said with a faint smile, and Robbie laughed.

"The wagon with our things is still over at the Settlement Office holding pen," Rennie put in. "We —"

"Your father and Robbie can go with Brant to pick them up tomorrow," Mama told her before Rennie could get any further. "You've had a long trip, and you need a quiet evening. If you don't have enough with you to get through the night, I'm sure we can find something in the attic. Lewis is too old to need any of the baby clothes I passed on to Nan, and most of the things for older children are still there."

Mama and Allie spent the rest of the meal going over details with Rennie, deciding which rooms Rennie's family would have and tiptoeing around the question of what they might need, in case asking straight out or waiting for Rennie to ask would make her feel worse than she already did.

I wasn't as worried as Mama. It wasn't as if Oak River had failed and left Rennie and her family with nothing more than the clothes they were wearing. Oak River was actually one of the more successful settlements, and Brant had been one of the founders. He and Rennie might not have brought much home with them, but if the settlement was buying them out, they should have a fair stake to start over with.

The real question was why they had to start over at all. The settlement had been founded by the Society of Progressive Rationalists to prove that people could manage well without magic, and they'd always been strict about making people avoid using spells even if they were only visiting. Every year, the settlers had gotten stricter about making sure no one used magic, and by my last visit, most of them had just about stopped speaking to Brant and Rennie because Brant didn't think they should be so firm about making folks abide by their rules if the folks were just passing through. I hadn't thought the settlers were worked up enough to kick someone right out of the settlement, though, especially not someone like Brant.

I didn't find out what had happened that night, nor the next day (which was mostly occupied with getting Rennie and the children settled in). Neither Brant nor Rennie would talk about it, so it wasn't until Saturday, when I cornered Lan in Papa's library, that I got the whole story.

The problems at Oak River had started with the mirror bugs. They hadn't been drawn to Oak River the way they were drawn to all the other settlements, because it was magic that drew them and the Oak River settlement didn't use magic. You'd think that the settlers would have been pleased, but I'd already figured out that the Rationalists weren't any more rational than most other folks. Sure enough, a lot of them hadn't been happy. The spells the other settlements used had attracted the mirror bugs, keeping them away from Oak River, and some of the settlers didn't like feeling that they'd benefited from spells, even if they hadn't been the ones to cast them.

Then Professor Torgeson found out that the mirror bugs hadn't just been using whatever magic was around them, the way normal magical creatures did. They absorbed it and took it with them, and it didn't go back into the surroundings until they died. The mirror bug traps that the Settlement Office set up had really high levels of magic around them, and would for a few more years until the magic evened itself back out.

When they found that out, some of the more dedicated Rationalists at Oak River had taken the notion that they should find a way to get rid of all the natural magic anywhere in their allotment. Unfortunately for them, there was no way to do that without using magic or magical critters, and it wouldn't have lasted, anyway. They'd backed off from that idea, but now they were talking about keeping all of the magical plants and wildlife away from their land, as well as not using any spells themselves.

"That's crazy," I said. "Even the settlement protection spells can't do that, not completely. They only try to block out the dangerous things. And are the Rationalists going to stop growing hexberries and calsters in their gardens? Or Scandian wheat, or meadow rice?"

"They're scared," Lan said softly. "Scared people do crazy things."

Something in the way he said that made me narrow my eyes at him. "How crazy?" I demanded. "And how did you end up traveling with Brant and Rennie, anyway? I thought you were riding the middle settlements with Paul Roberts. Oak River is part of Wash's circuit."

Lan flushed and kicked at the floor. "We finished the circuit early, so I talked Mr. Roberts into taking me through Oak River on our way back. I wanted to talk to Brant."

"To . . ." I stopped, thinking hard. There had been a point, a few years back, when I'd thought that giving up magic and becoming a Rationalist was the best way to keep from ever doing harm with my magic. I'd almost done it, and I'd only been worried that I might hurt someone. Lan had actually killed his professor by accident. "You wanted to talk to someone who doesn't use magic."

Lan nodded without looking at me. "Mr. Roberts tried to talk me out of it, but I thought it was just because the normal Rationalists don't like magic. I told him I'd been to Oak River before and it hadn't been that bad, and he finally gave in. I didn't realize how much they'd changed.

"When we got to Oak River, we found out that Brant and Rennie were the only folks who were still letting magicians stay with them. If a group came through that was too large, the rest of the settlers made some of them stay outside the palisade wall. Without protection spells."

I was horrified. "But their charter says that magicians can stay in the settlement, because they don't have a wagonrest. They did it that way on purpose! And now they're going back on the agreement? Does the Settlement Office know about this?"

"They do now," Lan said grimly. "Anyway, the second day I was there, I went for a walk. There were a couple of boys playing marbles . . . remember that game Robbie and William invented, with the marbles changing color? I showed them how to play."

"Lan, you didn't!"

"It's just a game!"

"It's still using magic."

"Not for anything important."

I gave him a stern look, and he shrugged. "All right, I did know better. But I was angry. And I really didn't think there was any harm in it. None of the Rationalists I know ever minded using magic for little things that don't count. It's only useful things that they insist on doing by hand."

"How many Rationalists do you know? Besides Brant. And how many of them care enough about Progressive Rationalism to leave everything and go off to live in a settlement, just so they can get away from magic?"

"I know, but . . ." Lan shrugged again. "The point is, the boys' mother caught me at it. She threw a fit right there in the street, and next thing I knew, practically everyone in the settlement was out there threatening to get a rope and string me up."

My eyes widened. "No wonder you didn't want to tell Mama! She already worries about the wildlife; if she took a notion that the people out West are dangerous, too, she'd never let any of us get within a mile of the Mammoth River, ever again."

"And it wouldn't do any good to tell her that even if they'd actually tried to hang me, they couldn't have done a thing," Lan said. "Not without magic."

"They didn't try, then?"

"No. Brant got there first. He was just in time to hear them muttering about ropes, and he blew up." Lan paused. "You know, 'blew up' probably isn't the right way to put it."

"What did he *say*?"

"He . . . well, he tore strips off them," Lan said. "And he did it without even raising his voice. He told them they were a disgrace to the whole Rationalist movement, talking about hanging someone without a trial, and then he went on about how magic wasn't against the law but murder was, and a bunch of other things about Rationalist philosophy.

"The boys' mother went red in the face and yelled at him that I'd been corrupting her sons and she didn't want me in the settlement, wildlife or no wildlife. Quite a few folks had drifted off by then, but most of the ones who were left agreed with her. One of them called out that Brant should be ashamed to call himself a Rationalist, supporting a magician the way he had.

"Brant went real quiet for a minute, and then he said that he wasn't ashamed to be a Rationalist, but he was sure as anything ashamed to belong to the Oak River settlement. Right about then, Mr. Lewis showed up."

"And?"

"After he heard what happened, Mr. Lewis told everyone to go home while he had a talk with Brant and me." Lan shook his head. "Brant said he didn't have anything to hide, and went on some more about Rationalist philosophy. He finished up saying he and his family were leaving Oak River, and Mr. Lewis just looked . . ." He paused again. "Tired and stricken."

"Brant is his nephew," I said. "I always thought they were pretty close. He must feel like Mama felt when Rennie ran off, almost."

Lan nodded, but he didn't look as if he'd really thought on it much. "There was some more talk, and Brant and I went home. I apologized for putting him in such a situation, but he said he and Rennie had been talking about leaving the settlement since early spring, and it was better to go now than to wait and maybe get caught by an early winter. Rennie gave me one of her scolds, and we spent a couple of days packing up. Mr. Lewis came around and talked some more with Brant — I think that's when they worked out how the settlement would buy out Brant's share — and we left."

I thanked Lan for telling me, and we agreed that neither of us would say anything to Rennie or Brant unless they brought it up first. I was pretty sure that Rennie was glad to be back, but I wondered how Brant felt, and about how my niece and nephews would feel when they saw the rest of the family using spells.

I was right to worry. The first couple of weeks were difficult. Seren Louise got terribly upset the first time she saw Nan use the dusting spell, and Albert lectured everyone about how wicked it was to use magic for anything until Brant told him it was bad manners. Rennie alternated between flinching whenever someone cast a spell, and using spells herself even for the littlest things. Brant just looked tired all the time, and a little sad whenever he saw Rennie doing spellwork.

The third week after Rennie came home, two more families arrived from Oak River. They'd left for the same reasons as Brant and Rennie, and they brought letters from Brant's uncle. Having them around seemed to make Brant and Rennie feel better, though they didn't spend a lot of time together that I knew of.

Gradually, things settled down. Albert and Seren Louise started at the day school, and Brant found a job at one of the riverboat companies. Rennie started acting more like her old self, and stopped making such a point of casting spells in front of Brant, though she didn't hide that she was doing it.

The trouble was, I'd never much liked Rennie's old self, and I liked her new-old self even less. She'd always tried to boss us younger ones, and as soon as she was back to feeling better, she started in trying it again. Having Rennie around made Allie's bossing worse, too. Between the two of them, I wished more than once that I could move into Mrs. Jablonski's rooming house just to get away from them, but I knew Mama and Papa would never allow it, even once I turned twenty-one come June.

I started staying as late as I could at work, though there wasn't much to do. The Frontier Management Department had lied about getting started on the medusa lizard in November; by the end of the month, they didn't even have a preliminary list of people who they thought would be good choices to study Lizzie, much less an actual schedule of folks to show up and do things.

By mid-December, winter had settled in for sure. With the ground frozen, work on the study center had stopped. Work on the medusa lizard still hadn't started. I spent most of my time at the office sending letters to the Frontier Management Department asking when their so-called experts would arrive, or trudging back and forth through the snow to the Settlement Office to see if they had any news. At home, I watched the childings for Rennie and Brant and helped with the extra laundry and mending that came with having so many more people in the house.

And every night as I fell asleep, I wished I were back in settlement territory. Facing saber cats and medusa lizards might be a lot more dangerous than minding childings and writing cranky letters, but it was also a lot more interesting.

CHAPTER ·3·

RIGHT BEFORE CHRISTMAS, A MAN CAME UP FROM THE SOCIETY OF Progressive Rationalists in Long Lake City to talk to Brant and the others who'd left Oak River. The Long Lake City branch of the society were the ones who'd provided a lot of the people and money to start up the Oak River settlement in the first place. Mr. Lewis had been sending them progress reports for years, and the Long Lake City Rationalists were very unhappy about the turn the settlement had taken. The man they sent up to Mill City spent a week talking to all three of the families who'd left the settlement and then spent another couple of days talking to Mr. Parsons at the Settlement Office, and he wasn't any happier when he left than when he'd come.

Rennie and Brant stayed on at the house after Christmas, though Brant had been with the riverboat company for over two months and they'd gotten their settlement buyout. I didn't bother asking why. I wasn't sure I wanted to know. I felt snappish all the time, the way the golden firefoxes at the menagerie acted when we had to put them in the small cages in order to clean out their usual pen.

Even the Frontier Management Department deciding to let us start dissecting Lizzie at last didn't help, though at least

24

I finally had something to do at work besides write letters. Actually, it made things even harder. I'd spend my day taking notes and making sketches while Professor Torgeson and Professor Jeffries eased the preservation spells back from one bit of the medusa lizard or another so they could work on it. We'd talk and speculate about the lizard's magic and development, and I'd help write up the report of their findings.

And then I'd go home to Rennie's childings and Mama's chores and Allie trying to make rules for everything and everybody. Lan was the only one who ever asked about the medusa lizard or the menagerie. Robbie and my sisters weren't interested, and Papa didn't have to ask me because he and Professor Jeffries and Professor Graham always got together to talk at the end of the day, so he'd already heard. And if Mama or Brant wanted to know, they talked to Papa. It was like I was still thirteen and too young to know what I was doing.

Early in February, the first batch of experts from the Frontier Management Department came out to look at the medusa lizard. There were so many that they couldn't all fit in Professor Torgeson's laboratory at the same time, and a lot of them didn't have anything useful to say. As far as I could see, most of them had talked their way onto the list just so they'd be able to tell folks back home they'd actually seen the lizard.

"Good riddance," Professor Torgeson said when they left a week later. "Eff, we're taking the morning off."

"We are? But —"

"I have an important letter to write. You're helping."

It took us most of the morning to put together the letter she sent to the Frontier Management Department, and I learned a lot about how to be frigidly polite and still leave somebody feeling like they'd been spanked.

That was Thursday. On Friday, Roger Boden arrived back from Albion. I'd met Roger a little over a year before, when he'd started coming around to help out at the menagerie after taking one of Professor Jeffries's fall classes. We'd gotten to know each other pretty well, but then he'd had an offer to study advanced magic in Albion that was too good for him not to take. We'd been exchanging letters for the past year, and I'd been looking forward to seeing him again.

Roger stopped by the house on Saturday afternoon and Mama invited him to stay and have tea. I introduced him to Lan, who'd been away from home when we got acquainted, and to Brant and Rennie and the childings. Lan asked about his studies in Albion and they ended up having a long, energetic talk with Papa and Robbie about magical theory. I was especially glad to see Lan getting all emphatic and waving his arms around to make a point. He hadn't been that excited about anything in months.

I wasn't so sure what to think about Roger. His red-blond hair was a little longer than it had been, and he'd grown a small mustache that made him look older. He'd always seemed solid and reliable, but he was more sure of himself now, and less quiet than he had been. He'd picked up just a hint of an Albion accent, too. He didn't flirt or pay me any more attention than was courteous, but every so often during that tea, I felt his blue eyes following me for just a little longer than they followed anyone else.

Mama and Allie must have noticed that extra bit of looking, because the minute he got up to leave, Mama said, "It's so good to see you again, Mr. Boden, and we haven't come anywhere near catching up yet. Won't you stay for supper?"

"Yes, do," Allie put in. "You can't go back to a rooming house meal on your first night home! Tell him, Eff!"

Rennie frowned slightly, looking from Allie to me and back. I shot Allie a glare, but I didn't say anything.

Roger smiled at Mama. "Thank you kindly for the invitation, Mrs. Rothmer, but I really need to get back to my unpacking. I think the trunks must have multiplied on the journey — I swear there are twice as many as I remember sending off."

"I'm glad you took the time to stop by," Papa said. "I enjoyed the discussion."

"I'll admit to an ulterior motive, Professor," Roger said. "I'm hoping you can make time on Monday to start assessing the work I did in Albion. I'd like to finish my degree this year, and the sooner I know what I still have to take —"

"Say no more," Papa said, laughing. "I'll be in my office at ten thirty in the morning. Bring your papers along then, and I'll see what I can do."

Roger nodded. "Thank you, sir. I'll see you Monday." He bade us all good evening and left in a flurry of good wishes.

The minute he was out the door, Allie pounced on me. "Eff! Why didn't you help us persuade him to stay?"

"Because she didn't want to help you make a spectacle of yourself," Rennie said, frowning. "Honestly, Allie, you can't run after a fellow so obviously and expect to get anywhere."

Allie's eyes went wide. "But . . . I'm not . . . It's not me, it's Eff!"

"What?" Rennie gave her a puzzled look.

"She thinks Mr. Boden's sweet on Eff," Robbie said, snatching the last two cookies from the platter on the table as he left to do his studying.

Lan paused in the doorway and gave me a startled look. Rennie studied me for a moment, then turned and frowned at Allie. "What were you trying to do, then, ruin her chances?"

"You can both stop that right this minute," I said, alarmed. The last thing I needed was for Rennie to decide Roger Boden was courting me; whether she was for it or against it, she'd want to mix in and make things come out her way, and never mind what I thought of it. "Roger came to see Papa."

"Right — that's why *Roger* spent the whole afternoon staring at you," Allie said scornfully. "And after a whole year of writing letters between you, too."

"I've been writing to William for longer than that," I said, feeling my face go hot. The thought flashed through my mind that if I did marry Roger, I wouldn't have to come home to Allie's nagging anymore, and if I could have gone any redder, I would have. "Mr. Boden is a friend, that's all," I snapped, hoping to make that picture go out of my head.

Lan was looking back and forth between us, like he wasn't sure which of us had the right of things. "Eff, if you like Mr. —"

"You stay out of this!" I interrupted. "Whether I like him or not is my business, and what I choose to do about it — or not to do about it — is even more my business. And that goes double for the two of you," I added, turning to Allie and Rennie.

"'Choose to do about it'?" Allie snorted. "You're going to end up an old maid like that professor you work for if you dither around much longer."

"There are worse things than being an old maid," Rennie said softly.

Allie and I just stared at her for a minute. I remembered how unhappy Rennie had seemed both times I'd been in Oak River, and some of what she'd told me the one time we'd talked about why she ran off with Brant. Still, I'd never expected to have Rennie on my side in this kind of argument.

"I like Professor Torgeson," I said finally. "I wouldn't mind turning out like her. And anyway, I told you already that it's my business."

"Besides, isn't that a bit of the pot calling the kettle black?" Lan put in, tilting his head to study Allie. "You're three years older than we are. If anyone is getting long in the tooth —"

"I have plenty of prospects!"

"You do?" I said. "Well, I'll certainly remember how to help you out if you ever bring one of them home."

"I think you should leave each other alone," Rennie said firmly. "Eff's right; it's her business." Lan looked at me, then at Allie, and nodded.

Allie glared at us, but she knew better than to keep up arguing. "You just think hard about what you're doing, Eff, that's all," she said, and went off, leaving Rennie and me to finish clearing up the tea things.

I was more annoyed with Allie than I'd let on. I'd known what she thought about Roger, but I'd been hoping that she'd forgotten in the year he'd been away. Now she'd gone and gotten Rennie and Lan interested, and even if they were on my side today, there was no saying how long they'd stay that way.

Sometimes I couldn't help thinking that the unluckiest thing about being a thirteenth child was having all those older brothers and sisters telling me what to do.

CHAPTER

· 4 ·

I DIDN'T SEE MUCH OF ROGER UNTIL THE MIDDLE OF THE NEXT WEEK. Roger was helping in the menagerie until he graduated in the spring, and I was in the laboratory with Professor Torgeson when he and Professor Jeffries came in on a blast of freezing-cold air. They were both so crusted in snow that you couldn't tell what color their mufflers were until they started unwinding them and some of the clumps fell off to melt on the floor.

"I see it's started snowing out," Professor Torgeson commented.

"Since noon, and it's still coming down hard enough to make an ice dragon happy," Professor Jeffries replied, carefully shaking out his coat. "You might want to head home early. There's two inches on the ground already, and if the wind picks up . . ." He didn't have to finish the sentence. Anyone who'd spent a winter in Mill City knew better than to go out in a blizzard unless there was a dire need. Even in the heart of town it was easy to get disoriented and wander in circles until you froze. Mr. Gallington had lost two toes to frostbite that way a few years back, and everyone said he was lucky to have stumbled against the edge of Mr. Stolz's store when he did, or he'd have frozen to death.

"I don't think it will get that bad," Roger said, hanging his coat on the hook next to mine. "It doesn't have the right feel."

"You're a weather magician now, Mr. Boden?" Professor Torgeson raised an eyebrow at him.

"Not exactly, but I picked up a few things in Albion from Dr. Wencell," Roger told her. "Weather patterns are closely related to esoteric geomancy, so practically all my projects involved weather in some way. Of course, the weather they get in Albion isn't anything like ours, since we're smack in the middle of the continent, but that's the point — you can tell a great deal from the differences." He broke off, looking chagrined. "Sorry, Professors. I did my geomancy comprehensives on these cross-connections with the weather, and I tend to get carried away sometimes."

Professor Torgeson looked suddenly thoughtful. "Just how much did your geomancy studies encompass, Mr. Boden? Was it all theory, or did you venture into practical applications?"

"It was supposed to be mostly theory," Roger said after a minute, "but on an island like that, you can't help but see plenty of practical examples. The weather changes a lot faster than they think, but they're so used to it being that way that they take it for granted."

"The advantage of an outside perspective," Professor Jeffries murmured.

"Just so," Professor Torgeson said. "Mr. Boden, I wonder if you would be willing to put your skills to use on our medusa lizard?"

"Me?" Roger's eyes widened.

"Oh!" I said at the same time. Roger looked at the professors and then at me. "Professor Torgeson has been wanting to get a geomancer to come and look at the medusa lizard for months," I explained.

Geomancy is a really difficult specialization that mixes geology with several kinds of magic, including divination, which means you have to have a talent for it on top of being really intelligent. There are only four or five geomancers in the whole country, and they were all too busy to come running out to Mill City to do a few checks on a medusa lizard, so Professor Torgeson hadn't even asked for one.

Professor Torgeson nodded. "Mr. Boden?"

"Certainly, Professor," Roger said. "What would you like me to look for?"

"Point of origin, natural habitat, and history," Professor Torgeson said. "Beyond that, I'd prefer not to prejudice your findings. What would you like to begin with? Will you need any special supplies?"

"The claws and feet, please. Or whatever it uses to stand and balance. And if the small rock samples that Professor Olivera uses in the introductory geology class are available, I'd like those, please. A map would make it a lot easier, too, if you have one you don't mind me marking up."

Professor Torgeson nodded to me to get the sample cases that held the parts of the medusa lizard that she'd finished dissecting, and Professor Jeffries went for the rocks. I was only in the storage room for a minute, but when I came out, Professor Torgeson had a medium-sized map of the North Columbian continent lying open at the end of the table, and Roger was sketching an off-center diagram on the tabletop just below it in pale red and green chalk. I watched him for a minute and then said, "Oh! It's a compass rose."

Roger nodded without looking up. "Don't jiggle the table, or I'll have to redo it," he said.

"Would it be better to align the map to true north, also?" Professor Torgeson asked.

"No," Roger said. "This is better, because it gives me two lines to work with. Like having two eyes."

"Where do you want the medusa lizard feet?" I asked.

That got Roger and Professor Torgeson started on a whole long discussion about the medusa lizard and the way it resisted magic and the effect of taking the preservation spell off the bits they were using. By the time Professor Jeffries got back with the rocks, they'd decided that the spells would have to be canceled while Roger cast his own spells. Professor Torgeson did that while Roger laid out the rocks along the edge of the table, so that they made a big circle around the map and the diagram.

"Ready when you are," Roger said. Professor Torgeson nodded and handed him the sample jar that held the medusa lizard's left rear foot. Roger dumped the foot out into the middle of the compass rose and cast the spell.

A dark brown rock flew from the edge of the table, right over to the lizard's foot. It hit so hard that it knocked the foot to the edge of the compass rose. Two other rocks wobbled and moved out of line, but only by about an inch. Roger nodded and cast another spell. This time, one of the smallest points of the compass rose, the one that pointed west-west-southwest, turned from pale red to black. The two points on either side of it turned dark gray, and the southernmost one after that went pale gray.

"There's the general area of origin," Roger said. "Mostly west, and a little south, in an area with a lot of igneous rock, and maybe a bit of metamorphic rock, too. Mountains, probably. Looks as if it has a pretty wide range. I'm going to try for habitat next, though it won't be as accurate as it could be. I don't have the right samples."

Roger brushed the compass rose away and chalked a new diagram in its place. This one looked like two triangles, drawn on top of each other to make a six-pointed star. Roger set the medusa lizard's foot in the center, then pulled a small case out of his pocket, made of heavy quilted cotton. It was a little larger than the magician's cases that Papa and Lan used, and when he opened it, I saw that it had an extra section.

Carefully, Roger took six vials from the extra section of his case and tipped a tiny pinch from each of them into one of the six points of the star. One looked like gray dust, one like grains of sand, three like dried leaves, and one like black powder. Then he backed away and began muttering under his breath.

For a minute, nothing happened. Then there was a popping sound and flames shot up six inches from four of the star points. I jumped, and so did Professor Jeffries. The flares died back as fast as they'd come, and Roger stepped forward to peer at the star.

"I was right about the mountains, or maybe foothills," he announced. "Somewhere with a lot of granite, anyway, and with bedrock very close to the surface. It's definitely not a plains creature. I can't tell for sure whether it likes to be above the tree line or not, though, and I certainly can't tell what sort of forest it prefers. If it prefers forest to open hills." He sounded a mite disgruntled. "I said I didn't have the right samples."

"That's quite all right," Professor Jeffries said. "Just knowing that it's not native to the plains is very reassuring."

"In one way," Professor Torgeson said dryly. "In another, it's very unsettling. Just what would make something like this travel all the way out of the Far West to settlement territory, if it prefers mountains to plains?"

"Perhaps its history will tell us more," Professor Jeffries said. He looked at Roger and frowned. "If you aren't too tired?"

"I'm fine," Roger said. He picked up the brown rock that had knocked into the lizard foot and set it in the middle of the map. He set the two rocks that had wobbled farther out toward the western part of the map, and scooped up the pinches of powder from the unburned points of the star and sprinkled them across the rocks and the map. Then he stretched his left hand out over the table and cast again.

At first, it didn't seem that much was happening. Then I saw a small, bright red spot appear on the map, a bit east of the Red River. It looked like right about where we'd shot the two medusa lizards.

An instant later, Roger collapsed.

We all hurried forward, but Roger was already sitting up. As he struggled to his feet, Professor Torgeson made an exasperated noise, dragged a chair over, and pushed him into it. I fetched a glass of water and handed it to him. "Thanks," he told me, and gulped it down like he'd been in the desert for a week.

When he finished, Professor Torgeson and Professor Jeffries were both glaring at him. "I didn't mean for you to exhaust yourself!" Professor Torgeson said. "What do you think you were doing? Mapping the whole of the Far West?"

Roger stared at her for a minute, then dropped his head into his hands. "I forgot," he said in a muffled voice.

"Forgot what?" Professor Jeffries asked, straightening up from studying the map.

"I forgot I was using an undelimited symbol set," Roger said.

"It wasn't the lizard's magic resistance?"

"No — well, maybe a little." Roger lifted his head, looking sheepish. "But the resonance doesn't pass through the primary focus object; the geologic samples are the real conduits, so the blockage was really inconsequential. The real problem was that I kept waiting for it to finish."

Professor Torgeson looked like the only thing keeping her from rolling her eyes was politeness. "You *were* trying to map the whole of the Far West."

"Of course not," Roger said. "I know better than to try anything that stupid; it'd take more power than you could get even with a team of Hijero-Cathayans. All I was trying to do was trace the creature back to its point of origin, which of course is out in the unexplored territory somewhere."

"What went wrong?" I asked.

"I forgot it was —"

"— an undelimited thingamabob," I said. "I know, but what does that mean?"

"The map he was using doesn't have a proper end," Professor Torgeson said. "It just fades out into the unknown."

Roger shook his head. "No, it doesn't." He pointed at the line of mountains drawn along the western edge of the map. "And that's the problem. We know there are mountains out there, but not how far away, or even whether there's more than one range. So the map isn't accurate. When you track something back into unknown territory or off the edge of an accurate map, the trace just stops. Using a map that's not accurate . . . well, you saw what happened. I'm sorry, professors."

"Nonsense," Professor Jeffries said. "You've provided a good deal of useful information, more than you realize. No, no, you sit there. We'll take care of cleaning up."

Roger looked doubtful, but he sat in silence while the rest of us put the rocks and the lizard's foot back where they belonged and cleaned off the table. He didn't speak up again until Professor Torgeson reached for the map. Then he said, "Er, Professor? There was one thing . . ."

Both professors turned to him, and he flushed. "The point of using maps and symbols in geomancy is to control and confirm the divinatory aspects. Because divination is unreliable." Roger sounded as if he were reciting something.

"And?" Professor Torgeson said a little impatiently.

"And because of that, geomancers aren't supposed to talk about anything that . . . happens during the spells, unless there's a physical reaction to confirm it. Like the flares, or the symbols on the map. Because divination is unreliable without confirmation. Only —"

"Only there's something else you think we ought to know," Professor Jeffries said gently.

Roger nodded. He looked down, then took a deep breath and said rapidly, "I think there are more of those lizards coming east. Quite a lot of them. I . . . felt them, right before the spell turned on me."

"That's not exactly a surprise," Professor Torgeson said after a minute. "Nobody really thinks there were only two of them in the whole of the Far West."

"Nevertheless, I think I'll have a word with Mr. Parsons at the Settlement Office," Professor Jeffries said. Roger straightened up in alarm, and Professor Jeffries made a reassuring motion. "Never fear, I won't bring your name into it. Though if we do indeed have additional medusa lizards moving toward the settlements, we have a good deal more to worry about than your professional ethics."

We finished cleaning up and went off into the snow. I didn't expect much of anything to come of Roger's information; after all, it was pretty vague, and in my experience, both the Settlement Office and the Frontier Management Department hated to take action until they absolutely had to.

This time, I was wrong, but I didn't find out about it for a while.

CHAPTER
· 5 ·

In March, the next batch of experts from the Frontier Management Department started arriving. This time, they came in ones and twos instead of mobs, and they were folks who actually knew something about Western wildlife. Senior Magician George Ingolseby came from the New Bristol Institute of Magic, and Professor Donald Peppins from Franklin State University, and Dr. Corinna Ivanova from the Ladies College of Arts and Magic in Virginia. Dr. Martin Lefevre from Simon Magus came, which was a surprise — I'd met him in Philadelphia when Lan was recovering from the accident, and he'd been real interested in the petrified animals that Professor Torgeson found, but I hadn't figured him for the type to come all the way West just to look at a dead lizard, even a brand-new magical one.

The really big surprise, though, came in the last week of March. I opened the door to Professor Jeffries's office and my jaw dropped when I saw the two people standing by his desk.

"Miss Ochiba!" I said. "William! What — When —"

William Graham was the first friend Lan and I had made when Papa moved us all to Mill City when I was five, and after all that time he knew me better than anybody except Lan. Miss Ochiba had been one of our teachers from the time we were ten, teaching us Avrupan magic in class and Aphrikan magic every afternoon after the day school finished up. Two years after I started upper school, she'd gone back East to teach at Triskelion University in Belletriste. William hadn't ever said, but I'd always thought that it was partly on account of her that he'd decided to defy his father and make his own way at Triskelion instead of attending Simon Magus College with Lan.

It was two years since I'd seen William, and four since Miss Ochiba had left Mill City. She looked just the same: tall, with darker skin than most other black folks and an enormous bun of crinkly black hair at the nape of her neck. William looked different, but I couldn't put my finger on exactly how. He was still thin and sandy-haired; he hadn't grown much, and he still wore the same thick eyeglasses. He didn't look as pale as I remembered; I figured that came from living in Belletriste, which was a good eight hundred miles south and bound to be sunnier than Mill City, even in winter. His shoulders were a bit broader from working summers building railroad cars, but that was all.

William pushed his eyeglasses up on his nose and grinned at me. "Hello, Eff. It's good to see you again, too."

"Just so, Miss Rothmer," Miss Ochiba said. "I trust you are doing well?"

"Yes, ma'am," I replied, still feeling half stunned.

"Professor Ochiba and Mr. Graham are here to have a look at Lizzie," Professor Jeffries put in from behind me.

Neither of them had made a point of Miss Ochiba's proper title, but I felt myself flushing. "Of course. I'm sorry, Professor Ochiba, I just —"

"It was an understandable error, Miss Rothmer," she said with a little smile, and I wondered if I would ever get to calling her "Professor Ochiba" in my head. I hoped so. If there were anybody in the whole wide world I didn't want to be impolite to, even by accident, it was Professor Ochiba.

"Miss Rothmer has been assisting me with the menagerie for several years now," Professor Jeffries said with a pleased smile.

"We'll have to get together this week, so you can tell us all about it," William said to me. "Letters just aren't the same."

"Your letters certainly aren't," I said, sticking my nose up in the air and pretending to be cross. "I sent you pages and pages about the trip Professor Torgeson and I took through the settlements last year, and I was lucky to get three sentences back."

"They were very good sentences, though," William said earnestly.

I smiled. "I'm so glad you're back, even if it's only for a week."

"We are staying at Mrs. Jablonski's," Miss — *Professor* Ochiba said. "Perhaps you could join us for dinner one evening."

"I would love to," I said, carefully not looking at William. So he and his father still hadn't made up. Not that I was surprised. Professor Graham, William's father, had a terrible temper, and he was almost as stubborn as William. "May I bring Lan? I'm sure he'd be glad to see you both."

"He still hasn't gone back to Simon Magus, then?" William said. "That idiotic —" He looked at me and cut himself off. After a minute, he said, "So how is he, really?"

"Better," I told him. "He still has ups and downs." William was the only person besides me and Lan who knew the whole story of Lan's accident. I'd been a little surprised to find out that Lan had written him about it — William had always been more my friend than Lan's, I thought — but then I reminded myself that they'd been at boarding school in the East together for a year, and that Lan had been the first person William told about going to Triskelion, so it wasn't as surprising as I'd thought.

"We will have plenty of opportunity to catch up with Mr. Rothmer's doings over dinner," Professor Ochiba said. "At the moment, I believe we have a lizard to examine."

We'd had a string of warm, clear days, so much of the winter's snow had melted and the walk over to the laboratory building was a pleasant one. As we passed the menagerie, Roger Boden appeared from in between the mammoth pen and the small field where we kept the small animals like the chameleon tortoise and the porcupine that weren't too dangerous and wouldn't eat each other. "Professor Jeffries," he called.

"Roger," the professor called back. "Come and meet our latest visitors."

"Beg pardon for interrupting," Roger said as he joined us, "but you said you wanted to be notified as soon as the daybats broke their hibernation."

"Excellent! You and Eff can move them to their summer quarters tomorrow, then." Professor Jeffries turned to the rest of us. "Professor Ochiba, Mr. Graham, I'd like you to meet Roger Boden. He's just returned from studying in Albion, and he was most helpful with the medusa lizard. You recall the geomancy notes we sent along? That was his work."

Roger shook hands with the two of them. "Welcome to the frozen North. The weather's atypical today, but if you stick around long, we'll try to arrange a blizzard for you."

"Roger!" I said. "Stop playing scare-the-Easterners. It won't work; William grew up here, and Professor Ochiba taught us both in day school before she went back East."

"Oh, is this the William you mentioned in your letters? I hadn't realized." Roger gave me a sideways look, then nodded a bit stiffly at Professor Ochiba and William. "Welcome back, then."

William tensed, but he returned the nod with careful politeness.

"Thank you, Mr. Boden," Professor Ochiba said. She sounded mildly amused about something. "It's nice to be in Mill City again, even if it's only for a few days."

"So you're a geomancer?" William's eyes drifted from Roger to the mammoth pen and then to Professor Jeffries.

"Not quite yet, but I will be," Roger said easily. "It's not a quick process. I'll need a couple of years of fieldwork after I finish my degree before they'll let me take the certification exam."

"Fieldwork." William's shoulders relaxed a bit, though he still seemed wary. I barely kept from snorting. The two of them were behaving just like my older brothers used to, when one of them wanted to impress the other. "Where are you planning to do it?"

"I'm hoping for a job with one of the Settlement Offices," Roger said. "I understand they have a hard time finding people willing to work west of the Mammoth River. Too many of the best people head back East for school and then stay there."

I frowned. I'd been back East twice since we moved to Mill City: once for my sister Diane's wedding and once when Lan was hurt. I hadn't enjoyed it either time. I looked at William uncertainly, wondering if he liked it out East better than I did. I realized I'd always expected him to come back to Mill City when he finished school, but now that I thought about it, his letters had never said anything about it one way or the other.

"We'll certainly be pleased to have you for as long as you're willing to stay, Mr. Boden," Professor Jeffries said. "I'll have a look at the daybats as soon as we're through with Lizzie; in the meantime, we'd best be on our way."

We left Roger to go back to the daybat cages and made our way to the laboratory where Professor Torgeson kept the medusa lizard. She was waiting for us when we arrived. Professor Jeffries introduced Professor Ochiba and William, then said, "Lizzie is over here. Can you work through the preservation spells? I'd rather not take them down unless I have to."

"Which preservation spells did you use?" Professor Ochiba asked, and the discussion got very technical for a while before she said she didn't need the spells removed. Professor

Torgeson nodded at me to get my notebook, and Professor Ochiba got started.

Watching Professor Ochiba work wasn't anything like as interesting as watching the Avrupan magicians who'd been through in the past couple of weeks. Avrupan spells are well-defined and precise; they need particular words and arrangements and ingredients to cast. The really powerful ones take lots of magicians working together, each one performing a specific part of the spell just so, so that each part fits everyone else's part perfectly, like the pieces of a steam engine. Watching Avrupan spells being cast is interesting, even if you aren't trying to feel what the magic is doing, because Avrupan magicians are always moving — saying something, or mixing and sprinkling ingredients, or making gestures, or shifting something else into the right position.

Aphrikan magic isn't showy like that. Aphrikan magicians don't look like they're doing much of anything, even when they're casting a really big spell. Unless you're extra good at sensing magic, you often can't tell they're doing anything at all. That's why the first thing an Aphrikan magician has to learn is world-sensing — being real quiet in your own head and at the same time letting your magic pay close attention to everything that's going on outside you. It takes a long time and a lot of practice to get good at it. I'd been working on it for seven years, ever since Miss Ochiba started teaching me when I was thirteen, and it was only in the last couple of years that I'd actually been able to use it for anything besides just watching.

Professor Ochiba had learned Aphrikan magic from her parents. Her mother had been an Aphrikan magician who'd been kidnapped and brought to North Columbia as a slave, and her father was a South Columbian magician from New Asante who'd been sent north to try to stop the slave trade. Mr. Ochiba had bought several shiploads of slaves and set them free. Most of them had gone back to Aphrika, or to one of the colonies in South Columbia, but Professor Ochiba's mother had stayed in the United States with him to work with the abolitionists. The professor and her brothers had learned Avrupan magic in day school like everyone else, but both her parents had taught them Aphrikan magic at home. So she was a first-rate Aphrikan magician as well as an Avrupan one, and I was real interested in what she'd do with the medusa lizard.

From the outside, it looked like she just stood there. At first, even my world-sensing couldn't tell that she was doing anything. Then she started talking, and I realized that she'd been using her own world-sensing. I felt a little better. World-sensing is a subtle kind of magic, and you have to be really, really good before you can feel someone else doing it.

Every magician and scientist who'd come to see the medusa lizard started by describing what it looked like, and Professor Ochiba was no exception. Her description was more detailed than most, though. She got through all the usual things — that it was fifteen feet and some odd inches, nose to tail-tip, with gray-brown scales, short front legs and long, muscular back ones, and a mouth like a bird's beak as long as a man's arm and full of sharp, triangular teeth — and then she started in on things no one else had mentioned.

"The scales lie in two layers," she said. "The scales in the top layer are thicker at the base than at the outer edge, irregular in shape, with a rough surface; they are also particularly resistant to direct magical interference and observation. In most natural environments, they would therefore provide both visual and magical camouflage as well as protection. The underlying scales are thin, smooth, and nearly transparent; they are covered almost completely by the outer scales and it is not clear what function they perform."

William and I scribbled away as she moved on to the lizard's teeth, pointing out that all of them were in perfect condition, which was surprising in an adult creature. She speculated that worn or broken teeth fell out and the medusa lizard regrew them, and she estimated its age as twenty-two to twenty-six years, which was a good ten years more than most of the other scientists had guessed.

When she finished at last, she looked at Professor Torgeson and said, "Internally?"

Professor Torgeson nodded and we slid the carcass around so that the slit in its belly opened up.

Looking at the lizard's innards took even longer than looking at its outside had. By the time Professor Ochiba was done with her observations, I had five pages of notes and it was late in the afternoon.

The next day was even more interesting. Professor Ochiba had finished with just inspecting the lizard and moved on to doing more active magic. It still didn't look like much from the outside, but with my world-sensing I could feel when she poked at Lizzie with her magic.

The trouble was that Lizzie didn't have a speck of magic to be poked, as far as I could tell. I'd been wondering about that ever since we started in studying her properly. A critter that could turn animals and people to stone had to have *some* magic, but Lizzie didn't feel any more magical than the young mammoth we had out in the menagerie.

Professor Ochiba asked to look at the lizard's innards again, but it was the same thing. She'd been at it for over an hour when she frowned and straightened up. "Professor Jeffries, Professor Torgeson, I'd like to try something a bit unusual, if you wouldn't mind."

"Try anything you like, as long as you don't damage the lizard," Professor Torgeson replied.

"Very good," Professor Ochiba said. "Would one of you be so kind as to cast the candle-lighting spell over there?" She nodded at the table at the side of the room, where we kept all the paraphernalia that the Avrupan magicians needed.

"How many do you want lit?" Professor Jeffries asked.

"Four should be enough. All together, please."

Professor Jeffries nodded. He glanced at Professor Torgeson, who smiled and cast the spell. I felt the magic gather around the candles in a cloud that slowly heated up. Just as the candlewicks popped into flame, I felt Professor Ochiba shove the spell, hard.

All four candles went out. The hot cloud of magic went flying over to the medusa lizard. It hit right at Lizzie's shoulder joint — and vanished without leaving so much as a warm spot.

My eyes widened, and beside me, William made a startled noise. Shoving magic around like that wasn't something you normally did with Aphrikan magic. Even when I'd been pushing at my Avrupan spells to make them work, I'd mostly just nudged things into place. And to have the magic vanish completely . . . well, magic just doesn't behave that way.

"What on earth . . ." Professor Torgeson was staring at the candles. Being strictly an Avrupan magician, I figured she had no idea why her spell hadn't done what she expected it to.

"I beg your pardon, professor," Professor Ochiba said. "I needed an outside source of magic, and your spell casting was the fastest and easiest way of getting one."

"Were four candles enough?"

"Yes, thank you. One more test, I think. Mr. Graham, would you hold the carcass open for a moment? Professor, if you would be so kind?"

The two professors repeated their spells. This time, I felt the cloud of magic head into the lizard's body, where it disappeared just as quickly and just as completely as it had before.

Professor Ochiba nodded at William to let go of the lizard, then dropped into a chair. She looked tired, but her eyes gleamed.

"You found something?" Professor Torgeson said.

Professor Ochiba nodded. "Your dead lizard is still absorbing magic. Inside and out."

CHAPTER
· 6 ·

THERE WAS A BRIEF, STUNNED SILENCE. "ABSORBING MAGIC?" Professor Torgeson said finally, half to herself. "How is that possible? The thing is *dead*."

"I don't know," Professor Ochiba said. "But every time a spell touches it, it soaks up the magic and converts it directly into more spell-resistance."

"No wonder no one's been able to get the evaluation spells to work," Professor Jeffries commented.

Professor Ochiba nodded. "And if people have been trying to evaluate this creature magically, I'm surprised your preservation spells haven't failed already."

"Perhaps it would be best to stop working on Lizzie directly for the moment," Professor Jeffries said. "We do have a few samples from the other lizard, and there are always the petrified animals."

For the rest of the day, the three professors left the whole medusa lizard in the main lab while they ran tests and looked at other bits. When they found that all of the other samples absorbed magic, too, Professor Jeffries got all excited and got out a couple of the dead mirror bugs to compare. It turned out that the dead mirror bugs didn't absorb magic as much or as well as the medusa lizard, but they still absorbed it.

That caused a whole flurry of talk, with nearly every professor of magic at the college weighing in with an opinion, and a couple of folks from the Settlement Office besides. Nobody knew what to do about it, and everyone was worried about what it would mean if more medusa lizards showed up.

Since Professor Ochiba's world-sensing was about the only magic the lizard hadn't soaked up right off, the Settlement Office let her do some more work on Lizzie while they argued about what to do next. Professor Ochiba and William never did find a way to keep the medusa lizard from absorbing magic, which was what the Settlement Office wanted, but on their last day in Mill City they did come up with a spell to drain the magic back out of the medusa lizard carcass after it had been absorbed.

"The trick was making it fast and not very strong," William told me. "And not trying to make it perfect."

"That doesn't sound much like Aphrikan magic to me," I said.

"It's the same kind of combination as your mirror bug spell," William said. "Aphrikan and Avrupan both. Anyway, it's Avrupan magicians who are going to be casting it most of the time, isn't it?"

"I suppose," I said. "What do you mean, it's like my mirror bug spell?"

I should have known better than to ask. I'd lived most of my life around the college, and I could usually follow the kind of explanations that Papa gave his students, but I got lost pretty quick when things got technical. William liked being technical. The part that made sense was that the spell had to be weak because the medusa lizard was absorbing it at the same time the spell was draining magic back out. They had to be sure that more magic was coming out of the lizard than the spell was putting in. The rest of it was something about combining a Hardison Relay with a Möbius twist according to the Nandelian Principles, and since I'd never heard of any of those things, it made about as much sense to me as Mr. Schwarz when he started cussing in Prussian.

Professor Ochiba and William took the train back to Belletriste the next day. I saw them off at the train station, which was about the only time we'd had to talk since the day they arrived. I found out later that on the last evening, Mama tried to get Professor Graham to come to dinner with all of them. I think she was hoping to get him to start talking to William again, but he refused to even consider it. I think if it had been anyone but Mama who suggested it, he'd have stopped speaking to them, too. William wasn't happy when he found out, either, though he didn't say anything more to Mama than what was polite.

The first thing I did after William left was to sit down and write him a letter, apologizing for Mama's meddling. I'd said it to him already at the train station, but it felt more true to do it in writing. I thought about asking whether he planned to come back to Mill City when he finished school, but I couldn't think of any way of putting it that didn't sound a whole lot nosier than I wanted to be, so in the end I didn't say anything.

Having had William around, even for a few days, made everything harder once he was gone again. Working on the medusa lizard was still interesting, but I couldn't seem to work up as much enthusiasm without him and Professor Ochiba. Going home was even worse. Rennie and Allie had taken to complaining that I wasn't doing my share of the chores, and they wouldn't listen when I tried to explain that I had to stay late at work to get the menagerie animals ready to move to the almost-finished new study center.

Lan was no help, either. Mama had started dropping hints about how Lan should be studying so he wouldn't be behind when he went back to Simon Magus College, and almost as soon as she did, Lan began staying late at the Settlement Office. I didn't blame him; I just wished I could do the same without getting an earful from Rennie.

And then, early in April, a party of circuit magicians showed up down in St. Louis with eight medusa lizard heads, and it came out that the Settlement Offices had been sending out hunting parties since mid-February. Apparently, Mr. Parsons at the North Plains Territory Homestead Claim and Settlement Office had taken Roger's warning seriously, even though there hadn't been any real proof. The day after Professor Jeffries talked to him, he'd sent telegrams out to the directors of all the Settlement Offices in the Middle and South Plains Territories, and then he'd called in every circuit rider and territory guide he could find and sent them out to hunt medusa lizards. And so had everyone else.

The Settlement Offices hadn't made a big secret out of what they were doing, but nobody had really noticed. Normally, the circuit riders and guides don't work much in mid-winter, at least in the North Plains, so nobody thought it was odd that they weren't around. It wasn't until they started coming back that folks finally caught on and got upset.

When more hunters showed up with more lizard heads, the lines of people wanting allotments from the Settlement Office evaporated. So many advertisements showed up in the paper offering to sell settlement shares for hardly anything that the paper had to double its pages. Most of the ads were from folks who'd paid their fees and gotten an assignment from the Settlement Office, but who hadn't actually gone West yet. The folks who were already out in settlements weren't so interested in giving up and coming back.

At first, I thought it was a little peculiar that it was the people who were safe on the east side of the Great Barrier Spell who were the most scared, but when I thought about it, it made sense. Folks in the settlements were used to dealing with wildlife; the medusa lizards were worse than most things, but not enough worse to make them pack up and leave, especially since the hunters all said they'd had to go quite a ways out to find the lizards they'd killed.

Mama alternated between fretting about my brother Jack, who'd been out in the Bisonfield settlement for four years, and remarking on how happy she was that Rennie and Brant and their childings were safe in Mill City. So she was more than a mite put out when Brant came home from the shipping company one evening and broke the news that the Society of Progressive Rationalists in Long Lake City was considering sponsoring another settlement.

"Now?" Mama said when Brant brought it up over dinner. "With the medusa lizards and goodness knows what else coming out of the Far West? Shouldn't they wait until it's safer?"

"The West won't get any safer unless people move out into it," Lan grumbled.

Brant nodded. "And right now, the society can buy allotments for less than the normal fees the Settlement Office charges."

"Why would anyone want to, with those creatures around?" Allie said, shuddering. "Imagine a whole herd of them, coming —"

"Oh, for Pete's sake, Allie!" Robbie interrupted. "They're predators; they don't travel in herds!"

"Packs, then," Allie said stubbornly. "Like wolves."

I couldn't stand it any more. "They're *lizards*, Allie. Not wolves or cows."

"Do you even bother to read the paper?" Lan added. "They don't travel in packs either; the biggest group the Settlement Office teams have found was three, and they're not really sure they were actually traveling together."

"And there can't be very many of them near the settlements," Robbie put in. "It's a long way from the mountains to settlement territory, with a lot of dangerous wildlife in between, so even if all of them headed east at once, a lot of them would probably be trampled by mammoths or eaten by swarming weasels before they got anywhere close. And the Settlement Office teams don't seem to be having much trouble bagging the ones that have."

"The hunting teams all went out with the latest long-range repeaters," Lan said. "Makes it a lot easier to kill the lizards before they get close enough to petrify people. They're still losing a lot of horses, though."

Allie glared at the two of them and subsided unhappily. She hated being outargued. Mama was still looking at Brant. "I'd have thought the Rationalists had had enough of settlements," she said. "Oak River proved their point, surely!"

"Oak River proved that it's possible for a settlement to survive without using any magic," Brant said. "But nobody considers it an unqualified success, for all it's still in operation."

Rennie snorted. "I should think not! The trouble Albert and Seren Louise are having adjusting to —"

"Yes, exactly," Brant cut in before she could go off on one of her rants. "We've been looking at ways to avoid those mistakes next time."

"We?" Mama set her fork down very carefully. "You're not considering taking your family West again, are you?"

Brant and Rennie exchanged looks. "Not at this time," Brant said carefully. "I'm happy to help the society plan its next settlement, but I've had enough of being beholden to them for my stake."

"A very reasonable attitude," Papa said, nodding.

"You should keep an eye on the ads, though," Robbie put in. "If the prices on allotments keep dropping, you might be able to pick up a share in one of the established settlements for cheap."

Lan frowned. "You'll have to be quick if you want to try that, though. Mr. Parsons said that he's already had trouble with land speculators trying to get him to swap the allotments they've bought for ones they think are better, and most of those are out along the western edge of settlement territory. They'll be all over anything closer in."

"Land speculators?" Robbie looked interested, and we ended up spending the rest of the meal talking about where the best places would be to buy up land, compared to which places were most likely to be selling. Allie got bored fairly quickly, but Mama had just as much to say as anyone else. She didn't have any objection to investing in settlements, only to any of us going off into danger.

All the uproar over the lizard hunts actually made things easier when the study center finally got finished enough to start moving the menagerie animals to their new home, because the ferry wasn't busy with all the spring settlers. We got almost all the smaller natural animals, like the porcupine and the prairie dogs, across the river in one trip, though we had to take the three bison one at a time on account of their size. The magical animals were harder, especially the scorch lizard and the pseudogriffin, because they reacted badly to going through the Great Barrier Spell.

The two biggest problems, in a manner of speaking, were the medusa lizard eggs and the mammoth. The eggs were a problem because the college still didn't want anyone to know that they had such potentially dangerous things anywhere east of the Great Barrier Spell, even if they were still under the professor's preservation spell. We ended up wrapping each one individually in cotton wool, burying them all in two crates of straw, and labeling the crates as special laboratory equipment for Professor Torgeson and Professor Jeffries. Professor Jeffries took them to the study center himself on the very last ferry trip.

The mammoth was a lot harder to deal with. It had been a baby when the McNeil Expedition brought it back to Mill City in 1850, and they'd had trouble getting it on the ferry and through the Great Barrier Spell even then. Nine years later, it was nearly full grown and much too large for the ferry. Professor Jeffries suggested hiring one of the grain barges to get it across the river to West Landing, but even he looked doubtful when he said it.

"A grain barge might work if that creature were thoroughly tame, and mild-mannered to boot," Professor Torgeson said, glaring at him. "But since it is neither, there's no point in discussing it."

"We could keep it here for another year," Professor Jeffries said. "When they finish the new bridge, it'll just be a matter of walking him across it." The territory governor had finally given in and let Mill City and West Landing start building a bridge across the Mammoth River to connect the two towns, but putting it up was a tricky business because they didn't want to do anything that might disrupt the Great Barrier Spell. They'd been working on it for a year and a half already, and they still had nearly a year to go.

Professor Torgeson shook her head. "Do you really think Dean Farley will let you keep that animal here for another year? Getting rid of the mammoth was half the reason he agreed to fund the study center in the first place."

"I suppose," Professor Jeffries said.

In the end, the only thing to do was move the mammoth overland — walking it upstream to a ford and then back down and out to the study center. Mama was not pleased when she found out that Professor Jeffries wanted me to go along with the crew that was moving the mammoth to its new quarters. She and Allie and I were in the kitchen, clearing up the breakfast dishes, when I finally got around to mentioning it.

"Haven't you had enough of running around out West yet?" she asked in an exasperated tone when I told her.

I sighed. "It's not really 'out West,' Mama. Half the trip is on this side of the Mammoth River, and we won't ever be more than a few miles from it when we come back down the other side. It's all territory that's been settled for years and years."

"It's still not safe," Allie said with a sniff as she set the last dry plate on the stack and reached for the first cup on the drainboard. "Look at all those lizards they've been catching. What if they miss one? And anyway, working with wild beasts is —"

"— not a proper way for a lady to behave," I finished along with her. "Maybe not, but it's my job and I like it. You're the one who cares about propriety, Allie, not me."

Mama looked from me to Allie and back, and her eyebrows drew together just a little. Allie went on without noticing. "Just tell Professor Jeffries that you can't go. I'm sure he can find someone else."

"Allie, I've been helping to care for that critter for a good four years now," I said. "Six, if you count the first two years in upper school when I was just helping out for fun. The mammoth is accustomed to me."

"That doesn't mean —"

"And when it comes to the spells for controlling it, I've had more practice than anyone but Professor Jeffries, just from working with it for so long." I'd had a lot of practice with the mammoth other ways, too. Ever since my first year in upper school, I'd been using it to practice Aphrikan magic on — nudging it to eat first and then drink, or to move from one part of its pen to another. I'd gotten pretty good at it, but I wasn't bringing that up in front of Allie.

"But I'm sure you —"

"Allie." Mama's voice had that firm, no-nonsense edge that meant you'd best sit up and snap to, right this minute. Nobody argued when Mama used that voice, not even my oldest sister, Sharl, who'd been married for over fifteen years and had four childings of her own. "I think you've made yourself clear. Why don't you run upstairs and help Rennie with her mending? I swear, those childings are harder on their clothes than the last six of you put together."

"Yes, Mama." Reluctantly, Allie put down her dish towel and left.

Mama picked up the dish towel and started in drying, right where Allie had left off. She didn't say anything until the swing door had settled and I'd finished washing the forks and started on the knives. Then she gave a little sigh and looked at me.

"I know you worry, Mama," I started, "but this really isn't so —"

Mama held up her hands and I stopped. "This trip may not be so bad, but it won't be your last, will it, Eff?"

I was quiet for a minute. "I hope it won't," I said at last.

There was another long silence. I finished the knives and spoons.

"I suppose we didn't raise any of you to walk a path other than your own," Mama said after a while. "And I can't rightly say that I'd wish you all to be unhappy just so you would keep from being hurt. But . . ."

"But you really wish all of us could be happy doing something safe," I finished.

Mama smiled slightly. "You'd think that watching your children grow up would get easier with practice, but it doesn't. And you and Lan are special."

"Because Lan's a double-seventh son," I said, nodding.

"Because you are the youngest," Mama corrected gently. "The last of my boys, and the last of my girls."

We finished the clearing up in silence. Afterward, I spent a good deal of time thinking about what Mama had said. She'd as much as told me that she wouldn't stand in my way if I wanted to go West again, no matter how much she hated the idea. I wondered if she'd feel the same if Lan decided to go; technically, he was the youngest of us all, though I could see where a few minutes' difference might not mean all that much to Mama. Next day, I told Professor Jeffries that I'd be pleased to help herd the mammoth to its new home.

CHAPTER
· 7 ·

IN MID-MAY, WE LEFT MILL CITY — PROFESSOR TORGESON, ROGER Boden and two other students who'd been helping at the menagerie, two guides, two muleteers, the mammoth, and me. Before we left, the professor had a harness made for the mammoth from leather-wrapped chain. Professor Jeffries had designed a series of spells to keep the mammoth calm and easy to control, and he got Lan and Roger to come and help layer them onto the harness. I could see why he'd asked Lan — the power of a double-seventh son would make all the spells stronger and more long-lasting — but I wasn't sure why he wanted Roger's help.

Enchanting the harness took nearly a week, mostly figuring out which spells to use and how to adapt them to stick to the harness. Every time someone mentioned it to Professor Torgeson, she grumbled that the mammoth was too large and too dangerous and ought to be let go instead of being moved to a new menagerie. Finally, Lan pointed out that we'd need the harness even if the college wanted to let the mammoth go, because we couldn't set it free east of the Great Barrier Spell, so we'd still have to get it across the river. The professor quit grumbling so loudly after that. I was a little surprised that she didn't suggest shooting it, the way she had when she first came, but I think she'd gotten used to it.

Putting all those spells on the harness turned out to be well worth the effort. The mammoth shied when Professor Torgeson threw the first straps over its back, but as soon as the leather touched it, it calmed right down and let us finish hooking and buckling everything in place. Then the first guide took the lead rope and the muleteers and the two students took the ropes on either side, and we started on our way.

We had quite a crowd to see us off, mostly because of the mammoth. Everybody knew about it because Mr. Brewster, the mayor, had closed off the streets we were going to use, the way he always did for the Fourth of July parade, so that the mammoth wouldn't spook someone's horses and cause an accident. Folks on the east side of the river didn't get much chance to see the more dangerous wildlife, and they lined up to gape as we went by. The crowd made the mammoth uneasy, even with the calming spells on the harness, and we were all relieved when we finally got out of town.

Once we were out of Mill City, we had more trouble with people than we did with the mammoth itself. The college and the Settlement Office had tried to let folks along the way know about the mammoth in advance, but we still attracted a lot of attention as we went up the river. A couple of times, farmers who hadn't heard came out with rifles or shotguns to see what we were about, and one town sent a whole group of men along with their sheriff to warn us to keep away.

On the third night, I had a dream, one of the ones that was too sharp and clear and organized to be an ordinary dream. I'd been having them off and on for over two years, ever since I'd gone out to the settlements with Professor Torgeson that first time to help with the wildlife survey. Even after so long, I wasn't sure what they meant, but I was positive they were important. After we got back with the medusa lizard, I'd taken to writing them down, in hopes of making sense of them. I had quite a collection of them by then, but I hadn't gotten very far with the making-sense part.

It started the way the dreams usually did, with me walking through an early-summer forest. A silver cord floated waist-high in front of me, stretching off between the trees. I thought about letting go of it and just following along by sight, but when I looked down at my hands, I saw that the cord disappeared six inches behind my fingers as usual, and it occurred to me that if I let go, it might disappear completely. Or I might. And it wasn't as if holding the cord was a bother. It slipped easily through my hands, like it was made of silk.

Just as I thought that, the feel of the cord changed. When I looked down at it again, it had become a strip of leather, like the one that held the wooden pendant I wore every day. I wasn't walking through a forest any longer, either — I was crossing a rolling plain. I didn't see any trees or animals, just grass, stretching out toward a bright glitter on the distant horizon.

I followed the leather cord straight toward the glitter. After a bit, I realized that the glittering was sunlight on water. At first I thought it was a lake, but then I realized that it was the ocean that I hadn't seen since we all went back East to Helvan Shores for my sister Diane's wedding when I was thirteen. I felt light and happy.

Abruptly, a thick fog closed in ahead of me, cutting off my view of the ocean. The cord twisted sideways in my hands. I hesitated. I wanted to head for the ocean, but that would mean letting go of the cord and walking into the fog. I kept my hold on the cord.

Ahead was a hill, with a wall of white fog on the left, too thick to see through. I followed the leather cord up the hill. At the crown of the hill was a wrought-iron post, sunk deep into the ground. It stood as high as my chest, and on top of the post was a ring about three inches across. As the leather cord ran through the ring, it split in two. On the opposite side of the ring, half of the cord led off to the right and disappeared into the fog after about two feet; the other half went left, back across the plain. In the distance, if I squinted, I could see a line of green. I wondered if it was the forest I'd been walking through for so long.

Hesitantly, I let go of the cord with my right hand and reached around to touch the two branches on the other side of the iron ring, one after another. Nothing happened. I frowned, then switched hands.

As soon as my left hand touched the cord that ran back across the plain, I felt warmth run up my arm, and smelled smoke and fresh-baked bread and the sharp scent of the pre-serving solution that Professor Torgeson used on her specimens. When I touched the second cord, the one that led into the fog, I smelled water and leaf mold, coffee and frying onions, and the musty wet-hair smell of the mammoth on a rainy day.

My eyes blinked open, and I reached for the pencil and notebook I kept next to my bed before I was quite awake enough to remember where I was. I blinked again to get the sleep-grit out of my eyes. It was near enough to morning that the sky was lightening, though the sun wasn't up yet. I slid out of my bedroll quietly, to keep from waking Professor Torgeson, and left the tent to check on the mammoth.

The mammoth was asleep, leaning up against a tree with the end of its trunk curled up and its long hair poking every which way through the gaps in the harness. The muleteer who'd been on night watch waved at me, but didn't say anything. I poked up the campfire and fetched a kettle of water from the river. I was always cold when I woke up after one of *those* dreams, and I wanted something hot to drink. I didn't think anyone else would mind waking up to find the coffee already brewed.

While I waited for the water to heat, I sat and thought. I might not know all of what those strange dreams meant, but sometimes I got a bit of a feeling. I'd figured out the year before that they had something to do with the wooden pendant that Washington Morris had given me four years before.

Wash was one of the Settlement Office's best circuit magicians, a tall black man with a touch of a Southern drawl in his voice. He was about fifteen or sixteen years older than me, I guessed — I knew he'd fought in the Secession War that ended the year I was born, though he'd had to lie about his age to get into the army. We'd been friends since my last year in upper school, when Miss Ochiba had brought him in to talk to our class.

He'd given me the pendant that summer, when I was still fretting over my magic maybe getting out of hand. He'd told me to use it as long as I needed it and then pass it on, and that it could only pass in one direction, teacher to student. The idea of me being anyone's teacher made me snort a little every time I thought of it.

I frowned. I'd been West three times: once with Papa and Lan and Professor Jeffries to visit Oak River and find out about the mirror bug beetles; once as Professor Torgeson's assistant when she went to survey the wildlife in the settlements for the college; and again just the year before, when Professor Torgeson went to collect more samples of the stone animals we'd found, and we'd gone on to discover the first two medusa lizards.

Wash had been there every time. He'd been our guide on the first two trips; the third time, he'd been the one to let the professor know that something was turning animals to stone up by Big Bear Lake, and we'd gone with him to find out what it was. He might not have done a lot of teaching of the sort I'd been used to, but I'd learned a lot from him. Maybe that was all that the pendant counted.

I sighed in frustration. Thinking about the pendant never seemed to get me anywhere. The kettle was boiling, so I set about making coffee. I poured a cup for myself and took one to the muleteer, then sat back by the fire to think about the dream itself.

Usually when the dream changed, it changed completely, right from the beginning. The first time I'd had one, I'd been in the well house back in Helvan Shores, where we'd lived until I was five. In the second dream, I'd been flying over Mill City, and there hadn't been any connection I could see to the first dream.

68

This time, the dream had started the same way the last few had, with me following the silver cord through the forest. I went over the dream in my head, trying to remember exactly when the forest had changed to the plain and whether there'd been any warning. The silver cord had changed to leather, and then I'd been on the plain. I wasn't sure whether the fog counted as another change or not. And what did it mean that the cord had split in two?

Changes and choices. I frowned. If I wanted to keep following the cord, I'd have to pick one branch or the other. I already knew which one I'd choose. I'd wanted to get to the sea; the left-hand branch led back across the plain. On the other hand, neither one of the cords had smelled like the ocean when I touched them.

As I was going over the dream in my head one more time, I heard a rustle behind me, and Roger's voice said, "You're up early."

"I woke up and couldn't get back to sleep," I said. I hadn't told anyone about the dreams, not even Wash or William, and I didn't feel comfortable explaining it all to Roger. "I figured that as long as I was awake, I'd come watch the sunrise."

Roger yawned. "It's pretty, but I could have done with another hour's sleep."

"You and Lan," I said. "Would you like some coffee?" He nodded. I passed him a cup, and we sat in silence for a while until the rest of the camp woke up and it was time to start moving again.

I half expected to have the dream again that night, but I didn't, nor the night after. We worked our way slowly up the

Mammoth River, looking for a place to get the mammoth across. The first ford we came to was wider and deeper than either Professor Torgeson or I liked. Even something as big as the mammoth would have had to swim partway, and we didn't know how well the calming spells would hold when they went through the Great Barrier Spell. Nobody wanted to be out swimming in the middle of the river with a suddenly angry mammoth. Also, the town at the east end of the ford wasn't too keen on the notion of letting a mammoth walk down their main street to get to the river.

We passed up two more crossings before we came to one that suited Professor Torgeson. The banks sloped down easily on both sides, and the water was low enough that the near side of the river was a muddy flat. The main channel — and the Great Barrier Spell that followed along it — was nearer to the far bank, so if the mammoth spooked, there was a good chance it would head up the west bank and not back where we'd have to start over.

I'd only ever crossed the Mammoth River by ferry before. Looking at the dark water made me more than a little nervous about riding across, even if it wasn't moving very fast and the guides said the water in the main channel wouldn't be more than chest-deep for our horses. The really difficult part, though, was getting the mammoth through the Great Barrier Spell.

We had two things going for us: first, the mammoth was a natural animal, not a magical one; and second, we were heading east to west through the spell. The Great Barrier was made to keep dangerous wildlife out of the east, so it was practically impossible for any wildlife that couldn't fly to get past the barrier coming west to east. When the McNeil Expedition brought the mammoth back, it had taken half a dozen magicians from the college and several of the ones from the expedition to get it through the barrier, and Papa said afterward that they'd only gotten away with it because the mammoth was still a baby.

Going east to west, though, we only needed Professor Torgeson, one of the guides, and Roger and the other student-assistants to cast the spells that would let the mammoth through, and we only needed that many because we wanted to be sure the mammoth wasn't hurt. The second guide, the two mule-teers, and I had to control the mammoth on the way across the river. We'd all had plenty of practice; the professor and Roger had done the crossing spell for all of the smaller wildlife in the menagerie, and the guide, the muleteers, and I had been handling the mammoth every day since we left Mill City.

We coaxed the mammoth up to the edge of the ford and Professor Torgeson started the crossing spell. I cast a calming spell at the mammoth and, after a moment's thought, an extra one at my horse, too. I dithered for a second about using my Aphrikan magic; the one time I'd gone through the Great Barrier while doing world-sensing, I hadn't liked it at all. But I was a lot better at using Aphrikan magic on the mammoth than Avrupan. In the end, I damped my world-sensing down until all I was feeling was a tiny trickle, hoping that I'd be able to work on the mammoth that way without being overwhelmed by the Great Barrier Spell.

Professor Torgeson's voice rose. As Roger and the others joined the spell casting, she waved us forward. The Great Barrier Spell shimmered in the air in front of us. It looked thicker than I remembered, and I wondered if that was because the river was narrower here or because there weren't ferry boats going back and forth through the spell every day.

I could feel the professor's spell building up behind us as we approached the main channel of the river and the cold river water rose up over my boots. Then the Great Barrier thinned right in front of us. The guide pulled on the lead rope to hurry the mammoth up, and I gave it a little nudge, the same way I did when I wanted it to finish eating from one feed trough so I could clean it while the mammoth started on the second one. The mammoth plodded forward.

The Great Barrier Spell shivered as the guide rode through, and a second later, the mammoth reached it. As it did, the Great Barrier rippled and bulged toward the mammoth, right where Professor Torgeson's spell had thinned it out. I could see little flashes of light all around the edges, as if the Great Barrier was trying to get to the mammoth in spite of the professor's spell.

The water under the thin spot began to swirl and bubble. The mammoth jerked back, raised its head, and trumpeted angrily. Water splashed everywhere, some from the mammoth's thrashing and some from the bubbling in the river. The lead rope almost pulled the guide's horse off its feet; the guide loosened it from around his saddle horn just in time.

The muleteers backed their horses, tightening the control ropes on either side of the mammoth. The water around the mammoth — and around all of us — was churning and seething. I could feel my horse fighting to keep his feet.

The mammoth trumpeted again and backed away from

the Great Barrier. It tossed its head from side to side, trying to catch the lead rope with its tusks and break it. Before it could pull free, I let my world-sensing expand, so that I could find the best place to nudge the mammoth forward.

I gasped as the feel of magic crashed into me. The Great Barrier Spell loomed just ahead, as large and strong and ancient-feeling as ever, like a huge, aged oak tree or a living mountain. I could feel Professor Torgeson's spell, flowing through a small part of the Great Barrier and pushing it aside, or trying to. It felt like the professor was trying to hold the river back from one particular spot with just her hands. I felt the mammoth, unhappy and frightened on top, but with some of the same ancient living strength as the Great Barrier underneath.

I felt the spells in the mammoth's harness like steel wire stretched almost to its breaking point. The Great Barrier Spell pressed against them, trying to get at the mammoth, while the mammoth tried to tear free of both the Great Barrier and the harness. Lan's spells hadn't been meant to stand up to that kind of strain, and they wouldn't last much longer.

Lan's spells.

I reached for the harness spells, wrapping them in my own magic. Then I took a deep breath and pushed my own magic *into* the harness spells, as hard as ever I could push. You aren't supposed to be able to do that with Avrupan magic. Once you cast a spell, you can't change it. If you want it to be more or less powerful, you have to stop the first spell and start over with a new one. You can't do anything directly to another person's spell at all, except break it. If you're a really good magician, you can fit a new spell around someone else's spell, but that's like two gears fitting together in a steam engine.

That's how Avrupan magic is supposed to work, anyway. But I'd been using Aphrikan magic on my Avrupan spells for years, tweaking them from the outside to get them to work properly. It didn't seem like much of a stretch to tweak them from the inside for once. And Lan was my twin; his spells felt as much like mine as my own spells did. Also, I was pretty desperate.

The spells on the harness flared and buckled, and for a moment, I thought I'd made a terrible mistake and they were going to collapse completely. Then the wooden pendant heated against my skin, and my grip on the spells steadied. They felt like lines of fire wrapped around the mammoth, holding and gentling it.

The mammoth stopped fighting and lowered its head. The guide pulled the lead rope tight, and this time the mammoth surged forward. The muleteers and I went with it. I felt the Great Barrier Spell looking me over, as it always did, and then we were through.

CHAPTER

· 8 ·

I RELAXED MY HOLD ON THE HARNESS SPELLS AND SAGGED IN MY saddle, hoping the mammoth wouldn't take a sudden notion to head elsewhere at speed. Dimly, I felt the Great Barrier Spell flow back into place as Professor Torgeson ended her spell. A few minutes later, we were all gathered on the west bank.

The head guide cast the travel protection spells and we started south along the river, so as to get far enough from the ford to avoid anyone else who might come across. We didn't go far, just a mile or two, and then we made camp, even though it was only mid-afternoon. It was the first camp we'd made on the west side of the river, so setting up was a lot more complicated than it had been so far.

Even though the west bank had mostly been settled for a good twenty years, it was plenty dangerous because the river attracted wildlife. We couldn't use the wagonrests — the mammoth just wouldn't fit, and we didn't want to be inside any walls with the mammoth if it got upset all of a sudden — so the professor and the guides had to cast extra protection spells, and we had to dig our own firepit and haul water from the river.

As soon as we were settled, Professor Torgeson and Roger came over to find out what I'd done out in the middle of the river. I explained as best I could, and when I finished, the professor sat quiet for a long while.

"Twins," she said finally. "One of them a double-seventh son, the other a seventh daughter. It has to be . . . unless . . . Eff, have you and your brother done anything like this before?"

"Lan and I tried casting spells together a couple of times, when we were really little," I offered. "It never worked, and —" I stopped short and glanced sidelong at Roger.

"And?"

"And after a while, we quit trying."

Professor Torgeson's eyes narrowed. "You quit trying? Just like that?"

"It was only a couple of times," I said. "That was the summer that Lan was off with the boys all the time, and besides . . ." I hesitated, but I could tell by looking at her that Professor Torgeson was going to keep on asking until she was satisfied she'd gotten to the bottom of things. "Besides, I was worried about messing up his magic then. On account of me being a thirteenth child."

Roger looked startled, then frowned. Professor Torgeson gave a disdainful sniff. "Avrupans!" she said, and added a string of words in Vinish that I thought might be swearing. "I am surprised that your father believes such superstitions."

"It wasn't Papa," I said indignantly. "It was everybody else!"

"Indeed?" The professor looked skeptical, but she let it go in favor of grilling me more specifically about what I'd done to the harness spells. When she finally finished with me, she went over to the mammoth and spent another hour casting spells to analyze the ones on the harness.

Roger hung back for a moment. "She's right, you know," he said a little hesitantly.

"I can't help it that it's not supposed to work that way," I said. "I had to do something. And it worked, didn't it?"

"I don't mean about the harness spells," Roger said, sounding even more uncomfortable than before. "I meant about the other business. The unlucky thirteen. It really isn't important."

I stared at him for a minute while what he said sank in. Then I smiled. "Thank you." He nodded and went off to help the professor, but I felt considerably happier for the rest of the day.

Next morning, the professor asked if I would be willing to experiment on a few other spells, to see if I could do the same thing I'd done with the mammoth's harness. I wasn't happy about the idea at first, but Professor Torgeson assured me that they'd be small spells, nothing dangerous. Eventually, I agreed to try.

Professor Torgeson set up a row of rocks along the far side of the camp and cast different spells on each of them. She had the two guides cast a couple, too. Then I went down the row, trying to push my magic into each of them, the way I had with the harness spells.

It didn't work, not even once. Most of the time, I just bounced off, but twice I broke the spell. By the time I finished, I had a tearing headache, and I told the professor I wasn't going to try anything like that again until I was somewhere where I could take a nap afterward.

The rest of the trip to the new menagerie and study center went well. The mammoth didn't give us any more trouble, except once, and then it turned out that he'd smelled a spectral bear sneaking around the edge of the protection spells to try to get to our supplies. Professor Torgeson shot the bear before it could break through and damage anything, so it was a good thing the mammoth had acted up after all.

We reached the new Northern Plains Wildlife Study Center fifteen days after leaving Mill City. It was built on a part of the original land grant that the National Assembly in Washington had offered to all the states and territories that had been on the side of the Union during the Secession War. The college had originally kept it in hopes that the land on the west side of the Mammoth would be worth more once the settlers started moving in, and then when the railroad bought up a good part of their grant on the east side of the river, they just hung on to it for lack of any need to do anything with it.

It was a varied piece of land, stretching from the marshes along the north side of Lake Le Grande across rolling plains with an occasional patch of forest. The study center had been built on the shore of a long, skinny arm of the lake that thrust through the marsh into the prairie. A low, thick-walled cluster of buildings made of fieldstone occupied the middle of the study center. The smaller ones were living quarters; the larger ones were laboratories and a few offices.

The central buildings were surrounded by a palisade wall with several observation towers, but the holding pens, cages, and fenced-in areas for larger animals were outside the palisade, along with a long building for supplies. Some of the pens were already occupied, but there were plenty of empty ones for new acquisitions.

The whole complex had been designed to use as few protection spells as possible, because you can't study wildlife if you drive it all away before you even get a look at it. The college had borrowed a lot of the tricks the Rationalists used to make their settlements safe without magic, like putting half the rooms underground and setting up a double palisade wall, and then adding just a few spells to make things even safer. There were a couple of guard spells on the living quarters, and an alarm spell out around the outer edges of the land, but that was all.

The guides, Professor Torgeson, and her students went off to the administration building to let everyone know we'd arrived, while the muleteers and I took the mammoth to the biggest pen and let it loose. I stayed to watch it explore its new home. A few minutes later, Professor Torgeson and Professor Jeffries appeared, walking out from the palisade. They looked like they were having an argument, but I couldn't make out what they were saying until they got quite close.

"— completely irresponsible," Professor Torgeson was saying. "If this had happened in Mill City —"

"It wouldn't have happened in Mill City," Professor Jeffries said calmly. "It was the trip back through the Great Barrier Spell that disrupted the preservation spells."

"They should have been checked and reapplied immediately. It was —"

"— completely irresponsible, yes, you've said that at least four times." Professor Jeffries sounded like he was getting irritated, which hardly ever happens. "It simply wasn't possible."

"You could have —"

"— unpacked the eggs right there on the dock, and checked each one in the middle of West Landing?"

Professor Torgeson paused. "Of course not," she said reluctantly. "But as soon as you got here . . ."

"By then the shells had cracked on those three, and it was too late to recast the spells," Professor Jeffries said. "At least it wasn't the whole clutch; we still have plenty of specimen eggs under preservation."

"It's not the ones that are still preserved that concern me!" Professor Torgeson snapped.

"Yes, yes, you've made that quite clear," Professor Jeffries said. "Good afternoon, Miss Rothmer! I see you brought our mammoth back in fine shape. Did you have a good trip? How do you like our new facilities?"

"Good afternoon, Professor," I said. "The pens look great; we'll have room for a lot more animals now."

Professor Torgeson muttered something I didn't catch, and Professor Jeffries smiled. "Yes, and you'll have to come and see our latest acquisition. We have three baby medusa lizards to study."

I felt my eyes go wide. "M-medusa lizards?"

"Baby ones," the professor said, nodding cheerfully. "Though at the rate they're growing, they won't stay that way for long. When they hatched, they were about eight inches long, nose to tail-tip, but they've doubled in size in the last two weeks."

"Samuel, you are quite mad," Professor Torgeson announced. "You're lucky they haven't turned you to stone, or —"

"Oh, I doubt that's a danger," Professor Jeffries said. "They haven't developed their third eye yet, the one that Lefevre thinks controls the petrifying ability. Besides . . ." He hesitated, looking embarrassed. "I believe they've taken me for their . . . parent."

Professor Torgeson stared at him. "Parent. You — how —"

"I was the first thing they saw when they came out of their eggs, and I've been feeding them since then," Professor Jeffries said. "Don't glare like that. Once it was clear that they were hatching, someone had to be there to observe, and I could hardly ask one of the assistant professors to take the risk, could I?"

"So you knew it was a risk, at least," Professor Torgeson said.

Professor Jeffries gave her a reproving look. "I am not an imbecile, Aldis. Still, it's quite convenient, the way things turned out. Think of how much we can learn from live specimens! Though I confess I am glad it was only the three; forty-eight of them at once would be a bit much. Come and see."

Professor Torgeson and I exchanged glances, then followed Professor Jeffries along the wall and into the long supply building. "I thought it would be best to keep them isolated from the other animals, just in case," he said, waving toward a cage at the far end of the room. "Though I imagine we'll have to move them outside in a few months."

The three baby medusa lizards looked like a cross between a bird, a snake, and a giant frog. Their heads were long and pointed like a bird's beak, and they already had teeth. Their bodies were longer and thinner than I remembered, covered in pale brown scales. Their front legs were short, and their back legs were long and muscular. As soon as they saw Professor Jeffries, all three ran to the side of the cage and began opening and closing their mouths in excitement.

"They haven't made a sound yet," Professor Jeffries said. "This one is Stheno, and that's Euryale."

"I suppose there's a certain symmetry in naming them after the three Gorgons," Professor Torgeson said. "I presume the third one is Medusa?"

Professor Jeffries shook his head. "A medusa lizard named Medusa would be confusing, and in any case, the third one is male. So I'm calling him Fred."

"Stheno, Euryale, and Fred." Professor Torgeson sighed.

"They already answer to their names," Professor Jeffries told her. "And they haven't shown any sign of turning things to stone yet. They do, however, resist and absorb magic just as their adult counterparts do."

Professor Torgeson straightened up and her eyes narrowed. "You're sure it's the same?"

"So far as I can measure," Professor Jeffries told us. "I'll show you my notes when we get back to the main lab. And that means —"

"— that we have something to test our spells on," Professor Torgeson said. She sounded grimly pleased.

"Exactly."

Before we left the building, Professor Jeffries took one of the medusa lizards out of the cage to show us close up. It was quiet as long as he held it, but when he started to give it to Professor Torgeson, it tried to bite her. He calmed it down and put it back, then showed me how to feed the lizards. Fortunately, they weren't too picky; they seemed to prefer meat, when they could get it, but they gobbled up just about anything we put in front of them. Then we finished up walking around the pens and went inside the palisade to see the labs and living quarters.

The two professors spent the rest of the afternoon holed up in one of the offices, going over Professor Jeffries's notes and planning what to do next. Professor Jeffries hadn't told anyone outside the study center about the live medusa lizards yet, so one of the first things I did was to copy out a letter from Professor Jeffries to Dean Farley, Mr. Parsons, and the Frontier Management Department in Washington to let them know.

The guides and muleteers left the next day, but the students, Mr. Olsen and Mr. Yarmouth, stayed at the center to tend the menagerie animals and help get all the supplies and equipment unpacked and set up or put away. Professor Jeffries and Professor Torgeson spent most of their time with the medusa lizards, making observations and testing spells.

Three days after we arrived, Mr. Siwinski showed up, to be the first of the permanent staff members at the study center.

He was a short, stout man in his mid-forties, with hair that was rapidly going gray. He had a thick accent from somewhere in Eastern Avrupa. He'd been educated in Prague, and as soon as he finished, he'd gotten his papers together and come to Columbia, hoping to study the wildlife. He'd worked his way across the states until he got to the territories and Professor Jeffries hired him.

Mr. Siwinski brought letters from Mama and the rest of the family. Mama didn't say anything straight out, but she was plainly none too happy about me staying at the center, even if it was only a bit over ten miles from the river and only for the rest of the summer. She hadn't heard about the medusa lizard hatchlings yet, and I wasn't sure I wanted to tell her.

<hr />

With Mr. Siwinski to help, we had things running smoothly by the end of the week. But just as the center started to settle into a routine, both Professor Jeffries and Professor Torgeson got letters on heavy, cream-colored paper, trimmed with gold and sealed with red and gold wax. I thought at first they were official notices from the Frontier Management Department; I'd seen one once before, though I didn't remember the gold wax. I was close. The letters came from the Department of State in Washington, and they told the professors that a visiting Cathayan, Master Adept Farowase, had expressed interest in the medusa lizard hatchlings, and she and her aides would be coming to look at them in a few weeks.

The letters caused something of a stir. Two days after they arrived, a whole team of folks from the college arrived to spruce up some of the living quarters for the master adept and her aides. Along with them came a whole stack of letters and notices from all sorts of people, from the mayor of Mill City to the territory governor, wanting to arrange meetings and parades and interviews while the master adept went through town on her way to the study center. I spent the better part of a week writing back to everyone to tell them that if they wanted to talk to the Cathayans, they'd have to arrange it with the State Department.

When I thought about it, I could sort of understand all the fuss. The Cathayan Confederacy was enormous, rich, and powerful, and their teams of magicians had a reputation as the best and most powerful in the world. Most Cathayans didn't travel much outside the Confederacy, and Cathayan magicians in particular hardly ever left Ashia. Add to that the fact that the Confederacy was halfway around the world from Columbia, and it meant that this was probably the one chance most of the folks in Mill City would ever have to see a Cathayan Adept in person. Still, I couldn't help feeling that it was rude, and wondering how much it would annoy Master Adept Farawase when she finally got to Mill City. It would sure as anything have annoyed me.

About the only people who weren't half crazed by the adept's coming visit were Professor Jeffries and Professor Torgeson. Professor Jeffries pretty much ignored the whole thing, though he was very sharp with the man from the State Department when he wanted to move the medusa lizards to one of the labs inside the palisade. The State Department man thought the laboratory building would be easier to get at, more comfortable, and more impressive than the supply building out by the menagerie. Professor Jeffries told him that there was a reason the menagerie pens were so far from the guard spells inside the palisade and that if the State Department man wanted to impress the Cathayans, he could do it in Washington on his own time. Professor Torgeson just grumbled about all the time everyone was wasting, and said that a master adept ought to know better than to expect luxury quarters in a field research station.

Between the two of them, the professors kept the fuss and bother around the study center from getting completely out of hand, but even they couldn't keep the college and the Settlement Office from insisting that they come back to give the adept a "proper welcome" when she arrived in Mill City. So, two days before the Cathayans were due to arrive, the professors and I went back to town to get ready to meet her.

CHAPTER 9.

LAN WAS WAITING AT THE FERRY DOCK WHEN THE PROFESSORS AND I arrived back in Mill City. I was glad to see him, but I was more than a little surprised, too. "What are you doing out here in the middle of the morning?" I asked once we had our hellos out of the way.

"The Settlement Office sent me down, to be your official liaison," Lan said with a grin.

"What do we want with a —" I stopped short as we came around the loading house and I caught sight of the street. "What on earth is all that?"

Right in front of the warehouse, two men on tall ladders were wrestling with the ends of a red, white, and blue banner, while a third man stood in the street yelling directions. The front of the warehouse had a fresh coat of whitewash, and most of the storefronts I could see were newly painted. There were sawhorses stacked along the side of the street, ready to be set out.

"Preparations for the adept's visit," Lan said. "We need to go around this way. They've already blocked off most of the streets between here and the train station."

"I always thought those people in Washington had a bee in their collective bonnet about the Cathayan Confederacy,"

Professor Jeffries said, shaking his head. "Now I know it for sure."

"Oh, it's not the Frontier Management Department, nor the State Department, either," Lan said. "It's all Mayor Brewster's idea."

Apparently, Mayor Brewster had gotten more excited than anybody over the idea that a Cathayan master adept was coming to Mill City. He'd tried to persuade the State Department that she should stay in town for a night or two, but the State Department said it wasn't possible, so the mayor had settled on making a parade out of the adept and her aides getting from the train to the ferry. He even had people washing the cobblestones along the route.

The professors and I were to be part of the group welcoming the adept at the train platform. The mayor and the territory governor and the president of the college were going to make some speeches and present the master adept. All we had to do was stand there and be introduced. They had a band learning a Cathayan song that somebody said was their anthem, and the army had sent some men and women to be an honor guard and make it more parade-like.

The professors thought it was a lot of fuss and bother, and no good reason to drag us all away from the study center. I had to agree, especially since I didn't see what they wanted me for. Lan said they wanted everyone who'd been up at Big Bear Lake when the first medusa lizards were shot, but they couldn't get Mr. Grimsrud down from his settlement in time, and they couldn't find Wash or Greasy Pierre. They had to settle for Professor Torgeson and Lan and me.

I still thought it was silly, but I didn't have much choice. Two days later, I was standing on the platform at the train station in my Sunday best, along with Lan and the professors and a whole lot of other people. It was a lovely sunny day, and it looked like most of the town was milling around, waiting for the adept to arrive and the speeches to start. That's what the mayor and the territory governor seemed to think, anyway; I was pretty sure that everyone was really there to enjoy the sunshine and a bit of a break.

A man from the State Department had come out a week in advance to make sure everything ran smoothly. He was right in front of the group on the platform, looking uncomfortably hot and sweaty in his black frock coat and beaver hat. I never got to meet him, but he must have been good at his job, because he'd gotten the reporters to back off and he'd persuaded the mayor to keep the speeches to a minimum.

The new express train arrived right on time. The State Department man boarded it almost as soon as it stopped moving, and everyone in the street crowded up close to the platform. For about five minutes, nothing else happened, except for the stationmaster and the conductors moving up and down along the cars, but then the adept and her aides finally emerged and everyone cheered.

There were six Cathayans, plus the State Department man and two men in overcoats who I figured for marshals sent out with them from Washington to make sure they managed all right. All of the Cathayans were wearing loose, high-collared shirts with long, straight sleeves, and wide-legged pants. The men's shirts were just barely long enough to sit on, but the women's shirts came all the way down to their knees and were slit up the sides to mid-thigh. Elaborate embroidery edged every collar, cuff, and hem.

The Cathayans looked around and began talking very fast in a language that seemed to be all vowels. The State Department man said something back, more hesitantly, and pointed in our direction, and the little group crossed the platform to meet us.

Even though I'd never seen her before, I knew right off which one was Master Adept Farawase. She was an erect woman of middle height, with a flattish face, golden tan skin, and dark eyes that tipped up at the outer corner. Her long black hair was gathered into a single thick braid that fell to the backs of her knees, just below the embroidered hem of her tunic. Two chin-length locks had been left out of the braid in front, framing her face, and three dragon-scale ornaments, each about an inch long and made of gold, dangled along the length of the right-hand lock. Unless you looked close enough to spot the few strands of white in her hair, she didn't look more than thirty, but I'd have known just from the confident way she moved that she was a lot older than that. The odd thing was, her magic didn't feel like anything special. After all the fuss, I'd expected her to be as strong as Lan.

She'd brought four men and a woman with her. One of the men was nearly as short as she was, with thick, wavy hair and skin that was almost as dark as Professor Ochiba's. He wore a mustache; the rest of the men were clean-shaven. He moved like quicksilver, examining everything and making comments in Cathayan. The second man was medium tall, with the same straight, jet-black hair, golden skin, and slightly tilted eyes as the master adept. The third was round-faced and stocky, and seemed suspicious of everything. He was the one who kept answering the first man's comments, and from his tone of voice, he was annoyed.

The fourth man was tall and broad-shouldered, with a rectangular chiseled face, a hawk nose, and teeth as even as piano keys. His skin was a warm, light brown, and he had dark brown hair that fell thick and loose to his shoulders. Like the master adept, he had an inch-long dragon scale woven into the hair on the right side of his face, but he had only one, and his was made of silver instead of gold.

The last member of the Cathayan group was a slender young woman with dark, wavy hair, black eyes, and a heart-shaped face. At first I thought she was as tall as Master Adept Farawase, but then I realized that under her wide-legged pants she was wearing high-button boots with the tallest heels I'd ever seen. As the group reached us, she said something to the adept, bowed, and then stepped forward.

"Permit me to introduce us," she said, bowing again. "I am Speaker Bizen Sayo; you would say Miss Bizen. I am honored to be translator for Master Adept Farawase Rin."

The State Department man stepped forward and bowed back. "We are honored in turn, Master Adept Farawase, Speaker Bizen."

Miss Bizen turned and went down the line of Cathayans, giving their names and positions and a string of titles for each of them. I got lost very quickly, so I made Lan get me a list from the Settlement Office later on. The only one I remembered right off was the tall man wearing the silver dragon scale. Miss Bizen introduced him as Adept Alikaket, the master adept's second in command.

The State Department man was a lot better at names than I was, or else he'd memorized them all in advance. When Miss Bizen finished, he bowed to each of the Cathayans and welcomed them by name. Then he presented us, one at a time, starting with the territory governor. Whenever he paused, Miss Bizen would turn and rattle it off in Cathayan; Master Adept Farawase would incline her head, and the State Department man would bow and go on to the next person. The adept didn't seem too interested in the governor or the mayor or any of the other dignitaries, but she gave the State Department man a sharp look when he got to Professor Jeffries, and I thought she was paying much closer attention when it finally came down to Lan and me.

The speeches that came next took even longer than the introductions, even though all of them boiled down to "Welcome to Mill City. We hope you like our town. Have a good time while you're here." The idea seemed to be that if the Cathayan master adept wouldn't stay in Mill City, they'd drag out the time she was there for as long as they possibly could. Finally, it was all finished and we got into the carriages for the parade to the ferry.

Since we weren't particularly important people, Lan and I were in a closed carriage at the end of the line. I was just glad they'd put us together, so I had someone to talk to while we waited.

"Do you think all of them are magicians?" I asked doubtfully.

"They must be," Lan said, half to himself. "A normal Cathayan circle has at least ten people. Adepts can handle twice that many, and a master adept can work with multiple circles. At least, that's what Professor Warren —" He stopped short. Professor Warren was the man who'd died when the Hijero-Cathayan spell had gone wrong at Lan's college.

"Maybe they couldn't all leave the Confederacy for so long," I said. "Or maybe she didn't figure she'd need all of them. It's not like she's going to be damming up a river or cutting a road through a mountain while she's traveling." Hijero-Cathayan spells are mostly large-scale; you didn't need ten magicians at once to light a cookfire or seal up a storage barrel. Cathayan master adepts handle the biggest spells of all, the kind that only a double-seventh son could cast on his own.

"What is she here for, anyway? She can't have come all the way from Cathay to look at the medusa lizards, but they apparently didn't think the Settlement Office needed to know about anything else." He sounded a mite disgruntled.

"Trains, the State Department man said."

Lan looked at me in disbelief. "Trains?"

I shrugged. "The Cathayan Confederacy is building railroad lines all across their country, and they want the best trains they can get to run on them. They came to the U.S. because they'd heard that the Rationalist engineers have made a bunch of improvements to the engine, and they wanted to see for themselves. I don't think they really believed that a bunch of folks who don't believe in using magic would come up with anything good."

"Who else would?" Lan said. "The Rationalists may have loony ideas about magic, but you can't deny that they're brilliant when it comes to machines."

"Well, I guess the Cathayans know that now," I said. "That was the new express train they came in on."

Lan nodded absently, like he'd already moved on to thinking about something else. "I wish I could talk to her," he said wistfully.

"About that spell?" I said, meaning the one that had gone so wrong the year before.

Lan nodded. "The Northern Plains Riverbank College doesn't have anyone who's really studied Hijero-Cathayan magic, and I . . . don't want to write anyone at Simon Magus. I need to know what went wrong."

"But you know —"

"I mean *exactly* what went wrong," Lan said. "But even if I could wrangle some time to talk to her, I'm not sure she could tell me what I need to know. Translating technical questions can be a problem."

"Why don't you write to William?" I suggested. "There have to be people at Triskelion who can answer your questions."

Lan squirmed and looked away. "Maybe I will," he said, and I knew that he wouldn't.

"Be that way, then," I told him. I wanted to smack him for his stubbornness, but I knew there'd be no point to it. If Lan was too embarrassed to ask William something, nothing I could say or do would change his mind.

When we reached the ferry at last, things started to speed up some. The adept and her aides were already on board, along with the two marshals; the professors were waiting for me. I gave Lan a hug and a last-minute reassurance for Mama, and went to join them.

As the ferry pushed off, everyone gave a sigh of relief, even the Cathayans. They immediately went forward to look at the shimmer of the Great Barrier Spell, and after a minute Miss Bizen came back to ask Professor Jeffries about it. He spent the rest of the ferry ride talking with the adept and her aides.

West Landing hadn't put on anything like the show that Mill City had set up, but there were still plenty of curious people lined up to get a look at a Cathayan master adept. The Cathayans seemed unsurprised by it. The one with the mustache amused himself by making faces at the littlest childings along the street until the master adept saw and stopped him.

By the time we got to the study center, it was late afternoon and everyone was tired. Professor Jeffries suggested that we all have dinner, and save the tour of the center and the medusa lizards for the next day.

———◆———

That night, I had a dream, one of the special ones. It was completely different from any of the ones I'd had before; the only reason I knew it was one of *those* dreams was because it was so sharp and clear and unforgettable.

I was standing at one end of a large, darkened room. The floor was covered with a thick wool carpet with a complicated pattern in dark red and brown and deep green, but there weren't any chairs or tables or lamps. The wall to my left was covered with built-in bookcases, floor to ceiling. Most of the bookshelves were full of books, but there were a couple that held little gadgets and mechanical toys, and in the dream, I knew what each of them did and what most of the books were about, even though I hadn't read them all yet.

I looked to my right. The wall on that side was paneled in a hundred different kinds of wood that made an even more complicated pattern than the one in the carpet. Every so often, the woods shifted into a new design, almost like something living. At intervals in the pattern, there were hooks holding pots of plants. Some were vines that trailed almost to the ground, and some were cooking herbs that we grew in the garden, and some were odd shapes and colors that I'd never seen before.

Directly in front of me, at the far end of the room, was a set of heavy, midnight blue curtains that covered the whole wall. I hesitated. I looked at the wall of books, and then at the wall of plants. Finally, I walked slowly down to the end of the room and pulled the curtains aside.

Light spilled into the room, blindingly bright. I raised my hand to block it out, and the movement woke me. I sat up, shivering in the darkness, and pulled at the comforter to wrap it more closely around my shoulders. The little wooden pendant that I always wore thumped against my chest, and I shivered again.

The dreams and the cold had something to do with the pendant, I'd figured out that much, but I didn't know what. Wash knew, I was sure, but he wouldn't tell me. I'd meant to ask Professor Ochiba, because whatever the pendant was doing, it pretty much had to be Aphrikan magic, but thanks to Mama's dinners, I hadn't gotten the chance to ask in person when she was visiting, and it didn't seem the sort of thing that would be a good idea to put in a letter.

After a bit, I stopped shivering. I tucked the pendant away and lay back down. I knew I didn't have to worry about waking up like that again; I only ever had one of *those* dreams in a night. It still took me a long time to fall back asleep. Right before I did, I remembered what I'd seen through the blinding light at the very end of my dream.

Mountains.

CHAPTER

· 10 ·

IN THE MORNING, I WOKE UP FEELING PRETTY GOOD IN SPITE OF NOT having had as much sleep as I should have, but I was still almost late to breakfast on account of taking extra time to write down the dream. Professor Jeffries and Professor Torgeson were already there, and the six Cathayans arrived a moment later.

While we ate, Professor Jeffries gave a summary of how we'd found out about the medusa lizards and what we'd learned about them from studying the dead one. It took the whole meal, because he had to keep pausing so Miss Bizen could translate. Every once in a while one of the Cathayans had a question, and that would have to be translated back and forth, too. I noticed that the master adept and her chief assistant were paying careful attention to Professor Jeffries while he talked, and I wondered whether they understood more English than they'd let on.

Once we finished eating, Professor Jeffries showed the Cathayans around the study center, and then we walked out to the supply building where the medusa lizard hatchlings were kept. They'd grown a lot in just the few weeks since I'd first seen them; they were nearly three feet long now, nose to tail, and we'd had to enlarge the pen we kept them in. They still got excited and ran to Professor Jeffries whenever they saw him. They didn't pay any attention to me, even though I was the one who'd been feeding them every day since Professor Torgeson and I had arrived.

We'd cleared the supplies out of the whole back half of the building to make plenty of room for the Cathayans in front of the pens. Master Adept Farawase looked around and gave a small, wintry smile of approval. Then she turned, gave a formal nod to Professor Jeffries, and said something in Cathayan.

Miss Bizen bowed to the adept, then to Professor Jeffries, and said, "Master Adept Farawase requests that you allow her to perform some close examinations of these creatures. Is this acceptable?"

One of the marshals stepped forward, frowning slightly. "What sort of close examination? If you please," he added.

It turned out the master adept wanted to get right in the pen with the lizards, which the marshals didn't think was safe. They ended up with a very polite three-way argument, and finally compromised on taking one of the lizards out of the pen for her to handle.

Professor Jeffries and I went in to get it. All three lizards ran to him and began jumping like overexcited childings on Christmas morning. I managed to distract Stheno and Euryale with a bucket of kitchen scraps, just long enough for the professor to grab Fred and get out of the pen. I followed a minute later, in time to watch him hand the baby lizard to the master adept.

Either Master Adept Farawase knew a lot about animals, or else even a medusa lizard knew better than to make a fuss in front of a Cathayan master adept. Fred didn't kick or wiggle or try to get away while she looked him over — and she looked him over very thoroughly. Every so often, as she inspected his claws and legs and tail, she made an observation in Cathayan. Adept Alikaket wrote down everything she said, the silver dragon scale glittering as he nodded, while Miss Bizen translated for me and the professors.

Finally, the adept set Fred on the floor and stepped back. She looked at her aides and nodded. All five of them bowed. The translator looked over at Professor Jeffries and said, "Master Adept Farawase wishes to perform some magical tests, if that is acceptable."

Professor Jeffries nodded. "We would like to observe, of course."

Miss Bizen checked with Master Adept Farawase. "You may observe. Please step back to be out of the field."

The professors and I moved back as near to the wall as we could get. The five aides lined up a few feet behind the adept, whose attention had been fixed on the medusa lizard the whole time. The creature hadn't moved, not even when Professor Jeffries moved away.

Master Adept Farawase raised her left hand, and all five of the aides began to move.

I leaned forward, fascinated. It was the first time I'd ever seen a Cathayan spell working, and it wasn't at all what I'd expected. The Cathayans, all except the master adept, looked like they were doing a slow, precise dance. At first, all five of them made the same flowing movements — side step, turn, bend, reach forward, turn, straighten up, step to the other side, and repeat, over and over. As they did, I saw a pale haze form around each of them. To my Aphrikan world-sensing, it felt like a warm halo around each of the Cathayans.

The haze got warmer and brighter and thicker as the five of them repeated the moves, and as it brightened, it changed color until each person was hidden in a colored bubble of fog. The color was different for each of them — one was a pale red, one was a deep green, one an equally deep blue, and one a light yellow-orange. Only the haze around Adept Alikaket stayed the same foggy gray.

I glanced at Professor Torgeson and asked in a low voice, "What is that foggy stuff?"

Professor Torgeson frowned. "Foggy stuff?"

I looked at the puzzled expressions she and Professor Jeffries were wearing, and realized that they weren't seeing anything unusual. I shook my head and went back to watching the Cathayans. The haze was so thick that I could barely make out what each of them looked like or what they were doing any longer. The only one who looked normal was the adept herself.

On impulse, I stopped doing the world-sensing. I'd gotten so used to doing it all the time that I had to think about letting it drop. It was like snuffing a candle; as soon as I stopped world-sensing, the haze around the Cathayans vanished.

I stared, bewildered. I'd been doing Aphrikan world-sensing for years, and I'd used it on a lot of different spells, but I'd always *felt* what they were like — cold or hot or sharp or wet, or some other sensation. I'd never *seen* anything before.

Miss Ochiba and Wash had never even hinted that seeing magic was possible.

Master Adept Farawase stretched out her hand and the Cathayans flowed into a new set of movements. Hastily, I started the world-sensing again. I'd have time later to think about what was going on, but if I missed seeing any of this spell, I didn't think I'd get another chance. The haze sprang up around them, and I saw that it had changed. Each blob of colored fog had stretched out a long wiggly piece like the body of a snake, right to the adept's raised hand. The adept's fingers were working, stretching and twisting and weaving the five individual magics into a bright white beam; apart from that, Master Adept Farawase didn't move.

The white beam reached out from the adept's hand and surrounded the medusa lizard. I saw it hesitate as it touched Fred's skin, but Master Adept Farawase twitched her fingers and the magic sank into the lizard like water sinking into garden soil.

After a few minutes, the adept called out a single word. Smoothly, the five aides changed their movements again. They were still slow and deliberate, moving smoothly and continuously from one direction to another, but each person was doing something different instead of everyone making the same movements. It still looked like a dance, but like one with different parts that fit together instead of like one where everyone did the same thing.

The colors of some of the fog bubbles changed. The red got darker and the green and blue got paler; the gray-white one lightened and the yellow-orange one brightened. The adept's fingers worked again, and another white beam poured from her upraised hand to the medusa lizard.

It went on like that for a long, long time. Master Adept Farawase would call out something, the pattern of her aides' movements would change, and she would weave the strands into a new spell. After the first two changes, I noticed that the adept seemed to be getting hazy, even though she wasn't moving. To begin with, the haze was mostly green, but every time the dance changed, a new color or two showed up, until the adept was completely hidden by a bubble of swirling colors.

Finally, she said a long string of syllables, and a moment later lowered her hand. The foggy bubbles around each of the Cathayans shrank as their movements became slower and slower. When they stopped at last, the fog was gone, except around Master Adept Farawase herself and around the medusa lizard.

I blinked in surprise. I'd been so busy watching the Cathayans that I hadn't paid much attention to the lizard, but it was glowing nearly as bright as the adept. It twitched, then skittered away from the Cathayans. Professor Jeffries jumped forward to catch it before it disappeared into the crates of supplies that were stacked around the edges of the room.

"Professor Jeffries?" I said. "Fred sucked up an awful lot of magic. Do you think that draining spell Professor Ochiba came up with would work on a live lizard? Because this might be a good time to test it." I didn't add that most of the magicians who'd studied the dead lizard thought that absorbing magic from outside was one of the things that let the lizards petrify animals, and we only *thought* the baby lizards were still too young to do that. Professor Jeffries knew as well as I did how dangerous the medusa lizards could be.

Miss Bizen turned to look at me, and so did Adept Alikaket. Professor Jeffries raised his eyebrows, but all he said was, "Hijero-Cathayan magic has a reputation for being powerful. Perhaps it would be best. Professor?"

He and Professor Torgeson and I stood around Fred and cast the draining spell, one after another. Slowly, the glow around the medusa lizard dimmed and went out. Professor Jeffries's eyebrows rose even higher when he felt the amount of magic coming off the lizard. "I believe you were right about that, Eff," he said. "All done now?"

"I think so," I said. "It looks like it's back to normal, anyway."

"Excuse me, please."

We turned to find Miss Bizen, the translator, straightening up from a bow. Her face had a sheen of perspiration, and she looked tired from the long dance. "If you would not mind, Master Adept Farawase is wondering what the spell is that you have been doing."

Professor Jeffries nodded and started explaining about the dead medusa lizard absorbing magic and needing to be drained after every magical examination, and that I'd suggested doing the same thing to the live one. The adept and her aides listened intently, and it took a while to answer all their questions. A couple of times, Professor Jeffries and Professor Torgeson had to go over things two or three times before they figured out a way to say something that would translate right. I listened as hard as the Cathayans did. Since the college built the classroom building and Papa moved his classes out of our front parlor, I hadn't had much chance to hear any discussions of advanced spells.

I thought they were just about finished talking, when Master Adept Farawase looked straight at me and said something. "You were the one to suggest working this spell?" Miss Bizen asked.

"Yes, ma'am," I said after a second of being too startled to speak. "Because of how much magic Fred soaked up while you were all working."

Miss Bizen's eyes widened. "You can sense our spells?"

"Not exactly. I, um, have a little training in Aphrikan magic, and I could tell with the world-sensing."

Miss Bizen turned to the adept and they had a brief, rapid discussion. Then Master Adept Farawase gave me a small smile and spoke a few words. "Aphrikan magic requires much patience, and it has more heart than head," Miss Bizen translated. "It is an interesting choice for one of Avrupan descent. May you do well with it."

"Thank you," I said, and gave a little bow to the adept because that was what all her aides seemed to do when they talked to her. The adept's smile widened, and she nodded to me, then went back to talking with the professors.

Master Adept Farawase didn't do any more magic that day. Over lunch, she finished up her discussion with the professors, then she and her aides went to one of the labs to look at the stone birds and animals that we'd brought back from Daybat Creek. They spent the whole afternoon there, though they didn't cast any more spells.

The next day, the adept and her aides asked to see the lizards again. When we got to the supply shed, Professor Jeffries took one look at the lizards and forgot everything else. Fred had grown, just enough to notice. As soon as I saw the look on the professor's face, I went for the observation notebook; by the time I got back, he was on his knees in the middle of the lizard pen with the measuring tape in one hand and the medusa lizard in the other.

The Cathayans talked excitedly among themselves while Professor Jeffries called out measurements and observations and I wrote them down. While we worked, Master Adept Farawase and Professor Torgeson talked, and when we finished, Professor Torgeson pointed at Stheno. "Grab that one, Samuel; that will leave us one as a control."

Professor Jeffries picked up the smaller lizard, which butted his arm like a cat and then opened and shut its beak a few times. "Yes, yes, I'll feed you," the professor told it. He looked back at Professor Torgeson. "Has Master Adept Farawase indicated what spells she'll be using today?"

"We would like to repeat the first sequence only, with minor changes," Miss Bizen said. She turned to me. "Miss Rothmer, we would be most grateful if you would note for us how much magic this lizard has absorbed after each spell."

I stared at her. "I'd be pleased to help, Miss Bizen, but I'm not sure . . . that is, I don't exactly have a way to measure."

The Cathayans started talking rapidly among themselves. The short man with the mustache waved his arms to emphasize something, and the round-faced man bowed, while the tall one gave them both a disapproving look. We stood there awkwardly, not wanting to interrupt, until Master Adept Farawase said something sharply and everyone else fell silent. The adept turned to Miss Bizen, who nodded and asked, "We would like to know if this lizard is the only one that is . . ." She paused, hunting for a word. "That can 'soak up magic,' as you said it."

Professor Torgeson's eyebrows drew together. "It appears to be an ability of the species. Over a dozen have been shot, and all of them have been able to do it. And as you can see, even the young ones have the capacity."

"I am sorry; I was not clear," Miss Bizen said. "Are there other creatures, not lizards, that do this?"

"Other animals that soak up magic?" Professor Torgeson said. "Not that we know of."

"There are the mirror bugs," Professor Jeffries said. "Though they are insects, of course, and not animals, and the ability manifests in a different way."

Miss Bizen bowed and turned to translate that into Cathayan. As soon as she finished speaking, there was another burst of discussion in Cathayan. Then the adept asked about the mirror bugs, what they were and when they'd been found and what we knew about how they worked. It took quite a while to answer her questions, because we'd been studying the mirror bugs for a good three years, ever since they first showed up, and the professors had learned a lot about their life cycle. The adept was especially interested in the fact that if there wasn't much magic around, the grubs developed into ordinary beetles and stopped there, but if there was a lot of magic, even the grubs could pop right straight into mirror bugs without becoming pupae or ordinary beetles first.

Eventually, we got back to the medusa lizards. The Cathayans cast their spells, though not nearly as many as they had the day before. After each one, I tried to figure how much brighter the medusa lizard looked, and wrote down what I thought. Everything went smoothly until they finished and Professor Torgeson stepped forward to cast the spell and drain off the magic that the medusa lizard had absorbed.

"Please do not," Miss Bizen said as the professor raised her hand.

"I beg your pardon?"

Miss Bizen looked at me. "This lizard has not absorbed so much magic as the other, has it?"

"No, ma'am," I said, though I thought that should be pretty obvious. They hadn't cast as many spells as they had on the first day.

Professor Torgeson's eyes narrowed, then she frowned uncertainly. "It's a good thought, but we don't know much about how these creatures develop, or how fast. If absorbing magic triggers their petrification ability, we could be in trouble."

Master Adept Farawase said something. "To take no chances is to die in spirit," Miss Bizen translated, and frowned as if that wasn't quite the right way to put what she wanted to say.

"We'll have to try it sometime, Aldis," Professor Jeffries

said. "Best to do it now, when we have so much help available if things go wrong."

"Very well," Professor Torgeson said. "But with precautions."

"Of course with precautions," Professor Jeffries said cheerfully. "What did you have in mind?"

CHAPTER
· 11 ·

WHAT PROFESSOR TORGESON HAD IN MIND, APPARENTLY, WAS A LOT more than we could manage. She had very firm ideas about how to treat dangerous wildlife, most of which involved killing it as fast as you possibly could and then studying it after it was dead. I think it came from being a Vinlander.

We finally settled on arranging a lot of the supply crates to make a barrier right in front of the medusa lizard pen, so that they couldn't turn anyone into stone at a distance. Then Professor Torgeson put a rabbit cage at the end of the barricade, where the medusa lizards could see it from one side and anyone coming in the door could see it from the other. The idea was to check whether the rabbit had been turned to stone before you walked around the barrier. If it hadn't, then it was probably safe to go into the pen.

While Professor Torgeson and I moved boxes to set up the barrier, Professor Jeffries took the Cathayans off to look at mirror bugs. Fortunately, we had plenty of specimens at all of the stages of mirror bug development, from the eggs to the grubs to the striped beetles to the mirror bugs themselves, even though none of them were alive.

The mirror bugs kept the Cathayans busy for the rest of the day. Professor Jeffries and I checked on the medusa lizards that evening, and both of the ones the Cathayans had used spells on were bigger. We made more measurements, and the next day we did all of it again.

The Cathayans stayed for four days, which was a day and a half longer than they'd planned. When they left, they took some mirror bug specimens and some samples of the stone animals we'd collected. Professor Jeffries almost gave them one of the medusa lizard eggs we still had under preservation spells, but Professor Torgeson pointed out that taking it through the Great Barrier Spell a third time would likely disrupt the preservation spell permanently, and hatching a medusa lizard on the east bank would cause all sorts of problems.

By the time they left, I was positive that Miss Bizen wasn't the only one in the group who spoke English, but it wouldn't have been polite to say anything about it. Once they had gone, I was so busy setting things back in order that I forgot about it.

We had a busy couple of weeks at the study center before fall classes started. The two medusa lizards that the Cathayans had cast spells at continued to grow much faster than the third lizard, which meant lots of measuring and taking notes to document exactly how fast they grew and whether there were any other differences between them. Professor Jeffries talked about designing a series of experiments to see how much magic a baby medusa lizard could absorb at once and how much difference the draining spell made, but nobody wanted to try anything like that without a whole lot more protection first.

On the last day of August, right before the professors and I were supposed to head back to Mill City, I was hauling a bag of feed from the supply shed to the mammoth pen when I saw a lone rider heading in from the northwest. Not too many folks travel alone through settlement country, even that close to the Great Barrier, so I stopped and shaded my eyes to get a better look.

At first, all I could see was a dark, man-shaped blob, no matter how I squinted. Just when I was getting irritated, I realized that it wasn't the sun in my eyes that was the cause. The face under the broad-brimmed hat was a dark brown-black. I grinned and waved, because I was pretty sure I knew who it was.

The rider saw and waved back, then angled his horse to come toward the mammoth pen instead of straight in to the main compound. Once he got a little closer, I saw that I'd been right: It was Washington Morris, the circuit magician who'd taken Professor Torgeson and the rest of us out to hunt the first medusa lizard, and the man who'd given me the Aphrikan pendant I'd worn for the last three years.

Wash looked even scruffier than he usually did when he was coming back in from the settlements, with his beard grown raggedy and his hair at least three inches longer than normal. His buckskin jacket was covered in dust, and when he got close in and dismounted, I could see that his dark face looked tired. The nod he gave me was as polite as ever. "Miss Eff."

"Hello, Wash!" I said. "What brings you by? Was Professor Jeffries expecting you?"

"If he was, I'm not aware of it," Wash said. "Is he still out here? I thought you all would be back to Mill City by now."

"We'd planned to be," I said, "but having the Cathayans come visit slowed everything down."

"Cathayans?" Wash asked.

So I told him while I finished filling the mammoth's feed bin, and then I took him into the storage building to show him the medusa lizards. He frowned when he saw the size of them — the largest was nearing waist-high by then — and asked, "How long are you all planning on keeping them?"

"I'm not sure," I said. "Professor Jeffries thinks they'll be safe for a while yet, and he wants to find out whether they hibernate, so probably a couple months more, at least. We're moving them to a new pen tomorrow, out by the lake where they'll be away from everything else."

Wash pursed his lips. "I'll be speaking with the professor, then. Is he up at the main complex?"

I nodded. "I wonder, sometimes, if that parent thing works both ways." At Wash's puzzled look, I explained, "He says that the medusa lizards think he's their parent, because he was the first thing they saw after they hatched, and that's why they haven't attacked anybody. Professor Torgeson thinks it's just because they're still too young."

"Could be, but it's not something I'd be inclined to rely on for long," Wash said. "Well, that's for the professor to explain. What all have you been doing, this last year? And how's that brother of yours liking his work at the Settlement Office?"

As we walked toward the main buildings, I answered Wash's questions and asked a few of my own about folks I'd met out in the settlements. About halfway in, I mentioned the strange dreams I'd been having.

"I know the pendant you gave me has something to do with them, but I haven't figured out what yet," I finished. I didn't ask Wash to explain, because he never had before, and by this time I'd figured out that a lot of Aphrikan magic was about learning how you yourself did things, which wasn't something other folks could help out with much. But I thought he ought to know what it was doing.

"Dreams," he said in a thoughtful tone. "That's different. Same one every time?"

"No," I said. "It's always at least a little different, and sometimes it changes a lot. I've been writing them down, but I still can't make sense of them."

"Magic doesn't make sense, if you think hard on it," Wash said. "Not even Avrupan magic, much as it tries."

"It's still more head than heart," I said. "Avrupan magic, I mean."

Wash looked startled, then nodded. "That's one way of looking at it."

"There's always other ways," I said, and grinned at him.

"Maybe you should find one," he said seriously.

I thought about that for a minute. Then I reached for the cord around my neck. I'd worn the pendant constantly for over three years, though most of the time I hid it under my clothes to avoid folks asking questions about it. The polished wood gleamed in the sunlight as I held it out toward Wash. "Has it changed any since you had it?"

For a moment, Wash stared at the pendant without any expression. I felt a brush of something, like a breeze against my hand, followed by an icy trickle down my back. Then he gave a slow smile that erased all the tired lines around his eyes. "It has indeed, Miss Eff."

"I don't suppose you'd care to explain how?" I said after a minute.

He reached out and brushed a finger across the pendant. I felt a tiny burst like Fourth of July fireworks, right at the back of my head. "Not quite yet," he said. "But I'll advise you to do some looking of your own."

I couldn't stop myself from snorting. "That's all you have to say?"

"For now." Wash grinned. "Getting irritated is part of the process."

"If getting irritated is that important, I should be done with it three times over by now," I said as I put the pendant back on.

"It's only part of it, not the whole," Wash said.

I thought about that while I stabled Wash's horse, and on my walk back out to the menagerie pens, and while I did the routine work of cleaning and feeding the animals. That night, I read through the journal where I'd written down all the dreams I'd had. I'd been over it before, trying and trying to find some rhyme or reason to the images, but I'd never managed.

This time, I spread my world-sensing out around me and just read, letting the dreams play over in my head without worrying about what they meant. When I finished, I sat and let my mind drift. The dreams were important, I knew, but they didn't feel like any kind of foretelling. The very first ones I'd had had been about the far past, when I was five and we still lived in Helvan Shores. And the next ones, where I'd been trying to cross the river and kept sinking in and drowning, certainly hadn't ever come true.

I sighed and pulled out the pendant itself. It sat in my hand, a dark whorl of wood a little smaller than a robin's egg, polished smooth with much handling. I wondered idly what kind of tree it had come from; I didn't recall ever having seen wood quite like it before.

A picture formed behind my eyes, of a tree with leaves like silver lace and a twisting, curling trunk. It wasn't much taller than an apple tree, but its roots spread wide and reached down toward the heart of the world. It felt strange and familiar, both at once, and I knew nothing like it had ever grown in Columbian soil.

After a minute, the image faded, and I was left staring at the pendant. I didn't move. I hardly dared to breathe. In the three years I'd worn the pendant, it hadn't ever done anything like that before. I wondered briefly whether it would answer other questions, but I didn't think so. I tried asking anyway, every way I could think of, but nothing else happened.

Finally, I reached out with my magic and poked at the pendant, the way I'd poked at my Avrupan spells to make them work properly. I'd felt the layers of spells around it before, but I'd never been able to tease apart more than the topmost few. There was a bit of my magic wrapped around the outside, and then some that felt like Wash's, and then several layers that were full of magic that felt like concealment and not-noticing, wound through with both Avrupan and Aphrikan magic. Past that, I'd never been able to tell much.

On the second or third poke, the pendant started to look fuzzy, and after a minute I realized that it looked like the Cathayan magicians had, when they were spell casting. The fuzz around the pendant was almost the same color as the wood itself, and not as foggy. It looked more like wool yarn that someone had wrapped tight around the pendant in compli-cated layers.

The layers seemed to have loosened up a bit in places, and if I held it right I could see straight through them all to the wood at the heart of the pendant. I wondered briefly whether Wash had done that when he touched it, or whether the loos-ening was something that just happened after the magic had a chance to get accustomed to a new wearer. I thought it proba-bly just happened after a while; almost all the magic curled around the pendant felt like Aphrikan magic, and Aphrikan magic often works more slowly than Avrupan magic.

I sat back suddenly, feeling as if I'd been very dense. I *knew* that pendant was Aphrikan magic, and I'd known that right from the minute Wash gave it to me. And yet I'd still been thinking about it as if it were Avrupan magic, something that I could take apart into neat piles that would tell me how it worked and what it did.

Oh, there was Avrupan magic wound around the pen-dant. I'd felt it. But Avrupan spells compel things to change and be the way the magician wants them to be; Aphrikan spells mostly nudge or coax things in the direction the magician wants — and the heart of the pendant was Aphrikan. Heart, more than head.

I set the pendant down and read through my dreams again. I still couldn't make sense of them, but I could feel that they'd been nudging me. I frowned and shook my head, knowing that wasn't quite right. The pendant didn't have a mind or personality or will. It was just a lot of magic, wrapped around the wood.

And then I understood. The dreams were mine; all the pendant did was pull them out and make me pay attention to them. I'd been nudging myself, without knowing.

That felt true, though I couldn't say why. Now all I had to do was figure out what I'd been nudging myself to do or think. Some of the dreams were different, so it was probably something different every time. I sighed. I'd have to start writing down a lot more than just the dreams, I thought. I'd need to know what I was doing and thinking, and maybe what I thought I wanted to know at the time.

Then I stopped, wondering if that was really such a good idea. It would be just the thing if I were working with Avrupan magic, but it might not be so helpful in understanding Aphrikan magic. I looked at the pendant and slipped the cord back over my head. I fingered it, and slowly I smiled. I wasn't Aphrikan, and I wasn't Avrupan, not really. I was Columbian, born and raised, for all my grandparents weren't. I didn't have to do things one way or the other. I could do either, or both, or mix them up until something worked.

That night, I dreamed of standing on a high rock in the middle of the ocean. The water changed constantly. One minute, the waves dashed furiously against the stone, showering me with spray; the next, the water was calm and smoother than the real ocean ever could be; the minute after that, it swirled and eddied around the base of the rock.

I tried to catch the spray, but there wasn't enough. I wanted more. I looked down into the shifting water, took a deep breath, and dove.

The water rose to meet me. As it closed over my head, I laughed and woke up.

CHAPTER

· 12 ·

A FEW DAYS AFTER WASH'S VISIT, PROFESSOR TORGESON AND I headed back to Mill City to get ready for fall classes. Professor Jeffries was staying at the study center until the very last minute, on account of the medusa lizards. He and Professor Torgeson planned to alternate weekends at the center through the fall, to check on the animals and see how Mr. Siwinski was getting on with all the observations.

Lan and Papa came to meet the ferry and bring me home. When I walked in the door, Allie hugged me, read me a lecture on how awful and unladylike it was for me to be running around in the settlements, and burst into tears. Robbie rolled his eyes and told her she wasn't Mama, and anyway I was old enough to decide things like that for myself, which got Allie started on scolding him instead of me.

In between all the talk, I got caught up on the family news. Robbie had finished his degree and found a job at Mr. Imhada's pharmacy while he thought about what he wanted to do next. Nan was in a family way again, and Robbie teased her about it constantly, which got both Nan and Rennie mad at him. Brant and Rennie were still staying in the big house with Papa and Mama and the rest of us, though it was nearly a year since they'd come back from Oak River. Brant was saving up from his job at the shipping company. He said it was for a house, but I noticed that neither he nor Rennie said much about where the house would be. I figured they wanted to go back out to the settlements and were avoiding arguments.

Mama had made a special welcome-home dinner, with roast chicken, chestnut-and-black-rice dressing, greens with hexberry sauce, candied beets, and bread pudding. She'd made sure the whole family would be there for it, too, at least everyone who was still in Mill City. In addition to Nan and her husband George, Mama had invited Professor Graham and Roger Boden to come for dinner, so it was almost as many folks around the table as we used to have when all of my brothers and sisters were home.

I was surprised to see Roger at first, but Mama said that he'd taken a job at the Settlement Office, and he and Lan had gotten friendly. I wasn't surprised. Lan might have decided he was done with schooling for good, but he'd always liked talking magic theory and finding out about strange and exotic new spells, and you couldn't get much stranger than the things Roger had specialized in.

Being the center of attention made me a little uncomfortable, but it wasn't long before one of the childings distracted Rennie. Then Papa, Lan, Roger, and Professor Graham got to talking about the latest experiments in the magic laboratory, and pretty soon there were a lot of little conversations all around the table and I could relax and not be noticed.

Or at least not until there was a lull in the conversation and Lan took a notion to quiz me about the Hijero-Cathayans.

I couldn't help rolling my eyes, but I described the adept's spell casting in as much detail as I could remember. He frowned when I told him about the way the adept's aides moved the whole time.

"Dancing?" he asked.

"Well, not exactly dancing," I said. "But not like the hand passes for third-declension spells, either. Slower and smoother, and moving their whole selves, not just their hands."

"I've never heard of anything like that." He sounded like he didn't quite believe what I was telling him.

"It's what they did!"

Roger leaned forward. "It's not that unreasonable. There are a couple of Scandian spells that work with whole-body movement."

"Those aren't coordinated magic," Professor Graham said. "You can't get the precision necessary for a group working by depending on physical movement alone."

"Besides, nobody could cast a spell the way you describe," Lan said in an infuriatingly superior tone. "It's too slow. The magic would leak away before you could do anything with it."

"The aides weren't casting the spell," I pointed out, holding on to my temper with both hands. "Master Adept Farawase was doing that."

Professor Graham frowned. "They had to be doing some spell to pool their magic. That's how Hijero-Cathayan spells work."

"I didn't see anything. They just . . . danced, all together. Except for the master adept herself."

"I'll have to be sure to ask Professor Jeffries for his write-up," Papa said thoughtfully. "It's a pity the adept was not willing to allow other observers. There are so few opportunities to see genuine Hijero-Cathayan spellwork in this country."

Professor Graham snorted. "Few? None, I'd say. To see genuine Hijero-Cathayan spellwork, you need a genuine Hijero-Cathayan team, and Farawase's was the first to come to Columbia that I've ever heard of."

"We may not have seen actual spell casting, but we know the theory behind Hijero-Cathayan spellwork," Lan said. "I spent most of that last year at Simon Magus studying it. And I never heard about anything like this dance of yours, Eff."

"One actual observation is better than a hundred theories," Roger said, like he was quoting someone. "Maybe the Hijero-Cathayans haven't told us as much about their magic as we think they have."

"Or maybe your professors didn't know as much as they might," I said before I thought. I froze for just a second. Then, before all the implications of what I'd said could really sink in, I went on quickly, "Why are you so interested, anyway?"

"Because of the expedition," Roger said instantly.

"Expedition?" I said, puzzled.

"Master Adept Farawase's expedition," Lan said. "Didn't you hear? Nobody at the Settlement Office has talked about anything else for the past week."

I frowned at him. "I've been out at the study center ever since the Cathayans left, and we didn't exactly get a lot of mail. Is she taking her aides out to the Far West?"

"Sending them, more likely," Roger said. "At least one."

"She's talked President Trent into sending out an exploratory expedition," said Lan. "The Cathayans are going to cosponsor it. She's been pushing the idea ever since she got back to Washington from Mill City and caught out the Secretary of State and the head of the Frontier Management Department in an argument about whether it would be worse for the country to have another failed expedition, or another surprise like the medusa lizards. At least, that's what Mr. Parsons said."

"It doesn't sound like an opinion he'd get from official correspondence," Professor Graham put in dryly. "Nor has there been any announcement of such an expedition. It's all just rumor and speculation, if you ask me."

"Interesting speculation, though," Papa said. "And it's high time the government got over losing those other groups and sent someone to do a proper job of mapping the territory, at least. The McNeil Expedition came back without a man lost, and it's been nearly ten years since then with no progress. I'd have thought we'd see two or three others go out in that amount of time."

"If it's a government expedition, they can't have a Hijero-Cathayan in it," Allie said, as if that settled everything.

"They can if the Cathayan Confederacy is sponsoring it," Lan retorted. "Weren't you listening?"

"Rumors," Professor Graham said with a snort.

Mama gave Papa a sidelong look. "It's been a while since you wrote your brother Gregory, hasn't it?"

Professor Graham and Roger and Brant all looked a little startled by what seemed a total change in topic, but everyone in my family smiled a little. Uncle Gregory lived in Washington and worked at the Bureau of Magic and Technology, and Papa always said that he was a worse gossip than my Aunt Janna. He liked to write long letters full of tidbits about all the important people he'd met and what they were doing. If anyone could find out what was going on and tell us, it would be Uncle Gregory.

Papa did write, and Uncle Gregory was happy to write back everything he knew. From what he said, Lan's rumors weren't far off. When Master Adept Farawase got back to Washington, she'd said nice things about our study center, but she hadn't been too pleased with the lack of information about the Far West in general. She'd made it clear that she expected someone to fix that, and fix it now. Within days, the plans for a Western expedition had gone from something that might happen in another five or ten years if everything went well and enough folks agreed, to being a settled thing that would leave next spring. It helped that the Cathayans had offered to provide money as well as the master adept's personal backing.

Talk of the expedition followed me to work, too. Professor Jeffries had three notes from the Settlement Office waiting on his desk, asking for his advice, and so did Professor Torgeson. It kept up like that all through the fall, while the folks in Washington argued and fussed and fumed and planned.

All the expedition work made it hard for Professor Jeffries and Professor Torgeson to get off to the study center every other week the way they'd planned, but they mostly managed. I stayed in Mill City, getting more and more uncomfortable with the situation at home. Mama and Rennie and Allie all expected things of me: not just chores and minding the child-ings, but what they thought I ought to do with the rest of my life. Except for Lan, Papa and the boys mostly ignored me unless something specific came up, and even Lan was more caught up in the expedition planning than interested in anything I had to say on my own.

I wrote a lot of letters to William that fall. Letters were better than talking, I decided, because I couldn't see if someone wasn't interested or notice when they stopped listening. Not that William didn't listen; his return letters always showed that he'd thought about what I'd said, even when he had a lot to say himself. I told him all the expedition news, and he told me that some of the professors at Triskelion had already been approached to see if they were interested in going. We both agreed that if it were us, we'd jump at the chance.

Somewhat to my surprise, I also spent a fair bit of time with Roger. If I'd thought about it at all, I'd expected that between the time he'd spent in Albion and his friendship with Lan, he'd have lost interest in me entirely, but I was wrong. The attention made me nervous. Part of me didn't want to be leading him on if Allie was right and he had an interest in being more than friends, but another part was glad for the excuse to get away from the chores and childings at home. It was very confusing. At least Allie had stopped pestering me on the subject.

In October, the mammoth nearly broke free of its pen out at the study center. It was always extra restless in spring and fall, when the wild mammoths were migrating, but this year it was especially bad. Professor Jeffries had to make an emergency trip to help control it.

When he came back, he and Professor Torgeson had a huge argument over the cause of the problem. Professor Jeffries thought it was the trip and being in new surroundings with new people, and that the mammoth would settle down once it got used to its new quarters. Professor Torgeson thought it was because the mammoth was nearly full grown and west of the Great Barrier, and that the problem would only get worse. They finally agreed to wait until spring and see how it behaved then. Professor Torgeson walked off muttering, "At least those medusa lizards haven't started acting up. Yet."

At the end of October, the Frontier Management Department finally announced that a new expedition would be going out to explore the Far West. By then, everyone had known for months that the announcement was coming, and it was only the details that folks were interested in. The expedition would leave from Mill City in April, following the path of the McNeil Expedition as far as they knew it and then heading on up the Grand Bow River toward the Rocky Mountains.

The minute the official announcement was made, everyone started talking about who, exactly, would be part of it. It was no easy thing to choose people to send on an expedition that would be gone for at least two years, maybe more, and that had a good chance of not coming back at all. Also, a lot of folks seemed to think that if there *was* going to be an expedition, they wanted in on it in some way, even if they didn't want to go their own selves.

The army and the Frontier Management Department were arguing worse than ever, each insisting that their people should be in charge. Master Adept Farawase wanted to send magical naturalists and scientists, and was even leaving one of her aides behind to go along. The National Farmer's Society wanted to send a geographer at the very least, and a geomancer if they could get one. The railroad company wanted to include a surveyor. The Agriculture Department wanted to send a plant specialist to look for edible plants that could make for new crops. The Bureau of National Development wanted a geologist along to look for mineral deposits. Even the new National Baseball League wanted to send someone, or at least a baseball that they could show off as the first baseball to reach the Rocky Mountains.

The Frontier Management Department didn't pay heed to most of the arguments, so far as I could tell. In late November, about three weeks after the announcement, another letter arrived from Washington for Professor Jeffries, sealed with red wax. It was an invitation to join the new expedition, and it set off quite a flurry of meetings at the college. I didn't find out what they were about until Papa came by the laboratory late one afternoon while we were cleaning up.

"I hear you've been asked to head West with this new expedition," Papa said to Professor Jeffries. "Congratulations."

Professor Jeffries looked at him suspiciously. "I expect you've also heard that I'm going to decline the honor."

"Dean Farley did say something of the kind," Papa said. "I believe he's hoping I can talk you into changing your mind."

"I don't think that's possible," Professor Torgeson said. "I've already tried."

I looked at Professor Jeffries in surprise. "Don't you want to go?" I asked.

Professor Jeffries looked sternly over the top of his spectacles at all three of us. "Yes, yes, it's a great honor, but it's simply not practical. I don't know why on earth they came up with such a ridiculous idea in the first place."

"Maybe because you're the foremost expert on Western wildlife in the country?" Professor Torgeson said.

"Don't exaggerate. There are at least half a dozen people who know as much or more than I do. Harlow has done groundbreaking work on silverhooves. Pachenski's findings on the relationship between arrow hawks and tiger mice is positively brilliant. There are plenty of other logical choices." Professor Jeffries sighed. "There's also the lizard study to consider. The three we have are fixated on me, and I wouldn't like to put them down until we've learned as much as we can. Besides, I'm too old to be setting out into the wildlands."

I looked at him, startled. I'd never thought of Professor Jeffries as being particularly old before, but he was one of the senior professors at the college. He'd been a professor for nearly forty years, since well before the Northern Plains Riverbank College was founded. His hair was gray, and he had a lot more wrinkles than I'd ever noticed. He was plenty spry, I knew; he'd ridden out to the settlements three years before when we went to look into the mirror bug infestation. But he hadn't been too far west of the Mammoth River after that, not since Professor Torgeson joined the department.

Papa seemed to be thinking some of the same things. "I'm sure the Frontier Management Department has taken that into consideration," he said, though he didn't sound all that certain to me.

"The Frontier Management Department can't see past the end of its collective nose," Professor Jeffries said. He smiled suddenly, with an evil glint in his eyes. "I'm recommending they take Aldis instead. Let's see what they make of that."

"Me?" Professor Torgeson looked thoroughly taken aback for a minute, then shook her head. "They'll never do it. I'm too young, I don't have the credentials, and I'm only an assistant professor."

"You're a Vinlander, which means you have more experience with North Columbian wildlife than any of the people born and raised on this side of the Great Barrier Spell," Professor Jeffries countered. "You also have experience traveling and studying in the unprotected settlements. You did fine work on the wildlife survey two years ago, and since you came on staff, you've collected more large specimens than anyone else at this college. Including, may I remind you, the medusa lizard that set off all this expedition talk in the first place. You're a strong magician and a crack shot — I heard about that rifle contest you had with young Anderson. You're a very logical choice."

"You're assuming I want to go on this snipe hunt," Professor Torgeson grumbled, but anyone could see her heart wasn't in it.

Sure enough, a week and a half later, Professor Torgeson got one of the letters sealed with red wax, inviting her along on the expedition. She had me write out her acceptance that very afternoon. So that was settled.

On the way home, I went the long way around so I could stop at the Post Office to pick up the mail for our family. Lan was usually the one to do that chore, because it was more on his way, but Mr. Parsons had asked him to stay late at the Settlement Office that day, so he'd asked me to take care of it. I smiled as Miss Jarlbrod handed me the stack of letters and glanced through them. And froze.

One of the letters was on heavy cream paper, sealed with red wax. I hesitated. With shaking hands, I turned it over to see who it had been sent to.

It was for Brant.

CHAPTER
· 13 ·

I WALKED THE REST OF THE WAY HOME IN A DAZE. I WASN'T SURE what Mama or Papa would think, but I was positive that Rennie and Allie wouldn't like the idea of Brant going on the expedition, not one little bit.

When I got home, I hesitated before I set the mail in the little wooden rack by the door. I didn't know whether anyone would recognize the letter from the Frontier Management Department for what it was straightaway, and I really thought that Brant should see it first. Luckily, he came in just a minute or two after I did, while I was still hanging up my coat and putting my hat and scarf away.

"You have a letter," I told him, and he fished it out of the pile just as Mama came into the front hall.

I saw the moment when he opened the letter and stiffened. Unfortunately, Mama saw it, too.

"What do you have there, Brant, if I may ask?" she said.

"It's from the Frontier Management Department," Brant said in a stunned voice. "They want me to go on this new expedition they're putting together."

"What!"

We all turned. Rennie was standing at the foot of the stairs, her eyes wide and one hand covering her mouth in horror. She stood statue-still for a moment, then reached forward. "Brant, you can't mean to go!"

Brant shook himself out of his daze. "I don't mean much of anything yet. I only just got the offer. I haven't had time to think about it."

"Think about it! What is there to think about?" Rennie said. "You can't —"

"What's all the fuss?" Allie walked through the rear doorway into the hall. She had a flour-sack towel in her hands, as if she'd been drying dishes.

"Brant wants to go out West on this expedition Lan's been talking so much about!" Rennie told her.

"No!" Allie looked almost as horrified as Rennie had.

"Nothing's been said about going or not going," Mama said firmly before Brant could open his mouth. "And your husband is right, Rennie; this isn't a decision to be made in the front hallway."

"But, Mama —"

"Come and help finish making dinner," Mama said. "Eff can watch the childings until it's ready" — she gave me a sharp look to be sure I wouldn't object — "and Brant can take a few minutes to think. You can discuss it later."

She sent Brant a meaningful look and nodded toward Papa's study, then shepherded Allie and Rennie back down the hall to the kitchen. I went upstairs to find the childings. I'd had the walk home from the Post Office to get used to the notion of Brant's invitation, but even so I'd been surprised by the look on his face, and on Rennie's. I sighed. There'd be an argument at dinner, for sure.

It was nearly an hour before Mama called us down, and at first I thought I'd been wrong. Oh, it was plain enough that Rennie and Allie and Brant were unhappy about something, but none of them said anything about the letter or the expedition. No one said much of anything at all for the first few minutes, though Robbie tried. Even Lewis and Seren Louise were more subdued than usual.

Then the front door banged and I heard Lan's voice, loud enough to recognize but too muffled to make out exactly what he was saying. A moment later, he came into the dining room. His cheeks were still red from the cold, and his eyes were bright and excited.

"I'm sorry to be so late," he said, "but you'll never guess what happened at the Settlement Office today!"

Mama smiled, looking relieved because it wouldn't be a silent dinner after all. "What?"

"The letters came about the expedition!" Lan said. "They've finally decided who they're asking to go."

The silence around the table got thick enough to cut with a knife, and little Albert whimpered. Lan went on, oblivious. "There was a letter for Wash Morris, of course, and one for us to send on to that trapper. *And* —" He paused dramatically, and I felt my heart sink. "Roger and I both got invitations! Isn't it great?"

Mama went pale, and Rennie's teeth clenched. Papa's eyes narrowed. Brant looked down at his plate, where he'd been pushing his shepherd's pie around without actually eating much. Allie glanced at Mama, then scowled and said, "Lan! How can you?" At the same time, Robbie grinned and said, "*You're* going to the Far West? I bet it's just an excuse so you don't have to go back to Simon Magus!"

Allie transferred her glare to Robbie. "Hush up! Honestly, don't you have any sense?"

"What?" Robbie said. He and Lan wore identical expressions of bewilderment. "Just because you don't think it's exciting —"

Allie got the look that meant she was going to start yelling, so I said as calmly as I could, "Brant got a letter, too, and Mama and Rennie are a little worried about it."

"You did?" Robbie turned to Brant. "Why didn't you say —" Right about then his head caught up with the rest of what I'd said, and he broke off.

"It's a great honor to be asked," Papa said, and his voice settled everyone else down. "And it's not one to be declined *or* accepted without careful thought." He looked at Brant and then at Lan, and finally over toward Rennie and Allie. "In the meantime, I would like to hear a few more details about this expedition. I presume the Frontier Management Office included some in your letters?"

Lan nodded. He sat down, looking subdued for a moment, but it wasn't long before he was waving his hands in the air with nearly as much excitement as he'd shown when he walked in the door. I listened wistfully as he told us all about it.

The people in Washington figured the expedition would take at least two years, maybe more; after all, the McNeil

Expedition had been gone for two, and they'd only gotten a little past Wintering Island in the Grand Bow River. It was a lot farther to the Rocky Mountains. They'd settled a lot of the arguments by dividing the expedition into three groups: one for the scientists and magicians, one for the army and support people, and one for the Frontier Management Department. They were sending thirty people, and each group got to pick ten. The Frontier Management Department had asked the Settlement Offices for recommendations.

Wash had been an obvious choice. He'd been almost to the Rocky Mountains before, traveling all on his own, and he was one of the best circuit magicians in the North Plains Territory. They'd suggested Roger because he had geomancy training, though of course he wasn't a full-fledged geomancer. And they wanted Lan because they liked the work he was doing, because he'd help kill the first two medusa lizards and had at least some experience in settlement territory, and because he was a double-seventh son.

Lan had a pretty good notion who else the Settlement Office had invited, but he wouldn't say; they weren't making any public announcements until they knew who'd accepted. He hadn't known anything about Brant or Professor Torgeson, though. The professor was obviously going to be one of the scientific magicians. Since Brant wasn't a scientist and certainly wasn't a magician, that meant he'd probably been asked by the people choosing the army and support people. Robbie said it must be because he'd been on the McNeil Expedition and come home a hero.

Right about then, Rennie got up and left the table without speaking. After a minute, Brant went after her. Lan and Robbie looked uncomfortable for a minute, then went back to talking about details of the expedition. It was plain they thought it'd be best to cover as much as they could while Rennie was out of hearing.

I didn't think it was all the expedition talk that had made Rennie run off like that. I thought it was as much about Brant going out with Dr. McNeil and coming home a hero, because that was what had attracted Rennie to him nine years before, and the reason she'd run off with him to live in a Rationalist settlement and ended up trying to keep house and raise her childings without using magic.

I didn't think she'd been particularly happy all that time. I wasn't all that sure that she was as happy now as everybody seemed to think she was. Before she married, Rennie had always liked being in charge of everything she could get her hands on. While she lived in the Oak River settlement, she hadn't been in charge of nearly as much as she wanted, and I didn't think that coming back to Mill City and living with Mama and Papa again had done much to cure that. Brant was in for a long, hard talking-to, I figured, and I didn't even want to speculate on what the outcome would be.

I avoided Rennie and Brant for the next couple of weeks, but I couldn't avoid Allie or Robbie or Lan. Allie bent my ear every chance she could, trying to persuade me to help her talk Lan into staying home. She was especially put out because Mama and Papa weren't pressing him any.

"Mama's worried and upset — you can see it," she told me. "I've told Lan and told him, but he won't listen! Why hasn't she said anything?"

"Maybe she has, but not in front of you." I remembered the talk Mama and I had had, right after Professor Torgeson asked me to help move the mammoth out to the study center. Mama hadn't liked the notion, but she'd made that plain and then made it even plainer that the choice was mine to make. "Or maybe she thinks that her being worried isn't a good enough reason for Lan to stay home, if he doesn't want to."

"Fiddlesticks!" Allie tossed her head. "Lan should go back to Simon Magus College and finish his schooling, the way Mama and Papa want. He's got no business traipsing off into the Far West and getting eaten by saber cats or petrified by a medusa lizard or who knows what else!"

"There's no saying that's what would happen," I told her. "And besides, it's his choice."

"I bet you don't feel that way about Roger!" Allie retorted.

"I do so!"

"Have you talked to him about it?" she demanded.

"Not really," I said. "It isn't any of my business." He hadn't seemed to want to talk about it, the two times I'd seen him since the letters came. He'd just accepted my congratulations gravely and changed the subject. I didn't push him to talk because along with the excitement and being pleased that he was getting such an opportunity, I couldn't help feeling a little jealous of him and Lan and Brant.

Allie glared at me. "Well, it should be your business! Anyway, Lan's your twin; *he's* your business, surely."

"Not the way you mean." I hesitated. "Lan likes the West, almost as much as he likes learning new magic, and going on this expedition means he can do both at once. Why should I stop him?"

"He should think more about his family!" Allie snapped. "And so should Brant!"

I looked at her really hard for the first time in a long time. I'd always thought of Rennie as the bossy one of my sisters, and Allie just as more determined and sure of herself, but it occurred to me that she'd been developing a bossy streak ever since Rennie ran off with Brant. I hadn't noticed because she didn't boss people to do things she wanted for herself, the way Rennie always had. Allie bossed people to do what she thought they ought to do for other people.

"Allie," I said slowly, "why do you think what Mama and Papa want is more important than what the Settlement Office wants or what Lan wants?"

"I don't!" she said, but her cheeks reddened.

"Well, you're sure enough acting like it."

"Somebody has to think about the family!" Allie said furiously.

"Yes," I said. "And somebody has to work in the Settlement Office and at the railroad. Somebody has to study medusa lizards and any other new wildlife, somebody has to invent new spells to take care of them, and somebody has to go to Washington to make sure the National Assembly knows what's happening in the territories. But somebody has to go West, too. And you don't get to decide for other people which somebody they're going to be."

"I'm not! I'm just saying that —"

"Yes, you are. Or at least, you're trying to." I took a deep breath. "It's right that Brant's wife has a say in what he does, but you're not Brant's wife. You're not Lan's mother, either. And if Mama is staying out of Lan's decision, I don't see that you have any business pushing your nose into it."

Allie stared at me for a minute, then flounced off. After that, she didn't talk to me about Lan's invitation again.

———◆———

In the second week of December, Lan announced over dinner that he'd accepted and would be going on the new expedition to the Far West. Allie gave him a disapproving sniff, but she didn't light into him, so I thought maybe our talk had done some good.

Brant was still considering. "I can't deny I'd like to go," he said with a sigh, and Allie frowned at him for even admitting so much. "But I don't know if I can justify the risk, or taking so much time away when I have three little ones that need looking after." He smiled across the table at his children.

Albert scowled ferociously. "I'm not little!" he said indignantly. "I'm almost ten!"

Everybody laughed, and after that things were a bit less uneasy around the house. Allie grumbled and glowered, but Rennie settled down and stopped pestering Brant to say no, even though he still hadn't made up his mind. I decided that it was because he was taking her seriously.

Right before Christmas, the Frontier Management Department published the list of people who'd accepted their invitation to go along on the expedition. There were still some gaps, especially in the list of scientists and magicians and support people, but most of the army and Settlement Office folks had been chosen.

I was surprised at how many I knew. Besides Wash, Lan, Roger, and Professor Torgeson, the list included Professor Ochiba, and Professor Lefevre from Simon Magus College. And of course there was the Cathayan magician, Adept Alikaket Shilin; he brought the total number of people to thirty-one. He'd been Master Adept Farawase's second in command, and I'd thought at the time that he knew more English than he was letting on.

I wondered how Cathayan magicians worked when they didn't have a team. I didn't think the master adept would send somebody along just to observe things, not to a place as dangerous as the Far West.

I went back to the list. Pierre le Grise, the trapper that everyone called Greasy Pierre, was among the people from the Settlement Office, and Dick Corman, who I remembered from back in day school, was in the army unit that was coming up from the South Plains. I wondered how he'd ended up down there.

And then I got to the list of assistants and support people, and my eyes went wide in surprise.

The third name was William Graham.

CHAPTER
· 14 ·

MY FIRST REACTION TO SEEING WILLIAM'S NAME ON THE EXPEDITION
list — after I got over being surprised — was to be cross and a
little hurt that he hadn't written and told me about it himself,
and a little jealous that I wasn't going with, too. My second
reaction was to wish I were back out at the study center and
away from all the talk that was certain to follow. William was
practically family; Mama and Allie wouldn't be any happier
about him heading West than they'd been when Lan and Brant
got invitations, only since William wasn't around, they'd be
able to fuss as much as they liked. And I didn't want to think
how Professor Graham was going to react.

Sure enough, when I got home from work, Papa was holed
up in the study with Professor Graham. Allie said Professor
Graham was almost as upset by seeing William's name on the
expedition list as he'd been when he and William quit speaking to begin with. When I asked her what she meant, it turned
out she hadn't been home when he arrived, so she didn't really
know any more than I did. She was just guessing.

Papa and the professor came out just before dinner, and
the professor didn't look all that upset to me. Mama invited
him to stay, but he declined politely. He wished us all a Merry

Christmas and left. Papa didn't say what they'd talked about, but he was very firm that evening about turning the dinner conversation whenever it started to drift toward the expedition.

Two days later, I got a letter from William. I felt absurdly pleased to find that he'd written to me before the list was published after all; the letter had just taken longer to get to Mill City than he'd expected. He'd been asked to go as a special assistant to Professor Ochiba.

The selection committee let the scientific personnel choose their own assistants, within certain guidelines, he wrote. *It's lucky I grew up in Mill City; that counted as "frontier experience," which neither of the other two candidates had. So Professor Ochiba chose me.*

I snorted. It was like William to make out that it was no big thing, but I knew better. Being picked out by Professor Ochiba meant even more than being picked out by the expedition committee, as far as I was concerned. I wondered who Professor Torgeson would pick for an assistant, and for just a second, I hoped it would be me. I had "frontier experience," no question, but the students who'd help move the mammoth had that, too, and all of them knew a lot more magic than I did, and they'd already asked Roger. I fought the hope down and went back to the letter.

It's an amazing opportunity, William went on. *Of course, I'd want to go even without the money, but the hazard pay certainly doesn't hurt. Between that and the experience, I'll be in a much better position when we get back.*

I frowned at the letter. Brant and Lan hadn't mentioned hazard pay, but I could see why it might interest William. Neither he nor his father ever spoke about each other directly, but everybody knew that Professor Graham had cut William off without a penny. William had expected it, too; he'd found a patron to pay his way at Triskelion even before he wrote his father about what he was planning. Having a starting-out stake for when he finished up his schooling would be a big help.

I wrote back right away. I knew William must have seen Lan's name on the expedition list already, but he wouldn't know about all the arguments, or about Brant still waffling over whether to go along or not. I almost said something about Roger going, too, but at the last minute I decided not to. They hadn't exactly hit it off when William came to help study the medusa lizard last spring. I finished up with all the news from Professor Torgeson's lab, and sent the letter off the day before Christmas.

———◆———

The holidays were uneasy. Everyone knew that this was the last Christmas we'd all be together for a long time, and if things went badly, it might be the last one, period. Mama worked hard at making everything extra special, but she couldn't keep the tension from showing in the way Lan avoided Allie, or the way Rennie's mouth pinched in whenever she looked at Brant.

Brant was still considering. He'd written to the Frontier Management Department, asking some questions, but he wouldn't tell anyone what they were. In fact, he'd pretty much stopped talking about the expedition at all, and he'd pick up and leave the room if anyone else started. It made things difficult, because Lan and Robbie didn't seem to want to talk about anything else.

Three days after Christmas, Roger Boden came by. I was the one who answered the door, so I got to warn him not to bring up the expedition in front of Brant or Rennie before he went on in to see the others. It didn't help any; practically the first thing Lan said when Roger walked into the sitting room was, "Have you heard yet who they're assigning as the expedition leader?"

"No," Roger said. He gave me an apologetic glance as Brant got up and left. I gave him a little smile to show that he wasn't the one I blamed for it, and he relaxed a little.

"It's only another four months until you leave," Robbie complained. "You'd think they'd know by now."

Rennie got up and followed Brant out. I glared at Robbie, who gave me a bewildered look. I sighed. At least all the people who didn't want to talk about the expedition were gone, so I didn't have the impossible job of trying to turn the conversation to other things.

Sure enough, Lan and Robbie kept on about it, speculating about routes and what new wildlife the expedition would discover. Roger was usually happy to join in, but that day he seemed distracted. He kept losing track of the conversation and having to be reminded what they were talking about. Finally, he shook his head and said, "My mind is fuzzy this afternoon. Maybe a good walk would clear it."

Lan looked puzzled, then shrugged. "I'm staying here, thanks. But if you want something to do, Mrs. Callahan was saying yesterday that the pond had frozen over and someone should check how thick the ice is before the young ones find it and start agitating to go skating."

I leaned over and poked him. "Lan!" I whispered furiously. "You shouldn't be shoving your chores off on someone else, and a guest, too!"

I thought I'd kept my voice down, but Roger heard me. "It's no trouble," he said, and hesitated. "In fact, would you care to join me, Miss Rothmer?"

"All right." I didn't have to think for even a minute; I was glad for a chance to get away from my brothers and all the expedition talk.

We got our coats and left. It was a clear, crisp winter day, warm enough to be comfortable walking but not enough to turn the snow to muddy slush. We'd had enough snow to whiten the ground, but not so much that it was difficult to walk through. "This is nice," I said as we started toward the pond. "Another week or two and it'll be too bitter cold to go out in unless you have to."

"That's one thing I didn't miss when I was in Albion," Roger said. "The cold."

"It's only a week, usually," I replied. "You can stand anything, if it's just for a week. And we've had a thaw in February the last two years to make up for it, and then there'll only be a month left until winter is really over."

"And then we leave."

I glanced over at him quickly, but his head was turned to stare westward and he didn't notice. "Are you having second thoughts?" I asked after a minute.

"Not exactly." Roger took a deep breath and turned to

look at me. "I'd planned to do this properly, but I don't think either of us would be too pleased if I went down on one knee in the snow out where anyone passing can see. Miss Rothmer — Eff — the one thing I regretted most when I went off to Albion was leaving you here, and your letters were the thing that brightened my days there the most.

"I know it isn't fair to ask you to wait two years for me to come back from the expedition, but I couldn't leave again without letting you know how I feel. I admire and . . . care for you greatly, and if you could see your way to it, I would be honored and . . . and . . . very happy if you would consent to be my wife."

"Roger, I . . ." I didn't know what to say. Roger had hinted some, back before he went to Albion to study, and I spent some time then deciding not to encourage him. I thought it had worked, and that he was dropping by mostly to visit with Lan and Papa now, but —

"I don't mean to settle things between us now," Roger hurried on as if I hadn't spoken. "Two years is a long time, and there's always the chance that . . . well, it wouldn't be right. But if . . . *when* I get back, I'll have a sizable stake to set up a household with, and everyone who goes will have their pick of jobs when we get back. I'll be well able to support a wife. So I hope — that is — if you would consider —" He stuttered to a stop.

"I don't know," I said, half to myself. Roger's face fell, and I said hastily, "I didn't mean it that way! I just meant that I wasn't exactly looking for this. I need to think about it."

His expression cleared. "That's all I . . . expected." He hesitated again. "Could you see your way to giving me an answer before the expedition leaves?"

I frowned. "I should hope so! It wouldn't be fair to leave you hanging all the time you're away."

He nodded. "Thank you. I — shall we see about that pond, then?"

We walked the rest of the way to the pond in silence. When we arrived, I couldn't help but stare. The pond was frozen over, all right, but the ice was flat and clear as window glass, with just a tiny bubble here and there where the water weeds had trapped a bit of air. You could only tell that it was frozen by the dusting of white where a bit of snow had blown across the ice.

"Black ice," Roger said, sounding surprised. "No wonder your Mrs. Callahan wanted it checked."

We hunted around and found a couple long branches, and Roger and I used them to test the ice around the edges. When we were sure it was firm, we stepped gingerly out onto it, poking with the branches and bouncing every few steps to see if it was still solid. We both slipped a couple of times, just because it was so smooth.

"It's thick enough, in spite of the way it looks." He smiled. "It's like walking on water; you can see straight down to the bottom except in the deepest spots."

"The childings will love it," I said.

"So will everyone else, I expect." He gave me a sidelong look. "I don't suppose you'd be interested in joining me to test it out more thoroughly tomorrow? Between the weather and the skaters, it won't stay clear like this for long."

I nodded. We headed back to the house, talking almost normally about skating and the weather and my niece and nephews. Neither of us mentioned the expedition, or his proposal, and I didn't tell anyone about it when I got home. I wanted to think on it for myself.

I lay awake a long time that night. I couldn't decide whether I was truly stunned by Roger's proposal, or whether I was just trying to convince myself that it had been a surprise. My sisters had been saying almost since they met him that Roger was sweet on me, but they'd all been full of suggestions about how to catch him. Apparently even they hadn't thought he'd propose without me doing something on purpose to persuade him.

At least once Roger's name showed up on the expedition list, they'd quit pushing me to encourage him. I sighed. If I told Roger yes, I'd have two years of listening to the three of them fuss at me. Nan wasn't so bad — she had her own home, and another new baby any minute, so she wasn't around to nag very often. Rennie was busy with her own childings, and she and Brant were looking to find a place of their own as soon as might be. But Allie . . .

I sighed. Allie was going to fuss and fret the whole time Lan was gone anyway, but if I got myself engaged to someone else who was on the expedition, she'd have someone to fuss and fret at. I didn't relish the thought, but keeping an engagement secret for two years didn't seem right, either.

I told myself firmly that I was avoiding the real question, which was whether or not to accept Roger. I liked him. I liked him a lot. But did I like him *enough*?

Finally I shook my head. The expedition wasn't leaving until the second week in April; I had another three months to make up my mind. I didn't have to decide everything right then. I rolled over and resolutely shut my eyes, then had to untangle the cord on the wooden pendant. *Maybe I'll have one of those dreams tonight*, I thought. *Maybe it will give me an idea of what to do.*

No special dreams came to help me out, though, just the normal kind, full of Rennie throwing cups at the wall and breaking them, one at a time, while Nan built the fire in the stove so high that little flames came out the vents and Allie tried to fill a live swarming weasel with bread stuffing so they could bake it for dinner and I ran back and forth among them trying to persuade them to stop. I woke up feeling tireder than when I'd gone to bed.

I thought about Roger off and on for the next week, and the more I thought, the less I knew what I wanted to say. I was twenty-one; I wouldn't turn twenty-two until June. A lot of my upper-school friends were married already. Roger was nice, and it wasn't like I had a lot of proposals to choose from.

On the other hand, I remembered what it had been like when the McNeil Expedition came back. All the men had been mobbed by "expedition ladies" wanting their attention — Nan and Rennie had been among them, and Allie would have, too, if she hadn't been too young for flirting then. I didn't think Roger would have any trouble finding someone else if I turned him down . . . or even if I didn't.

That was the real problem, I decided. Two years was long enough to change someone, and change them a lot. Once the expedition got past the far end of settlement territory, we wouldn't even have letters. And the expedition itself would change everyone on it.

I thought about that for a while, and then one evening when Rennie was watching the childings and everyone else was talking expedition in the front room, I hunted Brant down. I found him in the study room, where Papa still taught some of his special students once in a while. He was sitting at the big round table in the middle with a big book in front of him. He closed it as I came up, but not before I saw that he'd been looking at an old map of settlement territory.

"Do you have a minute?" I asked. "I wanted to talk to you."

"About what?"

"The expedition." I saw his expression and hurried on. "Not about you. About Lan." I still didn't want to tell anyone about Roger's proposal, for fear of embarrassing him if I turned him down, but Brant wouldn't be surprised that I was worried about my twin. "He's going, and I want to know what it's going to be like for him. For when he comes back."

When I'd first thought of talking to Brant, I'd planned to be a lot clearer, but he seemed to understand me anyway. "Nobody knows what it's going to be like," Brant said. His lips twisted and he glanced upward, toward the room he and Rennie shared. "That's the difficulty."

"I know," I told him. "I didn't mean the details. I meant —" I waved my hands helplessly. "What it's like coming back, I suppose."

"Everything's different." Brant's eyes got a faraway look to them. "When you're out, there's just the few of you, and after two years in one another's pockets, you know everything about everyone, or nearly — from how they drink their coffee to the twitch that means they're annoyed about something. And there's a lot of annoying, believe me.

"Then you get back and there are too many people, and they're all too close, and there's too much noise. Even people you know — they expect you to be changed, but they don't really think about how much, or in what ways. And they've changed from the way you've been remembering them for two years, but nobody but you even remembers that they were ever different, because everyone else was there for it and has gotten used to it."

"It sounds hard," I said.

"It was harder for some than for others." Brant fell silent for a moment. "What bothered me the most were the little things. I'd known that there'd be some big things happening, like my best friend showing up at the welcome-home with a year-old baby, and I was more or less braced for those. But — well, I used to drink my coffee with a bit of sweet in it, but we ran short on sugar once the winter set in, so all of us got accustomed to taking it black. I almost choked when Aunt Lewis handed me a cup that she'd sweetened, the first night I spent with her and my uncle after the expedition."

"Was it the same when you came back from the settlement last year?" I asked.

"Some," Brant said. "But we were seven years out in Oak River, and nobody was expecting anything to be much the same. And we knew some of what had been happening here from letters — the big things, anyway. My parents moving back East, for instance, and your brother Jack going off to the settlements. And Nan getting married, and Lan coming back from Simon Magus for a while. There's no mail when you're out in the Far West."

He fell silent again, but it was a thinking sort of silence, like he was pondering on what he'd said. I thought about asking him something more, but I couldn't think of anything that wouldn't give away the fact that I was interested in more than just what Lan would be like when he came back. So I thanked him and left him fingering the spine of the book of maps and staring at the darkened, snow-speckled study window.

I spent the evening mulling over what Brant had said. I was still mulling when I went in to work. Around mid-morning, Professor Torgeson came to talk with Professor Jeffries. They spent half an hour in his office, and then called me in.

I picked up my notebook and a pencil and went in, figuring it was something about preparations for the expedition. Almost as soon as I sat down, Professor Torgeson glanced at Professor Jeffries and began.

"I don't know whether you know this, but the magicians and scientists who are going on the expedition to the Far West this spring have been asked to choose their own assistants, within certain parameters," she said.

"I'd heard," I said, thinking of Professor Ochiba and William.

Professor Torgeson nodded. "Good. Then you won't be surprised to hear that I've been discussing the matter with the Settlement Office, and I'd like you to come along as my assistant, Eff."

CHAPTER
· 15 ·

MY MOUTH FELL RIGHT OPEN AND I STARED AT PROFESSOR TORGESON, unable to speak.

Professor Jeffries laughed. "I would say that on the evidence, you are wrong about the surprise, Aldis."

Professor Torgeson gave him an annoyed look, then frowned at me. "Really, Eff, who else did you think I would choose? We already know that we can work together; you did very well on the survey trip."

"And you're one of the few in the scientific section who's had firsthand experience taking on unknown wildlife," Professor Jeffries put in.

"It's even worse than that," Professor Torgeson said tartly. "At present, Eff and I would be the only ones in the scientific section who have been west of the Mammoth at all, though I believe Professor Lefevre has visited parts of northern Acadia that are not protected by the Great Barrier Spell. I don't know what the selection committee was thinking."

"You could have anyone you wanted," I said, finding my voice at last. "And if you're looking for experience, Lan was there, too, when we shot the medusa lizards."

Professor Jeffries smiled. "But Mr. Rothmer has already been chosen to be one of the exploration-and-survey personnel. I don't think the Settlement Office would release him to the scientific section even if there were no alternative."

"I wouldn't ask them to," Professor Torgeson snapped. She started to add something, looked at me, and stopped. "Mr. Rothmer has a strong theoretical background, certainly, but I prefer to choose an assistant who I am certain will be personally compatible."

"An assistant's job is, after all, to assist," Professor Jeffries said, nodding. "And much as I will miss your assistance here, Miss Rothmer, I have to confess that I am not surprised by Professor Torgeson's choice . . . nor do I disapprove of it."

"Th-thank you, Professor," I stammered. "I —" I paused. I'd almost accepted straight off, but then pictures of Mama and Roger and Lan and Allie ran through my mind, and I realized that might not be such a good idea. "I wasn't expecting this at all," I said instead. "I'll have to think about it."

"It is a big decision," Professor Jeffries said. "Take your time."

"But not too much time," Professor Torgeson added. "I can easily give you a week, I think, but after that the Frontier Management Department will start insisting on my answer."

"I think a week will be enough," I told her. "It's just — it really hadn't occurred to me. And my mother is already unhappy about Lan going. I don't know what she'll say if I tell her . . ."

Professor Torgeson smiled, and I realized that I'd just as

much as said that I wanted to accept. Professor Jeffries looked thoughtful. "That aspect hadn't occurred to me," he said after a moment. "Still, I am sure that you will make the right choice, Miss Rothmer. Whatever that choice may be."

We talked for another hour about what my duties would be, about the precautions the expedition would be taking, and how everything would be organized. There would be ten people in the scientific section of the expedition, six of them experts in wildlife study or different kinds of magic and four of them assistants. Adept Alikaket, the Cathayan representative, had decided he didn't want an assistant, so they'd been able to fit an extra magician in, though they couldn't give him or her an assistant like the first four. There were only eight people in the exploration-and-survey section, and thirteen in the section that included the army and support staff.

The official head of the expedition would be Mr. Corvales from the Frontier Management Department, but Professor Jeffries said that the captain of the army unit would probably have just as much authority. Since the Cathayans were sponsoring the expedition and sending Adept Alikaket along, the professor figured it'd probably be three people actually making the important decisions for the whole expedition.

I left the office with my head in a whirl, and it wasn't until mid-afternoon that my mind started to settle. I didn't even try to pretend to myself that I didn't want to take the professor's offer. I wanted to be part of the expedition. I wanted it so badly that I could taste it like the sharp bite of fresh-ground pepper on my tongue. But the more I thought, the more I wasn't sure I should accept.

Mama was already worrying about Lan, and he hadn't even left yet. I could see how much Brant wanted to go; the only reason he hadn't said yes already was because of Rennie's nagging. I figured he'd accept eventually, and if I said yes, too, that would make three of us, which seemed like a lot from one family. Especially if no one came back.

Then there were William and Roger. They weren't family, but they were close enough that Mama would fuss about them at least a bit, especially if she found out that Roger had proposed to me. If I went, too —

My mind stuttered to a stop and backed up. For the first time in days, I'd forgotten all about Roger's proposal.

Right about then, Professor Jeffries came out and caught me staring at the wall with my dipping pen gone dry in the middle of the page I was copying. He smiled and told me to go home for the day, as I'd clearly be no use to him until I was done thinking.

I didn't go home right away; if I'd gone, I'd have had to explain to Mama why I was there early, and I wasn't ready for that. Instead, I went to the college library. People were used to seeing me there, picking up books for the professors or making notes on something they needed, so no one would think anything of me being there, and I'd have quiet and time to think.

I found a place at a long table near the clerestory windows at the back, and settled in for some more thinking. I still wasn't sure what to tell Roger, but whatever I told him, it was bound to make things awkward if we both went on the expedition. If we were engaged, it would cause talk even if we were in different parts of the expedition and even if Lan were along, too, and if I told Roger no, it would be awkward if we had to work together.

Of course, we still had time to get married before the expedition left, if we hurried. That way, there wouldn't be talk and it wouldn't be awkward. On the other hand, I'd have duties toward a husband that might take time away from what I was on the expedition to do. Also, I didn't know how Roger would feel about having his wife along.

I didn't come to any conclusion, but that night I asked Papa if I could talk to him after dinner. I told him about Professor Torgeson's offer, and that I thought I wanted to accept, but that I wanted to think on it for a few days before I told everyone else. "I don't want Lan and Allie fighting over it when I'm not sure myself," I said. "If I decide not to go, it'd be better not to say anything at all."

Papa nodded. "I think that's wise. And your mother?"

"I figured you'd know whether to tell her now or wait."

He smiled slightly and nodded. Then he gave me a long, searching look. "How long do you have to decide?"

"Professor Torgeson gave me a week. She needs to know soon so she can pick someone else if I say no."

"And do you really think you will be saying no, Eff?"

"I —" I didn't know how to answer him. "I think I know what I want. I just don't know how good an idea it is."

Papa sighed. "I can't say I'm happy about two of my children heading into the unknown with no guarantee of returning. Lewis and Clark never —"

"The Lewis and Clark Expedition disappeared nearly fifty years ago, Papa! The McNeil Expedition came back without losing a single man, and all the spells and guns are ten years better now."

"McNeil didn't go past Wintering Island," Papa pointed out. "This group is planning to go a lot farther." He paused. "Are you really sure about this, Eff?"

"Some of the time, I am," I said. "Some of the time, it's . . . I liked being out in the settlements with Professor Torgeson that summer we spent on the wildlife survey, and I liked taking the mammoth to the new study center. So I ought to like this. But it's —" I waved my hands, trying to find words for what I wanted to say. "It's *bigger*. And some of the time it scares me."

"Ah." Papa sat back. "It's not something you can take back if you change your mind in the middle."

I nodded. "And it's not like everything will stay the same while I'm gone. Anything could happen — Nan might have another baby, or Robbie or Jack might get married, or . . . or anything!"

"It's a hard thing to walk away from what you know, even when you're positive you're heading for something better," Papa said. "When you're not positive . . . well, it's just that much harder to decide." He sighed. "Remember when we moved to Mill City? It took me nearly a year to make up my mind to come. Your aunts and uncles thought I was mad to move so close to the frontier, and your oldest brothers and sisters weren't happy about us being so far away."

"Mama said you couldn't help coming to build the school," I said hesitantly.

Papa's eyes had a faraway remembering look. "The Northern Plains Riverbank College was barely four years old, and I knew I could make a mark on it if I came. But there weren't any guarantees that it would all come together the way I hoped." He shook his head and looked at me. "In the end, though, I knew that if I'd stayed back East, I'd have wondered all my days how it would have turned out. And I must say, I haven't ever been sorry we came, not even when things were . . . difficult.

"So think hard, Eff. Think about how you'd feel and what you'd regret in ten or twenty years, both ways — if you go, and if you don't go. Then make your decision, and I'll support it."

"Lan decided before he even got home from the office."

Papa laughed a little ruefully. "I hope I persuaded him to do some thinking after, at least. But his situation is a little different from yours. His decision may be, as well."

I nodded. Everyone in the family had always known that Lan would be going out to do new and dangerous things, because that's what seventh sons of seventh sons do. Nobody had thought specifically about him going out to the Far West, but it wasn't a huge and horrible surprise.

But me — I was the one in the family who'd always had the most trouble with magic, right through upper school, and I didn't have any special skills, like Roger's geomancy, that would make me a good choice for the expedition. Nobody had ever even suggested that I might be picked, not even after everybody knew Professor Torgeson was going.

Papa and I talked a little longer, and then I left. I didn't tell him about Roger's proposal, or how confused I was about it. I stayed awake most of the night turning things over and over in my mind. I pictured how it would be if I told Roger yes and went on the expedition with him, and how it would be if I said no and went. I thought about what it would be like to stay home and wait for him, and how it would be if I didn't wait.

It occurred to me after a while that I hadn't really been thinking about marrying Roger. I'd been thinking about how marrying him would affect things if I went on the expedition, or if I didn't. That didn't sound right to me. I sighed. I didn't want to hurt Roger, but I had to admit that not wanting to hurt him was a terrible reason to marry a man. Wanting things to work smoothly on an expedition was an even worse reason, especially since the expedition would only be two years and we'd be married for the rest of our lives.

That was when I knew what I would tell Roger. I still didn't know what I'd tell Professor Torgeson. I thought about Mama some more. I remembered the talk we'd had before I joined the group that moved the mammoth to the study center. She'd as good as told me straight out that she wouldn't stand in my way when I wanted to go out to the West again, even though she worried. *We didn't raise any of you to walk a path other than your own*, she'd said. I relaxed suddenly. I'd decided on my path a long time back, and though I hadn't really recognized it,

I was sure Mama had. I could put off following it for a while if I didn't go on the expedition, but that would only make it harder when I finally started.

It was right to think about what everyone else would think and how they'd feel about my decision, but it wasn't right for me to let that change my mind. I was pretty sure, now, what it was I wanted to do. I still had to figure out how to do it the best way for everyone.

I waited another two days to be sure, and then I told Mama and Papa that I wanted to join the expedition. Mama cried a little, but she said she was proud of me. Later on, she told me she actually felt better knowing I'd be along to keep Lan out of trouble.

Then I told Professor Torgeson yes, and Roger no. The conversation with Roger was especially hard. He came to Professor Jeffries's office to walk me home, and I could see that he was nervous. I told him about Professor Torgeson's offer first, and as soon as he heard that she wanted me to join the expedition, he frowned and asked if I was sure. "You do know how dangerous it is?"

"Roger, I've lived in Mill City since I was five. I've been out to settlement territory three times. The first time, my father and brother were almost drained dry by mirror bugs; the second time, Professor Torgeson and Wash and I fought off a pride of saber cats; and the third time, I shot a medusa lizard. Of course I know how dangerous it is."

"I wasn't trying to talk you out of it," he said quickly. "Just . . . some people have the oddest ideas about what we'll be doing."

"Like the 'expedition ladies' that made such a fuss when the McNeil Expedition came back," I said, nodding. "Thinking it's some kind of romantic adventure, when it's really just a lot of hard work and being uncomfortable."

"Yes." Roger sounded relieved. Then he cut his eyes sideways at me for a second, before he looked down and said, "If you're going on the expedition, it might — there'll be talk."

"It's not as if I'll be the only woman along," I said. "Professor Ochiba and Professor Torgeson are going, and Lan told me that there's a Miss Elizabet Dzozkic in the survey group, and maybe others in the support staff."

"Even so, you know how people are. I just thought maybe . . ." He took a deep breath. "If we got married before the expedition leaves —"

"I did think about that," I said gently. "But avoiding talk doesn't seem to me to be a good reason to rush into something that's going to last our whole lives long. Especially since we're not going to be here to hear the whispers."

"I understand," Roger said heavily. He stopped walking so he could look straight at me. "Your answer would be the same even if you weren't coming along, wouldn't it?"

"I —" I took a deep breath. "I'm really sorry, Roger. I just —"

"Don't try to explain," Roger interrupted. "It'll just make it harder."

We walked in silence the rest of the way. "Thank you for your honesty, Miss Rothmer," he said finally, just as we reached the house. "I think I won't come in this evening. Please give your mother my regards."

He reached up and very gently brushed a bit of my hair back from my face. Then he bowed and walked away. I stood there as the dark deepened and the cold soaked through my boots, feeling miserable and wondering whether I'd done the right thing.

I cried myself to sleep that night. Next day, I broke the news to my family that I would be joining Lan on the Joint Cathayan-Columbian Discovery and Mapping Expedition.

CHAPTER
· 16 ·

ALL MY GUESSES ABOUT HOW PEOPLE WOULD REACT WERE DEAD ON. Robbie's eyes got as big as teacups, and then he whooped right there at the dinner table. Rennie went white and Allie went red, and both of them yelled at me until Mama and Papa made them stop. Lan grinned in a way that made me wonder if he'd known more than I did. Brant went still and quiet, and waited for the ruckus to die down before he congratulated me.

Just as I'd expected, Allie was the most difficult. It took me nearly two days to make her understand that I wasn't still making up my mind and that she didn't have any chance to talk me out of it because I'd already told Professor Torgeson yes. When I finally got her convinced, she burst into tears. She spent the next two weeks giving me reproachful looks whenever we crossed paths. I was surprised that all I got were looks, until I found out that Mama had sat her down for a talking-to.

Somewhere in that first week, I made the time to write and tell William my news. I didn't tell him about Roger, though. He wrote back that he was glad we'd both be on the expedition, and he'd be looking forward to seeing me when he and Professor Ochiba got to Mill City for the send-off.

The day after I made my announcement, Brant took an afternoon off work and went down to the Settlement Office. That evening, he told us that he'd decided not to join the expedition.

Papa raised an eyebrow, but all he did was nod. Robbie frowned and said, "You're certain?"

"I'm certain that I'm not going," Brant said. "Mr. Parsons and I had a long talk, and decided that" — he paused, like he couldn't quite bring himself to say "it would be best." After a second, he finished — "that it's what I'm going to do. I signed the refusal. It's done and settled, and that's all there is to it."

Rennie burst into tears. Allie stuck her chin in the air and gave me a triumphant look.

"But I thought you really wanted to go," Robbie persisted.

"I did. I do. But I don't want to leave my family for two or three years." Brant put his shoulders back. "And there's no need for more talk on the subject. There's been enough talk and then some, and like I said, the decision is made."

Lan had opened his mouth to say something, but at that he closed it again. Allie gave him the same look she'd given me, but Lan ignored her. "We'll think of you, then," he said to Brant after a minute. Brant nodded, and that was the last they spoke of the expedition before it left.

Brant's decision made things harder and easier for me, both at the same time. On the one hand, Rennie and Allie were happy that he was staying, which meant they weren't so snappish all the time. On the other hand, they both seemed to think that it was their arguments that had persuaded him, which meant they went at Lan and me harder than ever. I took to working late when I could, and avoiding them as much as I could when I had to be at home.

Working late wasn't hard to arrange. For the next two months, I was almost too busy to think. A lot of it was on account of the newspapers and broadsheets. They made even more fuss over the Joint Cathayan-Columbian Discovery and Mapping Expedition than I recalled them making when the McNeil Expedition left, and they were particularly taken with Lan and me. Evidently they thought people were more interested in hearing about a pair of twins, one of them a double-seventh son, than in finding out what the expedition was supposed to accomplish.

The rest of my busy-ness had to do with the expedition itself. There was a lot of planning to do, and a lot of things to get together, and somehow Lan seemed to think that because I was going, I'd do his share of both of them as well as my own. I got that straightened out pretty quick, though.

In addition to my regular work, I had to make up a list for the Settlement Office of all the official supplies Professor Torgeson and I would need, and estimate how much space they would take up. I had to spend a couple of hours every week practicing with my rifle, and another couple of hours practicing travel protection spells.

The expedition was setting out from Mill City, which meant that all the supplies for it were being accumulated in Mr. Corcoran's warehouse down by the river. The Settlement Office was supposed to make sure everything was there, but

Professor Torgeson and I stopped in every few days to double-check, and twice she made them replace things that she didn't think were good enough quality.

The biggest problem, though, came from the Frontier Management Department itself. They had an enormous list of things that they thought we should take. "It looks to me as if they've taken the equipment lists from every party that's headed west in the past fifty years and added them all together," Professor Torgeson said when she saw it. "Idiots."

"It's even worse than you think," Professor Jeffries said. "I just came from the warehouse. They went and shipped us a railroad car's worth of supplies without bothering to mention it, and stacked them any which way because they were in a hurry to unload. Someone will have to go through them all, or you're likely to find yourselves halfway to the mountains with nothing but oatmeal to eat."

"At least we don't have to do all the work ourselves," I said. "Lan says the army is sending someone to take care of their part."

Professor Jeffries nodded. "Mr. Parsons mentioned that. I believe Quartermaster Solomon is expected next week."

"I hope he has more sense than this lot," Professor Torgeson said, waving at the stack of paper the Frontier Management Office had sent.

It took me several days to go over the list and sort out the parts that might actually be of some use. Then I had to add in the things that weren't on it, and check everything off that was already in the warehouse. It didn't take long to discover that some of the things we did need weren't in very good shape.

I was in the middle of going through a crate of sample

boxes and taking out all the ones whose preservation spells had stopped working, when I heard someone cough behind me. I turned and found a small, businesslike woman studying me with cool gray eyes. She looked to be in her mid-twenties, not so very much older than me. She had light brown hair cropped to just below her ears and pinned back to stay out of her face. She wore a plain gray skirt and jacket and a neat pair of high-button black-and-white boots.

"Excuse me," she said. "I'm looking for Professor Aldis Torgeson and Miss Francine Rothmer. The office said they'd likely be here."

"Professor Torgeson just left," I told her. "I'm Eff Rothmer."

"Sergeant Amy Solomon," the woman said. "Army quartermaster for the Joint Cathayan-Columbian Discovery and Mapping Expedition. I go by Sergeant Amy when it's not official business. I understand you've been having some trouble with the supplies."

I blinked in surprise. "You're the quartermaster? We weren't expecting you for another two days."

"I had a feeling this would be more of a mess than they were telling me, so I got the major to finish up the paperwork on my transfer a little early." She studied the stacks of crates and boxes and barrels, and shook her head. "I can see it was a good call. There isn't going to be room for even half of this, you know."

"It wasn't our idea," I said. "Half of what's here is useless, and a fair few of the things that we really do want are broken or have spells that don't work."

"Salvage goods and cheap suppliers," Sergeant Amy said, nodding. "Typical. The first thing is to get rid of the junk. We can probably sell or trade some of the things that are in good shape. That'll give us funds to replace the things that aren't."

"I've been sorting for the last three days," I said, and showed her what I'd done. Then we went back to the Settlement Office to go over the equipment lists.

I liked Amy Solomon from the start. In between looking over the supplies and lists, she told me that she'd grown up in a settlement in the South Plains Territory, near one of the forts the army had built to hunt the terror birds and gildenslinks that the settlement protection spells couldn't handle. She'd begun working for the army as soon as they'd let her, helping out in the office the same way I'd started helping at the college when I was in upper school.

A few years later, she'd joined up. She said that the army had been letting women sign up since the middle of the Secession War, when they needed magicians so badly. After the war ended, they'd never changed the rules, though there weren't a whole lot of women who took them up on it these days. Most army women were, like Sergeant Solomon, from the settlement territories, where people cared less about what you were than about what you could do.

Amy Solomon looked over my lists, spent a day in Mr. Corcoran's warehouse, and then fired off a bunch of telegrams. Two days later, three soldiers arrived on the train from New Orleans. They disappeared into the warehouse, and by the end of the week there was a lot more room and a lot more order.

At the beginning of the next week, Sergeant Amy showed up at Professor Torgeson's office, carrying all the lists and frowning. "Professor Torgeson, I have some questions," she said. "Particularly about this." She set a page on the desk and pointed.

I recognized it right off; it was the list I'd written of all the things we didn't need or couldn't get. Professor Torgeson glanced at where her finger was pointing and raised her eyebrows. "And?"

"Why are lizard-skin jackets on this list?"

"Because we can't get them," Professor Torgeson said.

"Why not? If it's a matter of cost —"

"It's not the cost," Professor Torgeson interrupted. "There simply aren't any around to buy. You have to understand, the medusa lizards only appeared two years ago. They are fortunately still uncommon near the settlements. There haven't been enough of them killed yet for medusa-lizard-skin jackets to be available in Mill City."

"Even a few —"

"The only one I actually know of is in the possession of one of the men who went out hunting medusa lizards last year," Professor Torgeson said sharply. "He killed the lizard and made the jacket himself. I don't doubt that the other hunters have been doing the same thing, even though we don't really know whether the lizard skin will repel the petrification effect. No doubt they feel that some chance of blocking the lizards' magic is better than no chance at all, and the hunters are the most likely to be exposed to it, after all."

Sergeant Amy made a face. "Reasonable. But in that case, what are the jackets doing on the equipment list at all?"

"I expect someone actually read the reports we've been sending," Professor Torgeson said. "As I said, we haven't been able to test the skins against the actual lizards, though I'm hopeful that we'll have field observations soon from this winter's hunt, but we did establish that the magic-resistance property outlasts the lizard's death and is not affected by the tanning process."

"And naturally no one considered anything else. Like availability." Sergeant Amy pursed her lips. "I don't suppose any of those hunters would be willing to sell if we put out word that we'll be buying on our way through."

Professor Torgeson shrugged. "Possibly, if someone has managed to kill enough of the lizards. I doubt that anyone would sell his only jacket. Money isn't worth anything to a statue."

"True, and from what you say, we're not likely to be able to outfit more than a fraction of the expedition members."

"I'd guess one or two of them, at most. Though I know that at least two of the guides have been hunting lizards; they may already have lizard-skin jackets of their own."

"Two is better than none, I suppose," the sergeant said. "But that brings up another problem. I haven't seen the reports myself, but what's the probability that we're going to run into these creatures ourselves?"

"High," Professor Torgeson said. "We think they're native to the Far West. Why they're moving east is anyone's guess, but it's only logical that the farther west we get, the more of them we're likely to find."

"West and north," the sergeant said absently, frowning. "We haven't seen any of the things in the south plains, thank goodness. Right, then. We'll just have to make our own lizard-skin jackets as we shoot the things."

Professor Torgeson seemed a little taken aback, but she didn't say anything outright. She had me give Sergeant Amy a copy of the summary report we'd made, then went back to her own preparations. I thought the sergeant had the right of it. We already knew we were likely to run into medusa lizards; if we ran into them, we'd have to kill them, because we didn't have a protection spell yet that worked. If we killed them, we'd have skins and we might as well make use of them if we could.

As March wore on, more and more expedition members began to arrive in Mill City. The next arrivals were Settlement Office and support people — Mr. MacPhee, the minerals expert, arrived first, then Mr. Zarbeliev, who'd been a circuit magician in the middle plains for three years. Miss Elizabet Dzozkic and Miss Bronwyn Hoel came in on the same train. They were actually a team, though Miss Dzozkic was a surveyor and officially one of the Settlement Office group and Miss Hoel was a dowser who'd been included with the support people for some reason.

Mr. Corvales, who would be heading up the expedition, arrived with Adept Alikaket two weeks before we were to set out. He was a short, round, cheerful man with a bald spot just starting in the back of his dark hair, and he made it a point to meet up with everyone who was going on the expedition, first thing, even though the territory governor and the mayor both wanted to talk to him.

Dr. Martin Lefevre and his assistant arrived right after Mr. Corvales, and the first thing he did was ask Professor Torgeson and Professor Jeffries if they could see the preserved medusa lizard parts. When he found out we had actual live lizards out at the study center, he insisted on going out to examine them right away. Even a three-inch snowfall the day he got to Mill City didn't discourage him.

"By tomorrow, it will have melted," he said confidently.

I almost pointed out that Mill City was a lot farther north than Philadelphia and he couldn't count on the snow melting that fast. In the end, I was glad I hadn't, because he was mostly right; the snow wasn't gone the next day, but it had melted enough to be muddy slush that didn't get so much in the way of riding.

Professor Jeffries had been looking for a good excuse to go out to the study center since early March, so he wasn't hard to persuade. When word got around, Mr. Zarbeliev and Adept Alikaket decided to go, too. Professor Torgeson and I sent them all off the next day and went back to preparing for the expedition.

Our biggest concern was all the supplies. Thirty-one people couldn't travel with just saddlebags and a couple of packhorses, especially not if we were going to do all the things the Frontier Management Department wanted us to do. The organizing committee had settled on covered wagons as the best option, packed as tight and full as we could manage. We could carry a lot that way; the trouble was that everyone wanted their own supplies right on top, where they would be easy to get at, and the only way to make sure that happened was to go down to the warehouse and help load.

After the third time Sergeant Amy caught someone re-arranging crates so as to put their gear on top and someone else's underneath, she threw everyone out of the warehouse.

"Since you can't do it properly yourselves, the army will load the wagons," she told us. "Each of you can give me a list of what you need, ranked by how often you expect to need it. I'll do my best to accommodate you, but anyone who gives me a list that says they need everything every day is going to find their equipment on the bottom layer in the very last wagon. Clear?"

Between that and the army unit's arrival the next day, things went a lot more smoothly for the next week. Then, two days before we were expected to leave, Dr. Lefevre and Adept Alikaket came back from the study center.

They brought the mammoth with them.

Nobody was particularly pleased to have the mammoth over in West Landing — Dr. Lefevre had at least been sensible enough not to try to bring it back through the Great Barrier Spell to Mill City — but nobody objected out loud in public on account of Adept Alikaket being involved. Even Mr. Corvales, who was supposed to be in charge of the expedition, only pursed his lips and said he'd have to talk to the adept right away.

Professor Torgeson wasn't so restrained in private. I think she really wanted to rip up at Professor Jeffries, but he'd had the sense to stay at the study center, so she couldn't get at him. Instead, she lit into Dr. Lefevre almost the minute she saw him.

"What were you thinking?" she demanded. "If you knew the work it took to get that beast out there in the first place —"

Dr. Lefevre's dark eyes narrowed and he drew himself up to his full height, which was considerable. "I do not owe you an explanation, madam."

"That's *professor*," Professor Torgeson snapped. "And *somebody* owes me an explanation. Who came up with this idea, anyway? Jeffries?"

"Adept Alikaket," Dr. Lefevre said with obvious satisfaction. "Require your answers from him, *madam*." And he left the room before Professor Torgeson recovered enough to blast him again.

Professor Torgeson was out of sorts for the rest of the day. We finally got some of the story at the expedition meeting the following morning, though it wasn't the whole tale by any means.

Mr. Corvales started off with basic information, like who would be in charge of what and suchlike. Then he introduced the captain of the army unit, Adept Alikaket, and the expedition doctor. Dr. Faber was a tall, thin man with a disapproving expression that made me hope that neither Lan nor I got sick for the next two years.

Captain Velasquez was an older man of medium height, with tight-curled black hair and skin only a few shades lighter. He spoke next, giving a little speech about cooperation among all the different sections of the expedition. Adept Alikaket went last and said least, just a few words about extending the horizons of knowledge and suchlike. I grinned to myself when he stood up to talk, and then raised my eyebrows when he spoke with only a light Cathayan accent. He knew a *lot* more English than he'd let on.

When the speeches were over, the three of them asked for questions, and naturally the first thing everyone wanted to talk about was the mammoth.

Adept Alikaket said that after talking with the college representatives (Professor Jeffries, presumably), he'd felt that the mammoth could be very useful to the expedition. It could haul a lot of the crucial magical supplies, which would mean one less wagon and a bit more space in the wagons we did take. The adept knew the spells the Bharat magicians used to train elephants, and he'd tried them out on the mammoth, and they'd worked fine. Professor Torgeson wasn't the only one to look skeptical, but nobody wanted to be the one to tell the adept that bringing the mammoth along was a bad idea. I looked over at the adept's expressionless face and couldn't help wondering whether he had more reasons for wanting the mammoth along than just hauling baggage. If he did, he obviously hadn't told anyone.

Once we finished with the questions, Mr. Corvales told everyone to get to know one another, especially the folks from the other sections of the expedition. He gave the army captain a rather pointed look when he said that, which made me think that maybe the captain wasn't in favor of a lot of mingling.

After the meeting was completely over, including the mingling, Professor Torgeson told me to wait. She and Professor Ochiba had done some organizing of their own, and gotten all the women of the expedition together to sort out sleeping arrangements. There were seven of us, in total: the two professors and me; Sergeant Amy; Mrs. Anna Wilson and Miss Bronwyn Hoel from the support staff; and Miss Elizabet Dzozkic from the exploration-and-survey group. Elizabet and Bronwyn were a dowser-surveyor team who had worked together for a long time, so they got the first tent, and it only made sense to put the two professors together.

That left me in the last tent with the sergeant and Mrs. Wilson. I thought that would be all right. I'd liked what I'd seen of the sergeant, and Mrs. Wilson was just as brisk and friendly as you'd expect from someone who was along as the expedition cook.

When I got home that afternoon, Rennie and Allie ambushed me. Allie was scowling and her lips kept twitching like she had a bad taste in her mouth. "You and Rennie have to talk," she told me, and shoved the pair of us into the front parlor.

"Allie . . . !" Rennie was too late; the door had closed behind her. "Drat that girl!"

"What is this about?" I demanded. "If you're making another try at talking me out of going on the expedition, I'm leaving right now. You have no business —"

"It's not that," Rennie interrupted. She opened her mouth and then closed it again, looking very uncomfortable.

"Then what?" I wasn't in any mood for more fussing, no matter what the subject.

"We thought — it's about going. On the expedition."

I waited.

"There's a spell you need to know," Rennie said very fast. "Mama should . . . but she won't . . . Allie and I decided . . ."

"Rennie, *what* are you on about?" I said.

Rennie took a deep breath. "You are going on an expedition out into the middle of nowhere with seven women and twenty-three men. You can't . . . Two years is a long while, and men can be very persuasive. You need to be prepared."

"Rennie, I don't —"

"There's a spell," Rennie continued with grim determination. "To keep from . . . getting in an interesting condition."

I was having a hard time believing my ears. I remembered the way Rennie had chased after Brant when the McNeil expedition came back; I really didn't think he'd been the one being "very persuasive." And I knew *somebody'd* been persuasive, on account of the way Rennie'd eloped with Brant so suddenly. I'd suspected the reason behind it for a while, and then Rennie finally let Papa record little Albert's birth date in the family Bible, and I knew for sure. Albert had been born barely seven months after Rennie and Brant ran off together. And here she was lecturing me about taking care! And . . . "You mean there's a spell to keep from falling pregnant?"

Rennie's face turned pink. She nodded. "It doesn't always work, but it's better than nothing, which is all the more those men are likely to have handy." She sniffed. "It goes like this —"

I just stood there gaping, while Rennie went over the words and demonstrated the spell. By the time she finished, her face was bright red, but she pushed on. "Now you try it," she said. "Go on."

"Allie put you up to this, didn't she?" I said, ignoring her commands.

"I'm married," Rennie said, trying to look dignified. "She isn't. It's more appropriate for me to do it."

"Appropriate?" I snorted. "Of all the nerve! What, you think that just because I'm going on the expedition, I'll turn into some kind of tart?"

"Of course we don't think that," Rennie said in a tone that made me positive that both of them had discussed just exactly that and were in complete agreement.

"The pair of you are the nosiest, most interfering, bossiest sisters anybody has ever had," I said. "And I'm not staying to hear more. Not from you."

I hadn't thought Rennie could get any redder, but she did. "My . . . history isn't important here! You need to know this."

"Well, you've shown me your spell, and that's enough." I could see that it'd be a good thing to know one day, though I'd no intention of needing to make use of it on the trip, but I wasn't about to tell Rennie any of that. I'd ask Sergeant Amy if I decided I needed to know more. She seemed like she'd be a lot better source of information than Rennie. Besides . . . I suppressed a sudden grin. "And if it's that important, you should teach Lan and William, too. You tell Allie that."

I left while Rennie was still sputtering and looking horrified. I didn't speak to her or to Allie for the rest of the day. When I finally got over being mad, I had to admit that they were trying to be a help, in their own way. I just wished they could have done it without being so annoying. Of all the ways to let me know they'd finally come around to the notion of me going on the expedition, they had to pick the most embarrassing one.

The next two days went by in a whirl. Mill City had given the McNeil Expedition a huge send-off eleven years before, and Mayor Brewster was determined to make this one bigger and better, especially since so many of the expedition members were from the town or the college. The mayor had wanted us to parade down to the docks the day we left, but Mr. Corvales put his foot down. He figured we'd have a hard enough time making our first day's mileage as it was, and he wasn't having a parade to run late and complicate things even worse.

So the parade and the big official good-bye dinner and the last round of fireworks all happened the day before we left. I thought at first that I'd rather have spent the evening at home, but Mr. Corvales said we should all be there if we could, along with any of our friends or family who wanted to see us off, and in the end I was mostly glad I'd gone. The whole family was on edge as it was; I didn't like to think how it would have been if it had just been the lot of us at home.

Rennie stuck close by Brant all evening, like she was afraid he'd change his mind at the last minute and come with us after all. Papa and Mama looked proud and worried at the same time. Allie couldn't seem to make up her mind whether to scowl and disapprove of everything or fuss over whether Lan and I had forgotten to pack something she figured we'd need, so she alternated between the two all evening long. Robbie and Lan were overexcited, and talked a mile a minute with anyone who'd stand still to hear; Brant made up for them by sitting in silence through most of the evening, even after Mayor Brewster finished with his good-luck speech.

The dinner was in the big meeting hall in the middle of town, and between the expedition members, their families and friends, and all the important folks from town, we pretty much filled the place up. A lot of the professors from the college came, and I was surprised to see Professor Graham among them. I worried a little that he and William would have another big blowup right there in public, which wouldn't be the best way to start off, but I couldn't really do anything about it if they did. I didn't relax until I saw that the two of them were sitting at different tables with their backs to each other.

After dinner, we all went out to the square for the fireworks, and I lost track of everyone but my family in the dark. William joined us on the wool blanket we'd brought, and he and Lan and Papa spent the whole time commenting on the spells that shaped the sparks into glowing pictures in the sky. There was one that was supposed to be a mammoth, but it looked more like a mastodon to me, and we had a friendly argument over whether it was because the magician doing the spell didn't know the difference (William and me) or whether he knew but hadn't gotten the illusion spell quite right (Papa and Lan).

When the fireworks were over, William said good night and then went off with Papa and Lan to speak with the expedition leaders. Allie and I stayed behind to pack up. As I picked up the blanket we'd been sitting on, I heard a cough behind me. I turned. "Professor Graham!" I said. "Papa's just off talking with Mr. Corvales; he'll be back in a minute."

"Actually, Miss Rothmer, I'd like to have a word with you, if I might," the professor said.

"All right," I said, a little taken aback. I finished folding the blanket and gave it to Allie to put into a carrypack, then followed the professor a little way to one side. There wasn't anywhere private to talk in such a crowd, but being surrounded by a lot of busy, happy strangers in the dark made it seem like no one was paying attention, which was almost as good.

"Professor?" I said after a minute. "What was it you wanted to say?"

"I just wanted to wish you and — and your brother the very best of luck," Professor Graham said quickly. "And the whole expedition, of course. It's a great honor to be chosen; I'm sure your parents are very proud."

"Thank you, Professor," I said. "I think they are, though I know Mama worries, too."

"Any parent would," Professor Graham said. "Whether they show it or not."

I couldn't help smiling slightly, but I was quite serious when I said, "We all know how dangerous it is, but it's — it's exciting to be part of something new like this."

Professor Graham was silent for a minute, then he said, "If this expedition is even partially successful, it will open up a lot more territory for settlement. It's an important thing you're doing."

"I understand, Professor, and thank you," I said. I hesitated for a moment, then added, "I'll be sure and pass your good wishes along to the rest of the expedition members when I get the chance."

"Thank you, Miss Rothmer, I'd appreciate that," Professor Graham said. "I probably should not have left it so late to express my opinion on the matter." He nodded as if that settled something, and walked me back to Mama and Papa.

I thought real hard all the way home, and only some of it was about Professor Graham. A good part was considering the talk I'd had with Brant right before I decided to accept Professor Torgeson's offer. Except for Lan, I wouldn't be seeing my family again for at least two years, maybe more. Nan's baby would be walking and talking by the time I got back. Brant and Rennie would likely be in a place of their own, here in town or maybe out in the settlements. And who knew what Allie and Robbie would be up to, or the rest of my family back East?

All the times I'd gone out to settlement country before, I'd missed my family, but it hadn't ever been too bad because I knew I'd see them again in a few weeks, or months at most. This was going to be a lot longer and a lot harder. I was missing them already, and I hadn't even left town yet!

I glanced over at Lan and saw him studying Albert and Seren Louise pensively. I wondered if he was thinking the same things I was. He'd been away at boarding school and then at Simon Magus for the best part of six years before the accident, but he'd had letters from all of us and the train from Philadelphia to Mill City only took two days if there'd been reason for him to come home.

Between being all excited about the journey and fretting over missing my family, I didn't sleep much that night. I gave up trying along about first light, and went down to the kitchen to start some breakfast biscuits. Mama was there before me, so the two of us made apfelkuchen instead. Neither one of us said much.

———— ◆ ————

Breakfast was a quiet meal. Lan was the last one down the stairs, but he didn't look like he'd slept any better than I had. As soon as he finished eating, the two of us had to leave for

West Landing. Mr. Corvales had asked us not to bring too many folks to watch the expedition actually leave, so only Papa came along to see us off. We hugged everyone good-bye, and Mama and Allie gave us lots of last-minute advice that I forgot by the time I was down the porch steps.

Most of our gear was already in the wagons in West Landing, but Lan and·I had a small carrypack each for the things we'd forgotten to pack. Lan's was a little fuller than mine, but we'd both been out in settlement territory before, so neither of us had brought much. When you have to haul everything along with you all the time, and unpack and pack it again every night, you figure out pretty quick that you don't need near as many things as you thought you did.

It was a clear day, but chilly — spring was late that year, and there were still foot-deep patches of snow in shadowed spots behind buildings. I wondered what it would be like when we got away from town. I hadn't ever been out to settlement territory this early in the year.

Crossing to West Landing was a lot easier than it had ever been, since they'd finally finished the bridge and we didn't have to wait for the ferry. The bridge was made of mismatched stone. The east half was built of large, dark gray blocks that had been squared up but not smoothed out except on top, where people and wagons would be traveling. The west half was built of a pale, sandy-gold stone cut into smaller, more rectangular blocks that were polished and that fit together so that from a distance you couldn't even see the seams.

The Great Barrier Spell ran across the bridge right where the two sides met in the middle. The Barrier Spell was the whole reason for building the bridge the way they had. All the stone for the east half of the bridge came from the east side of the river, and all the stone for the west half came from the west side, so that nothing from either side went through the Barrier Spell or created a link that might disrupt or weaken it in any way.

There were a couple of other bridges farther north, where the river was narrower, but they were all a lot smaller. Most of them were made of wood, too, so they didn't make the same kind of magical link between the two banks as a stone bridge would. It had taken the magicians months to figure out how to build a stone bridge that wouldn't create a thin spot in the Great Barrier Spell.

Papa explained all of this as we walked up the east half of the bridge toward the shimmer in the air that marked the place where the Great Barrier Spell was. I tensed up as we got closer. I'd been through the spell quite a few times by then, but I never liked it much. It always made me feel as if something old and strong and opinionated was looking me over to see if I was worth letting through.

This time, though, the feeling I got from the spell was a lot weaker and didn't last anywhere near as long. I frowned, and as soon as we were through, I asked Papa about it. He gave me a sharp look, then said, "The spell is strongest at the surface of the river. We're a good twenty feet above that, at least."

I nodded. Everybody knew the Great Barrier Spell didn't go up forever. Birds flew over it all the time, and there'd been a steam dragon once that did the same thing when I was fourteen. I'd always thought of the spell as a wall, though — something that went up good and solid until you got to the top of it and it stopped. I'd never thought about it being like the river, deep and hard to get through in some places, but getting shallower and easier to walk in if you went out to the edge.

"Does that mean that wildlife could get through the Great Barrier if they came over the bridge?" I said after a minute.

"The spell is still there, just as it is at the thin spot," Papa said. "And any wildlife would have to get through the protection spells around West Landing and then through all of the town and its magicians to reach the bridge. I doubt it's anything to worry over."

"Why are you worrying about it at all?" Lan asked. "It's not going to matter to us for at least two years."

"I was just wondering," I said, but I didn't stop frowning. Papa hadn't really answered my question — or had he? The thin spot was the place up north where the Great Barrier Spell cut across land so as to get from the top end of the Mammoth River over to the Great Lakes and from there down the St. Lawrence Seaway. Wildlife did come through it, though not often; that was why the Settlement Office kept extra magicians in the lumber camps and settlements even on the east side of the spell. If the Great Barrier Spell was the same on the bridge as it was at the thin spot, then wildlife could get through it here, the same way it did there.

I thought about it some more and decided that Papa was right; it wasn't anything to worry about. Most wildlife didn't like being around too many people, and West Landing was the biggest town on the west bank north of West St. Louis. What with all the people and protection spells, there hadn't been a wildlife incident since a lone prairie wolf had been spotted at the edge of town two or three years back. Nothing dangerous was likely to get anywhere near the bridge, much less cross it.

Still, I found myself thinking more about the Great Barrier Spell than about the expedition as we walked through West Landing. I'd taken it for granted all my life, but now I wondered. It was a powerful spell, tied to two rivers and the Great Lakes to keep it working even after all the magicians who'd helped cast it were gone, but no spell lasts forever. What would happen if — when — the Great Barrier Spell came down?

The west bank of the river was getting to be more like the east bank as people settled all along it. I'd seen that for myself when we walked the mammoth up one side of the river and down the other. Maybe by the time the Great Barrier fell, there wouldn't be any wildlife close enough to cause trouble. Or maybe the settlers in the West would have invented new spells so that the Great Barrier wouldn't be needed. I snorted. Somehow, I doubted that would happen.

By then we had reached the spot where the expedition was collecting. We weren't the first to arrive, but we weren't the last, either. Lan and I hugged Papa again, then went to saddle our horses and pack our carrypacks away. Then we had to split up to be with our groups, me with the scientists, Lan with the exploration-and-survey people. I was half expecting a lot of last-minute errands, but Mr. Corvales and Adept Alikaket and Captain Velasquez had everything running smooth as a brand-new pocket watch.

At ten sharp, I heard a whistle and a bugle call. I checked my rifle and mounted up as the first group of riders — army people and the first half of the exploration group — started moving. Lan and Wash and Roger were there, along with Mr. MacPhee, the minerals expert. Then came the nine members of the scientific party — Dr. Lefevre and Mr. Melby, Professor Ochiba and William, Professor Torgeson and me, Mr. Gensier and Mr. Tanzir, and Dr. Visser. Next the rest of the exploration-and-survey group — Pierre le Grise, Mr. Zarbeliev, and Miss Dzozkic. Last were the rest of the soldiers, including Sergeant Amy, and the support staff, which was Dr. Faber (the medical doctor), Mrs. Wilson (the cook), and Miss Hoel.

It made quite a long column, and I was glad Sergeant Amy and Mr. Corvales had arranged to pick up the wagons and the mammoth outside of town. I saw Papa standing in the crowd along the boardwalk, and I waved for as long as I could see him.

An hour later, we passed through the outer edge of West Landing's protection spells and out into open countryside. The Joint Cathayan-Columbian Discovery and Mapping Expedition was on its way.

CHAPTER
· 18 ·

ONCE WE MET UP WITH THE WAGONS AND THE MAMMOTH, THE RID-ing pattern shifted around some. Roger and Professor Torgeson and I rode near the mammoth; the rest of the scientists and most of the exploration-and-survey team bunched up around the supply wagons. Captain Velasquez rode in front, and the soldiers fanned out in a loose protective circle. Wash and Mr. Zarbeliev and Greasy Pierre rode even farther out, switching places periodically and scanning for trouble as only experienced circuit magicians and trappers could.

It wasn't much like my last three trips out West, but I didn't care. The trees hadn't leafed out yet, and there were only the barest hints of new green under last year's dead grass, but it still smelled more like plants and less like smoke and axle grease and people. Even with all the wagons and the horses kicking up dust, the air smelled different from the air in Mill City or West Landing.

We reached the first wagonrest around mid-afternoon. The expedition leaders had agreed to keep the first day's ride short, to give everyone some extra time to work out how best to set up camp. They'd also planned things out with the Settlement Office so that the expedition could head almost straight west, but still take advantage of the wagonrests that the Settlement Office had set up to protect settlers on their way out to allotments at the edge of settlement territory. The expedition was a little bigger than most settlement groups, but not too much, so there should have been enough room.

The big problem with that was the mammoth. The protection spells on the settlements and wagonrests made it irritable, and nobody west of the river wanted it anywhere near their towns or crops. That first night, Adept Alikaket tried to bring it into the wagonrest, and it started stamping and trumpeting and nearly broke free before he finally gave up. Then he suggested taking down the protection spells on the wagonrest so that we could bring the mammoth inside along with everyone else, but after the show the creature had already put on, nobody else thought that was a good idea.

While the adept and Mr. Corvales and Captain Velasquez were all arguing, I went over to the mammoth. It was still nervous and unhappy. Professor Jeffries and Adept Alikaket had rigged up another harness for it, one that you could hang bags and baskets on, and it was still fully loaded because nobody had dared try to get near it while it was so jumpy.

Three of the army men were holding the restraining ropes, and none of them looked any happier than the mammoth felt. One of them saw me and touched his cap. "You'd best get back, miss," he said. "He's mean."

"Eff Rothmer," I said. "It's all right. He knows me. I helped move him to the menagerie last summer."

"And she's worked with him for a good five years," a familiar voice said behind me.

"William!" I turned, smiling. "Did they send you over?"

William shook his head. "They're still arguing, and it's spreading. Your professor has opinions."

I rolled my eyes, because it was William. "She's from Vinland. As far as she's concerned, wildlife is something you shoot first and study later. She's been complaining about the menagerie animals since the day she got to Mill City, especially this one."

"What were you planning on doing with him?" William asked, nodding at the mammoth.

"Calming him down, for a start," I said.

"It's been a while, but if you'd like some help . . ."

I nodded before he finished speaking. William had started learning Aphrikan magic along with me, back in day school, and toward the end, before he went off East to boarding school, we'd practiced on the mammoth together.

"He's a lot bigger now," William commented as he stepped forward to study the beast.

"Big and mean," one of the soldiers muttered.

"He's not mean," I said firmly. "He's half wild. There's a difference."

"Less talk, more magic," William said.

I grinned and let my world-sensing flow outward. I felt the warm, sleepy magic in the ground, dusted with a spring urgency where sap was moving in the roots of the grasses and in the seeds that were just sprouting. There were a few short, bright prickles like a scattering of sparks from a fire, and I knew that if I bent to look for them I would find the tiny, pointed shoots of yarrow or pasqueflower just breaking through the earth under the dry, flattened remains of last year's grass. The air sparkled with our travel protection spells; the log wall around the wagonrest was a low, steady buzz.

I could tell where most of the expedition members were, even though none of them were actually casting spells at the moment. People's magic is much tidier and more organized than natural magic, so it's easy to pick out even when the person doesn't have a lot of magic to look at. Lan was the easiest to spot; he felt like a blacksmith's forge, with a core of white-hot metal surrounded by an intense fire, all collected behind thick, fireproof walls so that it couldn't escape or hurt anyone.

Most of the others felt like cookstoves or fireplaces, but there were three obvious exceptions. Professor Ochiba and Wash felt like strong campfires, open and uncontained, but still controlled. Adept Alikaket felt at first as if he had almost no magic at all, like a cold hearth. When I looked closer, I realized that his magic didn't feel like a cold hearth so much as like one with a fire that had been banked for the night. The adept's magic was quiet and shielded, like embers waiting for fuel.

I frowned and tucked that thought away for later. Right now, I had to deal with the mammoth. I stretched my world sense toward it and frowned some more. Lan hadn't helped with the spells on the harness this time, I could tell. They weren't as strong, and they felt rough and prickly. I reached past them and nudged the mammoth's magic, soothing him a little, but the harness spells rubbed at him and stirred it all up again.

Beside me, William shifted. "We have to get that harness off him," he said, and I knew he'd been doing world-sensing the same as I had.

"The harness is all that's keeping this thing under control!" one of the soldiers objected.

"It's making him cranky," I told him firmly. William nodded, and I felt a trickle of warmth as his magic reached out to soothe the creature. I looked over, impressed. He'd gotten a lot better at Aphrikan magic since I'd last seen him, and he hadn't exactly been bad then.

The three soldiers exchanged looks, and one of them shrugged. "We're just here to keep him from getting loose and trampling something."

"Let's start by getting him away from the wagonrest," William suggested. "The protection spells are making everything worse."

"We can't take him outside the perimeter," the first soldier said, frowning.

"Not outside," William said. "Just away from the center. It's . . . it's like he's too close to a fire; if we move him back, he'll be more comfortable and easier to settle down."

I looked around. The settlers had cut back most of the trees and bushes outside the walls of the wagonrest, so as not to leave any place for wildlife to hide, but they'd left one big flag tree off to one side. I pointed. "Over there."

The soldiers looked at each other doubtfully, but the tree was still well within the area protected by the wagonrest spells, so they urged the mammoth over. I reached out again, pulling at the natural magic in the tree. There wasn't much of it, this early in the spring, but there was enough to spread into a thin layer between the mammoth and the harness spells. It wouldn't last long, but for the time being, it calmed the creature right down.

"Go get Lan," I told William. "I'll get started unloading."

William gave the mammoth a doubtful look, but he nodded and walked back toward the wagonrest. I moved forward and started unhooking the bags and baskets, and after a minute one of the soldiers started helping. The other two looked uncertain, so I told them to stay and hang on to their ropes. "He's calm now," I said, nodding at the mammoth, "but even calm, he can be a nuisance."

The mammoth proved my point right then by snaking his trunk over to one of the baskets and knocking the lid off. I pulled the basket out of his reach and checked inside to make sure the contents hadn't been disarranged. The mammoth made a whuffling noise at me and started pulling at the dead grass around his feet, looking for new growth.

By the time we got all the bags and baskets unhooked and stacked alongside the mammoth, William was back with Lan . . . and half the scientists and a few more besides. I wasn't surprised to see Professor Torgeson or Professor Ochiba, but I was a bit taken aback to see Adept Alikaket, Captain Velasquez, and Mr. Corvales, and I wasn't expecting Wash or Roger or Greasy Pierre at all.

"What are you doing?" Adept Alikaket demanded, frowning. "Ah, I recall you. You were at the center when the circle went to remark it. You know this beast."

"Yes, sir," I said. "I'm trying to get it calmed down."

"For which you need your brother?" Professor Torgeson said, lifting her eyebrows.

"He did the harness spells when we moved the mammoth from Mill City to the study center," I pointed out. I turned to Lan. "Would you take a look at them, please? There's something off — the spells are trying to gentle him down, but they're chafing him at the same time. We didn't have that trouble when we moved him to the study center."

"Are you certain it's the harness, Miss Rothmer?" Captain Velasquez asked. "The beast has been wearing it all day, but it didn't start acting up until we reached camp."

"It's the harness, right enough," Wash's drawl broke in. "Well done, Miss Eff."

"The adept himself cast those spells!" Mr. Corvales objected.

"It is no matter," Adept Alikaket said with dignity. "The spells I used are from Bharat. The elephant and the mammoth are not wholly the same. A small difference can make much trouble."

Wash nodded. "It's no particular fault in the spell casting, any more than there's a flaw in a new pair of shoes that blister your feet when you wear them all day."

"Just so." Professor Ochiba had been studying the mammoth while the rest talked. "And there's no need to wear blisters on top of blisters when the spells can be recast. Mr. Rothmer, Miss Rothmer, could you use some assistance?"

In the end, nearly everyone stayed to help out or watch. William and Roger helped me get the harness off the mammoth, while Wash kept it calm and the soldiers retied their ropes. Then Lan and Professor Ochiba and Professor Torgeson spread the harness out on the ground and stripped all the old spells off. Professor Ochiba checked to make sure they were completely gone, and then the three of them went over the harness a section at a time, recasting the spells to strengthen the pieces of the harness and keep the mammoth calm and controlled.

Adept Alikaket watched closely, commenting occasionally. Once he made them pause while he and the two professors had a long discussion about a particular calming spell and the ways it was like and unlike the one he'd used on the first go-round. At one point, I thought they were going to get into an argument about comparing Hijero-Cathayan magic to Avrupan magic that would last all night, but Professor Ochiba pointed out that they had a job to finish and they'd have time to talk later.

Once they were finished, we put the harness back on the mammoth, and Wash and Professor Ochiba and William and I checked to make sure it wasn't still causing problems. Roger slipped away before we finished without saying anything to me. I was relieved and worried at the same time. I didn't think we could avoid each other for the whole two years of the expedition, but I wasn't real eager to get started dealing with him right away, either.

I didn't get a chance to talk to William that night about anything besides the mammoth and the harness spells. It was a bit frustrating, because the list of things I wanted to talk to him about was getting longer by the minute. I hadn't had a chance to tell him what his father had said at the good-bye dinner, and I was pretty sure he'd want to know as soon as possible. I wanted to ask him about the Aphrikan magic he'd obviously learned, and I wanted to talk to him about my dreams and the pendant Wash had given me.

As I lay down to sleep, it occurred to me that I hadn't had one of those dreams in a long time, not since — I thought back. Not since late summer, out at the study center. I fingered the pendant through my nightdress, thinking hard. I'd been using my world-sensing regularly, and I'd practiced up doing my Avrupan spells properly. I'd meant to look more closely at the spells around the pendant, but except for that one time, right after I talked to Wash, I hadn't done so. And it wasn't the first time I'd forgotten, either.

I thought about that for a minute, and I thought about all the don't-notice-it spells in the last couple of layers around the pendant. Then I reached up and pulled the leather cord that held the pendant up and off my head.

There wasn't much light in the tent, just a little bit that leaked in from the fire outside. Mrs. Wilson and Sergeant Amy were already asleep, and I didn't want to wake them by lighting a lantern, but I didn't really need to. I wasn't planning to look at the pendant with my eyes.

Slowly, I started the concentration exercise Professor Ochiba had taught me back in day school. When I was calm and centered, I let my world-sensing go just a little, just enough to feel the pendant and the layers of spells around it.

Before, I'd always studied the pendant as a whole thing, partly because that was the way I thought of it and partly because that was the way Aphrikan magic looked at most things. But the pendant and the spells weren't just one thing. Nothing ever was, really.

What other things is this? I thought, and started a mental list of everything I could think of. The pendant was an ornament, a necklace. It was an Aphrikan teaching tool — I knew that from what Wash had told me. It was a physical thing (the robin's-egg whorl of wood) plus a bunch of magic things (the spells that wrapped it). I paused and considered on that for a minute. A *bunch* of spells — not just one layer wrapped around a core, but lots of layers, like an onion.

The pendant gave me dreams . . . I stopped again. That was what it *did*, not what it *was*. That was where I'd gone wrong the last time I thought about it. I needed to understand what it was, really understand it, before I got to fussing about what it did.

So, layers. Onion layers, old ones and new ones, each a little different, some that felt purely Aphrikan and some that had an Avrupan feel mixed in, and some like nothing else I'd felt before.

Without really thinking, I checked the top layer of magic around the pendant. It wasn't anything as purposeful as spells, I realized. It felt a bit like Avrupan magic, and a bit like Aphrikan magic, and a bit like me.

And there wasn't any don't-see-it magic mixed up in that layer. I checked again, then went down to the next layer of spells. That was a mix of Avrupan and Aphrikan magic, too, though it wasn't much like the topmost layer, and it felt like Wash.

It made sense; Wash and I were the last two people who'd had the pendant. That probably meant there was a layer of magic for every person who'd worn it. I studied the Wash layer. There was a little bit of don't-see-it in that layer, but not much.

The next layer down was unfamiliar, more Aphrikan and less Avrupan, and there was a lot of the magic that didn't seem much like anything I'd seen before. And the don't-see-it spells were part of the magic that didn't feel Aphrikan or Avrupan.

I poked further down the layers, and saw that the next several were the same: a little Avrupan magic, and a lot of Aphrikan and unfamiliar magic. And the don't-see-it spells were always part of the magic that felt unfamiliar.

I was getting tired, which wasn't a surprise, so I stopped there. I thought some more, and then, before I let go of my world-sensing or the pendant, I resolved very firmly to keep studying the pendant and its magic the very next night, no matter how tired I was. Especially the don't-see-it magic. Then I hooked the leather cord back over my head and settled under the blankets with a sigh, hoping that this time, I wouldn't forget about trying again.

CHAPTER
· 19 ·

Mr. Corvales, Adept Alikaket, and Captain Velasquez got everyone up before dawn the next morning to eat and pack up, and we left the wagonrest shortly after sunrise. I could see that in a few more days we'd have the routine down, and by the time we got to unexplored territory, we'd be running like clockwork.

We moved faster on the second day, so much that we passed up the first wagonrest and went on to one a little farther out. Sure enough, settling in went better that night, too. After dinner, I hunted up William. I found him sitting alone by one of the campfires, making notes in a journal, but he set it aside as soon as he saw me. "Hello, Eff! Is it the mammoth again?"

"No, I just wanted to talk," I said.

William gave me a wary look, but waved at the log beside him. "What about?" he asked as I sat down.

I hesitated, but I didn't see any point in beating around the bush. "Your father talked to me at the good-bye dinner."

William stiffened. "If he said anything insulting —"

"No, no!" I said. "He wished us all the best of luck, and he said it was an honor to be chosen, and that *any* parent would be proud and worried both. I'm pretty sure he meant him and you. I mean, that he's proud of you and worried, too."

"Oh." William sat silent for a minute. The firelight reflected from his glasses, making it impossible to tell what he was thinking. After a bit, he sighed. "He couldn't just say it, could he?"

"He's as stubborn as you are," I said. "Maybe more, even. And his temper is a lot worse. But I think he meant it."

"Three and a half years," William said slowly. "He hasn't spoken to me in three and a half years. Or written, or . . . or anything. I was sure he'd never change his mind. But yesterday . . ."

"Yesterday?" I prompted when he didn't go on.

"He came to West Landing to watch us leave. I saw him at the back of the crowd by the feed store." William looked down. "Everyone else was waving and yelling good luck, even all the people who didn't know anyone in the expedition. He just stood there. I wondered —"

"He wanted to see you," I said softly. "Just . . . just in case."

"That . . . that . . ." William stopped and pressed his lips together. Apparently, he wanted to call his father something that he couldn't bring himself to say in front of a lady, even if the lady was only me. "What does he expect me to do with this?" he burst out after a minute. "We're going to be gone for two years! Maybe more!"

"We can still send mail for a while," I suggested. "Until we get to the end of settlement territory, anyway."

William snorted. "What would I say to him? 'I'm sorry I went against your wishes'? 'I'm glad I'm finally doing something you approve of'? Well, I'm not sorry, and I'm certainly not here in order to make him think well of me!"

I shrugged. "I can't tell you what to say," I told him. "Or even that you should write him. Just that if you want to, you only have another month and a half to do it in. There won't be any way to send mail after we get past St. Jacques du Fleuve."

William nodded. I sat with him a while longer while he stared at the fire, but neither of us spoke. After a bit, Professor Torgeson and Dr. Lefevre came by and took seats on the other side of the fire. They were in the middle of a discussion about magical theory, and it didn't take long before William was drawn in. I listened for a while, but I didn't understand more than half of it, so eventually I left.

Three days later, at the Mammoth Hill wagonrest, I saw William adding a letter to the mailbag. I didn't speak of it, and neither did he, but I could see he felt better after that, like something that had been hanging over him had drawn back.

The talk I had with William was practically the only time I had to draw breath during the first week of the expedition. Professor Torgeson and I were making observations and taking notes right from the start, even though we were passing through territory that was partly settled and pretty well mapped. Professor Torgeson wanted to compare what we'd found two years ago to the plants and animals we were seeing now; she said it would be useful to see the changes over time, and also how the plants and animals changed as we got farther west.

After that first evening, Captain Velasquez asked me to make sure the mammoth stayed happy. The harness spells didn't give any more trouble, but I got the feeling that the captain wasn't any better pleased than Professor Torgeson about having a great hairy wild critter around, no matter what Adept Alikaket said or how handy it was. So I had to check on him every morning and night, and regularly throughout the day.

Other people started in on their work right off, too. Whenever the train of wagons stopped to rest the horses, Elizabet and Bronwyn dashed to the rear and pulled out their tools — five or six dowsing rods for Bronwyn, each made of a different wood or metal, and a big box of mirrors and chains and measuring sticks for Elizabet. They worked like mad right up until Captain Velasquez called everyone to roll out again. Mr. MacPhee and Dr. Visser, the minerals and agriculture experts, ran around collecting rocks and plant samples at every stop. Mr. MacPhee left most of his rocks in a pile by the wagonrest gates the next morning, but Lan told me that was because he stayed up past midnight writing out notes and making sketches by lantern light.

I was determined to stick to my resolution about the pendant, but I found out pretty quick that studying it at day's end didn't work out so well. After the second time I fell asleep in the middle of the concentration exercise, I decided to try inspecting it at the other end of the day. On the third night of the trip, I asked Mrs. Wilson to roust me out when she got up to start breakfast for everyone. She looked a little doubtful, but she agreed.

Sergeant Amy frowned and told us both that as long as we didn't wake her even a minute early, she didn't care what we did. Mrs. Wilson winked at me and whispered that she'd make sure the sergeant got first go at the coffee. I wasn't sure that would pacify her, but I figured it was worth a try.

Much to my surprise, Mrs. Wilson and I weren't the only ones up earlier than we had to be. I'd expected the two men finishing up the night watch — Captain Velasquez had insisted that we begin as we meant to go on, so he'd posted guards even though we were still staying at wagonrests and were relatively safe. I hadn't expected so many people to be up and moving, though, and I certainly hadn't anticipated seeing Adept Alikaket over in a smallish open spot by the wagons.

Curious, I went nearer. He seemed to be just standing there with his eyes closed and his hands together. I watched for a moment, then let my world-sensing go. Right then, the adept stretched his arms wide and stepped sideways with the same slow, controlled, dancing motion as when he and the other aides had cast the spells at the medusa lizard back in the study center the previous summer.

Adept Alikaket's magic unfurled as he moved, changing and growing stronger with every step and gesture he made. The first day, with the mammoth, he'd felt to my world sense like the embers in a banked fire; now he felt like a baker's oven firing up to prepare for the day's bread making. He was nowhere near as powerful as Lan, but he had plenty enough magic compared to regular folks.

The adept went through a series of slow movements, over and over, while his magic settled into a pattern around him. Despite his strength, the pattern felt incomplete. Remembering the way the Hijero-Cathayans had worked at the study center, I figured his magic was meant to be used with a group.

I got so caught up in watching the patterns the adept's magic made that I barely noticed when he finished his dance and began to draw his power back in. When it was back to being banked embers again, he stood still for a moment or two, then bowed in the direction of the growing pre-dawn light. He walked toward me. I started, and then apologized for watching without asking first.

"If I had wanted you to leave, I would have spoken," Adept Alikaket said. "The way of boundless balance is not sacred or secret."

"It was very interesting, sir," I said. "I've never seen anyone who could . . . raise and lower their magic like that."

The adept's eyes narrowed for a moment, then he smiled slightly. "I remember now. You're the one Master Adept Farawase remarked, the Avrupan who studies the Aphrikan way."

"Columbian," I corrected without thinking.

"I beg your pardon?"

"I'm not Avrupan; I'm Columbian," I said, though by then I felt a little foolish for making such a fuss over it.

"Ah. Forgive me; I meant no insult to your young country." He paused, as if he were debating over what to say next, or how to phrase it. Then he said, "You haven't met a Cathayan magician before?"

"Master Adept Farawase was the first," I replied, nodding.

"Then you would not have seen the control of the heart of magic before," he said with absolute certainty. "It's very difficult to learn, and only Cathayan magic requires it."

"Why is that?" I asked before I could stop myself. I blushed. "I'm sorry. I don't mean to be rude. I just —"

"You are young and curious," Adept Alikaket said. "It doesn't matter."

"We don't learn much about Hijero-Cathayan magic in school," I said. "I don't mean to pry."

"Again, it isn't a secret. It is merely that few Avrupan magicians have the patience to listen and understand. Your Avrupan magic is a thing apart from yourselves — wood to be carved, stone to be shaped, metal to be melted and re-formed. The spell is outside you and separate from you, subject to your will."

I thought about my classes and the Avrupan spells I knew, and nodded. The adept was maybe simplifying some, but I didn't think he was far off.

"Aphrikan magicians also do not require such control, because their magic is also apart from themselves," Adept Alikaket continued. "Their magic is outside, but alive, to be shaped as a master gardener shapes his trees and bushes, not as a smith shapes metal or a carver shapes wood. Do you see?"

I nodded again. I wasn't as sure about his view of Aphrikan magic, but it was certainly one way of looking at it, and it fit comfortably with the way I felt sometimes when I was using Aphrikan magic.

"Our magic, the Cathayan magic, is us, and we are it, all together, as drops of water are a river and the river is made of drops of water. We flow together, and then apart, but it is still all the same. It is the harmony, the balance, that joins us to cast the elegant spells and then parts us once more. Do you see?"

"I think I understand what you're saying, Adept, but I don't quite see how it works."

"That is because you are Avrupan," Adept Alikaket said, but he sounded kind. "Always, Avrupans want to take things apart to see how they work. Cathayan magic doesn't come apart. Like the river, it simply *is*."

"People understand how rivers work," I objected.

"You Avrupans, you fill a bucket with water and think you know the river. But if you take the river to pieces, it isn't a river any longer."

"A steam engine isn't a steam engine once you take it apart, either," I pointed out. "A river is just . . . bigger, and more the same all over. Not made of all different pieces."

Adept Alikaket laughed and shook his head. "I fear you're too literal, Miss Rothmer. I mean only that Cathayan magic is not like your magic, and it isn't like Aphrikan magic. All your thinking will not understand it."

"More heart than head," I said, half to myself. But heart didn't feel right for Hijero-Cathayan magic. If Avrupan magic was mostly head, and Aphrikan magic was mostly heart, then Hijero-Cathayan magic ought to be a third thing, something that wasn't head or heart but that fit with both.

"That is a good way to look at them," Adept Alikaket said approvingly. "In fact —"

"Eff!"

I turned and saw Lan walking toward me. Behind him the whole camp was stirring.

"Morning, Lan!" I said as he came up to us.

"Good morning, Mr. Rothmer," Adept Alikaket said.

"I wish you good day, Adept Alikaket," Lan said, bowing.

The adept smiled broadly. "You've studied the customs of the Confederacy?"

"Only a little," Lan replied. "I was very interested in Hijero-Cathayan spellwork, and the class I took started with history and customs." He looked mildly annoyed. "There was a lot of history; it didn't leave much time for spells."

Adept Alikaket laughed again. "I think that many schoolchildren in the Cathayan Confederacy would agree with you."

"It was very interesting," Lan said, a little too quickly. "I was just — I'd been hoping —"

"You've heard that Hijero-Cathayan magic is the most powerful in the world, and you wanted to learn some of it," Adept Alikaket finished for him.

Lan flushed, but raised his chin. "Is that wrong?"

"It's very understandable, for an Avrupan."

"I'm still interested," Lan said, and I could hear the stubborn note in his voice.

"Lan!" I said. I'd expected him to corner Adept Alikaket sooner or later, but I hadn't thought he'd try on the third day of the trip, when everyone was still furiously busy.

Adept Alikaket looked from Lan to me and back, and smiled ruefully. "I should have known, when Farawase *daimacoch* asked if I would attend this expedition to complete my *shengmacoch*, that I would end by teaching after all."

Lan went beet red. "I'm sorry, sir. I didn't mean —"

"You aren't the first to ask, Mr. Rothmer," Adept Alikaket reassured him. "And as I said, I should have expected. All of your magicians have an admirable thirst for knowledge. It is my duty as *shengmacoch* to assist as much as I can."

"*Shengmacoch*?" I said.

"One who would become what you call a master adept, a *daimacoch*," he said. He looked at Lan. "I will speak to Mr. Corvales and the captain soon. In the meantime, you are welcome to join my morning practice."

"Practice?" Lan said, eyes wide. "But —"

"Not spells," I said quickly. "It's kind of like dancing. I told you, remember?"

"Dancing?" Lan looked even more appalled than he had before.

"I trust you will explain, Miss Rothmer." The adept's voice sounded solemn and serious, but his eyes crinkled at the corners in amusement. "In the meantime, I am to breakfast. I enjoyed our conversation." He bowed and walked away.

"Conversation?" Lan said. "Eff, what on earth —"

"We can talk over breakfast," I cut in. "I'm hungry, and I don't think Mr. Corvales will hold everybody up just because we're late finishing our meal. Come on." And I dragged him off toward the smell of wood smoke, coffee, and oatmeal-wheatberry pan bread.

CHAPTER
· 20 ·

AFTER MY ENCOUNTER WITH ADEPT ALIKAKET, I STARTED GETTING up early with Mrs. Wilson every day. Some days, I stayed inside the tent and studied the magic wrapped around the pendant. It took me two weeks to figure out how to get the don't-notice-it spells to leave me out, so that I wouldn't keep forgetting. It was a lot harder to do than tweaking my own spells, or Lan's, but the pendant had enough of my magic on and in it that I managed. After that things went a lot more smoothly.

Other days, I watched the adept do his morning "way of boundless balance." He never missed a day, and gradually I realized that it wasn't just about practicing the magic part. The spells he and the other aides had cast back at the study center had lasted over two hours; I remembered thinking then how tired they'd all looked. Turns out it wasn't just the spell casting. Repeating all those movements over and over, slow and controlled, was enough to tire anyone out, for all they didn't look so hard if you were just watching.

Lan came to watch, too, a couple of times, but after a few days he decided that he really wanted that extra hour or so of sleep most of the time, and quit coming every single morning.

As the word got around that Adept Alikaket didn't mind an audience, pretty near everyone got up early at least one morning just to see what he was doing. Most folks only came once, but a few came back over and over, and in the second week of the trip, some of us started trying to learn the pattern by imitating the adept's movements.

William joined up right away, and kept at it, the same way he had when Professor Ochiba started teaching us Aphrikan magic after day school when I was thirteen. Most of the magicians stuck with it long enough to learn the pattern, and Dr. Lefevre and his assistant, Mr. Melby, came almost every morning. Bronwyn did, too, and Mr. Zarbeliev, the circuit rider from the Middle Plains Territory. Roger only came once.

I wasn't sure why the others were interested; maybe it was just a way of working out the kinks before we got on our horses for the day's ride. I was interested in the magic as much as the exercise. Every day I used my world-sensing to watch as the adept's magic waxed and waned according to his movements. That was what I wanted to learn, not Hijero-Cathayan spells.

I'd spent a large part of my life being scared of myself and my magic. I'd mostly gotten over it, but there was a tiny part of me that still worried that I'd lose control and hurt someone, the way I'd almost done at my sister Diane's wedding nine years before. If I could command my magic the way the adept commanded his, I could let that tiny part go for good.

After what the adept had said to me on that first day, though, I didn't mention what I was after. I was pretty sure he'd tell me that I wouldn't be able to learn what I wanted, because Hijero-Cathayan magic was too different from mine.

Even though the way he described it made sense, I reckoned there had to be other ways to look at it. Adept Alikaket seemed to think that Aphrikan, Avrupan, and Hijero-Cathayan magic were three different things, but they didn't feel like that to my world-sensing. Magic all felt pretty much the same to me — sometimes it was stronger or weaker; and the ways Aphrikans, Avrupans, and Cathayans each used it were very different, but underneath, it was all the same power. So even if I couldn't learn to do exactly what he was doing, maybe I could understand it well enough to figure out an Avrupan or Aphrikan way of doing it instead.

I didn't have as much time to think as I'd have liked. Things did get easier and more of a routine as the days went on, but I still had more than enough work to keep me busy. In addition to watching out for the mammoth and making observations and notes for Professor Torgeson, Mr. Corvales asked everyone to keep a journal, even the soldiers and support staff. He said it was important to have as many records of what happened as we could, and everyone took it very seriously. I heard Sergeant Amy joking with the captain about running out of ink before we got to St. Jacques du Fleuve, if we kept up at this rate.

The speed at which we were moving kept all of us even busier. The plan for the first part of the trip was to get through settlement territory as quickly as possible, so as to get on into new territory where there were no wagonrests and we'd have to be more careful. Settlement territory was dangerous, and grew more so the nearer you got to the far edge, but we knew a lot about handling prairie wolves and saber cats and Columbian sphinxes and swarming weasels. We only knew some of the wildlife of the Far West, and all of the things we knew about, from mirror bugs to medusa lizards to steam dragons, were even more dangerous than the critters in settlement territory.

Everyone on the expedition knew that, of course, but some of us knew it better than others. In spite of the Frontier Management Department's rules, there were quite a few folks along who'd never been west of the Great Barrier Spell even once. Every group had some, even the exploration-and-survey people. Neither Roger nor Elizabet — Miss Dzozkic, the surveyor — had ever crossed the river.

The scientists and magicians had the least experience. Only Adept Alikaket, Professor Torgeson, William, and I had spent time in settlement territory, and Adept Alikaket's visit to the study center hardly counted. Professor Ochiba was like Roger — they'd both lived for years in Mill City, but they'd never actually gone through the Great Barrier Spell before. One of the other magicians was from New Orleans, so he knew about the wildlife in the Southern Plains Territory, though he hadn't personally seen or fought them. The rest of the magicians had plenty of book learning about the wildlife, but no more.

The army and support staff were kind of in the middle when it came to having dealt with wildlife before. The army unit came from one of the forts in the South Plains Territory, so they knew all about terror birds and saber cats and Columbian sphinxes and the other critters that roamed the whole of the Great Plains. They hadn't had any run-ins with spectral bears or giant beavers or other Northern wildlife, but they knew plenty about being cautious. None of the support people had been West before, though they'd all lived along the Mammoth River and had some idea what they were getting into.

Fortunately, we didn't have much trouble for the first two weeks. We had to detour around a nest of razorquarls on the second day, and at the end of the week Sergeant Amy ran off a black bear that went for the supplies in one of the wagons, but that was all.

By then we were deep inside the area that had been devastated by the mirror bugs four years before, and there wasn't as much wildlife to worry about. The mirror bugs had eaten everything bare and even chewed up the roots of the trees and killed them. That meant that almost all of the animals had left or starved to death, and while the prairie plants had grown back, the larger critters, especially the predators, hadn't moved back in yet. The animals that needed tree cover or magical plants wouldn't be back for a long time.

As we got closer to the far edge of settlement territory, wagonrests were scarcer and we had to plan our route more carefully. The newer settlements were still building their own palisades and barns and houses; they hadn't gotten to building shelter for travelers yet. The settlers didn't have room to put up thirty-one people, either, so when we couldn't make it to a wagonrest, we had to stop early to set up a protected camp ourselves.

We had good weather for the first week and a bit more, but after that the spring storms set in, and it seemed like every couple of days we ended up riding through rain. Mostly it was just steady drizzle, which was pretty miserable but didn't slow us down, but there were a couple of heavy rains when the wagons got stuck, and about once a week there were thunderstorms that made the mammoth nervous.

A few days before we reached St. Jacques, there was a particularly bad storm in the late afternoon. By the next morning, the mammoth still hadn't calmed down enough to load, and Mr. Corvales was muttering about losing time.

I wasn't exactly surprised; the mammoth had always gotten restless in spring and fall, when his wild cousins were migrating. Usually he started fussing around the start of April and kept it up all month, but I figured that walking all the way from Mill City had kept him from feeling so edgy this time. Professor Torgeson and William and Professor Ochiba and I worked on him for half an hour, but every time we got him tamed down, he'd raise his trunk after a minute and start shifting and dancing around again.

Just when I thought Mr. Corvales was going to come tell us to let the critter go, or stay behind until we got it under control, I saw Wash go up to him and say something. Mr. Corvales stiffened and looked north.

We'd been crossing an empty section of prairie covering a series of long, low hills, and we'd camped at the top of the highest rise we could find, so we could see pretty far. The hills and the prairie stopped at a dark, bare stand of dead trees along the northern horizon, one of the patches of forest that the grubs and mirror bugs had killed.

A haze hung just above the forest, barely visible in the pale post-dawn light. I squinted, then stiffened. "The forest is on fire," I said before I could stop myself.

Everyone's heads whipped around to look north. "No wonder he's nervous," William said after a minute, nodding at the mammoth.

"He has reason," Professor Ochiba said. "And now that we understand that, we should have better luck with him."

"I certainly hope so," Professor Torgeson muttered. She was the only one of the four of us who didn't use Aphrikan magic, so she'd been trying to get the mammoth loaded up while the rest of us held him calm.

Word of the fire spread quickly, and it didn't take long before the whole expedition was as edgy as the mammoth. Fortunately, we did manage better for knowing why the mammoth was uneasy. Aphrikan magic works by nudging things in a direction they might go anyway, but that's closer to what the magician wants to happen. The mammoth wouldn't stay calm while there was a forest fire burning only two and a half miles away, but we got it to stand still long enough to load up so that we could get moving.

By the time we finished, we could all see the flames and smoke to the north. Mr. Gensier thought that the fire had started during the storm the previous afternoon, by lightning striking somewhere among the dead, dry trees. Wash and Greasy Pierre said that the fire probably wouldn't come our way; the wind was wrong and there'd been enough rain that even last year's dead grass wasn't likely to burn easily. Still, we moved along at a brisk clip, and everyone kept a nervous eye on the northern horizon all day.

That night we had more rain, much to everyone's relief. Nobody even minded when the wind shifted and we spent the whole next day smelling damp ashes. When we got to St. Jacques du Fleuve, we found out that the fire had burned most of that section of forest and badly damaged one of the settlements at the edge of the trees.

"Damned fools figured on salvaging the timber the bugs killed," the Settlement Office agent in St. Jacques grumbled at Mr. Corvales when he asked for news.

"It does seem a shame to waste it," Mr. Corvales said mildly. He'd brought three of us along to the Settlement Office to collect the expedition's mail and send off our letters.

The agent shrugged. "Fine, if you take it down and clear a firebreak. Anyone with half a brain and normal eyesight could tell that there'd be a fire sooner or later, with all that wood standing around drying out, and it's only good sense to be ready for it. But that bunch kept putting it off, and now look at 'em. I'm not terrible fond of idiots."

"That's plain," Mr. Corvales said. He handed over a huge stack of letters to send back to Mill City and points east, and waited while the Settlement Office agent checked them over. It took him a while, as pretty near everyone on the expedition was sending more than one letter. St. Jacques was our last chance to write home, unless we got lucky and ran into a trapper out in the Far West who was willing to carry mail back for us.

"Which settlement was it?" I asked.

"Neues Freiburg," the agent said, and I breathed a quiet sigh of relief that it wasn't one that I'd visited, so I didn't know any of the people who'd been hurt or lost their houses. Then I felt guilty for not being as sorry about them hurting, just because I didn't know them personally.

We picked up the expedition's mail and left. Mr. Corvales handed me the letters for the scientists and magicians, and I took them back to camp to pass out. Everyone had mail, most of us more than one letter. I had four: a fat one from Mama, thin ones from Robbie and Nan, and one from Professor Jeffries. William had two. I could tell from the handwriting of the address that the first one was from Mama. I didn't recognize the other, but when William saw it, he stiffened and his hand shook when he took it from me, so I was fairly sure it was from his father.

We stayed three days at St. Jacques, refilling our supplies and getting everything in tiptop working order. St. Jacques was crammed with people, most of them trappers stopping in to trade the furs they'd collected in the winter. They all looked a little wild when they first arrived, and a fair few of them didn't bother to get themselves shaved and spiffed up, though there were plenty of places to do it.

There were two saloons, and they were open and full up all night and all day. Captain Velasquez made a point of telling the army folks that he'd court-martial anyone who pulled a gun, no matter what the provocation, but he didn't try to keep his men out of the drinking houses. I overheard him telling Mr. Corvales that it would do more harm to have the men grumpy and resentful because they hadn't been allowed to have a last bit of fun than it would to have them hungover on the first day out of St. Jacques.

I spent most of the time answering my letters, helping Mrs. Wilson and Sergeant Amy find the last few supplies they needed, and walking the mammoth around the outside of the camp to keep him calmed down.

On our last night in St. Jacques, Sergeant Amy came back to our tent hauling a giant canvas sack and wearing a grin that was just as big. "Take a look at these, will you, Eff, and tell me whether or not I've just been taken for a ride."

She turned the sack end-up and shook it out. Two jackets fell out, slightly smelly and crudely stitched. Mrs. Wilson wrinkled her nose. "If you didn't get paid to haul those things away, I'd say so."

"They're made of medusa lizard skin," I said. "They're real, if that's what you wanted to know. But . . ." I couldn't help making the same kind of face as Mrs. Wilson. From the look and smell, the skins hadn't been properly cleaned or tanned, and I could see places where the seams were already coming apart. "I don't think they'll last long. And even if they do, I don't know that I'd want to wear one, protection or not."

"As long as they're the real thing, I can deal with the rest," Sergeant Amy said confidently. "A couple of the men used to quick-tan gildenslink hides for fun, back at the fort. I'm sure they can fix these right up."

"Not if they try to use magic to do it," I said. "The skin is resistant, just like the lizards. That's the whole point of making it into jackets."

"That's probably where the fellow who made these went wrong," the sergeant said with unimpaired cheerfulness. "I'll warn them, never fear."

"I don't really care what went wrong or what you do with them, as long as you get them out of this tent," Mrs. Wilson said firmly.

"All right, all right, I'm going." Gingerly, Sergeant Amy gathered up the jackets and stuffed them back in the bag.

"And that one's your bedroll tonight!" Mrs. Wilson called after her as she left the tent.

"By the time I get back, I doubt I'll notice!" Sergeant Amy shot back just before the tent flap fell shut.

CHAPTER
· 21 ·

Leaving St. Jacques du Fleuve was harder work than I'd expected. Captain Velasquez had warned everyone that he wasn't making any allowances; whatever shape anyone was in, he wanted us on the road by sunup, just as usual. A couple of the soldiers decided that the best way to be on time was to stay up all night drinking; they were still plenty cheerful when we rode out, especially compared to the folks who'd quit early enough to have morning hangovers, but they weren't much actual use.

It wasn't just the soldiers who'd been taking advantage of their last night in town, either. The exploration-and-survey group wasn't in any better shape than the army folks, and several of the people in the science team looked to be under the weather. So it was no surprise that we didn't make very good time that first day.

Once everyone recovered from too much celebrating in St. Jacques, the days fell into a pattern. We started off every morning as soon as it was light enough to ride. Those first few hours were long and cold, especially when it was cloudy. We stopped at mid-morning to rest the horses for an hour, and then went on until about two in the afternoon, which was generally the end of the day's ride. Wash or Mr. Zarbeliev and some of the soldiers would go off to hunt while the rest of us made observations and did tests and set up camp. There was plenty of game, and the hunters nearly always came back with more than enough meat for dinner.

Every three or four days, we spent a full day in one spot, so the animals could get a good rest and all the scientists and survey people could work at the jobs they'd come along for. Nobody complained about how slowly we were moving. The horses were nearly as important as our rifles, and they were a lot harder to keep in good condition.

The maps we'd brought along from the McNeil Expedition were less help than you might think. West of St. Jacques, the land flattened out, and there were so few trees that it was hard to tell where the mirror bug plague had stopped. That really frustrated Professor Torgeson. She had a bunch of theories about the mirror bugs, and she'd been hoping to map out the far edge of the damage they'd done, but without all the trees they'd killed, it was nigh on to impossible to tell where they'd been.

One good thing about the lack of trees and hills was that you could see trouble coming a long, long way off. We had a couple of hours' warning when a thunderstorm was coming in from the west, and several times we shifted course to avoid attracting the attention of a flock of terror birds or pack of prairie wolves. Mostly, though, all we could do was loosen up our rifles and ride close in to protect the wagons.

The Western Plains were a lot more crowded than I'd ever expected. By the time we were three days out of St.

Jacques, we were sending curly-horned antelope bounding away from our path nearly every time we topped a rise, and there were so many mammoths and herds of bison and antelope and silverhooves grazing, the whole plain looked like it had freckles.

The mammoths made everyone uneasy. They wandered around in groups of ten or fifteen, which was too many for us to handle if they took a notion to ignore our protection spells and all charge at once. Mr. Corvales and Captain Velasquez had five men with elephant guns spaced out around the wagons, but nobody was quite sure that even an elephant gun would take down a mammoth in one shot. Also, they took a while to reload. If a whole group of mammoths attacked, they would flatten the wagons for sure.

We met up with our first medusa lizard on the fourth day. One of the soldiers spotted it crouched at the base of a low rise to the south, maybe half a mile away. It looked like an oddly shaped grayish-tan rock poking up out of the new green prairie growth. The soldier had just time to call a warning when the critter started moving toward us.

I'd never seen anything cover ground like that lizard did, not even the saber cats or the antelope. Those of us who'd been riding on the south side of the wagons barely had time to shoulder our rifles before it was in range. I heard one of the elephant guns boom, and a couple of rifles, but they all missed. I waited, tracking the thing as best I could, with my world-sensing stretched as far as I could make it go.

A few yards off, the creature paused. I heard more rifles, and saw the medusa lizard jerk, but I held my fire. I kept my eyes fixed on the knob in the middle of the lizard's forehead, waiting for it to open. As soon as it did, I fired.

I wasn't the only one who'd waited; at least half a dozen other rifle shots cracked off right along with mine. The medusa lizard's head snapped back from the impact, and it fell. I chambered another shot in case it wasn't quite dead or another one was around.

Distantly, I heard Captain Velasquez shout orders to his men. Two of them dismounted, keeping their guns ready, and approached the lizard from opposite sides. "It's dead," one of them called.

Some of the tension went out of the line of men, though everyone kept alert. Sergeant Amy rode up to the captain, and a minute later the captain gave orders to skin the lizard. Everyone was twitchy while we waited, and glad to get moving again.

As soon as we stopped for the day to set up camp, Mr. Corvales ordered extra watches, and Professor Torgeson and Professor Ochiba spent a fair lot of time setting up spells they hoped would detect medusa lizards from a distance. Dr. Lefevre thought that the lizards were daytime critters, and wouldn't come around at night, but nobody wanted to take a chance, and anyway Professor Torgeson wanted to test the spells.

I helped with the spells as much as I could, which mostly meant running back and forth to fetch candles and herbs and bowls, or to move them a few inches once they'd been set out. As soon as the casting was finished, all of the magicians and half the exploration team started talking about how to improve the spells, especially ways to make them work while we were moving.

That night, I lay awake for nearly an hour before I gave up and crawled out of the tent to sit by the fire. After a little while, I pulled out the wooden pendant. What with all the business of getting out of St. Jacques and into new territory, it had been a couple of days since I'd studied it. I'd tried a couple of different things, and I thought I had a fair notion of the sort of magic that made up each layer. Now I wanted to try working my way down through the layers one at a time.

The first layer, the one that felt like my magic, was more complicated than I'd expected. I couldn't sort out the Aphrikan spells from the Avrupan ones. Then I realized that most all the time I'd had the pendant, I'd been using both kinds of magic side by side, especially when I tweaked my Avrupan spells with Aphrikan magic to make them work. When I stopped trying to make them be two separate things, studying the magic got a whole lot easier.

Somebody sat down beside me. I pulled myself back from concentrating on the pendant and looked up. "Hello, Wash," I said, smiling. I hadn't seen him to talk to since the expedition started. He'd been too busy to spend much time with the magicians during the first part of our trip, because he knew that part of settlement territory so well.

"Evening, Miss Eff," Wash said. He glanced back at the tent. "Trouble sleeping?"

"Some," I said. "Mostly I'm just not tired. So I thought I'd work at this a while."

Wash smiled. "And?"

"It's a record of spell casting," I said. "Every bit of magic I've done is on there, so I can look and see what worked and what didn't and why."

Wash nodded slowly. He looked pleased, but he also looked like he was waiting for more.

"And every bit of magic that anybody else did while they were wearing this is here, too," I went on. "Not like spells written out in a book. It's how spells feel when you cast them, and . . . and the *shape* of the magic." I paused. "It works a lot better for Aphrikan magic than for Avrupan spells. For learning them, I mean."

"It *is* an Aphrikan study tool," Wash pointed out.

"Yes, but —" I frowned. "There ought to be a way to keep just a little more of the spell casting, so that when you study on it, you can tell what tools you need for the Avrupan ones. Just knowing that there's an Avrupan spell that shoos off blackflies doesn't help much with learning to cast it."

"Looking for that one in particular, were you?" Wash asked with a grin.

I started to shake my head, then paused. "Not exactly," I said. "But I was sort of checking to see if there were any spells that'd be of use to the expedition. And I expect that that one will come in real handy in another month or so."

"Very likely," Wash said.

"Now that I have some notion what it is, I thought I'd start working my way down, one layer at a time," I said when it was clear he wasn't going to say anything more. "Is that all right?"

"It's one way to tackle it," Wash said. "There are —"

"— other ways," I finished with him. "I don't expect you'd be willing to suggest some?"

"I've already done more explaining than is usual," Wash said, frowning slightly.

"All right," I said, but I didn't even try to pretend I wasn't grumpy about it. "I figured you wouldn't say, but I had to ask. Couldn't you at least have warned me about the don't-notice-it magic, though? It took me years to figure out that that was why I kept forgetting to work at understanding this."

Wash's eyes widened. "I do apologize, Miss Eff," he said after a minute. "It hadn't occurred to me that you'd have a problem with that, though it surely should have. I take it you've found a way around?"

I nodded. "I figured out how to make the don't-notice-it spells let me in."

"Just you?" Wash asked sharply.

"Just me."

"That's right useful," Wash said after a thoughtful pause. "Would you mind showing me?"

"I'd be happy to," I said. "But you'll have to do the don't-notice-it spell. I haven't figured out how to cast that yet, just how to change it after."

I spent the next hour fiddling with Wash's don't-notice-it spell, showing him what I'd done to the ones on the pendant. I found it a lot easier to work on his spells, now that I'd figured out the pendant ones on my own. Finally, Wash sat back and gave me a long, considering look. "That's well done, Miss Eff," he said. "I'd purely appreciate it if you wouldn't pass that trick along, though."

It sounded more like a command than a request, but I nodded. "Not if you don't want me to. Is that don't-notice-it spell a special kind of Aphrikan magic? It doesn't feel quite like the rest of it."

Wash hesitated. "It's not exactly Aphrikan, though it was folks from Aphrika who invented it," he said finally. "I suppose you'd call it slave magic. Back before the Secession War, plantation owners didn't take too kindly to their slaves working magic, especially a kind of magic they didn't know much about. Any magic a slave wanted to learn had to be . . . quiet. Or cast so that no one would notice."

"Oh." That explained a whole lot of things that had puzzled me about the pendant, from the way Avrupan magic suddenly started showing up to why there were don't-notice-it spells and magic in every layer after. And maybe why I'd had such trouble with the don't-notice-it spells — I was willing to bet money they'd been designed to work especially well on anyone whose family had originally come from Avrupa, rather than Aphrika. "Thank you for telling me."

"You're welcome, Miss Eff." Wash rose and brushed himself off. "I'll be heading back to catch some sleep now; I'd recommend you do the same. Mr. Corvales is right determined when it comes to getting an early start."

"I think I'm tired enough to sleep now," I said. "Good night, Wash."

He touched his hat brim and vanished into the darkness. I studied the pendant for a few more minutes, then tucked it away and went back to the tent to sleep.

We met up with three more medusa lizards over the next four days, and we lost a horse to one of them, but no people got turned to stone, not even partly. Every day, Dr. Lefevre and Adept Alikaket had some new spells to add to the travel protections, but none of them worked very well. The minute we came in sight, the critters would head straight for us, sometimes from over a mile away. It was a good thing the country was so flat that we could see them coming.

Finally, Mr. Zarbeliev suggested that maybe the medusa lizards were attracted to magic, the same way the mirror bugs had been. That caused quite a ruckus, on account of some folks wanting to go without the travel protection spells and others insisting on keeping them up. While they were all arguing, I pulled Wash aside.

"Do you think that the don't-notice-it spells would work on medusa lizards?" I asked. "And would it be all right to use them?" I figured that if he didn't want me telling other folks how to add Avrupans to the don't-notice-it spells on the pendant, he sure enough wouldn't want me showing everyone how to work them, especially if it wasn't going to help. On the other hand, it was pretty clear that we needed to do something different, and if the spells *would* work . . . .

Wash's eyes narrowed and he didn't say anything for a minute. Then he replied, "That's a good thought, Miss Eff, but let me consider on it some before you go saying anything."

"I figured you should do the saying anyway," I said. "I haven't learned how to cast them yet, and it'd be a mite hard to explain how I know them. And it's your pendant."

Wash frowned. "It's your pendant now, Miss Eff, and has been for quite some time."

"You know what I mean," I said, frowning right back at him.

A little while later, I saw Wash talking with Professor Ochiba. It was the first time I'd seen them exchange more than a word or two since the expedition started. I didn't hear what they said to each other, but the professor started off looking kind of stiff and disapproving and then unstiffened some and looked more interested as they talked.

After dinner that night Professor Ochiba went to talk with Adept Alikaket and Dr. Lefevre. The three of them stayed late by the fire, and the next day, they had another spell to add to the travel protections.

The new spell worked better than anything else we'd tried. The first day it was active, we managed to pass a medusa lizard that for sure was close enough that it would have attacked without it. After we were well and truly past it, I saw Wash catch Professor Ochiba's eye and tip his hat slightly. The corners of Professor Ochiba's mouth turned up a hair and she nodded once.

The new don't-notice-it spell worked on more than medusa lizards, which was a very good thing. It was a lot safer to test how far out it went by sneaking up on antelope and silverhooves that weren't dangerous and would just run away.

Adept Alikaket and the other magicians kept fiddling with the spell to make it stronger and easier to work. By the end of the next week, the spell kept critters from seeing or hearing us, as well as keeping them from sensing our magic.

Mr. Corvales made them teach it to everyone, even though they complained that they weren't finished improving it yet. After that, it took the hunters a whole lot less time to come back with dinner after we made camp.

Sergeant Amy had gotten skins from all four of the medusa lizards we'd killed, and she had three of the army men hard at work on them every evening. Eventually, we got six lizard-skin suits out of it, to add to the two she'd bought in St. Jacques du Fleuve. She wanted to send out hunting parties to get more, but after we lost the horse to the last lizard, Captain Velasquez said it wasn't worth the risk, especially with the new don't-notice-it spell. I think she was the only one in the expedition who was disappointed.

CHAPTER
22

As we worked our way west, we found more and more plants and animals that nobody had ever seen before. All the magicians and half of the survey folks got all excited every time we ran into something new, and Mr. Corvales had to keep reminding them that we'd be coming through the same territory on our way back, and it'd be a lot easier to pick up samples then than to take them now and drag them on an unnecessary round trip to the mountains.

By June first, we were almost to the Grand Bow River. The Grand Bow ran from somewhere way out in the Far West all the way down to St. Louis, where it joined up with the Mammoth River. Lewis and Clark had gone up it in 1804, and sent some of their men back with their maps when they stopped at Wintering Island at the end of that summer, so the first part of the river was pretty well mapped. Unfortunately, nobody knew what they'd found upriver from Wintering Island, because they'd gone on the next spring and never come back. There's a monument to them in Washington, right next to the one for all the folks who came from Avrupa to all the earliest settlements that failed, and the ones for the Lost Explorers — Jeremy Stokes, who was the first Albionese explorer in the

Northeast and who vanished in 1587, and Daniel Boone, who disappeared back before the Great Barrier Spell went up, on his third trip to map the parts of the country that are now the states of Cumberland and Franklin.

We planned to follow the Grand Bow, too, though we had wagons instead of boats. Going up one bank of the river meant we didn't have to worry so much about wildlife coming up on us from that side, and it also meant we'd always have water for the horses and the mammoth.

The day we reached the river at last, we stopped early to make camp. That night, we had a party, and Captain Velasquez passed out a little tot of rum from the stores to anyone who wanted one. Mr. Zarbeliev brought out his fiddle, and one of the soldiers had an English flute, and we sang until the full moon was sliding down the far side of the black and starry sky.

We'd planned to stay camped there for two days, so that the scientists and survey people could do a more thorough job than usual. I spent the first day with Professor Torgeson and Dr. Visser, examining plants and bugs down along the bank of the river, and making lists and sketches of them.

Dr. Visser was the agricultural expert who'd been added at the last minute, and he was mainly interested in plants that might make new crops. He had a bunch of specialized spells to check whether things were safe to eat or not. They worked fine for finding out whether you could eat something, but they didn't tell you anything about taste, so every once in a while he'd stop and nibble on something he thought was promising.

When we got back to the camp, Bronwyn and Elizabet were in the middle of a loud discussion with Mr. Corvales.

"The readings are too high," Elizabet was saying in a stubborn tone. She shook a small leather-bound book at Mr. Corvales for emphasis. Her bag of surveying tools sat half open at her feet, and both she and Bronwyn were covered in mud to the knees.

"Miss Dzozkic," Mr. Corvales replied in a harried tone, "by your own admission, they're only a point or two above normal. The natural variation from season to season —"

"I'm not an amateur!" Elizabet snapped. "I took seasonal variation into account."

"It's not just at the surface, either," Bronwyn put in. "I can feel it all the way down to the aquifer. And the flow is all wrong, too. It's tangled, which you don't expect around a river."

The raised voices had attracted a great deal of attention; most of the expedition members who weren't actually out doing something were sliding closer and closer to the argument.

"It's still only a few points," Mr. Corvales said. "And we don't actually know what normal is, this far west, do we?"

Bronwyn's lips thinned. Elizabet's eyes narrowed as she said, "There's no reason to expect that the coefficient of magic generated by a flowing river would be any different for the Grand Bow River than it is for the Mammoth River."

"But you don't *know* —"

"Excuse me, but we *do* know, and the coefficient *is* the same," Roger's voice broke in. "Or at least, it was when they measured it at the confluence just above St. Louis ten years ago. And surely one of the reasons we're out here is to find just this sort of anomaly?"

Mr. Corvales sighed. "Yes, of course. All right, we'll stay an extra day so Miss Dzozkic can take additional readings, but no more than that! And if you think any of the others can provide a useful perspective, Miss Dzozkic, feel free to draft them." His eyes cut sideways at Roger.

Bronwyn and Elizabet exchanged glances as Mr. Corvales left and the circle of onlookers began to break up. "Looks as if you're part of the team, Mr. Boden," Elizabet said. "At least for now."

Roger laughed. "I wouldn't miss this for all the tea in Albion. Would you mind if I looked at the readings?"

Elizabet opened the book she was holding and pointed. Roger leaned forward, his expression one of deep concentration. I hadn't seen hardly anything of Roger since the expedition started. Even though the three expedition groups tended to clump together when we made camp, we did a fair lot of mingling day to day, so I was pretty sure he'd been avoiding me. I couldn't honestly blame him, but I wasn't sure it was a good idea to keep on that way. I wasn't about to interrupt him while he was studying Elizabet's work, though.

Dr. Visser and Professor Torgeson walked over to Bronwyn. "What was that about?" Professor Torgeson asked.

"The magic readings along the banks of the Grand Bow are too high," Bronwyn said. "She checked in four places, and they're running consistently one point seven to two point two above the normal range. It's not an underground river; I checked."

"It's not a remarkable difference," Dr. Visser said, frowning. "Still, we know so little of the Far West that any deviation from normal is worth investigating, I would think."

"Two points above normal?" Professor Torgeson got a considering look. "That might be enough to affect the distribution of plant species. I didn't notice an unusual number of magical plants, though."

"It could be a subtle difference," Dr. Visser pointed out. "Perhaps you'll find something when you look at the statistics."

"It won't prove anything, one way or another, if we don't find anything," Professor Torgeson told Bronwyn. "But if there *is* an anomaly —"

"I'll go get started adding up the species," I said, suppressing a sigh. That was the part of my job I didn't like much — going through all the notes we'd made and making a list that showed how many of each type of plant we'd found. "You'll want them separated into natural, magical, and new or unknown, right?"

"Yes, thank you, Eff," Professor Torgeson said, and I went off to start listing.

<hr />

That night, I had a dream, the first one of *those* dreams I'd had since last summer. I was walking through trees, along the bank of a stream that got wider and wider until I stopped at the edge of an enormous lake. On my left was a cliff of gray rock, rising up into the clouds.

I looked across the lake and saw a wave starting on the far side. It swept slowly toward me, drawing up more and more water as it came, and I could see right off that if I just stood and waited for it, I'd probably drown. I started trying to climb the cliff, but I couldn't find handholds, and I didn't get far.

The wave was getting closer, and I was frightened and frustrated. I kicked at the cliff, and a piece of it fell off in front of me. I looked at the rock, and at the wave, and then I started kicking and hitting the rock. More rocks fell, piling up in front of me. The wave crashed into them; it showered me with ice-cold spray, but it didn't break through the dam.

I woke up shivering even harder than I usually did after one of *those* dreams. Sergeant Amy and Mrs. Wilson were sound asleep, and I crawled out of the tent very carefully so as not to wake them. The sky was lightening in the east, just enough that you'd notice that you could see fewer stars than if you looked toward the west. I sat on the grass by the fire, as close to the edge of the firepit as I could get without burning myself or setting my jacket aflame. As soon as I warmed up enough to think, I looked at the pendant.

The top layer of spells, the ones that felt like me, had changed. I considered for a minute. They'd never before done that after a dream, not that I'd noticed. I frowned and looked closer. It almost felt like I'd cast a spell in my sleep. Almost, but not quite — and there was no record of a new spell casting. "This is impossible," I muttered.

"What's impossible?"

I looked up and saw William. "What are you doing awake at this hour?"

"I could ask you the same thing." William plopped down beside me. "I woke up thinking it was time for Adept Alikaket's morning session. By the time I realized it was still too early, I was up and dressed and it seemed silly to go back to sleep. What's that?" He nodded at the pendant in my hand.

I hesitated. "I don't know if I should say."

William turned his head sharply, and the firelight flashed off his glasses, so I couldn't make out his expression properly. "It looks like an Aphrikan teaching ornament. Where did you get it?"

I gaped at him. "You know what this is?"

He nodded. "There's one in the magic museum at Triskelion; it has a bad crack, and the current holder didn't want to keep using it for fear it'd break all the way and lose the whole spell history. So he loaned it to the college to study. They only let a few people work with it, because it's so fragile."

"I'm going to murder Wash," I muttered, clenching my fist around the pendant. "All that mystery, and they have one at a college for studying?"

"Well, it's the only one like that, at least in North Columbia," William said. "Professor Ochiba says that in South Columbia, the folks who have one wear it openly, but here it's usually kept secret. Did Wash give you that?"

So I explained about Wash and the pendant and the dreams. "Please don't say anything to anyone else," I said when I finished.

"Not even Professor Ochiba?"

I thought for a minute. "If it's usually a secret, there's probably a reason. I think Wash might have told her already, though. He said something once . . ." I shrugged. "I think I'd better ask him straight out before either of us says anything. But it surely would be nice to have someone to talk to about it."

"If you're looking to get clear answers, I'm not sure talking with Professor Ochiba will help," William said. "She's always making me work things out for myself, even when I know she has the solution."

"I remember," I said, and sighed. "Wash does the same thing. Do you think it has something to do with Aphrikan magic, or is it just them?"

"It's them," William replied without hesitation. "The other professors at Triskelion aren't like that, not even the ones who teach Aphrikan magic." He looked suddenly thoughtful. "And Professor Ochiba's students generally do better than anyone else's. I bet that's a good part of why."

That turned the conversation to what Triskelion was like and what William had been doing there. I knew some of it from his letters, but there's only so much you can write down before your hand cramps up, so he had a lot of stories I hadn't heard before. The sky lightened rapidly, or that's how it seemed, and before we knew it, Adept Alikaket had come out for his morning practice.

As soon as we saw him, William and I stopped talking and got up to join him. We'd both been practicing long enough to know the motions by heart, and as I stepped and reached and bent in slow, smooth movements, my mind started to drift. I felt almost the way I did when I used the Hijero-Cathayan concentration exercise, except that instead of focusing on one specific thing, I was letting my mind drift wherever it wanted to go. It was very relaxing, even though by the end of the session I always felt like I'd just chased my nephew Albert down to the creek and back.

We stayed at that first stop on the Grand Bow for the full three days. By then, we were sure that Elizabet was right — the ambient magic levels around the river were just a little higher than they ought to be — but nobody had any idea why. Roger and Mr. MacPhee said that it didn't have anything to do with the geology of the area, and Bronwyn dowsed for water, oil, and every kind of metal anyone could think of to confirm that it wasn't on account of any underground mineral deposits.

Everyone else spent a lot of time trying to figure out what effects the higher magic levels might be having and what else strange might be going on. The lists I made for Professor Torgeson showed a few more magical plants along the banks than you'd expect, but not quite enough that it couldn't have been normal variation.

Professor Ochiba and Wash spent a long afternoon doing advanced world-sensing, and they both agreed with Bronwyn that the flow of magic in and around the river was unusual. Professor Ochiba said it felt like a skein of yarn that a pair of cats had been at, all tangled and knotted up; Wash described it as more like a fast creek with a lot of rocks and whirlpools and backflows that all interfered with each other until you couldn't figure out which way it was actually trying to go. Neither one of them thought it was dangerous for us, though everybody was sure we ought to keep a close eye on it.

We broke camp at last and went on up the Grand Bow. At every stop, Elizabet took readings, Roger and Bronwyn checked for underground changes, and Professor Ochiba spent time doing world-sensing on the river. It wasn't long before it became obvious that the magic level was climbing as we moved upriver. It wasn't climbing much, but Roger pointed out that we didn't know how long the Grand Bow was, and that if the river went all the way to the Rocky Mountains, as seemed likely, and if the magic level kept increasing at the same rate, then by the time we reached the mountains, the magic levels would be sky-high.

That worried everyone, for a lot of reasons. Rivers generate magic as they flow; that's the main reason why the Great Barrier Spell runs up the Mammoth River and down the St. Lawrence Seaway — so that the natural magic of the river can keep the spell going without any magicians needing to add power every so often. But the magic always flows the same way as the river, getting stronger and stronger as it moves from its headwaters down to the ocean. Nobody, not even Adept Alikaket, knew of any exceptions. Except the Grand Bow.

Mr. Corvales was especially puzzled because he thought that somebody would have noticed before now if the magic along the Grand Bow was behaving oddly. After all, a couple of hundred miles of the river flowed through settlement territory in the Middle Plains. Finally, Roger and Elizabet did some calculations on the rate of change and showed him that if the change in magic was consistent all up and down the river, the magic levels would be well within the normal range long before the Grand Bow reached settlement territory. And as long as they were normal, nobody was likely to notice that they were always on the high side of the range.

"Which is all very well," Lan said to me that night, "but it doesn't do anything to explain why this river is behaving so oddly." He sounded very cross, and I thought maybe it was because he'd been asking Roger questions and not getting answers.

"No, but everything we find out is important." I'd been working with Professor Torgeson for three years, and if there was one thing I'd learned from her, that was it. "You never know what is going to be the key thing that tells you what's going on."

"There's too much that we don't know," Lan grumbled.

I understood how he felt, but I couldn't help thinking that he ought to try coming to Adept Alikaket's practices more often. It'd help him calm down, or at least work off some of his mood instead of taking it out on the rest of us.

I knew better than to say so.

WE'D EXPECTED TO FIND A LOT OF WILDLIFE ALONG THE RIVER, COMING to drink, and we did. There were all the familiar critters — bison and silverhooves, terror birds and prairie wolves, mixed prides of saber cats and Columbian sphinxes, flocks of whooping cranes, piebald geese, and at least six kinds of ducks — but there were unfamiliar ones, too. Dr. Lefevre found a chameleon tortoise on the third day, and at the start of the second week, Wash caught a creature that looked for all the world like a horse that only stood waist-high, with long hair like a mammoth's. After that, new creatures started turning up at a great rate.

What we hadn't expected was how many of the new creatures would be magical, or that there would be more of them that absorbed magic, like the mirror bugs and medusa lizards. We found out about the first one almost by accident, when Greasy Pierre brought in a white ground squirrel, alive in one of the specimen cages.

Dr. Lefevre frowned at it. "White?"

"Animals go white in winter up here, don't they?" one of the soldiers suggested. "Maybe it just hasn't shed its winter coat yet."

"By June?" Greasy Pierre said derisively. "Also, it's larger than a normal ground squirrel."

"Maybe it's a sport, then. Albino, or some such."

"Nonsense," Dr. Lefevre put in firmly. "Look at the eyes." He glanced at Mr. Melby, his assistant, and gave him a brief nod of approval when he saw that the man was ready with his recording notebook and pencil. He set the cage on the ground and motioned to Greasy Pierre to stand back so he'd have room to do a sleeping spell. We only did that with the smaller creatures, so that we could examine them without getting bitten or pecked. As soon as everyone was far enough from the cage to suit him, Dr. Lefevre cast the spell.

The squirrel squeaked and turned brown and stripy. It didn't fall asleep at all.

Mr. Melby scribbled madly in his notebook. "What in —" Dr. Lefevre bit off his exclamation, and cast another spell. The squirrel squeaked again and turned white. It still didn't fall asleep.

"Mr. Melby!" Dr. Lefevre snapped. "Do me the favor of monitoring the next cast."

"Dr. Lefevre?" I said. "If you're trying to find out whether it's absorbing the spell, I can tell you it is."

"You were monitoring the spell casting?"

"Aphrikan world-sensing," I said. "It soaked up the first spell, right enough, but I think there was some left over the second time."

"You think." He looked annoyed, and he certainly sounded cross, but I got the feeling that underneath it, he was pleased. "And if I want exact numbers, I will still require the monitoring spell, won't I? Mr. Melby!"

I stepped back and let them get on with it. Sure enough,

the squirrel was soaking up any magic that was thrown at it. A bit more experimenting showed that it didn't absorb magic that wasn't cast directly at it. That was a relief, at first, because it meant that the ground squirrels were no threat to our travel protection spells — Dr. Lefevre checked that as soon as he was sure the critter was eating magic. But then someone pointed out that the ground squirrel probably wouldn't have developed a knack like that unless there was something that threw magic at it in the first place. That got everyone worrying again.

We found the critter that was throwing magic at the squirrels about two weeks later. It was a kind of small hawk that nobody'd heard of before, with wings that were cloud-white on the bottom side and a pale, speckled brown on top. When it dove down to catch something, it sent a burst of magic ahead of it that stunned whatever it was trying to catch. Mr. Gensier saw it first, so he got to name it. He called it a Priscilla hawk, after his wife back home. Everyone was pleased, because we'd already found two completely new magical animals, even though we hadn't passed the Lewis and Clark or the McNeil Expeditions yet.

Getting farther than the earlier expeditions was important to everybody, but especially to Mr. Corvales. For the first month, he kept us moving as fast as he could without stinting on the work or wearing down the horses. Near the middle of July, we finally passed Wintering Island. We had another cele-bration that night, though it almost felt more like we were trying to cheer each other up than like a party. Wintering Island was the very last point in the Far West that anyone knew anything about at all. From there on, we were truly on our own.

Once we'd passed Wintering Island, Mr. Corvales didn't push us to move quite so fast. "And that's a relief," Lan said. Then he added hastily, "Not that I'm not pleased to have finally beaten every other exploratory expedition that's gone up the Grand Bow."

"We may not actually have beaten them," William pointed out. "We don't know how far Lewis and Clark got after they passed Wintering Island. Or Turnbull's men, either."

"I don't think it counts until we get home," I put it. "Like the McNeil Expedition."

That sobered everyone up, but Lan was still grumpy about it for the rest of the day.

⸺⸺ ◆ ⸺⸺

Around mid-August, Mr. Corvales started looking for a good place for us to winter over. The easiest and safest spot would have been an island in the middle of the river. There weren't many kinds of wildlife that would swim out to attack an island, not with all the regular animals that lived on the plains, and even when the river froze over, the flowing water underneath the ice would add power to the protection spells.

Unfortunately, we hadn't seen anything but sandbars since we'd passed Wintering Island. That left us with two choices: We could push on and hope that we ran across an island before we *had* to stop, and then throw together as much in the way of walls and buildings as we could in whatever time we had left, or we could find a good spot along the riverbank and make a proper job of building winter quarters.

It wasn't really a hard choice, not if we wanted to be sure

of making it through the winter, but there was some grumbling when Mr. Corvales announced that we'd gone as far west as we were going to go for the year. He picked a spot where a smaller river joined up with the Grand Bow, so that we had water along two sides of our camp. Big cottonwoods grew all along the banks of both rivers, with a few oaks and birches and shredbarks mixed in, so we wouldn't have to go far to cut wood. In addition, the riverbanks rose a steep ten feet above the water where the two rivers came together, which meant that even if the river froze all the way over, any wildlife would have a hard time getting up to us on those sides.

We spent the next month and a half building a storage area, temporary quarters for ourselves and the horses, an outhouse, and a log wall with two sentry platforms. As soon as each part was finished, the magicians cast the strongest protection spells they had over it. The mammoth was especially useful for hauling logs, as it was large enough to move even the biggest trees, and we needed so many that even with all the growth along the river, we still had to move a lot of them a fair distance.

The wall and a medium-sized corral outside it were the only things we used logs for; there weren't enough trees to build more and still have firewood for the winter. We made the storage area and living quarters by digging out part of the rise inside the log wall and piling up squares of sod to make short walls around the edge of the hole. We roofed it over with small branches and more squares of sod. The inside was dark and cramped, but it would be warm, and that was the main thing.

As soon as the storage area was finished, Mr. Corvales and Captain Velasquez sent half the soldiers and explorers out every day to cut hay and hunt. We built a smokehouse next to the river, to smoke the bison and deer and silverhooves that the hunters brought in. Everyone who wasn't hunting or building walls spent at least part of every day gathering plants that would keep for a few months in a root cellar — cattail roots, late prairie turnips, sunflower and needlepoint seeds, elderberries, and so on.

Dr. Visser's lists came in real handy; there were a lot more things that we could eat than anyone had expected, and he found a slough a ways north that was full of a tall, reddish-purple grass, which he said would be particularly good feed for the horses. We spent three weeks cutting it and filling the wagons, over and over.

In mid-September, two of the soldiers left, along with Mr. Gensier, his assistant, and Greasy Pierre. They took copies of all the important notes and maps and discoveries the expedition had made so far, particularly including the things like the don't-notice-it spells that worked especially well on medusa lizards. Everyone sent letters, too, though there wasn't room in the saddlebags for more than two per person. Since the returning party knew where they were going and what to expect, and since they didn't have wagons to slow them down, they had plenty of time to make it to St. Jacques du Fleuve before travel got difficult, even if there was an early snowstorm in October.

Everyone was a little solemn for a few days after the small group left. It wasn't just because the expedition had been suddenly reduced by five people. We all knew that they'd been sent back so that we'd have a better chance of getting through the winter, with fewer men and horses to feed, and so that the things we'd learned so far would get back to people who could make use of them, even if we never did.

Right after the return party left, Mr. Corvales and Captain Velasquez had a big argument with Adept Alikaket over the mammoth, right in the middle of the compound.

"We're going to have enough trouble keeping the horses fed all winter," Captain Velasquez told him. "If we try to keep that creature around, we'll end up starving the lot of them."

"It has been of much use," Adept Alikaket pointed out.

"Yes, yes," Mr. Corvales said testily. "I admit the creature has been useful, but it's also caused us plenty of problems."

"None of which have been serious," the adept said, "and all of which were easy to deal with."

Captain Velasquez snorted. "Not serious? The day of that fire outside St. Jacques, we'd have been away at least half an hour earlier if it hadn't been for that thing. It was just luck that the fire went east instead of south. It could have been us burning up instead of that settlement, if the wind had shifted."

"But it was not."

"No," Mr. Corvales said. "But it could have been, and next time we may not be so lucky. And the captain here is right about the feed."

Adept Alikaket frowned slightly. "Mammoths live wild here, yes? There should be plenty of things for it to eat."

Right about then, Captain Velasquez caught sight of Professor Torgeson crossing the compound, and he called to her to come and explain things to the adept. "You're partly right," she said after Mr. Corvales and Captain Velasquez told her what the problem was. "The mammoth has been grazing all summer; we couldn't have brought enough feed along with us for it. Or for the horses, for that matter."

"Then —"

"There's a reason mammoths migrate south for the winter," Professor Torgeson went on. "Food. You won't find wild mammoths this far north much after mid-October. And if the past five years are anything to go by, we'll have trouble keeping this one here. It's always tried to break out of its pen during migration season, even back in Mill City."

"If we gather more food —" the adept started.

"Weren't you listening?" Professor Torgeson snapped. "Food or no food, it's going to try to take off after its free brethren, starting in about two weeks, and if there's a spell to stop it, we haven't learned it in all the years it's been in the menagerie."

"And we haven't the time to gather enough to feed it all winter, nor space to store it if we could gather it," Captain Velasquez added.

"*And* the thing is more trouble than it's worth." Mr. Corvales held up a hand to stop the adept's objection. "Yes, it's been useful, but it hasn't been useful *enough*. I don't understand why you insisted on bringing it along in the first place."

Adept Alikaket glared at the three of them. "I will think about this," he said at last. "If any of you have any other ideas, I hope you will let me know."

"Personally, I think we should shoot it now, smoke the meat, and tan the hide," Professor Torgeson muttered.

I could understand her saying that. Though it wasn't quite full-grown, the mammoth was large enough to provide meat for half the camp for a good part of the winter, and a mammoth-hide blanket would keep several people warmer than just about anything else. I hoped it wouldn't come to shooting it, though. I'd been working with the mammoth since my first year in upper school, and I'd much rather turn it loose to take its chances than kill it outright.

The argument continued, off and on, for several days, and pretty much everyone had an opinion. Most of the soldiers were with Professor Torgeson, and thought we should shoot it, at least until Mr. Zarbeliev told everyone that he'd had mammoth a time or two and it was stringy and rank and nothing you'd want to eat unless you were a good way beyond desperate. There were a few folks among the scientists and magicians who thought we should try to keep it — Dr. Lefevre was the most outspoken of those — but most everyone else thought we should let it go, and the sooner the better.

Professor Torgeson's remark about the mammoth getting ornery during migration put me in mind of how hard it had been to keep it contained, even when it was small. It had gone right through a rail fence once, early on when it was still a baby, and Professor Jeffries had had to improve the fence nearly every year after that. Finally, he got a bunch of his students together to build a stone wall, ten feet high and three feet thick, and after that we hadn't worried so much about the mammoth escaping. Now, though, I didn't think our log wall would be enough to hold the critter, and even if it was, the mammoth could do a lot of damage to it trying to get out.

I mentioned as much to Professor Torgeson, though I didn't expect much to come of it. She frowned and told me that I'd spent more time caring for the mammoth than anybody except

Professor Jeffries, and therefore if anybody was an expert on it, I was. Then she marched me off to talk to Adept Alikaket and Captain Velasquez. Adept Alikaket didn't look happy, but he had to admit that keeping the mammoth inside the log wall was dangerous as well as crowded. Eventually, he agreed to staking the mammoth in the corral outside the wall whenever we weren't using it. The corral had just as many protection spells on it as the compound, and if the mammoth did get restless and try to get out, we wouldn't have as much trouble fixing up the damage.

In the last week of September, just about sunrise, we woke to loud snarls, and the shouts of the sentries, and something slamming into the log wall around the compound. Everyone scrambled to grab a rifle and get out of the tents to find out what was happening.

I wasn't the first one out, but I wasn't the last, either. The first thing I saw was the front end of something hanging on to the top of the log wall. It had large, upstanding, triangular ears and a pointed muzzle like a fox's, full of teeth, but it looked to be almost as big as a saber cat. It was making noises like a cat, too. Its fur was dark brown, streaked with lighter brown in places. It clawed at the logs, leaving long gouges in the wood. Its hindquarters were still outside, and it didn't seem to have enough purchase to haul itself over and in.

As I rolled away from the tent, I heard two shots almost together, then another. The creature on the wall snarled and fell backward, disappearing behind the wall. A second later, something large and heavy crashed into the wall from outside. The timbers creaked and cracked, and there was a yowl.

"Three more outside!" the sentry shouted down from the platform.

Wash swung himself up to the narrow walkway that ran just below the top of the wall. "Concealing magic, too," he reported a second later. "Anybody have a neutralizing spell?"

"Me," Professor Torgeson said, climbing up beside him. I was right behind her, and the minute my feet were firm on the walkway, I looked around for something to shoot.

Right on the other side of the log wall, three of the giant fox-things were attacking the mammoth. The body of a fourth one lay at the foot of the log wall, twisted and unmoving. Now that I got a good look at the whole of them, they looked even more like giant foxes; they were tall and built for speed, and their tails were long and bushy.

Outside the corral, I spotted a ripple in the air, like a heat haze in high summer; if Wash hadn't said something, I'd never have noticed. I figured there were others, but I didn't look for them right then. I could only shoot one at a time.

I raised my rifle, keeping my eyes on the shimmer. Beside me, Professor Torgeson started muttering rapidly, her hands weaving an invisible pattern in the air. A rifle cracked, and one of the critters on the ground by the mammoth yelped and rolled head over tail as the bullet hit.

The mammoth lowered its head and made a sideways swipe faster than anything that large ought to have been able to move. When its head came up, the tips of its tusks were red and another one of the fox-things lay still.

Professor Torgeson finished her spell on a shout, and magic ripped outward from her in a great circle. The heat-shimmer in the air that I was watching blinked into another of the fox-things. I squeezed the trigger and chambered the second round without even thinking.

The giant fox-thing yowled and went down, injured but not dead. I looked for another target. Several more of the creatures had appeared out of nowhere when Professor Torgeson neutralized their concealing magic. They were moving too fast for me to get a good shot. I picked one and tracked it, waiting for it to pause long enough for me to be sure of hitting it.

One of the fox-things leaped onto the mammoth's back, digging in with its long, curved claws. The mammoth bellowed and shook itself. The thing on its back clung to its place, barely. Two of the creatures that had been concealed streaked toward the log wall; they seemed to know that their concealing magic was gone . . . and who to blame for it. I fired at one of them, but I missed.

More shots rang out, and more of the fox-things dropped. One of them made it to the log wall and leaped, but it fell short of the top. The mammoth moved again, dodging and shaking, and swept the fox-creature from his back at last. Then he swiped his tusks at the fox by the log wall, knocking the critter halfway across the corral. I shot a third time, and so did nearly everyone else.

And then it was over. We all stayed on the wall for a while, ready and waiting, until we were positive that there were no more of the fox-things, while the mammoth did his own check, stomping and snorting all around the edges of the corral. When we were finally sure it was safe, Captain Velasquez ordered a double watch along the wall, and the rest of us set about cleaning up.

CHAPTER
· 24 ·

WE COUNTED NINE OF THE CREATURES LYING DEAD IN AND AROUND the corral. The log wall needed repairs, and the protection spells on the corral were completely gone.

That last part worried everyone the most. The fox-things had not only gone right through the spells, they'd also taken them down without anyone noticing. Even the log wall hadn't been as much of a barrier as we'd hoped; from the marks on the outside, that first critter hadn't had any trouble clawing its way straight up it.

"We need an alarm spell," Mr. Corvales said when he heard about the protections on the corral being gone. "Something to tell us if the protection spells drop."

"We had one," Captain Velasquez told him. "The giant invisible foxes took it down along with everything else."

"Then we need something that won't go down if the rest of the spells do," Mr. Corvales said firmly.

Captain Velasquez looked like he was only just barely preventing himself from groaning, but nobody could argue that Mr. Corvales was wrong, so the captain and Wash and a couple of the magicians put their heads together and came up with an alarm spell that was anchored a ways back from the wall or fence that the protection spells were tied to. They figured that since it wasn't hooked to the same thing as the protections, it wouldn't go down at the same time, and we'd at least have notice that something was wrong. Nobody knew if it would actually work against the invisible foxes, though, and nobody really wanted to find out the hard way.

All of the magicians got busy with the dead foxes right away, dissecting them and studying them to find out what made them tick. We hadn't really had the need or time to examine any of our other new specimens so closely, and if it hadn't been so important to learn everything we could as fast as we could, studying the giant invisible foxes would have been a nice change of pace. Captain Velasquez's name for them stuck, though Dr. Lefevre complained every time he heard it that it was misleading, because the fox-things weren't actually invisible, just magically concealed temporarily. Nobody else thought it was much of a difference.

The other thing that the fox attack did was to settle the argument over the mammoth. It had pushed the log wall out of true and cracked a couple of logs, and it had just been attacking the invisible fox, not the wall. Everyone could see that the rail fence of the corral wouldn't hold it for a minute if it decided to get out, and nobody wanted to chance the mammoth making a serious attack on the wall. Adept Alikaket tried pointing out that the mammoth had killed two of the nine foxes, but you could tell his heart wasn't really in it.

So a couple of days after the attack, Wash and Professor Torgeson and I took the mammoth across the river and let it go. I had mixed feelings as I watched it amble away, but

Professor Torgeson grumbled that we should have shot it just on general principles. I never did find out why the adept had been so set on bringing it along on the expedition.

From then on, we were even more careful when we sent groups out to cut hay and hunt and gather for the winter. We didn't see any more of the invisible foxes, but Wash shot another medusa lizard.

As the days shortened and the weather got colder, there was less and less forage to be found, and everyone stuck close to the compound. The wall proved its worth more than once in those months. The terror birds had started south early in September, but the saber cats and Columbian sphinxes and prairie wolves didn't leave until the herds of bison and the migrating mammoths went south in October. Twice, a pride of cats tried to come over the wall, just like the invisible foxes, and once Captain Velasquez called out the whole army unit to head off a woolly rhinoceros. The first snowstorm came in early November. It was kind of a shock for the soldiers who'd been born and raised in the South Plains; they'd been complaining about the cold since September, and they hadn't really believed any of us Northerners when we told them it was going to get a whole lot worse.

Adept Alikaket still got up early every morning to do his practice, and as folks got less busy with gathering, more of them joined in. Even Lan started coming again. At first, I was pleased to see him, but by early November I could see that he was getting restless. And then suddenly he stopped coming.

I might have thought he'd lost interest, except that I caught him scowling at the adept when no one else was looking. He had the exact same expression he always got when he was sulking about something Mama had forbidden him to do. Nine times out of ten, he went off and did it anyway, and got into terrible trouble. I couldn't let him do that on the expedition, so three days after he stopped showing up at the adept's morning practice, I collared Lan and dragged him out to a corner of the compound where we could talk more or less in private.

At first, he didn't want to tell me what was up, but I kept at him. "You can't tell me it's nothing, Lan Rothmer — I know better. And you should know by this time that I'll get it out of you, sooner or later, so you might as well tell me now and save us both a fair lot of aggravation."

"All right," he said finally. "It's that Cathayan."

"Yes, I already figured out that much," I told him. "So what about him?"

"I asked him to teach me, and he said no."

I stared for a minute. "But he's teaching everyone, every morning. You just have to show up."

"Not the silly exercises!" Lan said, exasperated. "Magic! Proper Hijero-Cathayan spells, not the halfway theory that they teach — taught —" He stopped. I waited. After a minute, he went on, "Anyway, he didn't even consider it."

"The practice isn't silly," I told him sternly. "It's part of the magic. And I don't think he can teach 'proper Hijero-Cathayan spells' to anyone here, really. From what he said —"

"He's teaching William!" Lan burst out.

I blinked at him. "He is?"

Lan nodded.

"Then maybe we'd better talk to William."

"I don't want —"

"Maybe not, but we're going to do it anyway," I interrupted him. "Because if we don't, you'll keep stewing until you decide to go off and try something all on your own."

"I wouldn't," Lan said, but his eyes slid sideways.

"You were thinking about it, though, weren't you?"

"Maybe." He looked down, then straightened. "But I really wouldn't actually try to do anything. Not after what happened last time."

"I hope not," I said. "But I bet it will be a lot easier for you to not do anything if we talk to William and Adept Alikaket before you think yourself into a bowline knot."

William was working on the invisible foxes with Professor Ochiba. We still didn't know how they'd taken down the protection spells on the corral, or how they'd gotten around them in the first place, because most natural magic doesn't leave traces the way Avrupan spells do, so it's really hard to study unless you actually see it happening.

There were a couple of different theories. The most likely one was that the fox-things had followed the mammoth's scent from farther out, and then gotten through the protections when they cast around to pick up the trail. Professor Lefevre thought that the foxes were like the medusa lizards and mirror bugs — drawn to strong sources of magic — and that all the protection spells on the compound were enough to attract the pack. Some of the other folks thought that the foxes weren't affected by the protection spells at all.

Professor Ochiba and William had one of the dead foxes

laid out on the ground beside the trestle table we usually used for examining specimens. Professor Ochiba was sitting cross-legged next to it with her eyes closed, while William cast a small flea-repelling spell at different parts of the creature. Lan and I waited until William stopped and Professor Ochiba opened her eyes.

"Hello, Professor, William," I said. "Find anything interesting?"

"There is some residual activity," Professor Ochiba said. "Mainly around the head and long fur."

"Activity?" Lan said sharply. "What kind of activity?"

"It seems to resist magic indirectly," William replied, scribbling rapidly in the observations notebook.

"Like the medusa lizards?"

"No. Different."

"Different how?" Lan persisted.

"The mechanism is not the same," Professor Ochiba said as she stood up and stretched. "The medusa lizard skin actively resists and absorbs magic; it dissipates most of the spells that strike it, absorbing part of them to make its resistance stronger. It's a natural magical loop, which maintains itself even after the creature is dead. The invisible foxes merely redirect spells that strike them. I believe it would take less magic, but the effect disappears rapidly when the creature dies."

"They redirect spells?" I said uncertainly.

"You know how water beads up on oilcloth? Like that." William shoved his glasses back in place and then gestured at the dead fox. "When the spell hits, it doesn't sink in and affect the invisible fox. Instead, it slides off along the fur and into the air."

"Would it work the same way with stationary spells? Like the protection spells?" Lan asked.

"Possibly. But merely deflecting the protection spells would not have caused them to collapse completely." Professor Ochiba stretched again, then bent to collect the fox. "That will be all for today, William. We'll run the same series the day after tomorrow. That will give us three data points —"

"Four."

"Better still. We'll spend tomorrow analyzing what we have so far." The professor nodded farewell to us and walked off with the fox.

William closed his notebook and tucked his pencil through the loop of ribbon he was using as a bookmark. "I'd say I was happy to be finished early, except that going through all these figures tomorrow is going to be a miserable job." He shrugged and smiled slightly. "There's good parts and bad parts to anything, I suppose. What are you two up to?"

"Nothing much," Lan said. "Just . . . nothing much."

I heaved an exasperated sigh. "Lan's in a grump because Adept Alikaket won't talk to him about Cathayan magic."

William looked surprised. "That's odd. Sos Melby and Professor Lefevre and I have been asking him questions for weeks, and he's never been reluctant to answer. Maybe it's because you're in the exploration-and-survey section?"

"I knew it!" Lan clenched his fists.

"Why would it make a difference that Lan's in the exploration section?" I asked, frowning. "We're supposed to all be the same expedition."

"I don't know," William replied. "But Mr. Corvales has gotten snappy with Adept Alikaket a couple of times, and exploration-and-survey is supposed to be his section, so perhaps it's something to do with that."

"Mr. Corvales got snappy with the adept? I hadn't heard that."

William shrugged. "It's no big surprise, is it?" Lan and I looked at him. He shrugged again. "The three section heads are supposed to have equal authority, but the Cathayans put up half the money for the expedition, and Adept Alikaket is their representative. So it's more important to keep him happy than it is for either of the other two. It has to make things awkward."

"I never thought of that," I said slowly.

"It's stupid." Lan kicked at the ground, the way he used to when we were twelve and he was frustrated enough to want to hit something, only he had nothing to hit. "If I can learn proper Hijero-Cathayan magic —"

"Oh, we're not learning the actual spells," William interrupted. "It's mainly just discussions of theory. The way Cathayans think about magic is fundamentally different from the way we do. It's fascinating."

"Lan," I said suddenly, "when you talked to Adept Alikaket, what did you say? Did you actually ask straight out about learning spells? And did you tell him about the accident at Simon Magus, and Professor Warren getting killed?"

Lan turned bright red. "I didn't have a chance to tell him," he muttered. "I just — he just —"

"You didn't even try." I suppressed another sigh. Sometimes I felt like I was a lot more than just fifteen minutes older than Lan. "William, do you think it would make a difference if the adept knew?"

"It might." William gave Lan a long, hard look. "Why are you so keen on learning Cathayan spells, anyway?"

"I —" Lan took a deep breath. "I need to know what went wrong. With Professor Warren."

"You know what went wrong," I said as gently as I could. "You finished the team spell casting, and Professor Warren was the focus. He wasn't ready, and all that magic burned him out."

"I know," Lan whispered. "But what if there was something else? Something we could have done differently? We never learned anything about that practice dance thing the adept does every morning. What if *that's* what made the difference?"

Then it wouldn't have been your fault, I thought, though I knew better than to say such a thing straight out. Lan had been in a complete funk for months after the accident. He said he'd gotten over it, but what with this fascination with Hijero-Cathayan magic and the way he was still refusing to go back to school the way Mama and Papa wanted, I didn't think he was as over it as he claimed. I didn't want to upset him all over again by pointing that out, though.

William wasn't as kind as I was. "What made the difference was you pulling a stunt you should have known not to try," he said sternly. "Nobody but you was ready for that spell to go active; no matter what else could have or should have gone into it, they still wouldn't have been ready, because nobody knew you were going to activate it."

"All right!" Lan snapped. "I messed up, I know that! I just have to know whether there was something I could have done differently. *Besides* not finishing the casting in the first place."

"And that's all?" William stared steadily at him.

"Yes . . . no. I don't know."

"Good enough," William said after a moment. "Let's go ask the adept some questions, then."

"*Right now?*" Lan looked like he couldn't decide whether to be excited or frightened out of his wits.

I thought for half a second, and then linked my arm in his. William grinned and took Lan's other side.

"Why not?" I said cheerfully. "I think I saw him over by the storage cellar. Let's go."

CHAPTER
25

WE HAD NO TROUBLE FINDING ADEPT ALIKAKET. EXPLAINING WHAT we wanted was a little harder, because it was really Lan who wanted something, and he'd gone all tongue-tied and reluctant to talk. William and I had a silent agreement not to let him out of it, though, and after a few false starts we finally got through an explanation of the whole sorry mess.

Adept Alikaket's face didn't twitch a muscle the whole time we were talking, yet somehow he looked more and more stern as we went on. Oddly enough, the adept's disapproval made Lan more willing to talk, and he took over the story in the middle. Once he started talking, he didn't hold back or leave anything out.

"And you expect this story to persuade me to teach you?" Adept Alikaket said when Lan finished.

Lan flushed. "Not . . . exactly. I just . . . if there was something that would have made a difference . . ."

"Many things could have been done differently. Knowing them won't make your guilt less." The adept studied Lan, his face impassive. "If you continue to reach past your ability, you'll only create new disasters."

I could see Lan starting to get a mad on again, so I asked, "Excuse me, but what does that mean?"

"Cathayan magic is beyond you," Adept Alikaket said bluntly, holding Lan's gaze. "You cannot learn it, and if you keep trying, the best you can hope for is that only you yourself will be killed or injured."

"*What*? Why? You're teaching William —"

"You don't have the ability." The adept held up a hand to keep Lan from interrupting. "I see I should have explained more completely before. You are the seventh son of a seventh son."

Lan nodded warily.

"Your personal magic is very strong," Adept Alikaket went on. "Too strong. To learn Cathayan magic, one must be at one with the magic that is oneself. This, you cannot do without being buried under the mountain that is your power."

"There have to have been double-sevens born in the Cathayan Confederacy," William said. "You teach them, don't you?"

"No." We all stared, incredulous, and the adept sighed. "The double-sevens can learn the exterior part of the way of boundless balance, the movements, but they can't master the interior part. Their magic is too much."

"I'd still like to try," Lan said stubbornly. "Maybe it's different for Avrupans."

"I won't help you to destroy yourself," Adept Alikaket said flatly.

"Even just the theory —"

"No. For your Avrupan magic, there is distance between the theory and the practice; for Cathayan magic, there is not.

You've shown yourself headstrong and ambitious. I won't tempt you to further foolishness. Be content with the power you have. It's more than enough to bring you fame and honor if you use it well."

With that, Adept Alikaket nodded to us and strode off. We stood looking at each other for a minute. Then Lan kicked at the ground and muttered, "It's not fame and honor I'm after!"

"No?" I said, raising my eyebrows.

"No!" Lan glared when I still looked skeptical. "All right, maybe that's part of it, but what I *want* is to do something big. Just to have done it. Something nobody else can do." He kicked at the ground again. "Nobody else thinks that way. They have all these things that they want me to do because I'm a double-seven, but it's all just more powerful calming spells, wider-ranging protection spells — the same things everybody does, just a bit stronger and better. There has to be *something* that only a double-seven can do!"

"Like the Great Barrier Spell," I said without thinking.

"Exactly! Only I don't have another double-seven to work with, like Benjamin Franklin did."

"Benjamin Franklin was seventy-two when he did the working for the Great Barrier Spell," I pointed out. "And Thomas Jefferson was thirty-five. You're only twenty-two."

Lan made a face at me. "If I just wait around, nothing will happen. There've been five double-sevens in the United States since Thomas Jefferson, and none of them has done anything special. I have to get started."

"You're just impatient," I said. "Right, William?"

"Hmm?" William had been staring after Adept Alikaket with a frown of concentration on his face. "I'm sorry — what were you saying?"

"What has you off woolgathering?"

William's frown deepened. "I was thinking about something Adept Alikaket said. About theory and practice and Hijero-Cathayan magic." He hesitated. "I don't think he's right. At least, not all the way."

Lan looked up, his face suddenly alight with hope. "William! You can tell me what he's been teaching you!"

"What do you mean, he isn't right?" I asked at almost the same moment.

"It's that thing about there being a distance between theory and practice in Avrupan magic, but not in Cathayan magic," William told me, ignoring Lan. "It's the way he sees things, but —"

"— there's always another way to look at it," I chimed in, and grinned.

"What is going on with you two?" Lan demanded, looking from William to me and back.

"It's part of how you need to look at things when you're doing Aphrikan magic," I said. "Miss Ochiba taught us some of it in our very first magic class in day school, back before she was Professor Ochiba."

"I remember that speech," Lan said after frowning for a second. "But what does that have to do with Adept Alikaket and Cathayan magic?"

"I'm not sure," William said. "But I don't think he tries

270

very hard to see things more than one way. Maybe that's what you have to do in order to be a Cathayan magician, but . . ."

I nodded. "The one time we talked about it, he was very sure that Cathayan magic is completely different from Avrupan or Aphrikan magic. But they all feel the same to me, underneath. It's just different ways of making the magic do things, really."

The other two stared at me. "Underneath?" Lan asked finally.

"When I do Aphrikan world-sensing." I looked at William. "You know, the way magic feels, down under all the spells and the little differences because of where it came from."

"No," William said slowly, "I don't know. I don't sense anything like that when I do the world-sensing."

We all stared at each other again. "I think we should go somewhere and talk about this," Lan said after a minute. So we did.

By the time we finished, Lan and William had gotten everything out of me and then some — the dreams, the way I'd used Aphrikan magic to tweak my Avrupan spells for so long, the way I'd been able to tweak Lan's spells when we were taking the mammoth up to the study center, even some of the spells and techniques I'd learned from the pendant. There was a lot more of it than I'd thought, when you piled it all up in one spot like that, and both of them were annoyed that I hadn't told them any of it before.

"It didn't seem important," I said. They gave me identical exasperated looks. "It didn't! Especially since it didn't happen all at once."

"Can you show us?" Lan asked.

"Maybe," I said. "Not the dreams, of course. I'm not sure about the pendant — I'll have to ask Wash. But I can show you the tweaking, at least."

Right about then, Mrs. Wilson rang the dinner bell, so there wasn't time for any demonstrations. Next day, we got together again, and I showed them what I'd done to tweak my Avrupan spells. Or at least, I tried to show them. Neither one of them could tell what I was doing at first, not even William with all his world-sensing going. All they could see was that I'd cast a spell that had almost gone wrong, but then had steadied and settled and gone right after all.

It took William nearly two weeks just to see what I was doing. It was even harder for Lan, because he'd never learned any Aphrikan magic except for a little theory. All of us got frustrated, but we kept at it. I couldn't help wondering if it had something to do with the pendant, and I resolved to ask Wash about that, too, once we were all finished getting ready for winter and had more time to spend investigating things.

Winter sort of eased its way in that year. About a week after that first snowstorm, it warmed up and everything melted. It didn't keep the Southerners from complaining, though. We had a few days of gray, dry weather to fill in cracks in the longhouse, and then we got more snow. The first real blizzard didn't hit until mid-December, trapping everyone indoors for a day and a half straight. We got a foot of snow, and two of the tents that people still had set up collapsed.

That storm moved most of the holdouts into the longhouse, though Wash and Mr. Zarbeliev stayed in tents until

January, when it got cold enough that Mr. Corvales's thermometer froze. With nearly everyone inside, the longhouse was dark and crowded; sometimes it seemed that you could hardly move without poking someone or having to step over someone's feet. Wash and Mr. Zarbeliev were circuit magicians, used to being out in wild territory all on their own. Neither one of them cared much for towns or cities, even, and I didn't think it was odd that they didn't want to be cheek-by-jowl with all of us in the longhouse. For myself — well, I didn't much care for the crowding, but being warm made up for it.

I finally got the chance to talk to Wash right before Christmas. I told him everything Lan and William and I had been doing. I asked about showing them the pendant, too, as I didn't feel I could actually let Lan and William study it directly without getting his permission. Wash got real thoughtful, but all he said was "Does Miss Maryann know what you all are up to?"

"I was going to talk to her next," I told him. "If you say it's all right."

"Some things you can't tell about, going in," Wash said. "You just have to take your chances. But I won't be raising any objections, if that's your worry."

I thanked him and went off to find Professor Ochiba. She didn't seem surprised when I told her about the pendant, but she frowned when I told her about tweaking my spells, and she made me go over everything else very carefully. Then she looked even more thoughtful than Wash had. Finally, she said, "It appears that the three of you have stumbled into something, though whether it's something big or a dead end remains to be seen. I think you'd best go on as you've begun, but do keep me informed."

"You and Wash and Professor Torgeson," I said, nodding.

"Not Adept Alikaket?" she said, raising an eyebrow. "He is, after all, the head of the magical section of this expedition, and this project most definitely falls into that category."

"It's not really for the expedition, though," I said. "It's personal. And anyway, I don't think Adept Alikaket much wants to look at things different ways. Or maybe it's that Cathayan magic is so big and complicated that he hasn't got room to see it from different angles. I don't know enough about it to say for sure."

Professor Ochiba gave me a small smile. "Possibly," she said, and let me go.

So Lan and William and I kept getting together whenever we could. We didn't have a lot of time, to begin with. For the first few weeks of winter, all the scientists and magicians and survey people worked on organizing and tidying up all the notes we'd made since September, and all three of us were very busy. It was a slow process, because we didn't want to waste paper — we had a long way yet to go, and we couldn't get more if we ran out. The soldiers mended their personal gear and checked over the harnesses and saddles and wagon wheels to see if anything needed fixing or replacing.

After the first month, most of the urgent work was finished, and Mr. Corvales set up a sort of school for anyone who was interested in trading knowledge. It started off with Dr. Visser showing off his plant samples and then teaching everyone the basic spells he used to figure out whether or not people and animals could eat them. It was a lot more complicated than I'd thought. Some of the plants were fine for bison and mammoths, but they'd poison a person or a horse or a saber cat; others were only safe to eat once they'd been boiled. Then other people offered to teach whatever they were good at, from whittling to specialized cooking spells, and Lan and William and I finally had time to meet up more than once a week.

The other thing that happened once the work slowed was that a lot of the soldiers and survey men started hanging around the end of the longhouse where all of us women slept. The first time one of them tried to flirt with me, I was so surprised that I dropped the cup of coffee I was holding. Luckily, Sergeant Amy was standing right there; she laughed at him and sent him about his business. Then she took me aside and taught me a few things to say if I wanted them to leave, and a couple more things to do in case somebody wouldn't take no for an answer. It was a lot more useful than Rennie's nonsense about "taking care."

I didn't need any extreme measures, because all of the men on the expedition were pretty cheerful about leaving when we asked them to. Cheerful, but persistent; they left, but they kept coming back. Elizabet and Bronwyn took to going everywhere together, and Mrs. Wilson threatened to smack some of the men with the cooking ladle, as if they were two-year-olds.

The only one who wasn't bothered at all was Professor Torgeson, and that was because the first time somebody tried to flirt with her, she ripped strips off him, up one side and down the other, right in front of the whole camp. Everybody looked a bit stunned, even Dr. Lefevre, who usually wasn't impressed by much of anything, and after that all the men were very careful not to even look like they were thinking about taking any liberties.

Round about the last week in December, Lan came around and asked me a little awkwardly if the men were giving me any trouble. It took me a few minutes to figure out what he was on about, and then I could only shake my head.

"It took you this long to notice that the boys have been getting restless?" I asked him. Sergeant Amy called the soldiers "the boys," and I'd picked up the habit from her.

"What? You mean they really have been . . . been making improper advances?" Lan sounded horrified, as much by having to say something like that to his sister as by the idea itself.

"It's only a bit of flirting," I told him. "And it started months ago, really. It's just been getting more noticeable since there's less to do."

"Who?" Lan growled. "I'll talk to them."

"Lan Rothmer! You will do no such thing." I wasn't about to tell him that I was sort of enjoying all the attention, even though I knew that it was only coming my way on account of there only being seven women anywhere within a hundred miles and more. "It's harmless, and if it ever looks like being more than I can handle, I have Professor Torgeson and Sergeant Amy and Mrs. Wilson and Professor Ochiba to help. And Elizabet and Bronwyn."

"But I'm your brother. I'm supposed to take care of you."

"You do. And if I need you, I'll come ask. But please don't start anything unless I do. You know it won't end well."

"All right, if you say so." Lan actually sounded happy to have been talked out of taking any action, and I breathed a quiet sigh of relief. It had been a good long time since Lan lost his temper, and I wanted to keep it that way.

I didn't think anything more of that conversation with Lan until two weeks later, when William came around. At first I was cross because I thought he was worrying about all the flirting, same as Lan, but then I realized that it was his own behavior he was fretting over. I was a considerable way past startled, and I said so. "And we've been friends for upwards of fifteen years!" I finished. "Whyever would you start thinking you were . . . taking liberties now?"

"I didn't, really," William said. "I just thought you might think so. We've spent a lot of time together, what with working on the spell tweaking and all."

"Yes, and if there was any need for a chaperone, which there wasn't, Lan's been there nearly every minute." I frowned. "Lan put you up to this, didn't he?"

William hesitated. "No." He started to add something, then closed his mouth.

I narrowed my eyes at him. "If it wasn't Lan, who was it?"

"Roger Boden," William said after a long minute. "He works with Lan in the survey section, and if he —"

"Roger!" I broke in. "Well, I like that! He hasn't said two words to me since the expedition started, but he thinks he can . . ." I was so mad I couldn't even keep talking.

William gave me a considering look. "You mentioned him in your letters a couple of times."

"I didn't mention him having any right or reason to be

minding my business instead of his own, did I?" I took a deep breath. Then I took another. "I'm going to have to talk to Mr. Boden. Right away, I think. Where is he?"

"He went out with the hunters; everyone's getting tired of dried meat, and the sentry saw a herd of wallers off to the north this morning, close enough to be no trouble to —"

"All right." I knew William didn't deserve to be cut off like that, but I needed to take out my temper somehow. "I'll catch him as soon as he gets back. Don't you warn him."

For the first time since he'd started talking, William smiled just a little. "I wouldn't dream of it."

"And don't you worry about that other, either. If you do anything that bothers me, I'll tell you — but I won't have to. You won't do anything I don't like."

"I certainly hope not," William said, and there was a funny note in his voice that I'd never heard before. I was too busy thinking about Roger to pay attention to it right then, but it lodged in my brain for later.

"We're still going to practice tweaking after supper tonight," I told him. "You and me and Lan. Whether I've talked to Roger or not."

"Yes, ma'am!" This time William gave me a flat-out grin. I smiled back, pleased to have that settled, at least on his side. Now all I had to do was settle with Roger.

CHAPTER
· 26 ·

THE HUNTING PARTY WAS LATE GETTING BACK, BUT THEY'D BROUGHT a fresh-killed waller and a couple of sparklers, so nobody minded. Mrs. Wilson started a big kettle going to slow-stew most of the waller overnight and through the next day, and the mouthwatering smells filled up the longhouse in no time.

It took me until after breakfast the next morning to corner Roger. By then, my mad had gone down to just simmering, so I didn't begin by laying into him good and proper, though part of me wanted to try out some of the things I'd learned from watching Professor Torgeson and Sergeant Amy taking people down a peg or six. I just told him we had to talk.

Roger looked surprised, but he found a spot along one wall of the longhouse that was a little out of the way, and we settled down. "What is it?" he asked.

"Why did you tell William that he was spending too much time with me?"

"He told you?" Roger looked appalled.

"William has been my best friend since we were five years old — I know when he's not telling me something," I said. "And I know how to get it out of him, so I did. Answer the question."

Roger shifted uncomfortably. "Because he does. Spend too much time with you. Every few days, you go off together —"

"With Lan," I pointed out. "Who is my brother. In order to work at Aphrikan magic."

"If it's a real project, why isn't Professor Ochiba with you?" Roger said. "It looks bad."

I studied him for a minute. "Oh, for goodness' sake! You're jealous!"

"Of course I'm jealous!" Roger snapped back. "I wanted — I still want to marry you." He grabbed my hands. "We could — we don't have to wait until we get back, you know. Captain Velasquez could perform the ceremony."

"Roger." I tugged at my hands; after a minute, he let them go. "You've been avoiding me for months, ever since the expedition left."

Roger swallowed hard. "I thought if I kept away, you'd miss me and change your mind, or I'd change mine, or — I don't know. I can't stop thinking about you."

"But thinking is all you've done, for months." I shook my head. "How can you say you want to marry me?"

"I don't know, but I do."

"I believe you like the idea of me and of being married more than you like the actual me."

"No! I told you, I think about you all the time. I can't give up hope."

I sighed. "I'd be happy to be your friend, Roger, but I won't help you pin your hopes to something that isn't going to happen. Maybe I wasn't plain enough before, but I won't marry you, not now and not when we get back to Mill City, and I'd purely appreciate it if you'd find something else to daydream about."

"I can't change how I feel."

"You don't have to change how you feel in order to pay me the compliment of believing that I mean what I say," I told him. I knew that I wouldn't be changing my mind. I'd thought of him a time or two since the expedition started, mostly to notice that he was avoiding me, but I hadn't really missed his conversation or his company, and that was surely no good base for marrying a man.

Roger looked stubborn, but then his face fell and he nodded. I waited a minute more, but he just sat there looking dejected, so finally I stood up. "I meant what I said about being friends, too," I told him. "But I understand if you don't want to try that. Just think about it some."

He nodded again, once, and I left. I was feeling shaky inside, so I slipped behind the curtain that separated off the women's end from the rest of the longhouse, where there wouldn't be so many eyes on me.

I sat in the back for what seemed forever, trying to think and not getting any further than a wagonload of iron rails sunk axle-deep in a mud hole. About an hour later, Sergeant Amy poked her head around the curtain. "Eff! Just the one I want to see. Come out to the storehouse with me?"

It was a bitter day, so cold that the sky itself couldn't hold clouds. The sunlight was pale and frozen, but still enough to make me squint after the dimness of the longhouse. The sentries huddled on the platforms, with bison hides from the animals we'd killed wrapped overtop the layers of coats and sweaters. Even from the ground, I could see the ice that had condensed on their mufflers and eyebrows. I was glad I didn't have to be outside for more than a few minutes at a time.

The storehouse was a lot darker than the longhouse; we'd only left two small openings to let in light when we'd built it. It was colder, too, though nowhere near as bad as outside. Wash told me that making the buildings half underground the way we had kept them warmer than above ground, because the cold didn't get down so far and the snow piled up over the top and kept the heat in. We'd have to worry some about water when the snow started melting, but that wouldn't be until mid-March, at the earliest.

Sergeant Amy didn't light the lantern beside the door; she just plunked down on one of the flour barrels and waved me to the other one. "Best place in the compound for a chat, if you don't want to be overheard," she said when I looked at her.

I felt myself flushing. "You heard already."

"About that little talk you and Roger had?" She nodded. "Next time you want a private talk, bring him here. Or the barn — the horses won't repeat anything, and there are enough of them to keep it a little warmer just from their body heat."

"If I'd thought I needed to be private, I would have." I felt cross that everyone was talking already, even though I'd expected it, and even crosser because I couldn't really lay the blame on anyone. "I thought I was just going to yell at him for being as interfering as my sisters, and it wouldn't have been so bad for that to get around."

Sergeant Amy laughed. "It might have put the others off making the same mistake, I suppose. That is, if anyone was likely to make it after you set your brother straight."

"Everybody knows about that, too?"

"Of course they do. And there's only one or two of the boys that would even think of romancing a lady who'll talk back to a double-seventh son, and those two would think at least twice, and maybe more, believe me."

"Lan's my brother. I've been giving him what for whenever he needs it for all my life."

"Yes, well, that just makes it worse, doesn't it?" Her smile faded and she got a serious look. "The important thing is, what do you want to do now? About Mr. Boden."

"You mean that part didn't get out?" I said.

"If you mean the bit where you told him you weren't having the captain do the marriage anytime soon, yes, that was clear enough," Sergeant Amy replied. "What you meant by it — that's another matter."

"I meant what I said," I snapped. "Roger is nice enough, but —" I lifted my hands helplessly. I hadn't ever been able to convince my sisters that I wasn't inclined to marry Roger. I didn't see how I'd have better luck with somebody who'd known me for less than a year.

"Then you wouldn't mind if I had a go at him?" Sergeant Amy's tone was casual, but her gray eyes were fixed on mine, and they narrowed just a little at the corners as she spoke.

"You —" I shook my head. "I don't have any say in what Roger does!"

"Of course not," Sergeant Amy said, but she was still watching me with that concentrated expression. "But you're close enough to be on a first-name basis, and from what I heard, this isn't the first time he's expressed an interest. You might be waiting until the expedition is over."

"No." I sighed. "But if you think so, I bet that's what he thinks, too, drat it! You know, if you're right about the way folks feel about Lan, maybe I should have him talk to Roger." I didn't think Roger would take it well, what with Lan being two years younger even if he was a double-seven, but I was starting to feel desperate.

"All right," Sergeant Amy said abruptly. She sat back and smiled. "I'm glad. In my experience there's nothing so likely to cause trouble as a woman playing games with two men who're both hankering after her, and that's back home where everyone can get away if they want to. We're stuck out here for another year, at least, living in each other's pockets. So I needed to know."

"*Two* men?" I said incredulously.

Her eyes narrowed again. "You really haven't noticed?"

"Erm. No. I — Who is it?"

"William Graham."

"Oh, William." I smiled in relief. "We've been friends since we were childings, that's all. He's not courting me."

"No? From the way he watches you, I think he'd like to. I suppose I could be wrong." She paused to give me a sharp look, but I just stared at her, feeling as if I'd gone swimming in a shallow creek and had the bottom drop out from under me all of a sudden. William was sweet on me? I had a hard time wrapping my mind around the notion, but I couldn't truthfully say I objected to it. Certainly not the way I objected to the way Roger kept coming after me. In fact, it made me feel warm and happy — assuming Sergeant Amy was right.

After a full minute of me not saying anything at all, Sergeant Amy shrugged. "All right; Annie and I" — she meant Mrs. Wilson — "will make sure word gets around that you were serious about not marrying Roger. And discourage further speculation."

"Thank you," I said fervently.

Sergeant Amy grinned suddenly. "And I think I'll see if I can't give Mr. Boden's thoughts another direction. I'd been holding off because I thought there was something between the two of you, but since you're really not interested —"

"I'm not," I said. "But I don't know how much luck you'll have. He's real stubborn."

"Best kind. And they do say that the finest cure for a broken heart is a new interest." She winked at me.

I hesitated. "He and Elizabet have been working together a lot, because of the level of magic along the river, and I did think that maybe —"

"Oh, Elizabet isn't interested in Roger. Trust me on that." Sergeant Amy stood up and smiled cheerfully. "Now, unless you have something to add, I think we're settled. Give me a hand getting the ducks down — Annie wants six of them to bone for dinner — and then you can bring the onions and black rice."

I followed her instructions in something of a daze, and we went back to the longhouse. I felt unsettled, and I begged off the session with Lan and William that we'd planned for after dinner. I wasn't sure I could face either of them after that talk with Sergeant Amy, especially William.

Lan came around anyway, because he'd heard the gossip and wanted to know more than Roger would tell him. I dragged him out to the storehouse and told him that Roger had proposed even before I'd been asked to come with the expedition, that I'd turned Roger down, and that Roger was as stubborn about thinking he could change my mind as Lan had ever been.

"He doesn't know you as well as he thinks he does, then," Lan said, laughing. "When was the last time I actually got you to change your mind?"

"When we were three," I said, picking an age at random, "before I learned better."

Lan made a face at me, then grinned. He sobered fast, though, and asked seriously, "Do you want me to talk to him?"

"What did I say before?" I demanded. "I'll tell you if I need help!"

"All right — I was just asking." He let it go, for which I was grateful. I was even more grateful that he didn't ask if I was sure.

The gossip was a nine days' wonder, but Sergeant Amy and Mrs. Wilson saw to it that I didn't have to deal with it much. Lan didn't say anything, but he glared a lot, and that seemed to help. Roger went back to avoiding me, and since I was avoiding him, too, it worked about as well as was possible. With twenty-some people crammed into the longhouse, we couldn't keep from seeing each other, but Roger got real intense about working on all the figures he and Elizabet had collected, and I flung myself into working on the pendant spells, so we did pretty well at keeping out of each other's way.

William was a whole different matter. I couldn't get Sergeant Amy's words out of my head. I'd always thought of William as a friend, sort of like an extra brother, but better. We'd done nearly everything together, from learning Aphrikan magic to our first cakewalk at the church social. When he went East to school, I'd missed him even more than I'd missed Lan. I'd always figured I could tell him anything — but I just couldn't bring myself to tell him that Sergeant Amy thought he was sweet on me.

It made our study sessions a little awkward for a while. I kept watching William out of the corner of my eye, wondering if Sergeant Amy was right. I knew he'd heard about me turning Roger down — everyone on the expedition knew — but he never said anything about it. Not one word. If it hadn't been for that, I'd have figured that Sergeant Amy was completely wrong. Truth to tell, I'd have been disappointed if she was . . . but as soon as I realized *that*, I shoved it to the back of my mind and concentrated on the spellwork we were doing.

Both Lan and William had finally got the hang of the tweaking I'd been doing on my Avrupan spells, though the first time Lan tried it, he used too much power and melted the lantern he was trying to light. After that, we only worked on spells that we could cast at rocks or sticks or something else that we wouldn't have to go all the way back to Mill City to replace if something went wrong.

We didn't have as much luck with anything else. I'd added both of them to the don't-notice-it spells on the pendant, but it didn't make a lot of difference. Lan could tell there was magic on the pendant, but not much else; William could sense some of the layers, but he couldn't separate out individual spells. So I worked on learning those spells myself, and if something seemed useful, I'd try to teach it to them. Most of the time, that worked pretty well, though Lan had to ask Professor Ochiba for special tutoring in Aphrikan magic because he couldn't work any of the Aphrikan spells.

That frustrated both of us — Lan, because he was accustomed to doing pretty much any kind of spell he wanted straight off, and me because I could feel that the magic underneath was the same, and I didn't see that it should matter whether it was Aphrikan or Avrupan on top.

So the winter passed, and before we knew it, the days were getting longer and it was time to start thinking about what came next.

CHAPTER
· 27 ·

AROUND THE MIDDLE OF MARCH, THERE WAS A WARM SPELL, AND Captain Velasquez sent out a couple of small groups, one to scout the land ahead and the other to expand the area we had mapped away from the river. A week after they left, a blizzard blew up, and for a while we weren't sure we'd see them again. They showed up at last, one after the other, three days late and with four men suffering frostbite in their toes and fingers but all alive and otherwise well.

Some of the army men from down South had been agitating to get the expedition moving again, but that blizzard sobered them right up. They didn't say anything more about it, not even when the songbirds started showing up and the ducks and piebald geese flew over, heading north.

We finally left our winter quarters around the middle of April, when the prairie grass was starting to green up and the horses had something to graze on. We left a cache of things Mr. Corvales thought we might need on our way back, but didn't need to haul all the way to the mountains — extra saw blades and wheel rims and gun stocks and so on. We were careful not to leave any food to attract wildlife.

As we went on up the Grand Bow, Roger, Elizabet and Bronwyn kept checking the magic levels in and around the river. They were well above normal by then, and still rising. Nobody was too surprised that we were running into a lot more magical wildlife along the river; what was a surprise was finding more of them that absorbed magic.

"*Another* one?" Dr. Lefevre said when Wash and Mr. Zarbeliev brought back the first short-eared rabbit and explained that Wash had felt it sort of nibbling on the edges of their protection spells before Mr. Zarbeliev shot it. "You're quite sure?"

"'Fraid so, Professor," Wash replied. "Though if you like, we can keep an eye out for a live one for you to test."

Dr. Lefevre tapped his lips thoughtfully. By then, most of the camp had collected to see what Wash had brought. I slipped around to stand by Lan just as Mr. Corvales and Captain Velasquez pushed through to the front from opposite directions. They stepped up beside Wash in time to hear Dr. Lefevre say, "I believe that would be an excellent idea, Mr. Morris."

"No," Mr. Corvales and Captain Velasquez said at exactly the same time. They exchanged glances, and then Captain Velasquez went on, "We can't risk bringing wildlife that absorbs magic anywhere near the wagons or camp. They could interfere with the protection spells —"

"Or disrupt the spells on the equipment!" someone called.

Captain Velasquez nodded. "We don't know what these things are capable of. If —"

"Captain," Dr. Lefevre interrupted, "I appreciate your concerns, but that is exactly the point. We don't know enough, and we must learn. And I do not believe I said anything about bringing live specimens anywhere near the wagons or camp."

Mr. Corvales frowned. "What *are* you proposing, then, Dr. Lefevre?"

Dr. Lefevre frowned. "That I accompany Mr. Morris tomorrow to look for one of these creatures, of course."

Everyone looked startled, and Mr. Corvales's frown lines got deeper. "I appreciate your willingness to take such personal risk, Dr. Lefevre, but you must understand —"

"I understand that we have now found five creatures that absorb magic," Dr. Lefevre said. "The mirror bugs, the medusa lizards, the color-switching ground squirrels, the so-called invisible foxes, and now this one."

Beside me, Lan snickered. I frowned at him and he whispered, "That's just how he sounds when he's lecturing a class. Like everyone he's talking to is two years old."

I made a face at him and went back to listening. "— species outside North Columbia known to possess this ability," Dr. Lefevre was saying. "Three, in the entire world, and they are all closely related. Yet the Far West has produced five that we know of, from entirely different classes. We *must* understand more of how and why these creatures have come to have this magic-absorbing ability."

"You have one right there to study," Mr. Corvales pointed out.

I got the feeling that Dr. Lefevre was only just barely keeping from rolling his own eyes. "I shall, of course, dissect this specimen this evening, but examining dead specimens is unlikely to provide sufficient information about the way this creature uses its abilities. Field observation will certainly be required at some point, and it seems pointless to delay it, especially since this particular creature appears to be far less dangerous than, for instance, the medusa lizards."

Everyone looked at the critter Wash had brought back. It was about the size of a barn cat, with mottled black fur, a long, whiplike tail, and paddle-shaped front paws. Its head looked a bit like a squirrel that had run nose-first into a tree. "Size don't always mean much when it comes to wildlife," Mr. Zarbeliev muttered. "Swarming weasels are right about that size."

This time Dr. Lefevre did roll his eyes. "Swarming weasels are carnivores," he said in tones of exaggerated patience. "Meat-eaters. *That*" — he waved at the short-eared rabbit — "is a plant eater. You can tell from the teeth."

The discussion went on for a few minutes more, but I think that was when Mr. Corvales and Captain Velasquez decided it would be all right for Dr. Lefevre to go looking for more short-eared rabbits. So for the next three days, he went out with Wash or one of the other explorers. The third day, they didn't come back, and everyone was worried, but they showed up safe and sound around noon the day after. They'd found their rabbit, and Dr. Lefevre had a stack of notes and three more dead specimens to study, so he was pretty smug even when Mr. Corvales gave him a scold for scaring everyone.

We saw our first steam dragon near mid-May, curling lazily through a clear blue sky high above a herd of silverhooves about half a mile away. Wash called the warning, and everyone pulled back close to the wagons, hoping the don't-notice-it spell worked on steam dragons as well as it seemed to work on everything else. A few minutes later, the dragon dove toward the herd, its long, snaky body stretched out almost straight, like a knife blade flashing down the sky.

The herd took off across the grass, all but the one the dragon caught, and we moved cautiously on, keeping a careful eye on the silvery coils of the dragon curled up around the dead silverhoof. "Looks like a young one," Wash commented. He'd taken to riding near the magicians since we left winter quarters.

"How can you tell?" Adept Alikaket asked. He hadn't taken his eyes off the dragon since we first spotted it, and I couldn't help thinking that if he kept on that way he'd be trying to ride with his head turned backward pretty soon.

"Size, mostly," Wash said. "Not that I've seen too many of them."

"The one that fell on Mr. Stolz's feed store when I was eleven was a lot bigger around," I put in. "I'm not sure how long it was, though. I only ever saw it after it was all in a heap on top of the store."

"This was in Mill City?" the adept asked. "I thought your Barrier Spell prevented such invasions."

"The Great Barrier Spell can't block things that fly," Professor Ochiba told him.

"It seems a regrettable failing."

"Maybe so," Wash said with a sidelong look at Professor Ochiba, "but it keeps folks east of the river from getting too sure of themselves."

"Possibly," Professor Ochiba replied calmly. "But only among those living near the Mammoth River. Those who live in New Amsterdam or New Bristol or Philadelphia rarely give the wildlife threat a second thought. They've no need to."

"There is no wildlife in the eastern forests?" Adept Alikaket said, sounding skeptical.

"Of course there is some, but the forests have been hunted clean of the most dangerous and destructive animals, for the most part. Or they have moved out as people moved in."

"Indeed." Adept Alikaket glanced back at the steam dragon one last time and fingered the silver dragon scale that always dangled from the lock of hair on the right side of his face. "I did not think of that."

Wash raised an eyebrow inquiringly.

Adept Alikaket gave him a small smile and said, "Dangerous animals . . . predators . . . do not like to be crowded. It explains why your countries have grown so rapidly, here in the Columbias."

"Ah." Wash sounded pleased, like someone had given him a real nice compliment.

Right about then Professor Torgeson called me over to ask about the purple spotted rattlesnake we'd found the day before. It wasn't until we'd camped for the night that I got a chance to ask Professor Ochiba what the adept had meant.

"He meant that people are the most dangerous predators in Columbia," she said shortly.

———◆———

Two weeks later, we saw another steam dragon, though it didn't seem to be hunting anything, and after that we spotted one every couple of days, if the weather was clear. There were more medusa lizards, too, and we had to skirt around three swarming weasel burrows in five days. We lost a horse to the second medusa lizard, and one of the soldiers was badly mauled by an enormous silver-gray bear that we ended up calling a diamondclaw.

The more wildlife we ran into, the slower we traveled. Finally, Professor Torgeson and Dr. Lefevre suggested that we move away from the river for a while. They were mostly interested in finding out whether there was as much wildlife out away from the river as there was near the open water and high magic levels. Everybody else latched onto the notion of getting away from the wildlife, and didn't pay so much attention to the finding-out part, which made both of them a bit cross.

They were crosser still when it turned out that they'd been right. Away from the river, we passed plenty of bison and antelope and silverhooves, a couple of saber cats, and at least one pack of prairie wolves, but there weren't nearly as many of the highly dangerous magical creatures we'd been tangling with. We made considerably better time that day, and that evening the expedition leaders called everyone together to discuss the matter.

Captain Velasquez summed up the problems we'd been having, and Adept Alikaket went over Dr. Lefevre's theory about the high magic levels along the Grand Bow River having something to do with it. Then Mr. Corvales stepped forward and said, "So that's the situation. We have a couple of choices. First, we can turn back now."

There was a rustle of discontent, even among the soldiers, who you might expect wouldn't be too happy about keeping on. After all, their main job was to keep the expedition safe, and it was getting harder and harder to do.

"We've already come farther west than any successful expedition in the past," Mr. Corvales went on. "Turning back now would not be a failure."

The unhappy rustle was louder this time; I didn't think most folks agreed with him.

"The second choice is to keep on as we have been, following the Grand Bow. We'll be moving slowly and it seems likely that the risk from wildlife will only increase, so it is unlikely that we will reach the mountains that were our original goal before we have to turn back. But we will still map a great deal more territory, and in all probability we will make additional interesting discoveries."

Mr. Corvales paused to let everyone murmur for a minute. Nobody liked the idea of not getting all the way to the Rocky Mountains when that's what we'd set out to do. Still, there'd always been a chance we wouldn't make it all the way, as nobody knew what was between us and the mountains. If there were another set of Great Lakes out there, we'd never get around them in time to go back.

"Our third choice is to move away from the river and travel more directly overland. I think today's experience shows that we'll be able to travel faster and with less risk of attack, but we'll be taking the chance that we won't find water. Sergeant Solomon, how far can we get between water stops?"

"Right now, it'd be about two days, sir," Sergeant Amy said. "More if we cut back drinking water and lead the horses instead of riding, but that'll slow us down again. We only have two barrels, because we didn't figure on needing more, what with following the river."

Mr. Corvales nodded. "So there you have it. The floor is open for discussion, and I'm open to suggestions."

There was a moment of silence, then Mr. MacPhee scowled and said, "Sounds as if you don't think we'll make it to the Rocky Mountains no matter what we do."

Mr. Corvales nodded again with obvious reluctance.

Elizabet stood. "If we're not making it to the mountains, regardless, then I think we should stick to the riverbank so that Mr. Boden, Miss Hoel, and I can continue to take readings. If we can puzzle out the reason for the rise in magic, it may allow the next exploratory expedition to get farther, even if we can't."

"It don't make sense to come out here to do a job of work and then go where you can't do it," one of the soldiers said, nodding in agreement.

"And I don't like getting away from a sure water supply," another soldier put in. "Remember what happened that time out by Red Rock Canyon?" Several of the other soldiers nodded. "I say we stick to the river."

Professor Torgeson was frowning in the way that meant she was thinking real hard. "If the high level of magic around the river is attracting magical wildlife and making them more dangerous, perhaps we can make use of it as well," she said slowly.

Everyone looked at her. "How?" Dr. Lefevre demanded.

"We've been depending heavily on the new spells we've invented during this trip," the professor said. "At least one of them draws on ambient magic as much as on the spell caster's power. If we can increase that draw —"

"— then we can increase the power of the spell," Dr. Lefevre said, nodding.

"You're speaking of the *nontuamos* spell?" Mr. Corvales said. When Professor Torgeson nodded, he shook his head. "Not being seen is all very well, but I'd prefer not to depend so heavily on a single casting. Will this work for more than just the one spell?"

"The standard travel protection spells are based entirely off the caster," Dr. Lefevre said. "The only way to increase their effectiveness is to have someone stronger perform the spell. As a double-seventh son, Mr. Rothmer is the strongest member of the expedition, and he is already casting as many of the travel spells as is wise."

"There's other spells," Wash's deep voice put in. He was standing at the back, and in the firelight it was hard to see his expression.

"And other ways of seeing." Professor Ochiba didn't turn her head to look at Wash, but tension crackled between them, thick enough to cut with a knife. I looked away, wondering what they meant. I hadn't found any other spells in the records on the pendant that seemed like they would be useful for the expedition, though I'd hunted through them more than once.

"Maybe some of that special Ashian magic would help," one of the soldiers said with a pointed look at Adept Alikaket.

Adept Alikaket's expression did not change; only the shadows cast by the fire moved, flickering across his face. "I have nothing at hand, but I will consider." He looked at Lan. "We will speak later, Mr. Rothmer."

"Yes, sir," Lan said.

To my surprise, the adept's eyes turned to me. "You and Mr. Graham as well, Miss Rothmer."

William and I nodded. The discussion kept on, but I lost track of it for a while. I was thinking back over the several journeys I'd made west of the Great Barrier Spell. When Professor Torgeson and I had traveled with Wash, he'd used the standard protections with a light hand. The second guide we'd had was more inclined toward stronger magic, but he'd still used common variations and I was sure we'd already tried those. The first trip —

"Speed-traveling," I said softly.

CHAPTER
· 28 ·

I didn't think anyone had heard me until Professor Torgeson said, "What was that, Eff?"

"The first time I went West with Papa, we had to use a speed-travel spell to get to the wagonrest by nightfall," I said. "Something like that —"

"Speed travel interferes with protection spells, doesn't it?" Dr. Visser asked.

"Yes, but if we moved fast enough that the wildlife couldn't catch us, it wouldn't matter," William said thoughtfully.

"It's a possibility." Mr. Corvales looked around. "The consensus seems to be to continue on, following the river. We'll head back to the Grand Bow tomorrow, fill up on water, then back off and camp out here for a day so that the magicians can look into as many of these suggestions as possible without worrying so much about the wildlife. Anything else? Very good. Thank you all."

A hum of conversation rose around the fire. A few folks stood up and wandered off, but most stayed to talk among themselves. I saw Wash disappear behind the last wagon. Professor Ochiba rose and pointed William in my direction, then followed Wash.

Lan caught my eye and jerked his head toward Adept Alikaket. The adept was talking with Captain Velasquez, so the three of us waited for him to finish before Lan said, "You wanted to speak to us, sir?"

"Yes," the adept said. "I have watched the three of you all winter, what you are doing with the skills . . . ways . . ."

"Techniques?" Lan suggested.

"Yes, techniques, of Aphrikan and Avrupan magic. It is a possible solution to this problem of the protection spells."

"You want to try casting the travel protection spells the way Cathayans cast?" Lan said, frowning. "But you said —"

"Of course not, Mr. Rothmer," Adept Alikaket interrupted. "It would be foolish . . . foolhardy to cast even a simple Cathayan spell with untrained magicians, and the training takes years. And I have said before — you are not one who can learn Cathayan magic. Also, your Avrupan spells are not suited."

"Then what do you have in mind, sir?" William asked.

"The difficulty is holding the travel protection spells over so large a group at once, yes? But if you take the spell in pieces, as you Avrupans are so fond of doing, it will not be so difficult."

"If we could do that, we'd have done it before," Lan said.

"The spells have to overlap in order to protect everyone properly," William put in. "And they interfere with each other wherever they overlap. So it ends up being a lot more work to keep up two or three small spells than it is to keep one large spell going."

"As I thought." The adept nodded. "But you three have been changing spells from the outside."

"Just each other's spells, sir," I pointed out. "And it was really hard to get the hang of that. I don't know if any of us could tweak the spells of someone we hadn't practiced with."

"But could you manage not to — tweak? — the spells, but simply hold them apart from each other where they overlap? In the opposite way from Cathayan casting."

"So they wouldn't interfere with each other?" William's face went expressionless, the way it did sometimes when he was thinking real hard. After a minute, he looked at me. "I bet you could do it. I'm not sure I could do it with just anyone, but if Lan were holding one of the spells —"

The three of us started talking over the top of one another, and it was a few minutes before the adept could get another word in edgewise. We spent the rest of the evening working out the details, and we roped in Professor Torgeson and Professor Lefevre to help us test it. Holding the spells apart turned out to be a lot easier than trying to make them do anything; all three of us made it work on the very first try, even if Lan wasn't one of the magicians holding a protection spell.

Once we were sure the adept's idea would work, we told him, and he told Captain Velasquez and Mr. Corvales. We tried it out the next day, with Lan holding the protection spells over the middle section of the group and Professor Torgeson and Professor Lefevre on either end, while William and I kept the edges of the spells from interfering with each other where they overlapped. It worked really well, and between that and the speed-travel spell, we got a lot farther than we had in a long while.

We worked our way up the Grand Bow in little arcs, camping out in the plains each night, swinging back to the river at mid-morning to water the horses and fill the barrels, then moving back out to travel quickly through less crowded and less dangerous country until it was time to make camp again. Between Bronwyn's dowsing and Roger's geomancy, we had no trouble following the river even when it was well out of sight. William and I were exhausted every night from holding the spells apart all day, and even Lan was tired. The other magicians could trade off casting and holding the protection spells, but the three of us were the only ones who knew how to do what we were doing.

The magic levels along the Grand Bow kept rising, until all of us, even the ones who weren't particularly strong magicians, could feel it on our skin like a constant case of goosebumps. Elizabet and Roger got more and more worried about it, especially since they couldn't explain why it was happening. The number of dangerous critters we saw leveled off after a while — Professor Torgeson said it was because there was a limit to how many of them the land would support, magic or no magic — but they started getting larger. At least, the magical ones did.

On the second of June, Wash came back two hours late from scouting out ahead of us. The soldier on watch saw him coming, and right away, most everyone who could scare up half an excuse was hanging about, hoping to find out what had happened. He had a Columbian sphinx slung across the saddle in front of him that was nearly as big as a saber cat, and the minute they laid eyes on it, Professor Torgeson and Dr. Lefevre launched themselves straight into an argument over whether it was a whole new giant species or whether it was just an ordinary sphinx that was overgrown on account of the high magic levels. They'd barely gotten a good start when Wash cleared his throat.

"Excuse me, Professors, but I do believe that can wait. I was hoping for an opinion on something else." He wrestled the dead cat down from his horse (which was purely glad to get away from the critter, in spite of all the calming spells I could sense on it) and turned the carcass over.

An eight-inch-wide strip of fur was missing all down the sphinx's side, from the base of its black mane to its hindquarters. The skin that showed as a result was purple and twisted up into knots and ridges, and right smack in the center of the strip was a thin white scar like the slash of a razor blade.

"Would either of you happen to have a notion what sort of thing might have done this?" Wash said into the sudden silence.

"Whatever it is, I don't want to meet up with it," one of the soldiers muttered.

Dr. Lefevre squatted to examine the dead sphinx more closely, and Professor Torgeson followed suit. You'd never have known they were almost at each other's throats a moment before. "Burn scars," Dr. Lefevre said, tracing some of the knotted skin with one finger.

Professor Torgeson nodded. "Old ones. This, though —" She gestured at the long scar. "It has to have happened at the same time as the burns; it's too perfectly centered for it to be otherwise. But —"

"— it's too straight." Dr. Lefevre leaned forward precariously. "I think the slash was shallow, barely a glancing blow, really. I'm surprised the creature survived." He frowned. "Unless the burns were not as serious as the scarring would indicate."

"I don't see how that could be possible, not with scarring like this." ·

"For ordinary burns, that would be true." Dr. Lefevre sat back. "If the injury was magically induced, the surface damage might be far greater than one would expect."

"You're theorizing in advance of your data," Professor Torgeson said reprovingly. "We won't know how deep the scarring goes until we do the dissection."

Dr. Lefevre gave her an exasperated look. "Speculation is also part of the scientific process. And a shallow, magically induced injury would be consistent with the slash scarring, and also with the animal's survival." He turned to Wash. "It's an old injury, thoroughly healed —"

"That's healed?" someone said, sounding horrified.

"— and I have no idea what could have made it. Assuming it was another animal —"

"— which is quite an assumption," Professor Torgeson put in. "It could have been a plant, or a bird, or some natural feature we have yet to discover."

"*Assuming* the injury was caused by an animal . . . well, if this was the work of a horn, the unknown creature is probably half the size of this sphinx or smaller."

"And if it was a claw?" Wash said.

"Unlikely," Dr. Lefevre said. "There's only one slash mark, not four or five. However, I'd guess such an animal to be roughly the same size as this sphinx, possibly a bit larger."

Professor Torgeson snorted and started scolding him again, and I slipped off to set up for the dissection I knew they were going to want to do next. I was just laying out the last of the tools when they showed up with three men carting the dead sphinx.

The dissection didn't prove anything, to hear Professor Torgeson tell it. Dr. Lefevre almost agreed with her, as much as he ever did; he said it didn't tell him nearly as much as he'd like. The whole incident made everyone even warier than they'd been before. Columbian sphinxes are good at hiding, yet something had got at this one anyway — and had caused a great amount of hurt with a swipe that hardly touched it. Mr. Corvales doubled the watches and kept the elephant guns handy, just in case.

A few days later, we came to a spot where the Grand Bow split into two, and we had to stop to decide which branch to follow. Captain Velasquez and Mr. Corvales argued about it for a bit, and then they sent Wash and one of the soldiers out along the river that went mostly west, and Mr. Zarbeliev and another soldier out along the river that went mostly south. After another argument, they offered to send one of the elephant guns along with each of the groups. Mr. Zarbeliev allowed as how he thought that was a fine idea, so he took one, but Wash said he'd rather stick with the rifle he was accustomed to.

They were supposed to be gone four days. Wash and his companions showed up at the end of the fifth day; the soldier who'd gone with him had slipped on a rock by the river and busted his arm, so they'd had to come back a bit slower than they went out.

On the sixth day, we had storms in the morning, with rain so heavy that the waterproofing spells on the tents had to be reinforced twice, and thunder rumbling back and forth across the sky. The storms cleared off after a couple of hours, but they came back again in mid-afternoon, making everyone so miserable that we almost forgot to worry about Mr. Zarbeliev.

About mid-afternoon the next day, a week after he'd left, Mr. Zarbeliev showed up at last. He was alone and on foot, with a bad burn all down one leg that he'd covered in a paste made of plantains and blinkflower to keep himself going.

"Steam dragons," he said when the flurry of his arrival died down and someone thought to ask what had happened.

"Dragons? Plural?" Mr. Corvales said.

Mr. Zarbeliev nodded. "Three of them at once. They got Jonathan, and both horses."

Everyone was silent. We all knew we'd been awfully lucky to come so far and only lose a couple of horses, but facing that first death was still a hard shock. Even for those of us who hadn't known Jonathan Miller particularly well.

"We should have turned back when we saw the first one," Mr. Zarbeliev went on after a moment. "It was too close and too low. But we were barely a day out, and Jonathan stood on his orders."

Captain Velasquez nodded heavily. "Private Miller was a good man."

"So we kept going. We saw three or four more before the group that spotted us. The big one must have been forty feet long, and the other two were about fifteen feet each. Not that I got out of my hidey-hole to measure exactly, you understand."

"Youngsters," Wash said.

"Must have been. The three of them were out hunting early. We were just saddling up to head back when they hit.

"The littler ones whistled as they dove. Saved my life, that whistling did. I had just time to dive for the pile of rocks next to the camp."

"Whistled?" Mr. Corvales said, frowning. "I never heard of a steam dragon doing that."

Mr. Zarbeliev shrugged. "They sounded a bit like my ma's old teakettle going off, but not as loud. Maybe it's just the young ones that do it. Anyway, I saw quite a few more on the way back."

"How many?" Professor Torgeson asked.

"I wasn't counting," Mr. Zarbeliev said sourly. "I was mostly worried about keeping out of their way. Lucky for me, I passed a herd of mammoths heading southeast, and the dragons all went after them. There must be a — a steam dragon colony or a rookery or whatever you'd call it, somewhere farther south. I wouldn't recommend heading that way."

"I should hope not," someone muttered.

"I realize the steam dragons were distracting," Adept Alikaket put in, "but did you notice anything along your route that might explain seeing so many of them? Larger herds of silverhooves, or an additional increase in the ambient magic levels, for instance? You are the only one who has seen that area."

"Huh." Mr. Zarbeliev frowned. "I disremember seeing anything unusual, but now that you mention it, I slept a lot better that last night, on account of not feeling prickly all the time."

Elizabet pushed forward, her face intent. "So the ambient magic level was perceptibly less, going up that branch of the river?"

Mr. Zarbeliev shrugged. "I don't know about that. But it was real nice, getting that extra sleep."

"Mr. Corvales, Captain Velasquez, Adept Alikaket." Elizabet turned toward the expedition leaders. "Would it be possible to send another party up that branch to take proper readings? No more than a day's ride, perhaps less. I would —"

"You want us to send men back toward a colony of steam dragons?" Mr. Corvales interrupted, frowning. "I won't ask Mr. Boden or anyone else to do that."

"I believe Miss Dzozkic was volunteering to go herself," Captain Velasquez said. His tone was mild, but his eyes were slightly narrowed as if he disapproved of something. "And the protection spells —"

"— are obviously not perfect, or your man would have come back along with mine!" Mr. Corvales retorted.

"Perhaps we three should speak of this tonight," Adept Alikaket put in. "I can see good reason to acquire more information, but I would like to understand the dangers more."

That ended the argument, at least in public. The upshot of their talking was that we settled in to camp for a couple of days while Elizabet, Bronwyn, Wash, and two privates went out along the south branch of the river and came back. Mr. Corvales looked sour about it, and absolutely refused to let Roger go along, too, but even he had to agree when Professor Torgeson pointed out that Mr. Zarbeliev could use a couple of days to rest and heal up a bit before we went on. Captain Velasquez, on the other hand, went out of his way to make it clear that he had no objection to Bronwyn going along with.

Adept Alikaket didn't say much of anything either way, but I thought he had a small smile on his face as he watched the group of them leave.

THE WHOLE CAMP WAS JUMPY UNTIL THE SURVEY TEAM GOT BACK.
Luckily, they didn't spend nearly as much time away as we'd
expected. It was just a little before noon of the second day that
they turned up again, and from the minute they were close
enough to make out their faces clearly, it was plain as day that
Elizabet was excited about something.

"Roger!" she yelled as they reached camp. "Roger, come
here and look at this!" She swung down from her horse as she
spoke and started rooting in the saddlebags.

"A little decorum, Miss Dzozkic, if you please," Mr.
Corvales said, frowning, but Elizabet ignored him. He frowned
harder and cleared his throat. "If you could present your
findings —"

"We're not certain yet what we found, Mr. Corvales,"
Bronwyn told him. She smiled at Elizabet, who had pulled her
black surveyor's notebook out of the saddlebag at last and was
flipping rapidly through it. "Excuse me — I believe they'll be
wanting my notes as well."

People were collecting, as they always did when something interesting seemed to be happening. Roger arrived at last,

with Lan trailing behind. Roger shoved through to Elizabet's side and she thrust the notebook at him.

"Look there! Allowing for the usual effect of running water, the readings drop to normal along exactly the same curve as they do heading out into the plains."

"You're in my light," Roger said absently to Lan. He turned slightly.

I saw Lan glance at the page as he started to step back out of the way. He froze and his eyes went wide. "Miss Dzozkic, what's this column for?" he asked, pointing.

"Nothing important," Elizabet replied. "It's just the difference between the normal sequence up this river and the readings we've been getting on the Grand Bow. I thought the intervals might tell us something useful, but they aren't consistent."

"No," Lan said in a tight voice. "They're the base numerancy sequence for the Great Barrier Spell."

There was an excited murmur from the scientists and magicians. Roger studied the page and his eyes slowly went as wide as Lan's had. "You're right," he said after a moment. "Why didn't I see this before?"

Elizabet leaned past his shoulder and shook her head. "It wasn't just you. None of us saw it. I even did the calculations, and I didn't see it."

"And what does this mean, Mr. Boden?" Mr. Corvales asked.

"We can't be sure just yet," Roger said absently. "I'm going to have to run some tests. But I *think* I may finally have an idea why the magic along the Grand Bow has been getting so . . . intense."

"An idea?" Elizabet looked pointedly from her notebook to Roger.

Roger didn't seem to notice. "It's a branch of resonance theory that I studied at St. Edmund's. It's pretty new, but it's held up under laboratory conditions, and I think it would explain our observations."

"How long will your tests take?" Mr. Corvales put in.

"Couple of hours, if I start now." Roger didn't raise his eyes from the page. "Elizabet —"

"Yes, you may hang on to my notes that long, provided you let me help," Elizabet said.

"Miss Dzozkic —"

"Good — it'll go faster with two of us." Roger's answer drowned out the beginning of whatever disapproving thing Mr. Corvales had been about to say. "Or three, if you'll get in on it, Lan?"

Lan's eyes lit up, and he nodded. Mr. Corvales relaxed. Roger nodded sharply and closed the notebook with a snap. "Let's get going, then."

In the end, about six people followed Roger off to unpack his geomancy supplies, including Lan and Adept Alikaket and Sergeant Amy. Mr. Corvales shook his head slightly and went over to Wash, and everyone else went back to their normal duties.

Roger's tests took a bit longer than he'd expected, because it turned out that the protection spells interfered with them, especially the don't-notice-it spell. Mr. Corvales and Captain Velasquez were in complete agreement about not taking the spells down, so Roger, Lan, and Elizabet had to go a ways past the edges of the spells on the camp, and cast inside a ring of nervous guards. They came back even more excited than Elizabet had been when she rode into camp, and that night they explained it to all of us.

"It's a side effect of the Great Barrier Spell," Elizabet said.

"I think they did it on purpose," Lan put in.

"I don't see how they could have," Roger objected. "Nobody is really sure how to create a sustained effect like this, even on a small scale."

"Nobody is really sure how they created the Great Barrier Spell, either," Lan retorted.

Adept Alikaket cleared his throat pointedly. Lan and Roger settled back, looking slightly sheepish, and Captain Velasquez raised a hand to hide a smile.

Elizabet waited another few seconds, then went on. "We don't know nearly as much about the Great Barrier Spell as we'd like, but we know that it's sustained along the north side by the magic of the Great Lakes and the flow of the St. Lawrence Seaway, and along its west side by the magic that the Mammoth River generates."

Everyone nodded, some of them with impatient expressions. "There aren't very many sustained spells of this nature," Elizabet continued, "but they've all been cast using the flow of the rivers that they follow. That's how the spell is tied to the river in the first place.

"The Great Barrier Spell had to go up the Mammoth, across the lakes, and down the St. Lawrence as it was cast. The trouble is that the Grand Bow River is longer than the upper

Mammoth, and drains a lot more territory. That makes it the true main channel of the river. The upper Mammoth River, from the confluence north, is really a tributary."

"And that means that when President Jefferson and Mr. Franklin cast the Great Barrier Spell, the spell would have naturally wanted to head up the Grand Bow," Lan said, taking over smoothly from Elizabet. "So they had to have done something to force the spell to head north up the Mammoth, instead of west along the Grand Bow.

"Whatever they did, it obviously worked, and once the whole spell was in place, it was anchored in the Atlantic Ocean and the Gulf of Amerigo, and it couldn't be pulled up the Grand Bow anymore." Lan looked at Roger.

"But the pull is still there," Roger said. "And in addition, the Grand Bow itself generates magic, which ought to flow into the Mammoth where the two rivers come together. Some of it does, enough that when we take readings, it looks like the Grand Bow is an ordinary tributary river like all the others that flow into the Mammoth."

"But it isn't," Elizabet reminded us. "It's the main channel. So instead of pulling the Great Barrier Spell off to the west and up the Grand Bow —"

"Which can't happen because the barrier is anchored," Lan put in.

"— the river has been sucking most of its own magic all the way back up to its source. And it's been doing it ever since the Great Barrier Spell was established," Elizabet finished. "That's why the magic levels have been rising. That's what we've been feeling."

There was silence as everyone absorbed what they had said and did mental calculations. "So there's eighty-three years' worth of the Grand Bow's magic piled up at the source of this river?" Captain Velasquez said. "We must be getting close to it, then."

Elizabet and Roger both shook their heads. "Based on our calculations, we still have two hundred miles before we reach the headwaters," Roger said. "Possibly more."

"You mean this prickling is going to get even worse?" someone said on the other side of the group.

"Maybe, but we don't think so," Lan said. "There's a balance between the pull that tugs the magic upstream and the natural tendency for the magic to follow the flow of the river downstream. We think that's why it's so strong this far from the source of the river."

Mr. Corvales was looking at the three of them with narrowed eyes. "And what is the problem you haven't mentioned yet?" he said.

Lan, Elizabet, and Roger exchanged looks. Then Roger said, "There are several problems, sir. The first is that the longer this situation lasts, the farther down the Grand Bow the high magic levels reach. We have a few years before it gets to current settlement territory, but once the Frontier Management Department starts sending people West again, I'm not sure how long it'll actually be."

"And we already know that the high magic levels along the river attract the most dangerous of the magical wildlife," Lan said. "Which means —"

"The river will act like a road bringing them east to the settlements," Dr. Lefevre said.

Lan nodded. "The second problem is that we aren't sure that the situation is stable."

"Not stable?" Mr. Corvales said sharply.

This time, Roger nodded. "When I was in Albion, some of us did laboratory tests of this effect. All of them collapsed after a short time, letting the reservoir of magic that had been built up flow back along the generating conduit all at once. The surge always overloaded the desired spell, causing it to collapse — sometimes with unpredictable side effects. My lab partner's test cut a pattern of three-inch holes in every piece of furniture in the building; Dr. Wencell's collapsed a large section of floor. We have no idea if that pattern will hold under field conditions, of course, but —"

Mr. Corvales paled. "But if it does, over eighty years' worth of magic is going to slam into the Great Barrier Spell just north of St. Louis."

Roger nodded again. "The barrier *might* not collapse. We don't know much about it, and we do know that it's completely different from any of the spells we tested at St. Edmund's. But —"

"But if it does collapse, there'll be panic," Captain Velasquez finished. "And that's even if there aren't any strange side effects." He rubbed his chin thoughtfully. "Any idea how much time before all this happens?"

"I'm afraid not," Roger said. "We aren't even positive how far it is to the headwaters, and a lot of the other calculations depend on that."

"We have to get word of this back," Mr. Corvales said. Captain Velasquez nodded in agreement, but several of the scientists frowned.

"Weren't you listening?" Dr. Lefevre said. "We have to go on, at least far enough to determine whether this . . . condition is indeed unstable, and if so, how urgent it is to prepare for the worst."

That started an argument that lasted until long past full dark. Captain Velasquez and almost all his army people wanted to head home right away with the news. The exploration-and-survey group was split unevenly; everybody agreed that getting word back was important, but Lan and Roger and Wash favored going on, while Mr. Corvales and Elizabet and Mr. Zarbeliev thought going back was better, and Mr. MacPhee kind of waffled in the middle. Most of the scientists favored going on, though Adept Alikaket didn't venture an opinion. He just watched everyone intently, his face expressionless.

Nothing got settled that night, but next morning the three expedition leaders holed up in a tent for a couple of hours and came out with a compromise. We'd split the expedition, sending a small group home with the news and as much other data and information as we could pull together fast, and the rest of us would go on toward the headwaters to see what else we could learn.

That set all the scientists (and everyone else we could spare) to work copying notes and diagrams. The most important ones, of course, were the series of readings Roger and Elizabet had been taking, so those got first crack at our dwindling supply of paper, but everyone else had things they wanted to let people know about, too. I ended up copying out Professor Torgeson's notes on the rocket trees and blinkflowers and other new plants we'd found, as well as most of Dr. Lefevre's descriptions of the giant invisible foxes and other magical wild-life, because I could write smaller than Dr. Lefevre's assistant.

The next question was who to send back to Mill City, and that caused a whole new argument.

"A single man can ride farther and move faster than a group, even a small group," Captain Velasquez said.

"And if a medusa lizard gets that man, no one will ever know," Mr. Corvales retorted. "A small group may move slower, but it has a better chance of getting back."

"We've already reduced our numbers once," the captain objected. "We can't afford to send a large enough group to be sure they'd get back, not without seriously reducing the chances of everyone who goes on." Captain Velasquez sounded like he was going to start yelling in another minute; I hadn't seen him so worked up before.

"Who would we send?" Adept Alikaket put in. "We have not many choices."

"If you're sending one man alone, it should be one of the circuit riders," Sergeant Amy said into the silence that followed. "They have experience getting through the wildlands alone. Next best would be Private McCormick, though he's used to working with a group."

"I'd be willing to try, ma'am," Private McCormick said.

Captain Velasquez ran a hand over his beard. "Good man. All your experience is on the Southern Plains, isn't it?"

"And on this expedition, yes, sir."

"Well, it's an option."

"No, it isn't," Mr. Corvales said. "It's too likely that one man will be lost."

319

"If I recall correctly —" Captain Velasquez broke off and looked across at Wash. "Mr. Morris, I believe you did some solo exploration before you became a circuit magician. What's your opinion?"

"When it comes to this sort of decision, I'm a belt-and-suspenders man," Wash said. "One man alone is one sort of risky; a small group is a different sort. Send both, and I think the word is a lot more likely to get back, one way or the other. Choose the right folks to send, and I doubt it'll change the odds for the rest of us appreciably."

Captain Velasquez looked unhappy, like he'd expected Wash to say something different, but Mr. Corvales smiled. The argument went on a while longer, but in the end, Mr. Corvales and Adept Alikaket overruled Captain Velasquez and decided to follow Wash's advice. We'd send one rider on the strongest horse we had, to move as fast as he could, and a small group to follow him.

Then they had to decide who to send.

CHAPTER
· 30 ·

EVERYONE COULD SEE THAT SERGEANT AMY WAS RIGHT; THE BEST choice for the lone rider would be one of our circuit magicians, and it'd be good to have one leading the small group, as well. Unfortunately, we also needed one with the expedition that was going on, and we only had two: Wash and Mr. Zarbeliev. Mr. Zarbeliev was still limping from the steam dragon's burn, so Wash seemed like the logical choice to head back alone . . . except that Wash had the most experience with the Far West, so he was also the best choice to stay with the main expedition.

Another problem was who'd go in the small group. Mr. Corvales didn't want to just send the data; he wanted to send someone who could explain the problem with the magic levels firsthand and answer questions. That meant sending Roger or Elizabet or maybe Bronwyn, but when Mr. Corvales suggested sending Elizabet and Bronwyn back, both of them and Roger insisted that they all needed to go on and continue making readings. And both the group that was heading back and the group that was going on wanted Lan, because the sheer strength of his magic could make the difference if either group ran into serious problems with the wildlife.

Finally, Mr. Zarbeliev pointed out that his having a bit of a limp wouldn't slow his horse down any, and that he'd made it home in much worse shape before, even if it wasn't over quite such a distance. Wash laughed, and they started swapping stories of being out on their circuits, and in the end Captain Velasquez reluctantly agreed that Mr. Zarbeliev would be the single rider.

Sergeant Amy issued Mr. Zarbeliev one of the jackets made of medusa lizard skin, and a pair of pants to go with it, and he left next morning. Adept Alikaket and Mr. Corvales and Captain Velasquez took another day to decide for sure who'd go with the small group. In the end, they sent Mr. MacPhee, the minerals expert, because he was a geologist and could explain what Roger and Elizabet had found, even if he wasn't the one who'd actually found it; Dr. Visser, the agricultural magician, and Dr. Lefevre's assistant, Mr. Melby, because they were both good with the travel and protection spells and because the rest of the expedition could get along all right without them; and Private McCormick and another soldier, to have some people with a bit more experience of wildlife and the Far West (though by then all of us had plenty).

The small group left the next day, with one of the elephant guns, another one of the medusa-lizard outfits, a copy of Elizabet and Roger's data, and all the research notes. Mr. Zarbeliev had only taken the data on magic levels, because that was the most important, and anyway, we didn't have time or paper to make a third copy of everything else for him.

The rest of us cached the last wagon so as to travel faster and started upriver again in a sober frame of mind. We were down to nineteen people: the three expedition leaders, five magicians, four exploration-and-survey people, five soldiers, Bronwyn, and Mrs. Wilson.

Over the next week, the river got shallower and rockier. We stuck close to the bank, so that Bronwyn and Elizabet and Roger could take readings every time we stopped, but we didn't have as much trouble with the wildlife as we'd expected. Nobody thought anything of it for the first few days, but on the fourth day, we passed a big bison herd, five elk, two small families of silverhooves, and a pack of prairie wolves, all heading east at a steady pace. I saw Wash talking to Mr. Corvales after the fourth batch of animals went by, and as soon as they finished, we were asked to double-check the protection spells and make them even stronger if we could. From then on, we rode closer together than usual, so that the magicians didn't have to cover quite so much space with the spells. Captain Velasquez doubled the guard shifts, and nobody even complained.

The lack of complaining wasn't just on account of people being nervous. It was excitement, too, because on the fifth morning, we rode to the top of a rise and caught our first sight of the mountains we'd spent so long heading for.

We heard wolves howling off to the south that night — proper howls, not the yippy noise that the prairie wolves make. The howls got more distant, then faded away, as if the wolf pack was moving away from us the same way the herds had been. I don't think anyone slept well, even after the howling stopped.

Around mid-morning of the sixth day, we reached a tumble of boulders along the riverbank. Most were just big enough to be a nuisance, but some ranged from sitting-on size to bigger than me and my horse put together. One had a tall, skinny pine tree growing out of a crack in the top. A stand of pines grew a ways back from the water, but the ground around the boulders had only some stunted blinkflowers and a bit of windthistle.

As soon as he saw the boulders, Wash raised his hand to bring us to a halt. We stopped about thirty feet shy of the rocks, crowding our horses together so we could hear what he had to say.

Wash was frowning, a wary, puzzled frown the like of which I'd never seen on his face before. "Miss Maryann," he said to Professor Ochiba, "would you do me the favor of making a careful examination of that batch of rocks up ahead?"

Mr. Corvales's eyebrows drew together, but Professor Ochiba just looked at Wash, then closed her eyes. I felt something brush past me and through the protection spells I was helping to hold. Professor Ochiba's expression didn't exactly change, but it hardened up. After a moment, she opened her eyes. "That's —" She shook her head.

Professor Lefevre frowned and cast a couple of wildlife-detection spells. "There's nothing there," he announced. "Nothing living, that is."

"So it seems," Professor Ochiba said. "But the flow of magic isn't . . . quite right. I think we should give those boulders a wide berth." She never once took her eyes off the boulders as she spoke, and neither did Wash.

"So do I," he said, "and I do thank you for the confirmation."

"How far do you recommend?" Captain Velasquez asked with a small sigh. I could tell he didn't care for the notion, but he wasn't going to overrule a circuit magician's advice without a darned good reason. Mr. Corvales looked from Professor Ochiba to Wash and back, but he didn't add anything.

"I'd suggest —"

Right then, I saw something moving at the edge of the pines. I couldn't make out what it was, and a second later it was too late. One of the boulders unfolded into a blur of gray-brown teeth and claws and wings, and pounced on it.

"Holy God, what is that thing?" one of the soldiers whispered.

The critter turned as if it had heard, and we all got a good look at it. It was smaller than a medusa lizard — about the size of a cougar or a saber cat, if you didn't count the batlike wings. It had a lean, long body, with powerful back legs and a thick tail that rested on the ground between them like the third support on a tripod. Its front legs were shorter, though still long enough for it to run on all fours, and they ended in long-fingered paws that had a long spike on the back side and two-inch claws at the end of each finger. The head looked like a giant snake, with big yellow eyes, slits for a nose, and a mouth full of needle-sharp teeth. The whole thing was covered in a pattern of bumpy scales the same color as the gray boulders around it.

Beside me, Professor Torgeson gasped and went for her rifle. Wash and three of the soldiers raised theirs at the same time as the professor; the rest of us were a hair behind. The critter was faster than all of us; it blurred into movement and dodged in among the boulders before anyone had a chance to fire.

I had my own rifle out by then, and I didn't lower it. I reached out with my world-sensing, hoping to get some warning of which way the creature was going.

I couldn't sense anything. Well, I could feel the ordinary magic of the rocks and the river and the trees, but as far as the world sense was concerned, there was nothing else out there.

That had never happened before, not even with the chameleon tortoise. I hesitated, then sank deeper, down to where everything was just magic swirling in slightly different directions. At that level, I wasn't sure I could tell which swirls were river and which were rocks and which were the travel protection spells we had up, much less which bit was tied to a brand-new kind of wildlife, but I didn't figure it would hurt anything to try.

For a minute, I thought it hadn't worked. All the magic felt the same; it was like diving into a full-up washtub and trying to tell one thimbleful of water from another. Then I felt a kind of sucking, and I shifted my aim and pulled the trigger just as the creature burst out of the rocks, heading straight for us as if the protection spells and *nontuamos* spell weren't there at all.

My shot scored a long gash down the thing's right side and dug into its wing. I heard the *crack-crack* of other shots as I chambered the next round, and felt a series of shivery zings as Lan and some of the others cast spells. The creature shuddered under all the impacts, but it didn't stop coming, or even slow down. Then there was an even louder crack as Captain Velasquez fired his elephant gun.

That shot threw the critter back on its haunches, its wings beating against the air as it tried to keep from going right over backward. Almost as one, we all fired again. The critter screeched and fell at last, but it still wasn't dead. Its claws scored deep gouges in the ground as it tried to claw itself closer to us.

"Hold," Captain Velasquez snapped, and all of us stopped firing. He kept the elephant gun trained on the dying creature, so I kept my rifle aimed and ready, too. We all watched, silent and tense, until the thing stopped thrashing. Even then, nobody lowered a weapon until the captain signaled his men and then lowered the elephant gun.

There was a long silence, and you could feel some of the tension going out of the air. Then Wash swung down off his horse, and the tension spiked again.

"Mr. Morris?" Mr. Corvales said tentatively.

"Somebody has to make sure it's dead," Wash said calmly. He didn't move forward; instead, he reached down and picked up a handful of dirt and pebbles and started tossing them ahead of him, getting closer and closer to the critter with each throw. The thing didn't twitch, even when he hit it a couple of times directly, but nobody really relaxed until he walked cautiously forward, examined the body, and announced that it was well and truly dead.

"Rope that thing to a horse," Captain Velasquez commanded. "We need to examine it, but we're not stopping here."

Wash and a couple of the soldiers went for rope, and everyone else shifted so as to be out of the way. I heard a whoosh of breath behind me and turned in the saddle to see Lan rolling his shoulders. "Phew!" he said when he caught me looking. "That was even worse than that first time with the medusa lizards."

"Aldis?" Dr. Lefevre's voice sounded almost concerned. I turned to see him frowning at Professor Torgeson, who was staring at the critter, her face white as a sun-bleached sheet.

"Professor?" I said.

Professor Torgeson shivered and looked up at last. Her eyes were dark. "Ice dragons," she said. "That thing is related to ice dragons."

"What?" Dr. Lefevre gave her a stern look. "Impossible. Ice dragons are tied to areas of permafrost; I doubt that one would be able to come so far south even in midwinter, and certainly not at the height of summer."

The professor's eyes narrowed and some of her color returned. "I didn't say it was an ice dragon," she snapped. "I said it's related. The pattern of the scales is unmistakable."

"It bears a certain resemblance to the diagrams," Dr. Lefevre conceded, "but —"

"It's an exact match. If you'd ever seen an actual sample, you'd know that."

"You've seen actual ice dragon scales?"

"Vinlander, remember? Dragons can't cross open water to get to us, but they come down to the mainland coast nearly every winter. Back in my grandfather's day, when we got back in contact with Avrupa, we bought a batch of cannons and tried them out one winter. It took two volleys and they lost three men, but they managed to kill a dragon, and the skin's been hanging in the meeting hall ever since."

Dr. Lefevre looked thoughtful. "That may be useful to know. If there are similarities —"

"There are plenty of similarities!" Professor Torgeson snarled. "About the only differences I can see is that this thing is smaller, faster, and even meaner than an ice dragon, it's obviously not limited to areas with permafrost, and it's the color of rocks instead of ice-white."

"So we've got rock dragons, then," Mr. Corvales said heavily. "Wonderful. Just the news I wanted to hear."

"Happy to oblige," Dr. Lefevre said. "Now, how far are you planning to drag that thing? I certainly don't object to working on it elsewhere, and it's clearly too large to get up on a horse even if one would put up with it, but I'd rather not have it any more battered than it already is, if that's possible."

While Mr. Corvales and Dr. Lefevre argued about that, Wash went off to the pine stand and cut a couple of branches. He lashed them together and got the rock dragon up on them so it wouldn't be dragging straight across the ground, and we were ready to go. Mr. Corvales and Dr. Lefevre seemed almost put out that they couldn't keep on arguing, but even they didn't care to hang about when they didn't have to.

Captain Velasquez took us two miles out onto the plains before we stopped and made camp. He made a point of choosing a site that didn't have a rock anywhere near it that was bigger than my fist.

Dr. Lefevre, Professor Torgeson, and Professor Ochiba went to work on the rock dragon right away. Since it was obviously a magical animal, rather than a natural one, Professor

Ochiba worked on getting a feel for its magic, while Professor Torgeson and Dr. Lefevre dissected it and argued about what they were finding and what it meant. William and I took notes for all three of them, since Dr. Lefevre's assistant had gone back to Mill City with the last group.

As near as we could tell, the rock dragon was pretty much just like Professor Torgeson's description: fast, mean, and deadly. Dr. Lefevre found two sacks in the roof of its mouth that Professor Ochiba warned him to be extra careful about the minute she saw them. When he finally teased them out and cut a slit in one, it oozed a thin, oily liquid that melted the tip of Dr. Lefevre's knife and set fire to the wooden trestle table he was working on. Water kept the fire from spreading, but the part where the oil fell went right on burning until every bit of magic in the venom was used up.

After that, we moved the dissection right to the edge of the protection spells, as far away from everyone else as we could get, and Dr. Lefevre was even more careful than he'd been before. He claimed it was because he didn't want to ruin another one of his dissecting knives. None of us believed him, but nobody wanted to say so. He was cranky enough already.

The rock dragon had more venom sacks in its front legs, set so that the oil could squeeze out of the long spike that rose from the back of its hands. Dr. Lefevre pressed his lips together when he saw them and said, "I believe we have discovered the source of that strange injury on the sphinx Mr. Morris brought in some weeks ago."

Professor Torgeson frowned. "That's just a guess."

"Provisional theory," Dr. Lefevre corrected.

The only good news was that the dragon's venom had so much concentrated magic that Dr. Lefevre was sure it had to stick to highly magical areas to maintain it. Professor Ochiba wondered out loud whether this was why so much of the magical wildlife we'd run into could absorb magic, which made Professor Torgeson mutter some more about speculations.

We did a test on one of the venom sacks, and established that sucking all the magic out of it did neutralize the venom inside. Professor Torgeson said that still didn't prove anything, but at least it gave us a way to fight it if another rock dragon got near enough to someone to spit venom at him.

"Which is highly unlikely," Dr. Lefevre explained when he told Captain Velasquez, Adept Alikaket, and Mr. Corvales what we'd found. "A predator such as this needs a large territory, and would not tolerate others of its kind within the area it claims."

"Any idea how to tell how big an area that would be?" Captain Velasquez asked.

"I'm afraid not; not exactly," Dr. Lefevre replied. "Given its size and speed, however, I believe it unlikely that we'll cross into another dragon's territory for a day's ride, at least. However, when we do, the rock dragon's need for high levels of magic means that it will very likely be hunting near the river."

"Well, at least we know what to expect now," the captain replied with a sigh. "Would you ask Miss Dzozkic and Mr. Boden to step in? I'd like to know if they can estimate how much farther we have to go before they're satisfied."

We had just left the tent to look for them when one of the guards shouted, "Rock dragons!"

CHAPTER
· 31 ·

THERE WERE NINE OF THEM, COMING STRAIGHT FOR US ACROSS THE plains from the south, and if we hadn't camped on a rise, we wouldn't have seen them until they were on top of us. They moved with the familiarity and coordination of a pack of wolves, and I realized that nobody had thought of dragons hunting in packs. Why would we? Ice dragons and steam dragons were solitary hunters; so were the extinct mountain dragons of Ashia and the sand dragons of the Sahara.

Rock dragons were, apparently, different from other dragons in more than size and meanness. I ran for my rifle, like almost everyone else who wasn't carrying theirs around in camp. The guards were already firing. I heard the deep boom of one of the elephant guns, and then another.

"It's flying!" someone yelled.

A hand grabbed my arm and spun me around. It was William, panting like he'd run after me. "The venom," he gasped out. "We have to neutralize it. Magicians' job."

I stared at him for a second, then nodded. I'd never really thought of myself as one of the magicians; I'd always figured that I was better with a gun than with spells. But I was one of the six people left in the magicians' section of the expedition, even if I was only Professor Torgeson's assistant, and except for the folks we'd just told, we were the only ones who knew about the venom and what to do about it. And with nine rock dragons —

The air trembled and I felt the same sucking I'd felt by the river. The protection spells around the camp shivered and shrank. "Fall back to the shield line!" Captain Velasquez shouted behind me, and the row of people with guns moved back until they were inside the protection spells again.

I felt another pull, and off to one side I saw Elizabet Dzozkic collapse, along with the protection spells. *She must have been the one holding them*, I thought. Then I felt a familiar surge, and the protection spells were back, stronger and solider than before.

"Lan!" I gasped. "What's he doing?"

"Never mind!" William said, and pointed past the line of soldiers facing the rock dragons through the protection spells. Two of the dragons had taken to the air and were almost to the soldiers. "You do that one; I'll get the other. Then go for the ones on the ground."

I nodded and reached out with my world-sensing. It was a lot harder with live rock dragons; at first I couldn't find any of them. Then I realized that I was feeling a rock that was up in the air and moving, and I latched onto it and cast the spell Dr. Lefevre used to drain magic from the venom sacks of the one we'd dissected.

The spell took hold, but slowly. Too slowly. The rock dragon would be on us before the venom's magic was fully drained, and the rest of the pack was right behind it — there wasn't time to take care of all of them.

I sank deeper into the magic, looking frantically for a way

to tweak the draining spell so that it would work faster and cover more of the rock dragons. And then, suddenly, I fell through into the quiet that was just magic and no spells.

It was like being deep underwater, knowing that above me there were fish swimming, and higher up there were boats and people fishing and swimming and splashing, but none of it could reach where I was. It felt like the ocean in my dreams. It felt *right*.

I took a deep breath, struggling to keep a sense of the world around me as well as all the magic. All the magic . . . I had more magic than I'd ever need, but I didn't know how to make it do what I wanted. I didn't know enough, and there wasn't enough time for me to figure it all out. But there were other people who knew.

I reached out, up through the currents of magic, until I felt the spells that people were weaving. I recognized Lan's magic first, holding the protection spell around the camp with every bit of power a double-seventh son had. Pushing more magic up to him was easy, because he had so much already that I didn't have to worry about burning him out.

The protection spells solidified into a glimmering dome. I saw the first of the airborne rock dragons crash into it and bounce off, hissing. It spat, but the venom hit the barrier and ran down it like raindrops running down a windowpane. The ground at the bottom smoked and bubbled, but the spell was undamaged; magic couldn't burn magic.

William came next, because I'd worked with him enough that his magic was almost as familiar as Lan's. I tried to be more careful with pushing magic at him, but the minute I started, he sort of slid down through all the water to join me.

"What on earth —?" I heard him say.

"It's just magic!" I said aloud. "Use it!"

"Right."

I felt his world-sensing spread out, shaping the raw magic to drain the rock dragons' venom. That gave me an idea, and I looked up. Sure enough, Wash and Professor Ochiba both had their world-sensing working as hard as ever they could make it go. I reached for both of them, and this time, instead of pushing magic at them, I pulled them down through all the types and layers of magic to the place where I was, where it was all the same.

I didn't stop to see what they'd do with it; I looked around to see who I could pull in next. I saw Adept Alikaket, practically glowing from bringing his magic up as high as it would go. I saw him blow the wing off a rock dragon that had just launched itself into the air, and I hesitated. The adept was doing just fine without any extra power, and I didn't want to distract him. On the other hand, he probably knew more about using extra power than anyone else there, what with the way Hijero-Cathayan group spells worked. I stretched up.

It was harder with Adept Alikaket, because I didn't know him the way I knew Lan and William, and I didn't know much about the Cathayan magic he was using, not the way I knew the Aphrikan magic that Professor Ochiba and Wash used. Then he seemed to sense what I was trying to do, and a bit of his spell opened up to let me in. I didn't go in; I grabbed the edges of the opening and pulled him down to join the rest of us.

I did Dr. Lefevre and Professor Torgeson next, then looked for anyone else who was using magic to fight. Roger was standing next to Sergeant Amy; she was reloading a repeater rifle while he threw blasts of fire at a dragon who hissed and spat against the protection barrier, less than three feet in front of them. I shoved magic at him, and his next blast charred the dragon's leg to the bone. Mr. Corvales was using his magic to aim the elephant gun; I waited until he'd finished the shot, then pushed magic at him, too.

I was running out of magicians, and I still didn't know how to work with all the magic. I let myself float up to the surface of the magic, figuring I could let everyone else handle the spells now, while I got my rifle.

I didn't need it. The pack of rock dragons were all dead. Some had been shot; some had been burned or crushed by spells; one of the flying ones had crashed into the ground from too high up. The shimmering dome of Lan's protection spells slowly faded back to normal as I watched.

All around me, people lowered their guns or relaxed from their spell casting and started taking stock. We hadn't gotten off scot-free. Elizabet was still unconscious, with Bronwyn minding her. Wash had a burn down one side where he'd been caught by a spray of venom, one of the soldiers had been badly clawed, and two of the horses were dead. All of the magicians were wobbly on their feet, though it was hard to tell whether it was from what I'd done to most of them, from too much spell casting generally, or just from having been in a big fight. Still, we hadn't actually lost anyone, which was a lot better than it could have been.

"Well," Mr. Corvales said loudly after a moment. "I believe that settles it. We are *not* going any farther west."

There were a lot of shaky laughs, and Wash's voice called back, "I do believe you won't get much argument on that, Mr. Corvales."

"We're moving out as soon as we can," Captain Velasquez announced. "We've a few hours yet till sunset, and I don't want to spend the night fighting off the scavengers this lot will draw."

Everyone nodded and most folks began moving toward the tents. I sat down right where I was and put my head in my hands.

"Are you all right, Eff?" William asked.

"Just wobbly, like everyone else," I said.

"What *was* that? That thing you did?"

"I think we'd all like to know that, Miss Rothmer."

I looked up. Adept Alikaket, Dr. Lefevre, and most of the other magicians I'd pulled into the deep levels of magic had come over to me instead of starting to take down their tents, and they were all looking at me expectantly. The only one missing was Wash, who'd gone off to get his burns fixed up.

I sighed. "I'm not sure how to explain it. It's just . . . remember how I said all magic feels the same underneath? That's what I meant. That was underneath."

"*That's* your explanation?" Lan said indignantly.

I glared at him. "It's all the explanation I have! I don't know how it works; I just *did* it. You're the one who knows magical theory — *you* explain it!"

"I suspect you have just revolutionized our basic theories of magic, Miss Rothmer," Dr. Lefevre said with a sidelong glance at Adept Alikaket.

The adept's lips tightened, then he shook his head ruefully.

"Theories aside, do you have any idea why and how you were able to do what you did?" he asked me.

Professor Ochiba looked at me with a tiny smile. "She is the seventh daughter —"

"— of a seventh son," Lan put in, and grinned at me.

"— making her a double-seventh child," the professor continued with a small frown in Lan's direction. "And she is the twin sister of a seventh son of a seventh son, and a thirteenth child."

I shivered, then remembered the conversation I'd had with Professor Ochiba back in day school, when she'd explained that different places didn't all see being a thirteenth child as a bad thing the way Avrupans did. And there were all those other things, too.

"Unprecedented, in other words," Dr. Lefevre said in a very dry tone.

"That is one way to look at it," Professor Ochiba said. Lan, William, and I all looked at each other and tried not to smile.

"We'll have plenty of time to study this phenomenon on the trip back," Professor Torgeson said, and I wasn't quite sure whether she meant me or the magic. "In the meantime —"

Before she could finish, something shivered through the air, making all the hairs on my arms stand up like a bad thunderstorm was blowing in real fast. Everyone froze, looking south toward the river. "Now what?" Lan said crossly.

There was a distant rumble off to the south, and the prickly feeling of magic rose up all around us like a wave and then fell back. Roger went white to the lips.

338

"It's the river," he said, barely loud enough for all of us to hear. "All the spells we were throwing around — they must have finished destabilizing the magic that's been piling up along it."

"Destabilizing —" Dr. Lefevre looked at Roger, and his eyes widened.

Roger nodded. "Eighty-three years' worth of magic, and it's about to go pouring down the river like an avalanche down a mountain. It'll hit the Great Barrier Spell where the rivers come together, and . . ."

His voice trailed off, but he didn't have to say anything else. He'd told us what would happen next; it was why we'd sent Mr. Zarbeliev and the others home ahead of us. Only now there was no chance that they'd arrive in time for a warning to make any difference. Even if they got back to Mill City before the wave of magic hit the Great Barrier Spell, there wouldn't be time to get a warning to St. Louis or New Orleans or any of the other towns along the river.

I remembered some of the accidents that had happened in the practice laboratories at the college, and shivered. If a mistake in a college student's experiment could punch a duck-shaped hole in every window on the west side of a building, what would eighty years' worth of raw magic do when it hit something? And what would happen if the Great Barrier Spell collapsed and released all *its* magic?

From the expressions everyone wore, they were all thinking the same thing. Lan looked at Roger. "Can we do anything to stop it?"

Roger licked his lips like they had suddenly gone dry. "No," he said.

LAN SCOWLED. "THERE HAS TO BE *SOMETHING!*" HE SAID. "SOME way to prop it up, or freeze it in place, or send it in a different direction, or use it up, or . . . or something."

"Are you crazy?" Roger practically shouted at him. "We're talking about enough magic to keep the Great Barrier Spell itself going for eighty years! All we can do is get out of the way."

"How long?" Dr. Lefevre demanded.

"What?"

"How long do we have before this avalanche of yours starts?" Dr. Lefevre said impatiently.

Roger took a shaky breath. "I don't know. But it's not going to be long — hours, maybe a day or two, at most."

"Have you any way of narrowing the time down quickly enough to do us any good?"

"Knowing exactly when it's going to collapse won't help," Roger said, but his forehead furrowed and his frown changed from the scared-and-angry sort to the thinking-very-hard sort. "There isn't anything we can do about eighty years' worth of magic."

"It's not eighty years' worth," I said suddenly. "It can't be."

"It *is*," Roger insisted. "Ever since the Great Barrier Spell went up —"

I shook my head. "That's not what I mean. You said this backup has been going on for eighty-three years, but all the magic can't have just piled up and stayed put. The magical wildlife all along the river has to have used up some of it, and some of the rest of it has to have gone back into the earth and air, the way magic from regular spell casting does."

"Not enough to make a difference," Roger said, but he didn't sound like he was paying careful attention to the conversation anymore. "At least, I don't think . . . Where's Eliz — oh, that's right; she was holding the protection spells. Where's Bronwyn?"

"Miss Hoel is with Miss Dzozkic," Mr. Corvales said from in back. "I thought you were all supposed to be packing up?"

"This is more important," Adept Alikaket said, and explained.

Mr. Corvales went as white as Roger had, then yelled for Captain Velasquez. Roger hadn't waited for Adept Alikaket to finish; he'd gone off to find Bronwyn before Mr. Corvales had even finished his first question. The rest of us looked at each other, then Lan and William and Professor Ochiba and I went after Roger, leaving Professor Torgeson and Dr. Lefevre to answer whatever other questions the expedition leaders had.

When we caught up with him, Roger and Bronwyn were sitting on the ground next to Elizabet (who was gradually recovering) with their heads bent over their notebooks. Roger was muttering about energy gradients and mass equivalence and Turnik's equations and a bunch of other things. Sergeant Amy appeared a moment after we arrived with a steel-tipped dipping pen and a small bottle of ink. Roger grabbed them without looking up and said, "The very first anomaly — what was the Jivaili ratio?"

Bronwyn flipped a couple of pages and read off some numbers. Nobody wanted to interrupt, so we all stood there silently. Gradually, the rest of the expedition members began to collect around us — first Mrs. Wilson, then one of the soldiers pretending to have a question for Sergeant Amy. Wash came next. His shirt was half off to make room for the bandages on his right arm and across his right side. There were pain creases around his eyes, and he didn't look as if he ought to be up running around. Professor Ochiba gave him a narrow-eyed glare when she saw him, but he just smiled.

Roger and Bronwyn didn't seem to notice any of us. After what seemed a long time, Roger sighed and set the dipping pen aside. There was silence as he recapped the ink bottle and looked up at last. A ripple of dismay ran through the group as everyone took in the expression on his face.

"There's really nothing to be done?" Mr. Corvales said.

"I don't believe so, sir," Roger said. "For a minute, I thought — but there's just too much magic piled up. There isn't any spell I know of that could stop it once it starts moving."

"Once it starts moving?" Captain Velasquez said quickly. "Then there's still time —"

Roger was shaking his head before the captain finished his sentence. "No, sir. It's already started. Right now there's just a trickle heading downstream, but according to my calculations, that's enough to throw off the balance that's been holding the large mass of magic up at this end of the river for the past eighty years. Within thirty-six hours, the rest of it will break loose."

"Can't we stop it before then, if it's only a trickle?" Mr. Corvales said.

"It's a trickle of *magic*," Roger told him impatiently. "It's not as if a dam made of cottonwood logs and mud will hold it back. We'd have to use magic . . . and that would mean putting *more* magic into the system. That will destabilize things even faster."

Beside me, Lan stiffened. "A dam," he breathed. Then, "Mr. Corvales!"

"Mr. Rothmer?" Mr. Corvales said as everyone turned.

"What if we take magic *out* of the system?" Lan said. "We've been tapping it for weeks to strengthen the protection spells. If we can use up enough of it —"

"Use it up?" Roger interrupted. "Lan, there's too much of it! Even with all of us casting every spell we know, we wouldn't be able to use up more than a fraction of that magic in thirty-six hours."

"That's with spells *we* know," Lan said, looking at Adept Alikaket. "But Hijero-Cathayans use massive group magic all the time. For draining lakes and building roads over mountains. For damming up rivers. If we use one of those —"

Adept Alikaket was already shaking his head. "To use up so much magic would take something like the spell that raised the Great Wall along the northern border of the Cathayan Confederacy, and that took thirty circles and ten years."

"Maybe we can dam it up," William said.

Roger scowled at him. "I just said —"

"Dam the river, I mean," William added hastily. "The magic follows the river; if we dam the river, the magic won't have anywhere to go. Well, at least until the dam fills up, but that would take at least a couple of years, I'd think."

"It'll buy us some time," Mr. Corvales said. He looked at the adept. "Can you do it?"

Adept Alikaket pursed his lips. "I have no circle to work with, and even if I had, raising a dam large enough to stop so large a river is work for two circles, at least."

Professor Torgeson gave him a reproving look. "The question is not what you might do with more time and more resources."

"Can't you use some of the magic that's built up around the river, the way Mr. Rothmer suggested?" Mr. Corvales asked.

The adept pursed his lips. "Perhaps. Natural magic is difficult to work with."

"Is it?" Wash said. When the adept looked at him, Wash quirked his lips. "We make do with what we have."

"Ah," Adept Alikaket said. He smiled suddenly. "I suppose that under the circumstances, I will . . . make do." He shook his head. "Still, I think you Columbians are more reckless than you need to be."

"I'll take that as a compliment," Wash said.

"There remains a problem," the adept went on. "To dam a river, especially one so large, needs a place that is suited, somewhere that the river cannot spread out too far and flow around it. This area" — he waved his hands to indicate the way we had come up the river — "is not well suited, and we have no time to look farther ahead."

Something was niggling at my mind. I tried not to listen to the conversation while I concentrated on remembering, and then I heard Roger's voice again, and I had it. "The undelimited thing!" I said out loud.

The argument broke off and everyone looked at me. I ignored them all, except for Roger. "Right after you came back from Albion, when Professor Torgeson asked you to look at the medusa lizard in the lab and the map went funny, she wanted to know if you were trying to map the whole of the Far West, and you said it would take more power than a whole team of Hijero-Cathayans, even. Did you mean it?"

Roger's eyes went wide. "It might work," he said, half to himself. "Especially if — Lan! Do you know the Laurencian Protocols?"

"Of course," Lan said. "Why? And would you explain what you two are talking about?"

"Mapping spells," Roger said. "If I understand Adept Alikaket correctly, the problem with damming up the river is finding the right place — a gorge or canyon that we can block off, for instance — which we can't do because we haven't mapped the rest of the river. And everybody knows that mapping spells only work with a well-defined symbol set; it takes too much power to cover an undelimited space."

"But we have plenty of power here," Dr. Lefevre said with a slow smile. Then his eyes narrowed. "Even so — will you be able to control it, Mr. Boden?"

345

"I don't know that I could if it were just me," Roger said. "But if Lan helps . . ."

"That's why you asked about the Laurencian Protocols!" Lan said. "Coordination!" The two of them went off into a technical conversation that had most of the senior magicians nodding and everyone else looking confused. When they finished talking, Mr. Corvales asked how soon they could start, obviously meaning for them to begin right away.

"I don't think that would be wise," Adept Alikaket said just as Roger shook his head. "We are all tired already from fighting the rock dragons; it would be better to rest before we try another major spell casting. Also, I think we will only have one chance to do this. We must be careful."

Roger switched from shaking his head to nodding. "The spells we used against the rock dragons are what started the destabilization," he said. "Tapping the built-up magic directly could make it much worse, very quickly. We'll want to have everything ready to cast, one spell right after another, before we start any of them."

"And we have another day," William pointed out. "More. Thirty-six hours, didn't you say, Roger?"

"He says that like it's a lot of time," Dr. Lefevre muttered, but too softly for very many people to hear.

"Well, then, let's get started planning," Captain Velasquez said briskly.

For all Adept Alikaket's talk about resting, Wash and Elizabet were the only magicians who got much that night. We camped where we were, despite the worry about more rock dragons finding us, because moving to anywhere else would have taken time that we didn't have. Roger and Lan went over their plans for the mapping. First, Lan would cast a spell to define the edges of the map they were making, so that Roger's spell wouldn't try to just keep going and going. Then Roger would work the primary spell, tapping into the vast pool of magic around the river to power it and keep it working until the map was filled in. It sounded simple enough, but Lan said that the amount of power rose too rapidly compared to the size of the area being mapped for it to be a useful way of mapping most places.

Meanwhile, Adept Alikaket gathered up the rest of us to plan the spell to dam up the river. That was complicated, because the Hijero-Cathayan spell he said would work best was one that normally needed a large circle of Cathayan magicians to do the casting, not just to provide power, and all the magicians we had knew only Avrupan or Aphrikan magic. Professor Ochiba and Professor Torgeson stayed up most of the night with him, going over the spell and breaking it down into parts, while Dr. Lefevre tried to come up with spells that would do each part without interfering with each other.

By dawn, they'd worked out a sequence of spells that everybody agreed would probably work. Captain Velasquez didn't like the "probably" part, but it was the best anybody could come up with. Lan and Roger would do the mapping spell; as soon as enough of the river was mapped, Wash would use Aphrikan magic to find a spot for the dam. Professor Torgeson and Dr. Lefevre would cast the spells to anchor the ends of the dam to either side of the river, while Adept Alikaket worked the main spell that collected material and moved it into place.

By then, Lan and Roger would be finished with the mapping spell; Lan would do the spell that welded all the rocks and other things into one solid structure, while Bronwyn anchored the base of the dam to the bedrock and Roger carved a spillway. Professor Ochiba and Wash would be checking with their world sense to make sure the dam was solid and that we'd contained both the river and as much of the stored-up magic as possible. William and I were the balancers; our job was to tweak any of the spells that looked like it was wobbling or starting to interfere with another one, so that the whole process would go smoothly.

The biggest difficulty was the timing. The mapping spell had to come first, but after that, a lot of the spell casting would overlap. That meant that we had a good chance that the spells would interfere with each other, as well as the chance that everybody drawing on the stored-up magic at once would set off the very flood of power that we were trying to prevent. Of course, we'd be using up a lot of magic, too, but nobody seemed to think we could use up anything like enough to make a difference without the dam.

Once we had the spells and sequence worked out, Adept Alikaket made all the magicians have a good meal and then sleep for a few hours. I tried, just like he said, but I was too keyed up to nap. I just lay in the tent with my eyes closed, worrying about all the things that could go wrong and feeling the distant trembles in the magic around the river as it shifted and prepared to break apart.

After about an hour, I got up again and went out to help set up the spell-casting area. Mr. Corvales had already brought out the big maps he'd been using to chart the expedition's progress, and Captain Velasquez had his men clearing and leveling a big patch of ground, with Elizabet directing them. She said she still had a splitting headache from the backlash of whatever the rock dragons had done to the protection spells, and she didn't think she could actually help with the big spell casting directly, but measuring and leveling land was her job and she could do that much, anyway. She sounded quite fierce, which made me think that maybe Mr. Corvales had tried to get her to lie back down and she wasn't having it.

So I helped cart rocks out of the spell-casting area, and then I held one end of Elizabet's measuring chain wherever she told me. By the time we finished, the other magicians were drifting back out to join us. Roger and Lan and the other Avrupan magicians started setting up the things they needed for the various spells they would be casting; the rest of us stood and watched in silence.

Finally everything was nearly ready. Lan gave one last critical look at Mr. Corvales's map, spread out on the bare ground in the middle of the diagram Roger had scratched. He looked up and gave me a tense smile. On the far side of the spell-working area, Elizabet gave Bronwyn a quick hug and stepped back. Beside me, William cleared his throat. "Eff —" He stopped short.

I tore my eyes from the preparations. "What?"

"I . . ." He hesitated. "If anything goes wrong . . ."

"It won't," I told him firmly.

He gave me a long look, then nodded in sudden decision.

"Right. We can talk after this is all finished." He paused again. "I'd better get in place. Good luck." He offered me his hand.

I took it and gave it a small squeeze instead of shaking it. Neither of us let go right away. "Good luck," I echoed. "Be careful."

William gave me a grin over his shoulder as he walked away. Theoretically, it didn't make any difference where we stood. As long as we could see the casting and sense the spells, we could tweak them if they needed it. We'd never tried working on anything as complicated as this, though, so we thought we'd better stand on opposite sides of the spell-casting area, in case it made more difference than we thought.

Dr. Lefevre made one final adjustment to the iron ring that lay in the upper-right corner of the square-and-circle diagram in front of him, then straightened up and nodded.

Roger looked at Lan. "Whenever you're ready."

Lan nodded. He took a deep breath and began to recite the first spell. On the fifth word, Roger joined him, repeating the same thing Lan had said, but one line behind, like two people singing a round. That was the First Laurencian Protocol, one of the spells that Avrupan magicians sometimes use when they have to work on an especially tricky joint casting. Lan said it would pull their spells together more closely than they could otherwise get and then keep them there, like putting a large book on top of two sheets of paper to press them together.

As soon as they finished the Protocol spell, Lan went straight on into the spell that would put edges around the map to contain Roger's spell, and William and I started the world-sensing to keep an eye on the spells. We didn't expect to have to do anything for a while yet, but we might as well be prepared.

Roger raised his hand and cast the mapping spell. I felt it surge outward, and then the edges of Lan's spell contained it and sent it back. The blank parts of Mr. Corvales's map started filling in, like a reflection appearing in a curtained mirror as the curtains were slowly drawn back. I could feel the spell building as Roger drew on the piled-up magic around the river and poured it into the mapping spell.

Just behind Roger, Wash closed his eyes and reached out. "Got it," he said after a moment. "There's a canyon just upriver. Here." He pointed, and his magic followed his pointing finger into the map, and through the map to the actual place. Adept Alikaket and the professors cast the spells to follow Wash's, so that they could start actually building the dam. The mapping spell shivered and tilted as all those other spells went through it, and I felt it starting to slip out of Roger's hold. I nudged it and it steadied. I felt a broad grin spread across my face. It was working!

Distantly, I heard Adept Alikaket's deep voice calling words in Cathayan. A moment later, I sensed him groping for more magic. I left the mapping spell for William to take care of, and tweaked the bit of the adept's spell that wasn't in quite the right place because it was normally fed magic from a circle of Cathayan magicians instead of having to draw from a huge built-up pile of natural magic. A second later, the spell took hold.

Power roared up into the adept's spell, so much that I couldn't help looking over to make sure he wasn't burning up.

I had to squint and look away almost at once; Adept Alikaket was surrounded by a blinding white cloud. I could feel his spell shaping the power, reaching out to the rocks and dirt near the canyon and moving them into place. I wondered briefly what it looked like to the critters that were right on the spot.

Dr. Lefevre and Professor Torgeson started their spells, to anchor either side of the dam. Bronwyn began casting hers a moment later, to firm up the base. Roger's mapping spell slowed and stopped; he cast the final part to make the new map permanent, then started to disengage.

And then I felt the built-up magic shake and shift like loose rock underfoot, and knew that in another instant it would fall in an unstoppable flood that would sweep away the dam and all of us.

CHAPTER
· 33 ·

"WILLIAM!" I SHRIEKED.

He didn't answer me in words, but I could sense him shoving the magic back into place and holding it there, just as I was. Unfortunately, it wasn't like tweaking a spell. Spells are organized; they're supposed to be just so, and you can feel when something isn't where it's supposed to be and shove it back into place. This was like a big pile of dirt — no one bit of it was supposed to be anywhere in particular, and trying to shove one part into place just made a gap somewhere else. And it didn't help any that everyone else was still draining magic out of the pile and making new gaps.

We'd delayed the collapse for a moment, but I could tell that we wouldn't be able to hold it for long — certainly not long enough for the others to finish. I could only think of one thing to do. I gave the magic one last shove, hoping it would stay put for a few seconds, and stretched out my world-sensing, looking for some way to keep everything in position. I just knew there had to be a key spot, a balance point that had been knocked off kilter by all the magic we'd been drawing.

It was like trying to see through a mud wall. I stretched and shoved and reached as hard as I could, but all I sensed were the spells that Adept Alikaket and everyone were busy casting, winding over and under and past each other in a complicated dance.

Dance . . .

An image flashed through my mind of Adept Alikaket slowly doing the dancelike moves he called the way of boundless balance, out at the edge of camp at sunrise. Something he'd said —

Your Avrupan magic is a thing apart from yourselves — wood to be carved, stone to be shaped, metal to be melted and re-formed . . . Aphrikan magic is outside, but alive, to be shaped as a master gardener shapes his trees and bushes, not as a smith shapes metal or a carver shapes wood. Our magic, the Cathayan magic, is us, and we are it, all together, as drops of water are a river and the river is made of drops of water.

And then I knew why I couldn't find the balance point I was looking for. I was used to tweaking spells — magic that had been shaped and organized by magicians. Even Cathayan magic was shaped and organized; the real difference was in how the magicians got at the magic for their spells and what they did to shape it, not in whether or not it was shaped. Natural magic, the kind that grew from rivers and plants and animals, was organized, too, just according to whatever grew it, instead of on purpose the way some magician wanted.

This magic — the magic that had been piling up along the river for eighty years — wasn't organized at all. It must have started off with as much order to it as any magic that a river produced, but when it got trapped up at the high end of the river for so long, whatever order it had to begin with must have broken down. Now it was just an enormous heap of raw magic, with no more form or shape to it than the sky or the ocean. We could tap the surface of it to power our spells, but we couldn't get down to the heart of it. Not with any of the ways magicians usually reached magic.

A stream of images ran through my mind: Lan at age ten, staring up at William, floating treetop-high above the stream near our house; Miss Ochiba, explaining Aphrikan world-sensing to me and my classmates after school; Papa and Professor Jeffries and Lan, casting the Fourth of July illusion that showed George Washington and his men crossing the Delaware; Wash, sitting patiently beside Daybat Creek, nudging the water through the fallen rock so that it wouldn't break loose all at once and flood settlements downstream; Master Adept Farawase, holding a stream of magic at the baby medusa lizard while her aides moved through the way of boundless balance. Last of all came an image from one of my dreams, of me standing on a high rock above an ever-changing ocean, then diving in.

I narrowed my eyes. "William!" I yelled across the murmur of everyone else working their various spells. "Can you hang on by yourself for another couple of minutes?"

Light flashed off William's glasses as he nodded. "Not long," he cautioned, and I nodded back to let him know I'd heard. Then I took a deep breath and instead of trying to sense the huge pile of magic, or nudge it, or use it, I dove straight into the middle of it.

It felt like the ocean in my dream: calm one minute, swirling chaos the next. I didn't try to shape it or nudge it. I just let it carry me wherever it went.

After a second, I started sensing a pull on the magic, or rather, a whole lot of different pulls. Most of them were scattered; I figured those were the magical plants and animals that were drawing on the magical buildup. There was a cluster of strong tugs that had to be Adept Alikaket and the professors and everyone using the magic to power their spells. And there was a strong, steady suction off to the west that felt a bit like the Great Barrier Spell. I thought it must be the resonance that Roger said had made all the magic back up in the first place.

From inside the magic, I could feel the way the river held the magic, and the way all the spells we'd cast had unbalanced it. I couldn't find any way to hold it all in place — there was just too much of it, and for a moment, I almost gave up. *There has to be another way to look at it*, I thought, and then I had it.

I couldn't hold the mass of magic in place, because we'd already pulled too much of it away from one side, and nobody was strong enough to replace that much. But I might be able to drain enough magic from the other side of the mass to bring it back into balance again.

I reached out and found a weak spot farther up the river and to the south, probably a place where a smaller stream joined the Grand Bow. I paused just long enough to make sure it wasn't pointing back downriver toward the Great Barrier Spell, and then I poked at it. The magic gave a little, then sprang back into place, like a swing door when you don't shove it hard enough to stay open. I pushed harder. Raw magic swirled and started to leak past me.

"What the — ?" Roger said from off to my left.

"Hang on, William!" Lan shouted.

I braced myself and shoved, trying to make sure the flow of magic wouldn't stop, and suddenly I was caught in a rush of magic, like water gushing out of a drain hole that's just been unplugged. Just when I thought I would be completely swept away, someone grabbed my arm. I blinked and my awareness of the magic faded. "William?"

"What do you think you were doing?" he said, giving my arm a shake.

"Never mind that. Did it work?" I asked.

"If it was supposed to take some of the pressure off, then yes," William said, letting go of me. "Lan's holding it now."

I felt the blood drain from my face; even a double-seventh son wasn't strong enough to hold up that much magic. William shook his head and added hastily, "Not holding it — balancing it, I should have said. It's still not completely stable, but he can — oh, drat, the anchors are going again. You take Dr. Lefevre's end. I'll work on Professor Torgeson's."

I nodded. I couldn't help glancing over at Lan, and I breathed a sigh of relief when I saw that he wasn't trying to block the mass of magic all at once, by brute force. Instead, he was giving it a little push here and an extra spin there, like a child adding spin to a top that was starting to wobble. I grinned and went back to tweaking spells.

I kept an eye on the "opening" I'd made upstream, though I was careful to stay far enough away from it that I wouldn't get sucked into it accidentally. The pile of magic had burst through the weak spot I'd made like the river itself washing out a levy or a sandbar, flooding up the secondary river and out through the canyons and plains around it. For a while, I was afraid I'd made things worse by giving the magic a way around the dam we were building, but when the flooding settled down, I could tell that the magic had spread out to the south instead of coming back to the Grand Bow.

Building the dam took most of the rest of the day, and used up a whole lot of the built-up magic. We had several more tense moments when it seemed like everything would collapse, but each time the wobble was less and it was easier for us to stop it.

Finally, the adept finished moving rocks and earth. One by one, the other magicians finished their parts. As they did, William and I had less tweaking to do, so we started letting what was left of the built-up magic settle into its new place, a bit at a time. We'd used up a lot of it, but there was still enough left that a collapse could wreck the new dam after all, not to mention the damage it would do once it got down to the Mammoth River, so letting go of it all was a tricky business. Everyone breathed a sigh of relief once it was all done.

"Well," Dr. Lefevre said, once we were all sitting around the fire with tin cups full of the first really strong coffee we'd had in a while. (Sergeant Amy had been rationing the coffee ever since we left winter quarters.) "That was certainly a unique experience. This may revolutionize group spell casting, once we get back to publish the methodology."

"*Unique.*" Adept Alikaket spoke slowly, like he was tasting something to get every last flavor out of it. "Yes, I suppose *unique* will do, if that is the strongest word your language has for such things." He looked more exhausted than anyone, but pleased, too.

"Tomorrow, Mr. Boden and Miss Dzozkic should check to make sure this . . . experiment has worked as well as we hoped," Dr. Lefevre went on. "Once they've rested, of course."

"Some of it worked even better," Roger said with a tired grin. "Have you looked at that map yet, Mr. Corvales? I think I got just about everything we could want — topology, watersheds, mineral deposits, wildlife, and habitat."

Mr. Corvales nodded with evident satisfaction. "Yes, it's very well done. Though there seem to be a lot more wildlife indications on the northern half than farther south. Is that accurate, or was the spell losing strength at that distance?"

"It's accurate," Roger said.

"We already knew that the magic buildup along the river was attracting magical wildlife," Captain Velasquez put in, frowning at Mr. Corvales. "This is consistent with that finding."

"Theory," Professor Torgeson muttered.

"It's more than just attracting them, sir." Roger held out his cup for Sergeant Amy to refill. "I think there are more of them than there should be, especially the predators like the rock dragons and the giant invisible foxes. Everything felt a bit . . . off center, up around the river. I don't know what's going to happen now."

"Now?" Captain Velasquez asked.

"The magical wildlife around the river appears to have adapted to the high levels of available magic caused by this peculiar buildup," Dr. Lefevre said in his lecturing tone. "Building the dam has caused a significant drop in the level of available magic around the river, and while it's certainly not back to what we would consider normal levels, the change is bound to have an equally significant effect on the adapted species."

"Though exactly what that effect will be is unpredictable," Professor Torgeson put in. "It depends on how each species utilizes the ambient magic. Those that require high levels of magic for reproduction will no doubt see significantly smaller population growth in the next few years. Predators that use magic to hunt will have much greater difficulty in catching their preferred prey, and so on. It is a pity we can't stay to observe it."

"We're heading back as soon as we can," Mr. Corvales said firmly. "I don't think we could handle another pack of rock dragons."

Captain Velasquez nodded reluctantly. "As you say."

"Also, we'll need to let folks know about the dam," Wash pointed out.

Adept Alikaket nodded. "It's only a temporary solution. You'll have to get another batch of people out here to deal with this magic buildup for good."

"What?" Mr. Corvales looked taken aback. "I thought — how temporary?"

"It'll take a few years for the water — and the magic — to fill up behind the dam," Roger said reassuringly. "But Adept Alikaket is right; the river is still producing magic, and the resonance with the Great Barrier Spell is still making it pile up at this end of the Grand Bow. Eventually, there will be too much again, dam or no."

Lan nodded agreement. "It'll take longer because of that thing Eff did, but it'll still happen."

"'That thing Eff did'?" Adept Alikaket said, raising his eyebrows.

"Draining off so much of the pileup," Lan replied. "Didn't you feel it when the pressure let up?"

"That was *you*, Miss Rothmer?" Dr. Lefevre said, looking at me in disbelief. "What did you *do*?"

"I made a . . . a hole to let some of the built-up magic spread out away from the river," I explained.

Dr. Lefevre relaxed. "Ah. *Not* another groundbreaking change to accepted magical theory, then, just an extension and application of the previous one. Would you mind going into more specific detail?"

It took me quite a while to explain so he understood it, and a couple of times Lan and William had to help out. By the time I finished, Mr. Corvales was frowning and muttering again. "If this means that the dam hasn't solved the problem —"

"Building a dam was never going to be more than a temporary answer," Adept Alikaket interrupted.

"And thanks in part to Miss Rothmer, we have plenty of time to find a more permanent solution," Professor Ochiba said firmly. "Not that that is an excuse for delay, of course. Still, under the circumstances, I will be surprised if it is at all difficult to raise funds for another expedition. I shall certainly recommend that Triskelion participate in any future investigation."

Wash gave her a surprised look, then grinned. "One way or another, I imagine we'll work out something."

The corners of Professor Ochiba's mouth turned up, as if the words Wash said meant more than they seemed. "Just so."

"You Columbians." Adept Alikaket shook his head, but he was smiling, too. "So sure of yourselves."

"I believe 'overconfident' is the word you are looking for," Professor Torgeson said in a dry tone.

Adept Alikaket laughed. "Possibly."

"It's not overconfidence if you can actually do it," Lan pointed out.

"It remains to be seen whether we can," Roger said. "Until then —"

"Don't be a wet blanket," Lan said, and gave him a shove as if they were both ten years old.

"That's enough coffee for you," Sergeant Amy told Lan. "Anybody else who wants some, speak now. This is the last of the pot, and tomorrow we're back to regular strength."

There were groans of dismay, and Lan made a face, but most of the grumbling was good-natured. The soldiers who were going on night watch got first crack at the last of the coffee, and Adept Alikaket and Roger and Bronwyn split what was left. The rest of us nursed our cups for a while longer, then slowly drifted off to our tents.

CHAPTER
· 34 ·

WE STAYED CAMPED WHERE WE WERE FOR ANOTHER TWO DAYS, SO that Roger and Elizabet could check the ambient magic levels again, and so Wash and Professor Ochiba and Adept Alikaket could double-check the soundness of the dam. The extra time gave Dr. Lefevre and Professor Ochiba and Professor Torgeson a chance to do some more studying on the rock dragons we'd killed, so William and I were busy taking notes and packing samples until almost the last minute.

We left on July 17. We hadn't made it all the way to the Rocky Mountains, quite, but between the giant invisible foxes and the rock dragons, we had a pretty good notion why nobody else had, either. We were also pretty sure that there wouldn't be as much dangerous wildlife following the magic down the Grand Bow — at least, not for quite some time.

Even though Roger had told everyone that the dam worked just the way we'd wanted, it was a relief to get back to the river and see that there was still water in it, though it was considerably lower than it had been. Roger pointed out that the dam only blocked the main river, and there were a lot of tributaries still bringing water in. The main thing, though, was that the ambient magic levels were noticeably down; my skin didn't prickle with it the way it had, and some of the drifts of blinkflowers and sandwort along the riverbanks already looked wilted.

As soon as she saw the sandwort, Professor Torgeson started muttering about changing the balance of the wildlife and unforeseen consequences, but Dr. Lefevre pointed out that it was putting up the Great Barrier Spell in the first place that had created such unnaturally high magic levels to begin with, so from one point of view we'd just put things back the way they were supposed to be. Professor Torgeson retorted that we'd only lowered the magic levels temporarily, and we didn't know what effects such an abrupt up-and-down change would cause. They argued over it most of the way back to St. Jacques du Fleuve, when they weren't complaining about the speed-travel spells making it hard to collect samples.

Since we knew exactly where we were going and what was there, it didn't take us nearly as long to get back to settlement territory as it had to get out to the Far West, even with picking up samples of plants and wildlife along the way. We had another run-in with the giant invisible foxes in late July, a Priscilla hawk went after one of the prairie dogs we'd caught to take back for the menagerie, and we had to chase off some prairie wolves, but otherwise there wasn't a lot of excitement. Which was fine by pretty near everyone; we'd had all the excitement any of us wanted.

A week out of St. Jacques, we ran across the first person we'd seen besides other expedition members in over a year. He was a trapper, heading out to get his cabin and trapline in repair, and he was happy to spend the evening telling us all the news.

We had a new president, as Mr. Johann Bryce had beaten out President Trent when he tried for a second term. That got everyone excited right off, as nearly everyone had an opinion about President Bryce, or about his vice president, Mr. Abraham Lincoln. Captain Velasquez said that the important thing was that they both understood military matters, since they'd both fought in the Secession War almost thirty years ago; Mr. Corvales snorted and said that the important thing was that President Bryce knew how to make good decisions.

Then the trapper said that President Bryce and Vice President Lincoln had cooked up a scheme to divide up the Northern and Middle Plains Territories and let some of the more settled parts into the Union as states, even though they were on the far side of the Great Barrier Spell. That got everyone excited again, since so many expedition members were from the territories, and someone wanted to know why they weren't doing the same for the South Plains Territory. The trapper said it was because we might have new neighbors to the south soon, as the Ottoman colonies along the Gulf of Amerigo were negotiating for independence with their new sultan, and President Bryce wanted to be sure everybody agreed about where the country borders were before he started carving out states.

Once they got that settled, the trapper went on. Gold and silver had been discovered in the mountains of South Columbia, and a lot of folks had rushed out to get rich and been killed by the wildlife. There'd been considerable speculation over whether we'd bring back news of similar riches in the Far West. I frowned, thinking of the map Roger and Elizabet and Bronwyn had made. I hoped no one would go rushing out after gold and get killed by rock dragons, but I supposed that if people wanted to be stupid, I couldn't stop them.

The Long Lake Northern Railroad Company and the Atlantic St. Louis Railroad had gotten together and agreed to build railroad bridges across the Mammoth River at Mill City and St. Louis so that both railroads could expand into the West. And the baseball league was spreading; there were new teams in Washington and New Amsterdam.

After hearing all that, we made quick time to St. Jacques. The town had a celebration when we arrived, which mainly amounted to nearly everyone in town heading down to the saloons for three days running. Professor Torgeson said that was just what you'd expect from a trapper town. Most of the men from the expedition joined the rowdy celebrations, but it wasn't as bad as on the way out, because everyone was more interested in getting a hot bath in the tub at the general store, or in reading the piles of mail we had waiting, than in staying up all night drinking.

Lan's stack of mail was twice as tall as mine; he had letters from nearly everyone he'd ever met, including all the men who'd been at Simon Magus with him. I had three from Professor Jeffries and a couple from my friends from upper school, but all the rest were from family. I was surprised to see a few from my cousins and aunts and uncles back East; I suppose going off on a big expedition was enough to overcome the fact that none of them had seen me in years, and none of them had liked me particularly well before that. I set those aside and started with the ones from Mama and Papa.

Mama's letters were mostly family news: Nan had had another baby, a girl this time, and Rennie'd had another boy. Allie'd left her job at the day school and taken another one helping outfit new settlers, and she was keeping company with an older gentleman who'd come to Mill City to build a carriage factory. Brant and Rennie had signed on with another settlement group; Mama spent two solid pages not liking it one bit, but after that she allowed as how it would probably work out better than the all-Rationalist settlement at Oak River. She said Jack had come home for most of last winter, and gone back to his settlement with a nice girl, but Robbie was still flirting with nearly anything in a skirt. He'd been talking about moving to St. Louis; she hoped he'd still be in Mill City when we got back.

Rennie's letters were mostly about the childings (she and Nan both sent letters from my nephews and nieces; even the ones who couldn't write yet had sent drawings or scribbles), and a little about the new settlement she and Brant had joined. After the way Oak River turned out, the Rationalists in Long Lake City had decided not to try sending another group that was nothing but strict Rationalists. Instead, they were sponsoring three mixed settlements that would be half Rationalists and half other folks, so there'd be some magicians around and people wouldn't get so nervy and cross about magic.

I spent most of a day answering all those letters, though I knew they probably wouldn't get to Mill City much before we did. Most everyone in the expedition did the same, so it was a real quiet day. Late in the afternoon, I came out to find

William sitting on a big log by the cookfire, staring into the flames and turning a letter over and over in his hands.

I went and sat down next to him. "Bad news?" I asked after a while.

"No. Not exactly." He went silent again. I waited. Finally he said, "My father wants to see me when we get back."

I nodded. After the way Professor Graham had acted those last few days before the expedition left, I wasn't really surprised. I didn't think William would be, either, so I figured there was more to it than that. I waited some more.

"He wants me to come home. To stay there."

"Will you?"

"I —" William took a deep breath. "Not right away, I think. Maybe after we've talked. If he'll talk to me once he finds out I'm not doing exactly what he wants. Again."

"If you write him and tell him now, he'll probably have at least a few days to get accustomed to the idea."

"I suppose it'd be better than showing up and having him slam the door in my face," William said. He rubbed his nose like something had actually hit it.

"I don't think Professor Graham would do that," I said. "Not without a whole lot of yelling first, anyway, which would give you plenty of time to get out of the way."

William looked at me and grinned suddenly. "He would yell, wouldn't he? Even if people could hear him six houses away. My father has never cared much what other people think of his behavior." He sounded almost proud.

"Not when he's fussed about anything that's important to him," I agreed.

William looked down at the letter, then folded it up and tucked it in his shirt pocket. His grin had faded, but he was still smiling, and he looked a lot more relaxed than he had. "I'll write him later tonight," he said. "Once I think how to put what I want to say."

"Don't wait too long, or we'll be back before the letter."

"I know." William slid down the log to sit on the ground, so he had something to lean against. We sat in companionable silence for a few minutes. Then he asked, "What about you, Eff? Have you thought about what you're going to do when we get back?"

I shrugged. "I'll probably go back to work at the college, if Professor Jeffries still has a place for me. It's going to be hard, living at home again, but I certainly don't want to move in with Nan or Allie. Allie'd nag me to death, and Nan's got two childings now. I had enough of minding childings that last year when Rennie and Brant were living with us."

William tilted his head to look up at me; the light reflecting on his glasses made his expression hard to read. "You could . . ." He broke off and looked away.

"I could what? If you have any ideas, I'd surely like to hear them."

"When we get back, we're both going to have nearly two years of expedition pay coming," William said slowly. "That's enough to get a good start pretty much anywhere, if we're careful. Professor Ochiba thinks everyone who came will have a lot of offers. Positions and such."

We? I nodded slowly. "Professor Torgeson said the same thing. Lan's been talking about going back to school, only at

Triskelion instead of Simon Magus. He wants to work out the theory behind all the spell tweaking and such that we've been doing."

"I'll have my degree, and I'm not looking for more than that, no matter what my father thinks," William said. "Not yet, anyway. I'd like to do some practical work on the things we've found — the magic buildup and the spell tweaking and getting all the different types of magic to work together the way we did when we built the dam."

"That sounds like you," I said.

"Dr. Lefevre thinks that they'll send another expedition out next year or the year after," he went on. "Well, they'll have to, if we're going to do anything about that magic buildup on the Grand Bow. I don't know that I'll be ready to go back that soon, but I think I'd like to eventually. If that would be all right with you."

I whipped my head around, but he was staring into the fire and I couldn't read his expression. "All right with me?" I said cautiously.

William nodded.

"Why would I get a say in what you do?"

"I was hoping you'd come with me," he said in a low voice.

"Come with — William Graham, is this your idea of a proposal of marriage?"

"I'm afraid so," he said with a shadow of a smile. "Sorry. I'd intended to wait until we got back and do things properly, with a ring and everything, but then I got the letter." He touched his pocket. "My father wrote something about all the fuss there'll be when we get back, and I started thinking about the way everyone was after the folks who went on the McNeil Expedition, and I figured I'd better say something before then."

"Hmph," I said. "It'd serve you right if I said yes and then threw you over for somebody else the minute we get home."

"You wouldn't do that," William said seriously. "If you didn't want to marry me, you'd tell me straight out, right off. Though I suppose you might throw a shoe at my head for going about this so badly. Will you?"

"Yes, I'll marry you." I didn't have to think about it. I didn't have any doubts, the way I'd had when Roger proposed. I felt warm and happy, and not just from being in front of the fire. I felt *right*. I didn't have to worry that we'd disappoint each other when we got to know each other better. We'd already known each other for most of our lives.

More than that, I knew that with William, I'd never have to choose between being who I was and being who he wanted me to be. The only times he'd ever yelled at me were when I was trying to do things just because other folks thought I should, and not because I wanted them myself.

William curled his arm around my shoulders, and I leaned against him. We sat there for a while without saying much. Finally William stirred. "I suppose I'd better write that letter to my father," he said. "At least now I have some good news to tell him; maybe it'll be enough to make him forgive me for the rest."

"He'll think that the two of us getting married is good news?" I asked doubtfully.

"He likes you," William said. "He thinks you're level-headed."

"He *does*?"

William grinned. "More level-headed than me, anyway. What about your family?"

"Papa and Mama will be pleased," I said. "So will Lan, I think. Robbie and the rest of the boys probably won't care, one way or another, so long as Papa and Mama think it's all right, and the same for Nan. I think Allie will be unhappy, but mostly because it wasn't her idea. Rennie — I don't know what Rennie'll think. I gave up on figuring what she'd think a long while back."

"Shall we tell Lan now?"

I could tell that William really wanted to tell *somebody*, and Lan was the only family either of us had in reach. So I nodded, and let William pull me to my feet for the pure joy of taking his hand, and we went to look for my brother.

Lan was startled by our news, and by the time he got over being startled and gone on to being pleased, half the camp had heard. Professor Ochiba and Wash were the first to offer their congratulations, and I could see they meant them. Professor Torgeson said all the right things, but I could see she was more hoping I'd made the right choice than sure of it. Roger came over just long enough to wish us happy in a stiff tone.

Dinner turned into a party; Captain Velasquez even brought over a fiddler he'd run into in town, so there was music and singing and even a little dancing, though that was mostly circles and reels on account of the difficulty of finding partners. I saw Roger dancing with Sergeant Amy several times, and I was pleased they were enjoying themselves. Neither William nor I ever did get a proper letter written; I had to scribble a quick note the next morning to give to the post rider before we started packing up to leave.

Getting through settlement territory took longer than I'd expected. Since it was autumn, the weather was especially uncertain; we even had an early snow halfway to Puerta del Oeste, though it was barely enough to coat the grass in slippery slush before it melted. It felt a little odd to be able to trade for food instead of sending out hunters every few days, but the variety was more than welcome.

We stopped briefly at the study center to leave the live specimens we'd collected — two prairie dogs, a chameleon tortoise, a porcupine, and a young Priscilla hawk. There wasn't any point in trying to take them through the Great Barrier Spell when they'd have to come back out to the menagerie eventually.

Except for the gray skies and bare trees, going back through West Landing was a lot like leaving it on our way out. People lined up along the boardwalks, waving and gaping like we were a circus come to town. The mayor met up with us at the edge of town and rode up front along with Adept Alikaket, Captain Velasquez, and Mr. Corvales all the way to the bridge. I heard later that the mayor had wanted to make a speech, but had the good sense to figure that a cold November day wasn't the best time for a lot of fuss out of doors.

They'd cleared the traffic on the bridge so that we could ride straight across from West Landing to Mill City. William, Lan, and I rode over the bridge together, though technically Lan should have stayed with the exploration section until Mr. Corvales officially dismissed everyone. The mayor of Mill City was waiting on the east bank, along with more curious folks, but they didn't get much of a show. Mr. Corvales, Adept Alikaket, and Captain Velasquez got to the far side of the bridge, dismounted to shake hands with the mayor, and then signaled that we were dismissed. Right away, the train of expedition horses and people started breaking up and mixing with all the folks who'd come to welcome us back. By the time Lan and William and I got there, there wasn't much left in the way of organization.

Papa and Mama were standing with Professor Graham off to one side. I saw them first and turned my horse toward them, and a few minutes later we were all home.

THE JOINT CATHAYAN-COLUMBIAN DISCOVERY AND MAPPING Expedition was considered a great success by almost everybody. We'd gone nearly eight hundred miles, which was over three hundred miles farther into the Far West than any other expedition. Thanks to Roger, we'd brought back a detailed map of the whole North Plains Territory and then some, a lot of which wasn't plains at all. We had brought back specimens of twenty-three new plants and eleven animals, and sketches of dozens more. And we'd dammed up the westernmost end of the Grand Bow River and kept the Great Barrier Spell from collapsing, hopefully for long enough so that somebody else might be able to do something more permanent.

There was at least as much fuss made over all of us as there'd been over the members of the McNeil Expedition. Adept Alikaket put up with it for about three days, then informed everyone most politely that he really had to go home himself, and left for Washington. He stayed there for a couple of months, talking to people from the State Department and the Frontier Management Office, and then went back to Cathay.

A year later, William and Lan and I each got a package containing a strip of silk painted with odd, finger-shaped hills. Beside them was a row of symbols that looked like someone piled up a bunch of boxes and triangles and straight lines in little heaps. The translation that came with it announced that Adept Alikaket Shilin was now Master Adept Alikaket Shilin. There was a little card, too, that Master Adept Alikaket had written himself, acknowledging his friendship and saying that we would be welcome if we ever came to visit the Cathayan Confederacy.

Mr. Corvales went back to Washington as soon as the fuss in Mill City died down. He was still pretty worried about the magic piling up at the far end of the Grand Bow River, and wanted to get someone started working at a way to solve the problem for good and all. He was pretty successful, one way and another: They're already planning to send more people out next year, and if all goes well, they're hoping to put a permanent research outpost somewhere between the spot where we overwintered and the dam we built.

Professor Ochiba and Dr. Lefevre both stayed in Mill City for the rest of the winter, working with Professor Torgeson to organize and write up all the notes we'd taken. Wash stuck around, too, right up until Professor Ochiba left to go back to Triskelion University. Then he went out to ride circuit for the settlements. He showed up again as soon as Professor Ochiba came back to start organizing the new research outpost. Mama and Allie shake their heads and say that the two of them — Wash and Professor Ochiba — ought to make up their minds whether they want to marry or not, and then just do it, but I'm not so sure. They seem happy as they are.

Roger and Sergeant Amy eloped six weeks after the expedition got back, which surprised everyone. Amy mustered out of the army (though most people still call her Sergeant Amy, anyway), and now she's organizing all the folks who want Roger to do geomancy for them now that he has his certification.

Elizabet and Bronwyn stayed in Mill City for a few weeks (like everyone else, they had notes and observations to organize), then went off to Washington for a while to help Adept Alikaket and Mr. Corvales convince people about the dam. Last I heard, they were thinking of joining an expedition to map the South Plains Territory.

Lan spent the winter working partly with the Homestead Claim and Settlement Office and partly with Professor Ochiba, Professor Torgeson, and Dr. Lefevre. When Professor Ochiba went back to Triskelion, Lan went along with her. Papa and Mama are pleased that he's finally going to finish his schooling; William's father, on the other hand, can't make up his mind whether that means that Triskelion really was a good choice for William, or whether William was a bad influence on Lan. Mostly, I think he just doesn't want to admit straight out that he was wrong.

And William and me? We were married just after Christmas, a little less than two months after the expedition returned. We spent the rest of the winter helping the professors with their notes, then went out to the study center to work with all the specimens the expedition brought back. We don't expect to stay there for too long, though. Neither of us is suited to the settlements, but we're both hoping to go along on the new expedition, and if they do build a research outpost, we're certainly going to try to get a place there.

Once the Far West gets into your blood, it's hard to get it out again.